PRAISE FOR THE *NEW*
REAPERS MOTOR

"Raw emotion and riveting characters, I fell in love from page one!"
—Katy Evans, *New York Times* bestselling author

"Seriously sexy . . . meltdown hot." —SeattlePi.com

"Sex that blisters the imagination, resulting in a thrill ride as raw as it is well written." —*Publishers Weekly*

"I'm a sucker for true bad boys . . . It's hot, explosive, intense and will leave you tingling in all the right places . . . For readers who like to be shocked and want to read something outside the box, this is definitely for you." —*Under the Covers*

"A gritty romance . . . raw [and] lusty." —*The Book Pushers*

"Hooked me so hard that I could not put it down. Ms. Wylde . . . will completely take you into the biker world where the motorcycle club has [its] own values, rules, laws, and ways of doing things." —*A Bookish Escape*

"[Joanna Wylde] knows how to balance great characters; a realistic, gritty storyline; [and] hot-as-hell men and women . . . with the perfect amount of romance and tenderness." —*Ana's Attic*

"Exactly what I've been looking to read." —*Maryse's Book Blog*

"Vastly entertaining." —*Dear Author*

"I am blown away by Joanna Wylde's writing and how much I love the Reapers MC books . . . [An] emotional roller coaster ride." —*Red's Hot Reads*

D0052027

Berkley titles by Joanna Wylde

Reapers Motorcycle Club
REAPER'S LEGACY
DEVIL'S GAME
REAPER'S STAND

Silver Valley
SILVER BASTARD

SILVER BASTARD

JOANNA WYLDE

BERKLEY BOOKS, NEW YORK

THE BERKLEY PUBLISHING GROUP
Published by the Penguin Group
Penguin Group (USA) LLC
375 Hudson Street, New York, New York 10014

USA • Canada • UK • Ireland • Australia • New Zealand • India • South Africa • China

penguin.com

A Penguin Random House Company

This book is an original publication of The Berkley Publishing Group.

Library of Congress Cataloging-in-Publication Data

Wylde, Joanna.
Silver bastard / Joanna Wylde.—Berkley trade paperback edition.
pages ; cm.—(Silver Valley ; 1)
ISBN 978-0-425-28062-1 (softcover)
1. Motorcycle clubs—Fiction.   2. Motorcycle gangs—Fiction.   3. Man-woman
relationships—Fiction.   I. Title.
PS3623.Y544S55 2015
813'.6—dc23
2014047383

PUBLISHING HISTORY
Berkley trade paperback edition / April 2015

PRINTED IN THE UNITED STATES OF AMERICA

10 9 8 7 6 5 4 3 2 1

Interior text design by Kelly Lipovich.

In memory of William "Backfire" Twardokus
Thank you for all you taught me.

ACKNOWLEDGMENTS

As always, thank you very much to everyone at The Berkley Publishing Group for making this book possible, particularly Cindy Hwang. Thanks also to Jessica Brock for her promotional work and the Berkley art department, which has given me yet another amazing cover. I appreciate your efforts so much.

I owe a special debt to Amy Tannenbaum, who never fails to return my calls no matter how disjointed my messages may be.

This book would not have been possible without the support of my crit partners, Kylie Scott and Cara Carnes. Renee Carlino and Kim Jones have nursed me through many a crisis as well, and Rebecca Zanetti has been an invaluable support when it comes to research (and the occasional celebratory lunch date!). I also appreciate the efforts of my beta readers, including Danielle, Hang, Sally, and Lori.

My online community is the only thing keeping me sane most days. Much love to my Sweet Butts, who always listen to me rant. Love also to the Joanna Wylde Junkies—may your dinosaurs frolic happily for all your days. Thanks to all the bloggers who have supported me all along during this journey, particularly Maryse, Lisa, Milasy, the other Lisa, and so many more. There are so many who have shown me kindness that I find it overwhelming. Thank you so much.

Finally, thanks to my family, including my endlessly patient husband and children. Yes, Mommy is finally finished with her book, and yes, we can go see a movie tonight.

AUTHOR'S NOTE

Thank you for choosing to read *Silver Bastard*, the first in my new Silver Valley series. The Silver Bastards Motorcycle Club was first featured in *Reaper's Property*, and the Reapers MC plays a significant role in this particular story. Having said that, this book stands alone, so don't worry if you haven't read the Reapers series first.

Unlike the Reapers books, the Silver Valley series won't be centered around motorcycle clubs, but a location. North Idaho's Silver Valley is located just east of Coeur d'Alene. It's a short drive from my home, and our family has been visiting the area for more than twenty years. It's an area rich in history, culture, and true stories so crazy you couldn't make them up if you tried. Miners, whores, con artists, and Wyatt Earp himself helped build the boomtowns that sprang up here when precious metals were discovered during the late 1800s. Those mines were so productive that the Silver Valley is among the top ten mining districts in world history, with total value of metals mined rising above $6 billion dollars.

Many of the major historical events and locations in the Silver Valley series are based in reality, although I've changed some names and shifted some dates. As always, I haven't let reality stand in the way of the story I want to tell. Having said that, my motorcycle club friends have reviewed this book for accuracy.

PROLOGUE

CALIFORNIA
FIVE YEARS AGO
PUCK

Mother*fucker* that burned.

The shot was a double, and the fact that it'd come cradled between two beautiful, giant tits attached to a stripper with endless legs and a tight ass didn't hurt one goddamned bit. Tequila hit my stomach, the alcohol shocking my system, and shit finally got real.

Freedom.

Fourteen months since the last time I'd had a decent drink—all but forgotten what it felt like, too. That sweet, harsh pain that comes from losing the surface layer of skin all the way down your throat? Gorgeous. Never felt better in my life, and that's a fact. Helped that the queen of body shots had sucked me off right after we'd pulled up to the party.

Spent the last year trying to decide what I'd do first when I finally got out. Kept going back and forth between getting laid and getting drunk, but God apparently has a soft spot for assholes because we'd found one hell of a good compromise.

I'd been free nearly four hours now. Still felt like a dream. The California Department of Corrections took its own sweet time with everything, up to and including processing a man out. I'd spent half the wait wondering if the cockwads would change their minds or if the club lawyer had forgotten something. Figured they'd find some way to fuck with my head.

FBI, state cops, even Homeland Security—they all wanted a piece of my club, the Silver Bastards MC, and not a week went by inside that they didn't try to cut it out of my hide. Guess they figured a prospect made an easy target.

Not fucking likely.

My old man *died* for the Bastards. If I turned, he'd haunt my ass the rest of my life because that shit does not stand in my family. I'd been born to wear a Bastard cut. And tonight? For the first time I finally had the right to show those colors off.

A hand slapped my shoulder, then a burly man caught me up in a hug so tight it hurt. My fucking ribs creaked.

"That patch feel right on your back, brother?" asked Boonie. He was the president of the Silver Bastards in Callup, Idaho, and I'd heard him call me a hell of a lot of things—but never brother. Felt good. Damned good. Until an hour ago, I'd been a prospect and I'd never gotten any special treatment because of my old man. That's how I wanted it.

"Best night of my life," I admitted. He pulled back, and his face grew serious.

"Proud of you," he said. "You did what you had to. Protected the club, took care of business. Painter told us how things were inside, how you took his back. You earned this, earned it with your life and your blood. I know you won't shame this patch, Puck."

"I won't," I replied, his words almost too much. Boonie grinned suddenly, then grabbed my arm and turned me toward the bar again.

"Drink up," he told me. "Then find yourself some pretty little thing to play with, because tomorrow we're ridin' home. Your bike's in good shape—took care of it for you."

"Thanks."

"Another shot, baby?" the stripper asked. She rolled onto her side, reaching out to catch my neck with her hand, pulling me in for a kiss. That brought me a little too close to her face. She was sweaty, and her mascara had started running. Didn't smell that great, either.

"More shots," I said, pulling away. I'd appreciated the blow job, no question. But she wasn't exactly the fantasy I'd been jacking off to the last year and I'd promised myself I wouldn't settle once I got out. I wanted someone fresh—someone clean and soft and sweet enough to eat. I'd play with her for a while before letting myself go, punching through all that softness until she screamed and begged for mercy.

Mouth, cunt, ass.

That'd been what got me through those long nights wondering why the fuck I'd let myself get caught.

Ignoring the bitch on the bar, I reached across and grabbed the bottle of tequila, chugging nearly a third of it down. Christ, there went the rest of my throat. Then I turned to look out across room. Four of my new Silver Bastard brothers had come down from Callup—Boonie, Miner, Deep, and Demon. Joining them were four Reapers and two Reaper prospects. They were here to welcome Painter, who'd gone down with me on a weapons charge. This sucked, but such is life. We'd been fighting for our clubs, so no regrets there. Through a combination of luck and well-placed pay-offs, we'd managed to stick together for the duration of our time served. The clubs provided the funds and the attorneys—to protect them, we matched that investment with our silence.

Painter caught my eye from across the room, grinning. After so much time together I could almost read his thoughts. I gave him a nod, one of those chin jerks that speaks volumes.

Congrats to you, too, asshole.

"You havin' fun?" a man asked. I looked down to find a painfully skinny, greasy little man missing half his teeth standing next to me. Tweaker called Teeny. His face was just a little too eager, his eyes a little too bright. Unfortunately, Teeny was our host for the night so I had to be nice to him. We were out in the middle of nowhere, tucked back in a canyon where this douche had somehow acquired a house. The Longnecks MC—one of our "allies," although their loyalty was questionable—had a warehouse set up in a shop right next to this guy's house.

This Teeny asshole wasn't even part of the club . . . apparently his brother Bax was patched in, though, so they used him as a pit stop. Something didn't quite add up about the situation, but fuck if I cared. In the morning I'd be riding for home. With luck my future association with the state of California in general and Teeny in particular would be extremely limited.

"See anything you like?" he asked. "That's my old lady, there. You want her? She's real good, welcome you home right."

I shrugged, glancing over toward his woman. She was probably in her midthirties, I decided. Pretty enough, but she had a hard, tired look around her eyes that didn't appeal. Not only that, she was wiry and skinny as fuck. Probably smoking meth to block out the fact that she had to live with this dickwad.

"No, she's great but not my type," I said, casually taking another drink of tequila. Wasn't burning so much now, which in retrospect should've been a sign to slow down. Maybe things would've turned out different.

Shitty thing about time—only runs the one direction.

"What's your type?" he asked. I shrugged. The day I needed some tweaker to find me pussy, I'd cut off my own cock and get it over with. Swallowing another drink, I glanced across the room, pointedly ignoring him.

That's when I saw her.

Now, I fuckin' hate clichés, and shit like this only happens in movies . . . but I swear to fuck, I think I fell for her in that instant. She was small, with long brown hair in one of those knot things on top of her head. Not dressed to show off her figure, either. I could still see she had a tiny waist, though, along with generous tits and the kind of round, healthy curves you just know will cradle your hips perfectly when you're pounding her.

I had to have her.

Like, needed her. Now.

"Good call," Teeny said. I ignored him, focusing on the angel I had every intention of owning just as soon as I talked her out of her pants. God, she was pretty. Kind of out of place, too. Not flirting with anyone, and not a ton of makeup. Just wandering around, picking up empties, and avoiding conversation. Fascinating.

"I'll introduce you."

Teeny walked across the room toward my Dream Fuck. I started after him, because I didn't want the asshole speaking on my behalf. Then Boonie caught my arm.

"Heads-up," he said, his voice pitched low, difficult to hear through the noise of the party. "We think somethin's going on with that guy. Don't be afraid to talk him up, okay? Can always use good information."

I nodded, wondering why the fuck Teeny had to pick me to buddy up with. Tonight was for relaxing, enjoying myself. Just looking at him made me feel dirty, and considering some of the shit I've pulled in my life, that's an accomplishment. Another hand slapped my back, then Painter caught me by the neck, squeezing me as he laughed.

"Never ends," he said. "Boonie cock-blocking you?"

I punched him in the gut—not hard. Just enough to make him back off.

"No, right now you have that honor," I muttered, glaring at him. "Christ, we just spent a year together in a fuckin' cell. Think we've covered everything, so let me get laid? Please?"

He answered by punching me back, and I reeled . . . damn, hadn't realized how drunk I'd gotten. Still, I wasn't about to go down easy. I swayed, watching him as our brothers started crowding around us. The wild gleam in his eyes—a mixture of almost manic happiness and pent-up energy—matched my own.

"Take it outside," Boonie said. "I got fifty on Puck."

"Hundred on Painter," Picnic Hayes, the Reapers' president, answered and then we were bundled outside for the fight.

I couldn't wait.

We'd sparred before, of course. Nothing but time to kill in the pen, so I knew Painter's moves like they were my own—and he knew mine, too. We were a good match, could go either way. Neither of us had much in the way of formal training but we'd both picked up a fair amount along the way. Hell, I'd gotten caught in my first bar fight when I was fourteen years old, seeing as my pop wasn't exactly Father of the Year material. Still loved the old bastard, though.

The sun was fading as we stepped outside, painting the sky in pinks and oranges shot through with smudged clouds. I paused a moment, struck by the incredible beauty all around me, and smiled, breathing deep. So fucking good to be outside again. Nobody knows what it's like, trapped in a cell like an animal. Nobody but the guys who've heard the sound of those gates closing behind them.

Fortunately for me, I wasn't exactly the first Silver Bastard to do time for the club, which meant my brothers got me. They knew what this was like.

"Okay, we got a circle here," Pic was saying. I blinked, starting to process the fact that maybe boxing with Painter while I was drunk might not be such a hot idea. Of course, he was drunk, too, and the booze would numb the pain . . . "Fight goes until one of you is down or taps out. Time to make your bets, brothers."

Boonie caught my arm, pulling me to the side and looking into my face.

"You ready?" he asked. I nodded sharply, because drunk or not, I wasn't going to pussy out in front of my president on the same day I got my colors. I glanced across the dusty circle to see Painter, who gave me a friendly sneer. Laughing, I flipped him off, then shook my arms out, loosening up.

That's when I saw her again. Off to the side, standing next to Teeny, who was talking rapidly and pointing to me. I frowned, because I really didn't need or want that asshole on my side. Knowing my luck, the fucker would send her running. I nudged my brother, Deep, who was standing next to me.

"See that girl?" I asked, jerking my chin toward her. "Make sure Teeny doesn't scare her off, okay?"

"Sure," he said. "I'll keep an eye out."

"Thanks."

Painter and I stepped into the circle together, and I felt the thrill of adrenaline cut through the haze of alcohol. My blood started pumping, pounding through me until I could all but taste it. Christ, but I loved to fight. Always seemed to clear my head, and I'd gotten good enough over the years that I won more than I lost. Inside, those skills had saved our asses, and I'd picked up my fair share of pointers from the very man I found myself facing.

Painter moved first, coming in with an experimental jab toward my stomach. This wasn't a real attack, just him testing my limits. I'd had a lot to drink, which would slow my reflexes. So had he. That changed the baseline, something we both needed to feel out.

"Can't believe they gave you a top rocker," he said, taunting me. I grinned.

"Try harder, old man. I know you too well."

Painter laughed, then came at me again, suddenly. He punched me square in the stomach and I doubled over. Shit. I fell back and almost stumbled out of the ring, catching myself at the last minute. I heard the shouts of my brothers urging me on.

Oh, hell no.

No fucking way I'd lose a fight tonight. Painter could fuck right off, because he'd had his colors for years. This was *my* night. I owned this bitch and he'd just have to suck it up and deal.

Still staggering, I lurched forward toward him like I was out of control. Then I attacked, and this time I caught him. One hit, two. Three. Right in the gut. Painter gasped and I moved in for the kill.

Somehow he pulled himself together, catching me across the chin. My entire head rattled as I staggered to the side. I felt blood in my mouth, then found a loose tooth with my tongue.

Asshole.

I thought of the pretty girl I'd just seen, which pissed me off. The anger was good. Cleared my head. Didn't matter if I won or not, she wouldn't want to suck face with someone bleeding like a stuck pig. This wasn't a fight—it was a cock-block.

Time to end it.

Painter waited for me, swaying. I'd gotten him pretty good. He was definitely favoring his left hand, which was great news because he was left-handed. Lucky me. I was ambidextrous.

I launched myself at him, turning that to my advantage.

He tried to block me but his arm was weak. I landed a blow to his gut followed by one that caught the side of his cheek. Pain seared through my hand, parting the fog of alcohol.

"Dick," he managed to gasp as I danced back, flexing my fingers. That last one had been bad—if I'd been any more off-center, I'd have a fist full of broken bones.

"You got him," Boonie shouted. I stretched my hand again. Did

I want to risk another head blow? I hadn't even wrapped my knuckles . . .

Fuck it.

I caught his chin again and Painter went down, falling hard. Blood dribbled from his nose and for long seconds I wondered if I'd actually hurt him for real.

Then he managed to roll onto his stomach, tapping out and flipping me off, all in one gesture.

"Congrats on getting your colors, Puck," he groaned. "I'll give you this one. Enjoy it while you can because next time I'm killing you."

I staggered back, grinning and raising my hands once I realized he wasn't seriously hurt. It'd been a lucky shot and we both knew it—we were well matched, could've gone either way. As I heard my brothers shouting in victory I didn't care. This was my night. I had my freedom and my patch.

Still needed that girl, though.

I looked around and spotted her standing next to Deep. Teeny stood on the other side of him, looking all sorry for himself. She was hugging herself with both arms, obviously nervous, and I felt my smile fade. Shit. I hadn't wanted her scared. I shook my head, wishing things weren't moving so fast. Waving off the men crowding around me, I headed toward her, half expecting her to run off.

She didn't, though.

As I came to a stop in front of her, she gave me a wavering smile, then spoke. "Can I help you find another drink?"

"Fuck yeah."

I took her arm and pulled her into my side, exchanging a satisfied look with Deep.

"Let me know if you need anything!" Teeny yelled after us, and I felt the girl shudder.

"Christ, but he's a nasty little shit, isn't he?" I asked her conversationally, and she gave a startled snort of laughter. I liked the sound. Sweet and sort of innocent. Made my dick happy, that was for sure. Still, I didn't want to fuck things up and push her too hard, because the skittish vibes were intense.

"Yeah, he is," she agreed quietly, and I leaned down to kiss the top of her head. She smelled good—fresh and clean, just like I'd been fantasizing all those months inside. Fresh and clean and perfect.

I wondered what she'd taste like.

"They're lighting a fire out back," she told me, her voice soft. "By the kegs. Maybe we should go over there?"

Hmmm . . . I could work with that.

"Okay."

She tried to pull away from me then, but I caught her hand playfully, tugging her back toward me.

"I can't get you a beer if you don't let me go," she pointed out.

Fuck. She was right. Still, I wasn't about to let her get away that easy—knowing my luck, Painter'd swoop in and take her, just to fuck with my head. If anyone could pull it off, he could. Fucker was pretty in his own weird way—even I could see it. I couldn't compete, not with the nasty scar on my face.

I'd just have to keep a close eye on her, I decided. Protect what was mine.

An hour later I found myself leaning back against the wall of the house, wondering how I'd gotten so lucky. My girl's name was Becca, and she was rapidly turning into my all-time favorite female. Not that we'd talked much—she was pretty quiet. But she was soft and warm, and now I had her tucked between my legs, leaning back against me.

"Skittish" hadn't been the right word for her, either. She'd been nervous as hell, so nervous I'd been afraid at first she'd pull a runner on me. Beer helped with that, and now she was relaxed into me, eyes closed, head turned toward my chest so that my chin brushed her forehead. I'd have said she was asleep if it wasn't for the little noises she made every time my fingers circled her nipples under her shirt, or slid down her stomach.

We'd pushed up the bra about ten minutes ago, and I'd explored down below just enough to know she wasn't sopping wet for me yet . . . but she was getting there. This was a good thing, because my dick was harder than a rock and ready for more. I shifted my hips, sliding my erection against her back, and groaned.

Feeling her up in the firelight was great, but time to move things along.

I pulled out one hand, catching her chin and tilting it up for a kiss. God, she was sweet. She tasted like sunshine and beer, with a hint of tequila mixed in for good measure. I could tell she didn't have a ton of experience, because when I slid my tongue into her mouth she wasn't quite sure what to do with her own.

Turned me on in a big way, gotta admit.

"Becca, you should take him on upstairs, don't you think?"

Teeny's voice cut through the kiss, and Becca stiffened. She pulled away from me, shutting down so hard I could practically feel the arctic chill. *Fuck.* For an instant I gave serious consideration to killing Teeny. It'd taken me nearly an hour to get her to this point, and he was *not* going to fuck it up for me.

I stared him down, eyes narrow.

"Is there a reason you're talking to her?"

He smirked.

"Just making sure it's all good here."

"Go away."

"Take him upstairs, Becca." If anything, she got more tense, and I groaned. Sure, I could just go find someone else. But I didn't want anyone else, and this asshole was ruining things for me. I wrapped my arms around her and pulled her into me, tight, making it clear that she didn't need to worry about Teeny.

"Now would be a real good time to disappear," I told him, my

voice full of a quiet menace designed to convey one message—fear.
Becca shivered, which pissed me off. Been hard enough to get
through to her, and now she had to see this. "Otherwise I'll make
it happen. Got me?"

Boonie came to stand next to us.

"We got a problem here?" he asked.

"No," Teeny said, glaring at me and Becca. Then he turned and
scuttled off like the fucking roach he was. She shivered, and I
rubbed my hands up and down her arms.

"Don't worry, babe," I told her absently. "Thanks, Boonie."

"No prob," he muttered looking after Teeny. "Glad we're leaving in the morning. There's something wrong here—been a very
educational trip."

I nodded, although I didn't have the full story. They'd fill me in
later, so until then I'd just follow Boonie's lead.

"Let's go inside," Becca said. "Find some privacy."

She pulled free and stood up. This startled me, but I wasn't
exactly unhappy about the development. I lurched off-balance as I
rose, and things were a little hazy around the edges. Wasn't messing
with my dick, though, so all good where it counted. She led me into
the house and up the stairs to a small room in the back. It had a
twin-size bed that was rumpled and stained. There was a puddle of
beer spilled on the floor next to a turned-over bottle. More cups
and bottles littered the area, and an ashtray was half full on the
bedside table.

"Guess we aren't the first ones looking for some privacy," I commented, but I didn't really care. Nope. I just shut the door and
locked it. When I turned back, she'd already stripped down to her
bra, and was busy unzipping her jeans.

Holy shit.

Becca was gorgeous.

I mean, I'd seen how pretty she was outside, but those sweet little boobs I'd been groping the last hour were even more perfect than I'd imagined. Somehow the fact that a plain cotton bra cradled them just enhanced the experience. Then she slid her pants off and I nearly died because I'd never seen anything sexier. I wanted to tie her down and take possession of every hole in her body. Twice.

Becca saw it all written in my face—clearly it scared her. She took a step back, and held up a hand. A deeply disturbing question flickered through my foggy brain.

"Are you a virgin?" I asked, the words tasting strange in my mouth. She gave a harsh laugh, then shook her head.

"No, I'm not a virgin."

She reached behind to unhook her bra and I saw her nipples for the first time. Pink and pointy and gorgeous, exactly the right size for my mouth . . . I stepped toward her and she surprised me, dropping to her knees and reaching for my fly.

"How long has it been?" she asked, her voice almost business-like. I groaned as she pushed down my jeans and briefs, cock springing free. I'd never been harder—wasn't entirely sure I'd survive the next ten minutes. Fuck, would I even *last* ten minutes? Then her hand wrapped around me and I closed my eyes, reaching out to lean against the wall because otherwise I would've fallen flat on my ass.

She started out slow and steady, wrapping her fingers around me and rubbing up and down. After a minute she paused. I opened my eyes to see her peeking up at me as she licked her palm, looking older and more seductive than I'd pegged her before. Fuck. *Fuck.* Then her other hand reached down to cup my balls as she started working me again with all ten fingers.

I gasped, falling into the sensation again. Definitely wouldn't be lasting that long, I realized. No way. But that was just fine, because tonight I had a lot more than one load saved up and ready to go.

"Use your mouth."

She obeyed, opening up and taking me in, her tongue flicking at me expertly. Almost too expertly . . . weird, and a little surprising, given how she kissed. Then she sucked me deeper and I stopped thinking at all. Everything was warm and wet and fucking perfect.

Thirty seconds later I blew up in her mouth without warning. Hell, it caught *me* off guard, it happened so fast, and I cringed. Reaching down, I caught her hair in my hand, pulling out the rubber band holding it so the long, brown strands fell around her face. She stood, wiping her face with the back of her hand, soft brown eyes meeting mine.

She looked like an innocent little angel again.

"Becca, that was . . ." I didn't have the words. God, I'd missed sex. Real sex, not just jacking off in my hand. Nothing in the world quite as sweet as the feel of hot wet woman wrapped around my dick.

She turned away, reaching down to grab a half-empty fifth of rotgut vodka off the bedside table, taking a big drink, and swishing it around her mouth. Then she spat it out on the floor so it mingled with the pooled beer before taking another swig.

Okay, not a total angel.

I reached out, and Becca handed the bottle to me wordlessly. Then she slid off her plain cotton panties and laid back on the bed.

"You ready?" she asked. I drank deep, my head spinning because I'd never been more ready for anything in my life. She didn't look ready, though. Her eyes were distant, and when I kicked off my pants and stepped between her legs, I could see her body wasn't with me, either.

Fortunately I knew how to fix that.

Pulling off my cut, I looked for somewhere safe to put it. The only available flat surface was the little table, but in the back corner was one of those hanging racks with some clothes on it. I walked over and grabbed a hanger, hung up the leather vest, and turned back to Becca.

She'd closed her eyes, and I'd have thought she was asleep if I didn't know better. Fuck, maybe she'd passed out.

"You awake?"

She nodded her head.

"Yeah, just sort of drunk," she muttered. "Don't worry about it."

Shrugging, I pulled off my shirt, then knelt down beside the bed and caught her legs up and over my shoulders. She squawked as I spread her pussy lips, giving her a long lick straight up to her clit.

"What are you doing?" she demanded, suddenly awake and alert. I licked her again, and Becca squirmed and gasped as her little nub started to harden for me. Nice. "Oh my God! I can't believe how good that feels . . ."

She fell back on the bed as I got going. I love pussy. Of course, most men do, but not all of them love going down on a nice, juicy cunt as much as me. I licked and tickled, every once in a while giving a little nip as Becca came to life under me. I think she was trying to keep still at first, but no way was I having any of that shit. Nope. I wanted her soaking wet and screaming, because I planned to ride her hard the rest of the night.

Then I slid two fingers deep inside, searching for just the right spot as I sucked on her clit like candy. Found it on the first try, and she blew up around me, crying out and sobbing. I pulled away, grabbing a chunk of loose sheet to wipe off my mouth, and she moaned, little shivers running through her body.

I'd been hard for her before—almost constantly, even right after I'd come in her mouth—but that was nothing compared to my cock now. Fluid seeped from the tip, and I reached across the floor for my pants, pulling out a condom. Along the way the vodka caught my eye and I took another drink, following her lead as I swished out my mouth and spat on the floor.

The place was truly disgusting, but I'd spent fourteen months in prison so a little filth was the least of my concerns. Tilting back my head, I sucked down the rest of the booze, swaying as I stood. I caught her under the arms and scooted her up the bed before I slipped on the condom. Seconds later I pushed deep into her. Fuck, this had been the right call tonight, because—I shit you not—never felt anything that good before in my life.

She moaned and I caught her mouth with mine, kissing her hard and claiming her. This time I didn't hold back. Nope. I just took as much as I could, savoring her sweet taste and wondering if she wanted to see Idaho . . . We'd be leaving in the morning, and the thought of throwing her on the back of my bike and taking her along worked for me in a big way.

Then she squeezed down on me hard and I stopped thinking altogether.

We slept for a while. Maybe we passed out. Dunno. Same difference. When I woke up, Becca was tucked into my side, one leg thrown over mine. Her hair trailed across my chest and her breath tickled my skin.

That's all it took.

I rolled her over onto her stomach, sliding a pillow under her hips and spreading her legs before grabbing a condom. She murmured, not really talking, but the sounds coming out of her mouth weren't unhappy when I found her clit again. Seconds later I pushed into her. I'm sure some man—somewhere in history—had enjoyed the feel of a woman's cunt more than I did in that moment. Hard to imagine how, though.

I'd taken off the edge earlier and now that I had her nice and warmed up, I was ready to do this thing for real. Grabbing her hips, I pulled back and slammed deep. Becca screamed and stiffened, now well and truly awake. Fuck, so hot and slick . . . I started pumping in and out of her hard, loving how she convulsed around me. Her arms reached out, clawing the sheets, and I lowered myself across her back, using my knees to spread her legs out even wider. Then I caught her hands in mine, nipping at the back of her neck before groaning into her ear.

"Reach down below and finger your clit."

"I can't," she gasped. I paused, catching her hand and shoving it down beneath her stomach as I lifted my weight. We found her clit together, then I shoved back into her roughly.

"Oh my God . . ." she moaned. "That's incredible."

Damn straight.

"Now keep it there," I ordered. "You're going to come for me at least twice, got it?"

She nodded into the sheets and I pulled my hand free, bracing myself as I started moving again. It wasn't gentle, but that was okay because I felt how wet and slick she was around me. Tight, too. Even better than I'd imagined back in my cell, and I have a hell of a good imagination. I leaned up on my elbows, catching her hair and jerking it back because I get off on that shit. Each twist of my hips took me closer, and when she started convulsing around me and crying, I nearly lost it. Not quite, though. I wasn't finished.

Mouth. Cunt. Ass.

I'd planned it all out in my head, dreamed about it for months . . . Now I finally had the staying power to finish it. As she shuddered and trembled, I pulled free and sat back on my heels. Becca's ass spread wide in front of me, and I smiled because it was fucking gorgeous. Heart shaped, pretty. Not too big, but not fucking skinny and nasty like a half-starved donkey, either.

Christ, I wanted to fuck her there.

My cock was still wrapped tight and dripping with her juices, but I spat into my hand a couple times for good measure, slathering it on for a little extra lube. Then caught her hips and pulled her up and onto her knees.

"Brace yourself."

She nodded, stretching out her arms in front of her like a cat, which was cute but totally inadequate under the circumstances. I caught her hair again, yanking her head to the side. Becca gasped.

"I said brace yourself," I repeated. "Gonna fuck your ass now."

She squawked, and her entire body stiffened.

"That a problem?" I asked. She shook her head quickly.

"No, do it."

Shit, could she sound less enthusiastic? I stilled, realizing my prison dream girl might not be up for the full porno fantasy in living color. Fuck.

"It's okay," I said, pulling back. I closed my eyes, running a hand through my hair and shuddering. I'd just fuck her cunt some more. I could do that. Then she shocked the hell out of me by reaching around behind to grab my cock. She pushed back with her hips, awkwardly trying to guide me to her asshole, which was funny and pathetic at the same time.

Because I'm a shitty human being, I went for it.

Not a complete dick, though. I could see the tension radiating off her.

"You never done this before?" I asked her. She shook her head violently, not looking at me.

"Okay, we'll go slow."

She nodded this time, but she still didn't give me her eyes. It bothered me for some reason, although why, I had no fucking idea. I dug my fingers deep into her hair, twisting her head around enough to kiss her. Hard. My tongue dug deep, forcing her to kiss me back and, I shit you not, I felt like fireworks were going off in my head. Clichéd as all fuck, but there you have it. After long seconds we came up for air, and I stared into her eyes, seeing how her pupils grew wide.

Slowly, steadily I found her opening with my cockhead, pushing in as she gasped.

"You okay?"

"I'm fine," she said, eyes wide, her lips trembling. I held her there, my heart beating so hard I thought it might come right out of my chest as I drove down deep. She was tight—really tight. Sure as hell hadn't been lying when she'd said she'd never done this before. I sank into her for what felt like forever before I hit bottom, balls resting against her pussy. Her heartbeat pulsed around my cock and I realized that I would be happy to die in that moment. *That's* how good it was.

Becca closed her eyes and turned her face into the covers, spasming around me. I didn't like the position—I wanted to watch her face—but she seemed to need some privacy. I got it. I've never been a nice, vanilla kind of guy, but this was a different kind of intensity than even I was used to. No screaming, no scratching, no fighting with each other until we both lost our minds . . . No, this was powerful on a whole new level, and looking into her eyes was probably too much for me, too.

I pulled back out, then slid in again. She gasped.

"Play with your clit some more."

She nodded without speaking, burrowing her hand back down until she found her target. I started moving, going slowly and carefully at first. But it felt really good, and I've never been one to take things slow and careful.

Looking back, I can't decide if that's when things really fell to shit, or if they'd been falling to shit all along and I was just too stupid to see it. Never have figured that one out, but what happened next was not my finest hour. I started moving faster. It felt fucking amazing. *She* felt fucking amazing. Then I was pounding her and she was shuddering and I thought she was coming and it was perfect.

Becca sobbed suddenly. Loud. Not a pretty crying kind of noise, and not one of those moans bitches give when they're getting off so hard they can't quite control themselves.

No.

This was the kind of noise a puppy makes when you kick it, and I felt it all the way down to my gut like a knife ripping me open.

Big. Fucking. Mistake.

I pulled out and caught her up and into my arms. She flinched and I hated myself, because even like that she was soft and pretty and I just wanted to keep nailing her ass. Becca knew it, too, because she tried to pull away from the press of my cock against her back. More sobs escaped and tears rolled down her face and I knew for a fact that I'd burn in hell for this.

Rubbing her head, I tried to think of soothing noises. Instead I was full of questions. Why had she let me do it?

'Cause you're a pushy, scary bastard.

Fuck.

"I'm sorry," I told her, my head starting to spin. Shouldn't have drunk so much. I had no idea what time it was, no idea how long we'd been up here . . . I heard noises outside, the sounds of music and the party still going, but that didn't mean much. A good party could last all night and into the next morning.

"It's okay," she finally managed to whisper, and I bit back a harsh laugh because that was a huge fucking lie and we both knew it. Then she did something that blew me away. Becca turned in my arms and pushed me down onto my back. Seconds later she had the condom off and was sucking me deep again, which made no fucking sense at all.

Unfortunately my dick wasn't the sensitive, caring type because it really didn't care that she was clearly so scared and drunk off her ass she'd lost touch with reality.

I could've stopped her.

I *should've* stopped her.

Instead I sank my fingers into her hair and blew up into her mouth and it was even better than the first time. The room was seriously spinning all around me as she tucked into my arm and stroked my chest.

"Tell him I did good, okay?" she whispered. "Just tell him I did good. Please?"

I passed out, wondering what the fuck she was talking about.

My bladder was about to explode.

Needed to pee. Maybe rinse out my mouth, too, because it tasted like something died in there and that was not an exaggeration. Shifting, I realized that Becca was still tucked into me, sleeping heavily. I managed to crack my eyes open, blinking. Faint light was creeping in through the window, although even now I could still hear music down below.

Great. Gonna be a long ride home with no sleep. Sliding carefully out from under Becca, I stood and pulled on my pants. My shirt had fallen into the sticky puddle of beer and vodka, so I stumbled out of the room half naked. The door across the hall was locked, although from the smell it had to be the bathroom—either that or people had started pissing and vomiting in the bedrooms, which I supposed wasn't entirely impossible. Felt great to be back with my brothers, but our hosts kind of sucked ass. Bunch of assholes and meth heads, so far as I could tell. No wonder Boonie didn't trust them.

I walked down the stairs into the living room, where despite the fact that music still blared, people were passed out all over the place. My brother Deep leaned back against the bar separating the living room from the kitchen area, arms crossed, a look of faint disgust on his face.

"Hey," I said, keeping my voice low.

"You look like death. Have fun up there?"

I shrugged, feeling like an asshole.

"She's perfect," I said. "But I think I hurt her."

His eyes narrowed.

"We got a situation? Should I go get Boonie?"

Shit.

"No, not like that," I said quickly. "I mean, I think I pushed her too far. Tried to fuck her ass, and it didn't go over so well. She's okay, but I still feel like a douche."

"We got a girl who's gonna cry rape?" he asked quickly, and I snorted.

"Probably should," I replied. "She told me to do it, though. Afterward she sucked me off. Feels wrong, somehow."

"You want another drink?" I turned to see Teeny standing there, his beady eyes bright and full of something I couldn't quite follow. God, I hated him—he was like a cockroach that wasn't smart enough to stay out of the light.

Anger replaced my disgust. He needed to leave me the fuck alone.

"Are you serious?" I asked him, turning and cracking my knuckles. The fight with Painter had taken off my edge, but it'd come back again as I told Deep about Becca. Hitting someone—anyone— would feel good, but hitting this guy? That'd be a flat-out pleasure. "God, don't you ever go away? Fucking piece of shit!"

I started toward him, but Deep caught my arm, pulling me back.

"Careful, bro," he said quietly. "This isn't about him. You're pissed about the girl. Pick your battles, because there's a lot more Longnecks than Reapers and Bastards combined. All he did was offer you a drink."

Fuck. I breathed deep, looking at the scared little shit and wishing desperately he'd do something—anything—to give me an excuse to take him down. My brothers would back me no matter what, but I wasn't stupid enough to think there wouldn't be a price for my actions.

"I'm going back to bed," I said after a tense minute or so, pulling free. "Talk to you later, brother."

Deep nodded, watching Teeny as I turned and stalked back up the stairs. This time the bathroom door was open. Sure enough, someone had missed the toilet, and I felt my own stomach heave sympathetically. For a sec there I thought I might lose it. Then I pulled it together enough to piss without barfing. Afterward, I turned to look at myself in the mirror. As always, the face looking back at me was ugly as fuck. Dark, ragged hair. Scar cutting across my face. Nose that'd been broken at least four times now . . .

Shit, no wonder Becca had been scared of me—I looked like a fuckin' serial killer. I wanted to punch the mirror and break it into a thousand pieces, which would accomplish even less than beating the shit out of Teeny.

Instead I went back into the room and found her still sound asleep on the bed. Her skin was pale and fragile, dark shadows ringing her eyes. Still gorgeous, but younger and more frail-looking now. Christ. What had I done? I crawled back into bed with her, sure I'd never get to sleep. I'd underestimated how much booze was still floating around in my system, because everything went dark again.

This time the sun was bright and harsh. I blinked, trying to remember where I was . . . Then it all came back and I looked around, wondering where my girl went.

Shit. Becca was gone.

What the hell really happened last night? I sat up, spotting my colors hanging from a rack next to . . . school uniforms? Fuck, some kid must live in this room, I realized. That'd suck, coming home to a mess like this. I turned and lowered my feet on the far side of the bed, figuring I'd open the window to air things out, check the lay of the land in the process. I stepped on a pile of books, which fell over. I reached down to pick one up.

Textbook.

I picked up another. Shit, it was another textbook, and under that was a notebook. That's when I started to get a very bad feeling in the pit of my stomach—something I wouldn't have pegged as possible, given how shitty I already felt about how the night had played out.

The notebook opened in my hands, and I saw the name *Becca Jones* written on the top of the front page, along with *English: First Period* and the date.

Below were notes.

Maybe she was in college, I thought desperately. Please, fuck . . . let her be in college. A piece of colored paper fell to the ground, and I dropped the notebook to pick it up.

What I saw nearly made me throw up.

It was a flyer for a dance—a *high school* dance.

Becca was still in school. Jailbait. *The fuck?* It didn't add up . . . Then her last words to me sank in, and it all added up far too well.

"Tell him I did good, okay? Just tell him I did good. Please?"

I flew down the stairs half dressed, my boots thudding loudly. My shirt was filthy from her floor, but my cut was still fine—safe and sound after a night spent hanging next to Becca's little school dresses. Fucking piece of shit pimp Teeny.

Had to be him.

This was his house. Who the hell was she? His kid? What the fuck kind of asshole pimped out his own daughter? But shit, I guess it happened all the time, all over the world. About halfway down I heard her scream, which should've woken up everyone all over the goddamned house. Most of them were still passed out drunk, though. I heard more shouts outside and knew my brothers were probably coming.

That turned out to be a good thing, because I came damned close to ending a man's life that day—fucking craptastic way to start parole . . .

Teeny stood in the center of the kitchen, Becca huddled at his feet as he kicked her. Then he whacked her across the head with a fucking soup pot, of all things, and I lost my shit.

"You cocksucking asshole!" I shouted, launching myself at him. "Fucking twat! I'll kill you!"

My fists destroyed his face with a crunch. It felt good—cathartic. He fell like a bag of concrete and some part of my brain noted vaguely that Becca was scrabbling away from us, chunks of her long hair torn loose and left on the floor. Blood, too. Another woman shouted and tugged at her, but I didn't turn to look.

Nope. I had work to do.

Specifically, I needed to kill Teeny with my bare hands. Then I'd tear him apart and eat his heart. Raw. He screamed like a bitch the whole time, and I heard Boonie yelling in the background. Then they hauled me off his ass, kicking and fighting because I'd well and truly lost my shit.

"What the fuck is happening here?" Picnic Hayes demanded. Beside him stood one of the Longnecks, a guy who looked a fuckuva lot like Teeny and I realized this must be the brother who was part of the club. Bax.

Bax wasn't a happy camper. Fair enough. I was pretty fucking unhappy myself.

Teeny moaned on the floor, rolling onto his back, and I spat at him. Then I heard a sobbing noise—one that'd already been burned into my brain. Becca was crying, and I looked over to find her huddled up against Teeny's old lady.

Shit. I hadn't seen it before because the woman was so nasty and used up, but under that scrawny, tweaker body was an older copy of Becca. Had to be her mother . . . Even with the meth eating her, though, she seemed too young. If that was the mother, she must've had Becca really fucking early.

"She his daughter?" I asked her, my voice like a knife. The woman shook her head quickly, lips quivering. "You let him pimp her out?"

She looked away.

"Damn," Picnic said. "This is a hell of a clusterfuck."

"I'm not leaving her here. He'll kill her."

Pic shook his head slowly, thoughtfully, but I could see it in his face—he knew I was right.

"Yeah, she can come with us," he said. "You up for that, Boon?"

My president nodded, eyes never leaving the huddled mass of blood and human filth crying on the floor.

"We'll head out in twenty minutes," Boonie said decisively. "Anyone got a problem with that?"

He looked around the room in challenge, and several of the Longnecks glanced away—apparently they weren't going to stand up for Teeny. Said a hell of a lot about them in general and Teeny in particular. I mean, I was glad that we weren't fighting our way out, but that's just pathetic. They were happy to party with him. When it came time to take his back, they were gone.

"C'mon, let's go upstairs and grab some of your shit," I said to Becca, reaching toward her. She gave a little scream and pushed back with her feet, sliding across the floor to get away from me. *Fuck.*

"I'll get her ready," the mother said suddenly. Her voice quavered, but her eyes were resolute as they met mine. "She'll go with you—just get her away from here. He'll hurt her bad for this. Real bad."

I nodded, watching as she drew her daughter to her feet, then pushed her toward the stairwell.

"Jesus, you can sure pick 'em," Boonie said. "How old you think she is?"

"She's still in high school," I said, my voice grim. "Fairly certain I'm up for statutory if this goes down wrong."

"Damn," Painter said, coming up behind me. "That's fast work—usually takes a little longer to violate parole, bro."

I met his gaze, and for once his face didn't hold even a hint of mockery. Fuck. This was really bad.

"Outside," Picnic said sharply. "Horse, Ruger—you stay here. Make sure the girl gets out safe, okay?"

He caught my arm and pulled me toward the door. Boonie flanked us, and I sensed real danger beneath their calm expressions. We walked over to the bikes as the others scrambled to grab their shit and pack up.

"I won't leave her," I told them again. "I know she's scared of me, but I don't give a fuck. That girl'll die if she stays here."

"Not gonna leave her," Pic said. "But we do need to get out fast, before they have time to figure out what happened and get pissed off. They decide to fight for her, things'll get ugly. Not sure we can take 'em."

"Thanks for standing with me."

Boonie snorted.

"You're our brother, Puck," he said, his voice casual. "This is what we do. You went down for us, you think we aren't prepared to do the same for you? Now pull your shit together. We can put the girl in the truck with the prospects, or you can take her on your bike. No time to fuck around."

Fifteen minutes later, I watched as Horse, Becca, and her mom walked out of the house. At least thirty members of the Longnecks MC stood watching, talking quietly among themselves. I kept waiting for one of them to reach for a gun or challenge us, but they didn't.

No sign of Teeny.

Becca had stopped crying, but her face was still covered in tear-smeared blood, and nasty bruises were popping up all over. Her breath sounded wheezy, too, and I hoped to hell she didn't have broken ribs.

"I don't want to go," she whispered, catching at her mom's arm. "I want to stay with you."

"You're getting out," the woman replied, her eyes hard and calculating. "Let him cool off, then we'll talk. Figure something out."

Becca shook her head, but when I caught her arm gently she let me pull her away.

"You want to ride in the truck or on my bike?"

Becca glanced at the truck, eyes widening at the sight of two Reaper prospects. "I'll stay with you."

I nodded and climbed on my bike, eyes alert as I monitored our audience. She climbed up behind me, and then her mother gave a satisfied nod. Becca wrapped her arms around me and I felt her tits press tight against my back. My cock stirred to life. What the fucking hell was wrong with me?

"How old are you?" I asked, my voice low.

"Sixteen."

Shit.

"Like, you're almost seventeen?"

"No, I turned sixteen last week."

Double shit.

Boonie kicked his bike to life, and we followed his lead, pulling away from the house in formation.

So that's the story of how I committed statutory rape less than twenty-four hours out of prison—on my birthday, no less. In retrospect, I probably should've stayed inside, served out my full five-year term. Would've been less work for everyone.

ONE

"Order up."

I turned to the window and grabbed the ticket, looking over everything to make sure Blake had gotten it right. He was a damned good cook, but sometimes he was a little loose in his interpretation of an order . . . especially if he was hungover.

And he was definitely hungover today.

In fact, I think he might've still been a little drunk when he dragged his ass through the back door at five that morning. I know Danielle was, because she was all giggly and unsteady when she'd started the breakfast shift with me.

"I think I'm going to barf," she whispered into my ear, leaning against the counter. Heh. Guess someone was finally sobering up.

"Can you cover my tables for a few? I can't let Eva catch me—she said she'd fire my ass if I fucked up again."

"I got it," I said, snatching up toast and throwing it onto a little plate, along with a couple of jelly packets. "Go take care of business—she's talking to Melba and you know how they get. You've got fifteen minutes at least, so make the most of it."

She nodded and ducked back through the kitchen. I heard Blake growl at her for getting in his way and had to smile. I didn't think it was a coincidence that they'd both shown up looking like hell. There was a story behind that growl, and if I knew Danielle, it'd be a good one.

Loading my tray, I hoisted it up and over my shoulder, carrying it out past the counter and into the main dining room. The Breakfast Table was the heart and soul of Callup, at least in the mornings. Everyone came in to see and be seen, because the food was good and it was cheap. We opened at five thirty a.m. so the miners and loggers could grab a bite before work, and we closed up again by two in the afternoon, although I was only on until eleven. At that point I'd hop in my car and drive over the pass to Coeur d'Alene to spend my afternoon at the beauty school.

Only six more months and I'd be ready to take my boards.

The thought put a little smile on my face as I hauled my tray over to Regina and Earl, an older couple who owned the old building downtown that held my apartment. The smile got bigger when I saw Regina was wearing the blouse I'd made her last week . . .

"Here you go," I said, feeling all sorts of pleased with myself. "One Belgian waffle with strawberries and bacon on the side. One pork chop with hash browns, toast, and applesauce. You good on coffee?"

"You're right on top of things, Becca," Earl said, eyeing his chop with anticipation. He had one every morning. Didn't seem like such a bright idea to me, considering he'd already had one heart attack, but every time I tried to talk to him about it he blew me off.

"These must be some of Honey's strawberries," Regina said, popping one into her mouth. "The store-bought ones aren't as sweet."

"Yup," I told her. "Enjoy them while they last—they'll be gone in a week or two."

"Order up!" Blake shouted, ringing the bell in the pass-through window.

"That's me," I said, leaning over to give Regina an impulsive hug. She'd been the one to take me in when I'd first arrived in Callup five years ago. I'd been bruised, terrified, and so lonely for my mother it hurt. And yeah, I realize it's crazy to miss someone who treats you like shit, but deep down inside we're all just babies crying for Mommy, you know? Regina took it all in stride, holding me tight through the nightmares as I slowly rebuilt myself into something human.

It took Teeny six months to "forgive" me after Puck and I rode north. Mom had called all excited, saying I should come back home. Earl declared I'd be leaving over his dead body, and that was the end of it. I'd lived with him and Regina through high school and while I spent a year working and saving up my money. After that they gave me one of their apartments over the old pharmacy building at the friends-and-family rate.

Regina and Earl were the best thing that ever happened to me, and I loved them for it.

"Lookin' good, Becca," said Jakob McDougal, settling himself at the counter. Today he had four of his buddies in tow. He was loud, rude, and one time he'd left me a penny underneath a turned-over glass of water for a tip because his breakfast steak was over-cooked. (I don't know if you've ever seen someone do that, but it's a straight-up dick move—one that takes real effort, too.)

Long story short, Jakob McDougal was an asshole.

He also wasn't real bright, because after pulling that shit he *still* thought he had a shot at getting me naked, no matter how many times I shot his ass down. Now I resisted the urge to flip him off because I was still six months away from dumping this gig to start cutting hair, and Eva could be a real bitch if we were rude to the customers, even if they'd earned it. (Eva could be a real bitch about a lot of things, which was part of why I was working so hard to get my license and leave the waitressing behind.)

"I'll be with you in a minute," I told him, my voice tight, because guys like him pissed me off. Giving him my back, I reached for the next ticket and prepped my tray.

"I'm tired and need some coffee," Jake said, ignoring the fact that I'd just told him I needed a minute. Dumbass. His friends Cooper, Matt, Alex, and one other I didn't know laughed like a chorus of braying jackasses. "I was up laaaate last night making Sherri Fields a very happy girl, and I want something to get me up again. I got needs, baby."

The jackasses grunted and snickered, giving each other high fives. One of them made a slapping noise and another moaned in a way that I suspected was supposed to sound like the unfortunate Sherri Fields in the throes of ecstasy. More like a dying elk, in my opinion.

I counted to ten and stared at the plated food in the window, jaw clenched. Blake caught my gaze, and his eyes narrowed. Uh-oh. Blake wasn't a big fan of customers giving the waitresses shit at the best of times, and he got mean when he had a hangover. I saw him reach for his big, flat metal spatula with the sharp edge on one side and my eyes widened.

Crap. Did I want Jake and his friends to suffer? Absolutely. But not if it got me fired.

"It's all good, Blake," I said quickly. He shook his head slowly as Jake and his friends laughed harder. That's when I remembered they'd gone to school with Blake, over in Kellogg. Seniors together on the football team. Then the other guys got jobs at the Laughing Tess mine . . . Blake had claustrophobia, so he slung hash browns in the mornings and went to community college in the afternoons. He was a smart guy, and personally I thought he had a much brighter future ahead of him than the losers behind me.

I felt his pain, though. Taking the high road can wear a person out.

"We got an issue here?" a deep voice asked, sending shivers all up and down my spine. I closed my eyes, wondering if the day could possibly get any more fucked up. That was the voice that haunted my dreams, although I hadn't heard it for six months. (Six months and eight days . . . give or take. Not that I was counting.)

The voice belonged to Puck Redhouse.

The same Puck Redhouse who—in one monumentally fucked-up night five years ago—made me come harder than I knew was possible, poked me in a most uncomfortable place, and then set me up to get my ass kicked when he complained about how bad I was in the sack.

I sort of hated him for that.

The next morning he'd hauled me all the way back to Idaho and deposited me on Earl and Regina's doorstep like a lost puppy. After that he disappeared into the night. I saw him around on and off, but the guy was mysterious.

Kind of like Batman. *On a motorcycle.*

In a weird way, I owed him everything . . . the man still scared the shit out of me, though. Scared me, turned me on, you name it, because if there was one constant derailing my quest for happy normalcy, it was Puck Redhouse and his stupid, sexy voice. The man was my own personal North Atlantic iceberg, lurking under the cold waters, just waiting to shred me wide open.

Fucking biker. I'd had enough bikers to last a lifetime—I didn't need him in my life.

Not that he'd ever said anything to indicate he *wanted* me in his life. But over the years he'd watched me . . . Sometimes I got the feeling he wanted to do a lot more than watch.

I shivered, because I'd never forget how he'd felt pushing deep inside, stretching and filling and blowing my mind all at once.

Unfortunately, there wasn't time to give my stupid body the lecture about why Puck was all wrong. I had a feeling we were one step away from a bloodbath right at the breakfast counter. Too much testosterone. I needed to do something—break the tension and smooth things over.

"No issues—" I tried to say, but Blake cut me off.

"Yeah, we got a fuckin' issue," he snarled, pushing through the swinging doors from the kitchen into the counter area. "These cocksuckers think you can come in here and treat the girls like shit. Outside, McDougal."

Across the dining room people fell silent, and then I saw Eva stand up and start toward us, her default scowl growing uglier than usual. Fuck. I was about thirty seconds away from unemployment, and believe me when I say there weren't exactly an abundance of work opportunities in a mountain town of eight hundred people.

"Blake, please go back into the kitchen," I hissed, deciding to ignore Puck because I just didn't have enough space in my brain to deal with him. "Let me get coffee for everyone, and a slice of pie. It's on me."

"Can I eat it off you?" Jake asked. Apparently he didn't have a highly honed sense of self-preservation. His friends burst out laughing as all hell broke loose.

I'm still not entirely sure what happened next.

I do know that Blake slammed his big spatula down on Jake's hand right as Puck punched him. Jake's jackass chorus might be idiots, but they weren't cowards because suddenly they were all up and fighting. That's when I discovered Puck hadn't walked in for breakfast alone—nope, he'd come in with two other Silver Bastards (Boonie and Deep), Boonie's old lady (Darcy), and another girl named Carlie Gifford. Carlie was about my age, and she'd been hanging around with the club for a while, which I knew because I knew everything about Callup. (I might not be a native, but the Breakfast Table was Grand Central so far as this town went—if something happened, I heard about it.)

As Eva started screeching at us to stop, Darcy grabbed me and jerked me out from behind the breakfast bar. Jake was shouting and clutching his hand, which dripped blood over everything. The big plastic sugar container with the funnel on top that I used to refill the sugar jars for the table went flying, showering all of us as Blake hurdled the counter to go after his former friend. Then Coop jumped Puck from behind and something inside me snapped.

This is where it's worth mentioning that over the years I've developed a bit of a temper.

Okay, make that one hell of a temper.

Puck might be trouble, but he'd also saved my ass big-time and I didn't want him getting hurt. Knowing he was around (*Batman!*) helped me sleep in a weird way. Nothing scares off a monster like a bigger, nastier monster, and every time I woke up screaming in the night after a dream about my stepdad, the memory of Puck beating his ass helped me keep it together. So long as Puck was in the region, I'd be safe . . . at least, I'd be safe from everyone but Puck.

I broke free from Darcy's grasp and reached for a glass coffeepot that'd been left sitting on the counter. Then I brought it down over Coop's head so hard it exploded, hot coffee soaking his shirt and coating his back. He screamed and fell down, so I kicked him in the nuts. Puck stared at me, obviously startled but impressed.

"Behind you!" I shouted, catching Alex lunging out of the corner of my eye. Puck ducked and spun around, punching the other man in the gut. Darcy caught me by one arm and Carlie grabbed the other one as an entire rack of clean water glasses crashed to the floor. Eva was shouting in the background and to my shock, I saw Earl lumbering toward the fight, a maniacal grin on his wrinkled face.

How did things get out of control so fast? And more important, where the hell was I going to work now? No fucking way Eva would keep me on after this.

Normal girls don't start fights in restaurants! my brain hissed. Crapsicles. This was exactly the kind of shit my mom was always getting herself into. Generally I tried to look at any given situation, figure out what she'd do, and then do the exact opposite. My theory was that this would turn me from trashy to classy.

Someday I'd be classy if it killed me—probably not *today*, though.

Pisser.

The fight was spiraling out of control as a body hit the hostess table, sending it crashing over with a splintering, cracking noise. Jake and his friends were tough, no question. The mountains bred hard men, and the mines tempered them like steel. But Puck, Boonie, and Deep were hard men, too. And Blake? I had a feeling this wasn't his first run-in with the boys . . . I'd always known he was a big, tough teddy bear, but suddenly he'd turned into a grizzly.

The crack of a shot cut through the air, followed quickly by a second and third. People started dropping to the ground and I heard Regina's voice ringing through the room.

"You boys settle right the hell down! This is a restaurant, you idiots, not some damned bar where you can tear things apart and nobody even notices because it's such a dump!"

Everything stopped, and I cautiously raised my head. Regina stood on a table in her purple track pants, chunky plastic jewelry, and tennis shoes, every gray hair on her head aligned perfectly. She looked like any other sweet old grandmother, but her eyes were like chunks of obsidian, sharp and brilliant.

Wowza.

"Now get out, all of you," she said. "Boonie, Eva will be in touch about the damages. I'm assuming the club will be good for it?"

"But they didn't start it!" I piped up, outraged. "Jake and his friends—"

"Let it go," Darcy said, pulling me to my feet. I looked at her, startled to see her eyes were dancing with laughter. How she could laugh I couldn't imagine. I was fucking pissed.

"It's not fair!"

Boonie came up behind me, his hand coming down on my shoulder with a thump. I jerked—startled—and then the anger drained out, replaced with that old fear I felt whenever I got too close to one of the bikers. What was I thinking, arguing with these people over the damages? I needed to get out before Puck cornered me—I couldn't deal with him. Not today.

"We got this," Boonie said in a low voice. "Jake and his boys'll pay, don't worry."

That sounded ominous. I swallowed.

"Go outside," he said over my shoulder, talking to Darcy. "I'll meet you in a few. Make sure Eva doesn't follow her, got it?"

I closed my eyes as the full ramifications of the fight hit me.

This is what happens when you let your temper take over. I could actually hear the high school counselor's words in my head, along with the smug, prissy tone of her voice. She'd been lecturing me about the way I'd coldcocked a guy who tried to cop a feel, but the same principle applied.

Hitting people rarely solved things.

I had a problem, but at least I'd stopped feeling sorry for myself over the years . . . Earl insisted this was a step in the right direction. Healthy, even. Looking around the trashed restaurant, I had to wonder if maybe he was full of shit.

So much for my job—I'd lost it for sure, or at least I would once the dust settled. Fucking sucked, because despite Eva's nasty personality, I had the perfect schedule, allowing me to get in a full shift every day and still go to school.

School was my future—*normal* girls go to school and support themselves. I couldn't afford mistakes like today, not if I wanted to make something of myself.

"This sucks," I muttered, following Darcy out to the parking lot, where at least half the residents of Callup were milling around, anxious to see what the fuss was all about. Now that the fight was over, they weren't leaving. Nope. They were standing in little clumps to whisper and point at me, and more looky-loos were pulling up to join them every minute.

News travels fast in Callup and this was the most exciting thing to happen since Regina and Melba had their confrontation in the beauty salon over who stole whose hairstyle.

Fuck, I hated it when people talked about me.

"You okay?" Carlie asked. I nodded, trying not to look at her. Carlie was everything I hated. She was tall, skinny, and gorgeous. Like a model. Exactly the type of woman who belonged with Puck, because they fit each other. Her eyes sparkled and her teeth were bright and straight and white. The only thing less than perfect about her was a tiny gap between her front teeth. Somehow that just made her look more interesting, though.

And she was nice.

Bitch.

"I'm fine," I replied, feeling my adrenaline fade a little. "Do you think anyone was really hurt?"

"No," she said. "Coop's probably got some burns, but nothing serious. It didn't keep him down for long. I have to give you credit. That took balls."

I shrugged, because she had no idea about the real me. I'd grown up surrounded by dangerous men—Jake and Coop were innocent babies compared to them. I could teach them all kinds of things about fighting dirty . . . But that part of my life was in the past, and I wanted to keep it that way. Boring was better.

Boring, comfortable, and safe. Words to live by.

Words I wished my mom would learn for herself. So far as I could tell, her favorite word was "drama."

"Don't worry," Darcy said, wrapping an arm around my shoulders and pulling me close. I think it was supposed to make me feel better but it kind of creeped me out. She was attached to Boonie, and Boonie was president of the MC. Not that I hated the Silver Bastards—they scared Teeny, which meant he wasn't a threat, and I appreciated that a great deal. I just preferred to appreciate it from a comfortable distance. "My old man will fix it. He always does."

Sure, he'd fix it for the boys. At the end of the day I'd still be out a job, though. Probably Blake, too.

Puck, Boonie, Deep, and Blake came sauntering out of the restaurant, laughing and slapping each other on the back like it was all a big fucking joke. This frustrated me, because it wasn't a joke—it was my life. Of course you could make the obvious argument that my whole life was one big fucking joke. But I'd read a book about the power of positive thinking last year, and had decided I wouldn't let myself wallow like that ever again.

Stop thinking about it, I told my brain, which of course made it worse. *You're a joke*, it hissed. *Trash. Who the hell do you think you are?*

Wait. That was *Teeny's* voice in my head.

He could fuck himself right off. So what if things had gone bad here? I'd lived through worse and I'd live through this because I was a winner.

Power. Of. Positive. Thinking.

"All good, baby?" Darcy asked, stepping toward Boonie. He wrapped an arm around her waist, pulling her in for a deep kiss. "Sure. Eva came right around. Jake and his boys will be heading home soon, where I suggested they practice their manners before showing their faces around town again. Let's ride down to Kellogg and grab some breakfast there. Sound good?"

I felt Puck's eyes touch me, although he didn't say anything.

He never did.

Five years ago, I'd felt him watching me like a physical touch. He'd been the seventh stranger Teeny told me I had to fuck. He'd been different from the others, though. It probably sounds twisted, but I remembered feeling a mixture of fear and excitement when Teeny gave me my marching orders. Puck was actually young and good-looking—in any other world, I might've even tried talking to him, or at least stalking him discreetly.

Of course, that was before I got close and realized just how big he was. Tough. Scary. And not just because he had that nasty scar across his face, either. Nope, even in that room full of dangerous, scary men there had been something different about him.

Then he'd started touching me, and I'd forgotten to be afraid.

I'd had no idea up to that point how good sex could feel, or that there might be a reason women let themselves go crazy for a man's attention. And when we'd sat near the fire and he'd held me, and later when he made me come for the first time ever? For a while I pretended I was a normal girl at a regular party, not just a biker whore's brat learning to earn her keep.

Yeah, Puck hurt me.

They *all* hurt me.

At least he didn't know, and once he figured it out he held me and then we'd slept together in one bed. I was safe for a while. Of course it didn't last, but nothing good ever lasted around the Longnecks MC. They were like a festering wound that oozed pus and spread infection to whatever they touched.

Case in point? My mom. After five years she and Teeny were still together, still fucked up, and still trying to use me. She'd called me last month with some story about a broken water heater, begging for money. Again.

I didn't hate her anymore, though. When things got truly bad, she'd done the right thing and sent me with Puck. She'd never defied Teeny like that before—I knew he'd beaten her after I left. Came close to killing her and kicked her out for a week . . . then she went crawling back to him. Unbelievable.

"You coming with?" Puck asked, stepping toward me. I jumped. *What the hell?* Puck watched me, occasionally said hello. Like, once a year. He never, ever invited me to do anything with him because we had strict boundaries. He prowled around, I pretended he wasn't there, and I lived life safe and sound where Teeny could never get to me.

Now Puck stared at me, obviously waiting for an answer. I shook my head, unnerved. Then Puck reached out to catch a lock of my hair and tuck it behind my ear.

What. The. Fuck.

Beside me Carlie stiffened, her smile fading. Great. Not only was Batman changing his M.O. without warning, he was doing it in front of his girlfriend. Just what I needed.

(Okay, that wasn't entirely fair. She obviously had a thing for him and I'd bet a hundred bucks they were sleeping together, but so far as I knew Puck never pretended or lied to get laid. He wasn't into commitment. This was well known to every woman in Callup foolish enough to crush on him. Essentially all of them who had a pulse and few borderline cases, too. I'd watched Melba checking out his ass once—you can't unsee something like that, trust me.)

"I really can't go to breakfast," I said, my voice shaky. "I need to talk with Eva."

"Don't bother," Blake said with a grin. "You're fired. Me, too."

"Did she say that?" I asked, feeling a little sick to my stomach.

"Oh yeah. She said it loud and clear. Repeatedly. I'll go back with you to pick up your check at the end of the week so you don't have to face her alone."

I closed my eyes, wondering why things couldn't have just stayed the same, even if it was just for another six months. Not that I should be surprised. My reality had never been smooth before, so why should it start now?

Think positive, I reminded myself.

Crap. Now I was bummed *and* I wanted to bitch-slap my brain for being so annoying.

"What the fuck happened out here?" Danielle asked, her arm suddenly around my shoulders. I immediately felt better. Danielle and I balanced each other out perfectly—she was batshit crazy and insanely optimistic. Make that dangerously, recklessly optimistic. As for me, I spent nearly all my time focused on staying sane and getting ahead. That didn't leave much time for things like actually *living* my life.

We'd met each other our senior year of high school, when she'd offered to drive me back and forth to town in her shiny new Jeep Wrangler. This spared me from the horror of sharing a battered school bus with every hormonal teen living in the greater Callup metropolitan area. After a particularly harrowing ride home in her car one night (long story short, it took us six hours to travel thirty miles and by the time we pulled into town, we had matching tattoos of chipmunks wearing scarves) I decided it was my job to keep her from accidentally killing herself.

In return, she pushed me to do fun things, reminding me at least once a week that I was only twenty-one and perhaps the fate of the universe didn't literally rest on whether or not I balanced my checkbook to the penny. Along the way, she taught me how to do smoky eye makeup, how *not* to freak out when a guy asked me to dance, and how to "borrow" music off the Internet. (When I pointed out that "borrowing" music was stealing, she agreed and started using iTunes for her downloads. To finance this, she "borrowed" her dad's credit card.)

"Well, apparently me and Blake no longer work here," I said, leaning my head against her. "I don't know if you're fired or not."

"Fuck that," Danielle declared. "Eva can kiss my ass. If you're out, I'm out."

"You weren't even part of it," I protested.

"I don't care. You're a *much* better waitress than I am. If she fired you, no way I'd last there anyway. Let's go get drunk!"

Blake laughed and caught me around the neck, hugging me from the other side. Puck watched us silently, his face grim. Just. Like. Batman.

The Dark Knight was easier to understand, though. Puck had treated me like I had the plague ever since that night five years ago, yet this morning he suddenly wanted to get breakfast? We weren't friends. I didn't even know where he lived, for God's sake. Sometimes he'd just disappear for months at a time and despite full access to Callup's sophisticated gossip network, I'd never been able to figure out where he was or what he was doing.

Not that I cared.

I didn't.

Although I had to admit, I slept better when he was in town. He made me feel weirdly safe in a terrified, trapped-deer kind of way. Puck was a wolf, but for the most part he left me alone while scaring away the other wolves. This was a good thing and it worked for us—if it ain't broke, don't fix it.

"I can't get drunk," I reminded her. "I have to go home and shower, and then it's time to head out for school."

"Okay, tonight then," Blake said. "We'll get together and share our misery. I'll bring my friend, the good Dr. Jack Daniels, and we can make a double date of it—you, me, Danielle, and our bottle. Sound good?"

I shot a quick glance at Puck, wishing he'd go away and stop listening to us. Ignoring my wishes, he studied me and Blake, his face turning thoughtful. Not the "oh, she should go out and have fun" kind of thoughtful. No—he was definitely having dark, broody thoughts. That's when it hit me. Puck didn't like the idea of me partying with Blake and Danielle.

That was exactly what I needed to tilt the scale.

"Tonight sounds great," I announced. "Might as well celebrate the fact that we won't be getting up at five tomorrow morning."

Danielle grinned happily, and I smiled back at her, pretending Puck didn't exist.

Eva stormed out of the restaurant at that moment, all angry and red in the face. Shit. She spotted me and started trucking across the parking lot under full steam, Regina and Melba behind her. Melba seemed to be egging her on, while Regina was trying to catch and hold her arm. Eva ignored both, and the look on her face convinced me that now wasn't the time to discuss my final paycheck with her. Danielle apparently came to the same conclusion.

"She's in a real bad mood," she said, her voice dry. "I think we should leave her alone."

"Um, yeah . . ." I agreed. "She looks like she's going to have a heart attack."

"You're not getting away with this!" Eva shouted suddenly. *Crap*. Danielle and I glanced at each other, and Danielle's eyes started to dance. She loved drama like this, crazy girl.

"Run!" she hissed. We sprinted across the parking lot, and I very sincerely hoped that Danielle had her keys ready to go. I heard a man's deep laugh behind us—Boonie? Sure as shit wasn't Puck. Not that it mattered. We'd committed our crime and now it was time to get the hell out of there before Eva tried to kill us.

We reached the back of the lot, where Danielle's Jeep waited. Thankfully, she'd taken off the doors for the summer, allowing us to jump inside. She stabbed the ignition with her key and suddenly the big tires were spinning as we pulled out of the lot and onto the old highway.

I grabbed the roll bar and turned around in my seat, climbing up onto my knees to see Puck standing next to Blake. He was scowling and Blake was smiling broadly. Eva had started screaming and shaking her fist at him like a cartoon character, which didn't bother our (former) cook in the slightest. I spun back down and dropped into the seat, looking over at Danielle. She giggled, and then we were both cackling like crazy—as shitty as it was to be out of work, seeing Eva like that was sweet, sweet revenge.

God, that woman was a bitch. Served her right for not protecting her waitresses.

TWO

By the time I got home that night the laughter had faded, leaving behind my cold, unpleasant reality.

School had been okay—I'd actually gotten there early enough to talk to my instructor about losing my job, which was good because I had no idea what my next work schedule would look like. Finding something compatible with classes might be hard . . .

My school advisor had suggested I move out of Callup and into Coeur d'Alene, where I'd have more employment options. Took me all of thirty seconds to rule it out. I didn't want to be away from Regina and Earl and Danielle and Blake. Not only that, there was the safety issue. Did I live in total fear? No. Did I still wake up some nights screaming? Absolutely.

I'd never have to worry about Teeny again, so long as I stayed in Silver Bastard territory. Throw in the fact that even the shittiest apartments in Coeur d'Alene cost three times what they were in Callup and it was a no-brainer.

I parked my ancient Subaru Impreza in the alley behind my

apartment and climbed out across the passenger seat. The driver's-side door had been broken as long as I'd owned it. Earl's niece had sold it to me for $400 three years ago, and while it might look like hell, it ran like a top—especially for a car that had nearly 200,000 miles. Earl helped me do most of the maintenance myself out in his shop. The important parts all worked great.

I could handle a broken door.

Popping the hatch, I pulled out my groceries and locked back up. Danielle and Blake were due in an hour. He was bringing booze, she was bringing salad, and I'd be providing the pasta to complete the meal. Danielle had emailed me while I was in school, saying that she had a line on a new gig for us already, God bless her. I couldn't imagine what it was, but figured so long as it was legal, I'd take it. When I'd checked my bank balance at the ATM there was only $22.63 left in the account.

I needed work, and I needed it fast.

Using my shoulder, I pushed open the door at the back of the building and started up the empty stairwell. The retail space downstairs had been for lease as long as I'd lived in Callup, but there weren't any takers. Most of the downtown buildings were like that. Callup's days of glory were long gone.

My front door was at the top of the steps off a little landing. There were two apartments, but one of them was currently uninhabitable because Earl had gotten a wild hair three years ago and torn out all the fixtures and cabinets. He'd decided to turn it into a luxury vacation condo, as if that would ever work. Then he got a new rifle and decided to go hunting instead, so now the place sat empty and collected dust like the rest of the town.

At least my apartment was in good shape. It was in the front half of the building, which was located on a corner, so I had lots of windows. There was a small kitchen in the back and a great big bathroom with a claw-foot tub.

I loved it.

The wooden floors were a hundred years old and the ceilings were high and covered in pressed tin. Best of all? The corner overlooking the street had a genuine turret built into it, curved glass window and all. It got bright, glorious sunlight almost all day.

That's where I put my sewing machine.

Regina had started me sewing right after I moved in, and sometimes I think it's what really saved me. I'd always loved fabrics and design, but she'd taught me how to take a shapeless pile of cloth and turn it into something beautiful. The first month I'd been afraid to leave the house, convinced that every motorcycle I heard carried Teeny. I spent my days torn between hating Puck and desperately wishing he was there to protect me. (Of course, when he came to check on me I couldn't even bring myself to look at him.)

Regina took my crazy in stride, assigning me sewing projects in a no-nonsense voice, offering hints and wisdom along the way. I'd made all new curtains for their house before I'd gotten brave enough to visit downtown Callup. After four sundresses (two for me, one for Regina, and one for Regina's cat—don't ask) I was ready to drive to Coeur d'Alene with her to get groceries.

It'd taken a full-on quilt to get me to the point where I could hear the sound of a Harley without panicking.

Through it all, Earl and Regina were as patient as the mountains. Regina homeschooled me until I got bold and registered for the high school when I turned seventeen. For the first time in my life, I belonged somewhere.

Regina had three sewing machines and a serger at that point. This was a good thing because Earl had been laid off at the mine, so she'd started taking in mending to make ends meet. One of the machines had a computer smart enough to pilot a spaceship but I didn't care for it. I preferred a delicate black Singer that was nearly a hundred years old—it'd belonged to Regina's mother. Right around the time I'd been born, she'd finally replaced the foot treadle with a tiny electric motor.

The day I graduated from high school, Regina gave it to me.

The best modern sewing machines might be more efficient than my Singer, but she was strong enough to sew leather and delicate enough to repair silk. The engraving and gold leaf gave her an elegance that transcended function, inspiring me and filling my heart with the soft presence of the generations of women who'd used her to clothe their families.

Now I lived in my very own home and it was beautiful. The furniture might not all match, but the curtains and pillows and other little touches I'd created tied my small, private world together into something that was homey, comfortable, and best of all, *normal*.

Too bad I couldn't convince Mom to join me. Whenever we talked, she insisted Teeny was better than he used to be. I didn't believe it for a minute. He still used her to get drugs, she still used him to get drugs, and they always needed "just another fifty bucks, baby" to make it through.

Whatever. She was old enough to make her own choices and I couldn't let her drag me down, too.

The blinking of the message light on my old-school answering machine caught my attention. Just one of the valley's many weird quirks was the fact that less than two miles off the interstate, we lost all cell service. I still had a cell phone, of course—every time I drove to Coeur d'Alene it would spring to life with random messages and texts that'd been locked in a holding pattern since the last time I'd come into range.

Then I'd drive home again and return those calls from my landline, which created all kinds of confusion on people's caller ID. It was inconvenient, but also kind of funny. I hit play on the message and Danielle's voice spilled out, full of excitement.

"Hey, Becca! We'll be over by six. I have great news!"

I looked at the clock—5:55 p.m. Well, crap. I ducked into the bathroom and gave myself a quick once-over. Not too bad, considering how fucked up my day had been. One of the best parts of beauty school was learning how to really take care of my appearance and I liked to keep myself together. Polished.

A quick run of the brush through my hair and a touch of lip gloss fixed me right up. I heard Danielle and Blake pounding on the apartment door and I opened it to find them wearing triumphant expressions. Blake held up two bottles, one of whiskey and the other of cheap red wine.

"So what's the news?" I asked, eyes darting between them.

"We've got jobs!" Danielle said. "Starting tomorrow! They even said they'd work around your school schedule."

I cocked my head.

"That was easy," I said slowly. "What's the catch?"

Danielle's smile faded, and Blake shrugged.

"It's down at the Bitter Moose." I opened my mouth to protest, but Danielle held up a hand, her face uncharacteristically serious.

"Don't get your panties in a knot," she said. "I know you don't like bars, but get over it. There's nowhere else to work around here and we all know it. Unless you want to work on the other side of the pass? I hear that new strip club is hiring in Post Falls . . ."

Ignoring the strip-club crack, I shook my head. Much as I hated to admit it, Danielle was probably right. There truly wasn't anywhere else to work near Callup—not for someone with my limited skill set.

Great.

I sighed and Danielle rolled her eyes unsympathetically.

"Look on the positive side," Blake said. "What are the odds a fight will start at the Bitter Moose on any given night?"

"There's a fight out there *every* night."

"Exactly. It's perfect, because they can't fire you or blame you when it happens," he said reasonably. "You can do this—I saw you throw yourself into the action this morning. Hell, you stay tough like that, you'll make a fortune in tips."

"Ooo, do you think we should sign up for the mud-wrestling championships?" Danielle asked, her voice excited.

"They have mud wrestling there?" I asked, my voice rising. Danielle laughed.

"No, you dork," she replied. "See what a civilized place it is? They're way too fancy for mud wrestling . . . Well, either that or they haven't thought of it. Now get your ass into the kitchen and start cooking some noodles. I'll open the wine. Blake, I expect you to entertain me."

"How am I supposed to do that?"

"Strip," Danielle demanded.

I snorted back a laugh at Blake's expression, holding up a hand.

"For the record, I'm broke," I told him. "If you start stripping, Danielle has to pay you."

"That should work out fine," he replied, waggling his eyebrows at her.

"Give me the wine," I demanded, deciding I might as well let go for the night and enjoy—Danielle wanted to party, and after everything that'd happened today, I was more than ready to join her.

Hell, I'd already blown classy for the day.

Might as well have some fun.

It was the smack on the ass that tipped me off Blake was drunk.

He'd snapped me with a towel at the diner plenty of times, but swatting my butt with his hand was a new level for us, one that probably would've bothered me if I wasn't feeling pretty festive myself.

Blake smacked me again. What the hell? I spun on him, then realized I was blocking the window and he wanted to go outside . . . Oopsie.

One of the best things about my apartment was the fact that the building next door was only one story—that meant I was able to use the roof as my own personal patio for important things like watching the sunset over the mountains. We'd already feasted like kings (well, more like two queens and a king, but you get the picture) and now it was time for lounging on the "veranda" to enjoy our after-dinner drinks.

Not that I needed more to drink . . .

"Get out here, slacker!" Danielle shouted at me, giggling when I stopped to glare at Blake.

"He copped a feel!" I accused loudly.

"I'm trying to go outside while I'm still young," he grumbled. "Christ, do we need to have a conference about this here, or you think maybe we can move it along before it gets dark?"

"Asshole," Danielle muttered, although her voice was anything but annoyed. Obviously she found Blake smacking me funny. I felt a twinge of jealousy—she had this laid back confidence around men, completely comfortable in her own attractions and more than ready to move on if it didn't work out. So far as I could tell, she was just using him for sex.

Wish I could do that. I'd probably gone out with three guys in the last two years, but they either made me anxious or left me cold. Even if things went well and we started making out, I'd flash back to Teeny and it was all over.

Reaching out, Danielle caught my hand and jerked me forward. I fell out onto the roof, landing on my face. This was apparently extremely funny—Blake couldn't stop laughing as I tried to right myself. Danielle joined him. Traitor.

"Laugh away, jerks," I muttered, holding up my wine bottle triumphantly. "You almost made me spill alcohol. That's a grave offense against the gods."

They sobered instantly.

"I forgot you were holding the wine," Danielle said, her voice serious. "I wouldn't have done that if I'd known the risk."

We pondered the severity of the situation before she started giggling again, which got me going. Life might be fucked up, but I had damned fine friends despite it all. Five minutes later we sat in a row on the roof's incline, feet braced on the low false front that someone thought would make the building look more impressive, once upon a time. It'd been a doctor's office back when Callup still had a doctor. His sign still sat out front, right next to the broken barber pole on the building next door.

"Your apartment used to be part of a whorehouse," Danielle said casually.

"I know. Regina told me about it."

"Did you know the girls liked to come out here to eat their meals? They wouldn't let them out to walk around town or anything."

"Really?" I asked, intrigued. "I thought it was anything goes back in the mining days. Seems weird that the hookers wouldn't be allowed outside."

Blake snorted.

"It didn't shut down until 1988," he said. My eyes widened.

"Seriously?"

He nodded, taking a swig from his bottle.

"Yup, my dad used to come here," he said. "Mom dumped his ass over it, I shit you not. There was one in the building on the other side, too."

I glanced over toward the three-story building rising above us, across the roof from my apartment. You'd be able to crawl out onto the roof from there, too, although I'd never seen anyone do it. That one just had one big apartment filling the whole second floor. Until recently, an old logger lived there. Six months ago he'd retired and gone south to move in with his daughter. Sooner or later someone else would rent it, but for now I had the roof to myself.

That's when I saw the flicker of a light inside.

"What's that?" I asked, my voice a loud whisper.

"What's what?"

"There's a light in the window over there," I said. "Or I think there is. They're so damned dirty it's hard to tell."

"Probably a ghost," Danielle replied, her voice sage. "You know, Wyatt Earp came through here, back during the gold rush. I'll bet he shot some prostitute in there, and now she's just waiting around to have her revenge on all men. You better watch out, Blake. She'll steal your dick and then you'll be no good to me."

"Fuck off," he said, his voice happy. The shadows had grown longer and the sun was already down below the ridgeline. Night fell fast here in the deep mountain valleys.

"You wish," she replied, crawling over me to lie down on top of him. I rolled my eyes.

"You guys are disgusting."

"Jealous?" Blake asked. "You're totally welcome to join in."

I flipped him off, then looked back toward the empty apartment across from mine. There was definitely a light in there, I decided. Between the dirt and the dark curtains it was hard to see, but apparently I had a new neighbor.

"Hope whoever moved in isn't an asshole."

Danielle and Blake didn't reply, and I looked over to find them swapping spit as his hand slipped up her shirt. Great.

"You know, you're hurting my feelings," I muttered. "Seems like just a little while ago your hands were all over me. What's a girl to think?"

They ignored me, and I giggled at my own little joke. Then I saw a shadow pass across the window.

Alcohol is fully to blame for what I did next.

Booze and that unpleasant, impulsive streak I'd inherited from Mom . . .

Setting down my bottle carefully, I crept across the roof on my hands and knees in full stealth mode. This wasn't exactly an impressive feat, given how old and soft the shingles were, but I still felt very sneaky and special when I reached the far window and tried to peek inside.

The grime blocked everything, so I spat on my finger and wiped off a little peephole. It worked surprisingly well but when I put my face up to it to look through, I was rewarded with a sight that shocked me. Oh wow.

It was an ass. A bare ass, with tight, sculpted muscles and thick, firm thighs. It'd been five years, but I recognized those thighs all too well. Even if I hadn't, the little tingle of arousal would've been a dead giveaway.

What in the name of hell was Puck Redhouse doing in the building across from mine? *And where the fuck were his clothes?*

I gasped as he slowly turned, revealing that it wasn't just his butt that was naked. Nope, that was a penis and it was every bit as big and hard as I remembered it being. I'd felt that thing push deep inside and it'd felt good. Total understatement. It'd been fantastic.

Well, fantastic until the pain, the beating, and the endless ride across the desert wondering whether my mom was still alive.

You'd think the memory of the bad would wipe out the good, but it didn't. In my head they were almost two separate incidents, unrelated. Regina told me once that we do whatever we have to when it comes to survival, including allowing our bodies to feel pleasure at the strangest of times. She said I shouldn't worry about judging my sexual responses, even if they were kind of fucked up.

This was easier in theory than practice.

I really, really didn't want to be attracted to Puck.

God obviously has a vicious sense of humor. Here I was, a walking, talking portrait of sexual dysfunction, and the only guy who really got me going happened to be the scariest biker I'd ever met. The motorcycle club was supposed to be a deal breaker. It wasn't personal—more of a "been there, done that, got my lifetime supply of psychological trauma" kind of thing.

Puck was exactly the opposite of what I wanted and needed, yet my stupid body just wasn't getting the message.

Unacceptable.

Then he reached down and caught that big cock in his hand, giving it a stroke. I stopped thinking and settled in for the show, figuring if God was going to betray me by creating a body that only responded to Puck, I might as well enjoy it. It didn't occur to me that maybe I shouldn't be spying on him. Not even a little. Of course, nothing good ever happens when you spy on someone.

Sometimes you get caught.

Sometimes you see horrible, horrible things . . . like Carlie Gifford stepping into view and dropping to her knees in front of the guy you absolutely don't want anything to do with under any circumstances— *not even a little*—and sucking his dick deep into her mouth.

I'd never been under any illusions about Puck. The night I'd met him, he'd fucked me harder than most women experience in their entire lives . . . but I knew I wasn't anything special in his world. Hell, he'd brought women to breakfast at the diner regularly whenever he was in town. Guess that made him a gentleman, because at least he fed them after a night spent hot and heavy under the sheets.

Still, knowing he was fucking around and seeing it in living color right in front of you are two very different things.

This was where I should've backed away. Scuttled off like a good girl, gone back into my apartment and gone to bed. Definitely the smart thing to do.

But when her mouth wrapped around him tight and he dug his fingers deep into her hair?

I couldn't have dragged my eyes away if my life depended on it. So I watched as her cheeks hollowed and sucked him in. So wrong on so many levels, and utterly compelling. Need and desire grew between my legs as her fingers dug into his ass. I still remembered exactly how it felt when he'd come deep into my own throat all those years ago.

It was wrong.

And when his entire body tensed before he pulled free and sprayed all over her face?

That's when I realized my fascination with Puck was deeply fucked up. I needed to meet some other man. *Any* other man. Maybe before I took a job down at the Bitter Moose, I should go check it out for myself. See who might be there. Somewhere in the world there had to be a guy as sexy as Puck who wasn't a biker. I just needed to find him.

There had to be a sweet spot between lonely cat lady and full-on biker whore like my mom. Not that I had a cat—yet. But one of Regina's was pregnant and she'd been talking about giving me a kitten.

When I got it, I'd already know how to make it sundresses . . .

No. *No more cat dresses.* I'd just have to suck it up and start screwing random guys until I found one that worked right.

Standing unsteadily, I backed away from the window, tripping as I knocked over the empty wine bottle with an unholy rattle of metal flashing. It startled Blake, and he sat up abruptly, rolling Danielle off to the side with a thud. She squawked in outrage. This would've been of far more concern to me if I wasn't suddenly teetering toward the end of the fake roof facade, hoping rather desperately that the two-foot-high barrier would be enough to keep me from going over the edge.

"Fuck," Blake muttered, diving for me. He caught the side of my shirt and yanked me back. Hard. The fabric tore wide open and we fell back down on the roof together with a thud.

When I caught my breath, I discovered that I was straddling Blake with both legs spread wide. His arms held my half-naked upper body against him—tight—and the tops of my breasts pressed firmly into his face.

"Are you all right?" Danielle asked, her voice short and breathy. I blinked, trying to figure that out for myself. Then Blake made a snorting noise and wiggled his head.

"Shit," I muttered, pulling back. I'd been smothering the poor man. "Blake, I'm so sorry! Thank you for saving me, though."

Blake took a deep breath and coughed, then gave a slow grin.

"If you really want to thank me, shove those tits back down into my face."

"Don't make me use my gun," Danielle muttered, her voice dark. I blushed fiercely, realizing that regardless of whether it was because he'd been making out with Danielle or because I was currently grinding my crotch deep into his, the man was hard as a rock.

Then Blake was rolling me to the side and I was lying on my back, wondering what the hell just happened. Shit. There was no way Puck could've missed all that noise outside the window.

Wasn't that just perfect.

I considered checking his window to see if he was watching. Did I really want to know? Uh-uh. Retreat was the better part of valor under the circumstances. Not only that, despite my crash into the roof, my bits were still a little tingly from watching Carlie suck him off, which was creepy and weird. Then I remembered my idea.

"Let's go to the Bitter Moose," I said, sitting up. "Get dressed up, go dancing or something. If I'm going to start working there, I should see what it's like at night. Maybe find a cute guy while we're at it."

"You've never been to the Moose at night?" Danielle asked, obviously surprised. "But you're always going on about how much you hate bars. How do you know you hate it if you've never been there?"

"I've heard stories. It's not my kind of place, but you know what? Maybe I need to get out more."

"I see what's happening here," Blake said, his voice sly. "You got a taste of Blake, and now you're ready to get back in the saddle, aren't you?"

"Jesus, do you never stop trying?" Danielle asked him.

"Hey, it's not my fault she threw herself at me," he said. "But seriously, if you want to go out, let's call my friend, Joe Collins. He can drive us, and he's been asking me forever to set something up with you, Becca."

Across the roof I caught the flare of a light. Crap. Puck had pushed open the drapes, and now I could see him all too clearly as he walked away from the window. Had he seen me spying on him? God, I hoped not. More important, what was he doing over there in the first place?

That apartment was supposed to be empty.

"We going out or not?" Danielle demanded.

"Yeah, let's go out."

"I'll call Joe," Blake said. "He's into you, Becca."

I shrugged, trying to picture Joe. I was pretty sure I remembered him—he'd come into the diner a few times.

"Doesn't he live up in Kellogg?"

"Used to," Blake replied. "But he's crashing with me right now. Needed a place to stay. He started at the Laughing Tess last month and got tired of the drive."

"Okay, we gotta find you something to wear," Danielle said, moving toward the open window. "Something sexy. I'm so proud— my little girl is finally growing up!"

It was nearly eleven before we reached the bar.

Danielle and Blake had gotten busy in the bed of Joe Collins' big Ford F-150 as we drove toward the Bitter Moose, which was illegal as hell. Fortunately the sheriff didn't make it out here very often, so they were safe enough. Well, as safe as two people can be while having sex in the open back of a truck that's driving sixty miles an hour down the highway at night.

"Glad you guys called me," Joe said, reaching over to turn down the music. I stole a glance at him out of the corner of my eye, noting that he was a lot cuter than I remembered. Joe was a big guy—well over six feet—and built like a bull. He had short, dark hair, classically handsome features, and a quick smile full of teeth just crooked enough to give him a rough charm.

Very attractive.

Unfortunately, my nether regions could care less—what would it be like to kiss him? Maybe it was time to stop waiting for tinglies and just get it on. I'd only tried dating a few times since I'd come to Callup and none of them had ended particularly well.

"I'm glad we did, too," I told him, which was true. Maybe he didn't blow me away but he seemed like a nice guy. We could have fun together. "I guess I'm going to be working at the Moose soon— at least, that's what Danielle says. I'll have to talk to the manager tonight while we're there . . ."

My voice trailed off as the implications hit me. Did I really want to meet my future boss for the first time while I was drunk? Wow, that was a super-stupid idea. But what else could I do? We were almost there and I didn't have any magical sobriety pills tucked in the little pocket of my phone case.

Crap.

"I can't believe I'm going to a job interview drunk."

Joe grinned at me, then reached over to catch my hand in his, giving it a squeeze.

"Don't worry about it," he said. "This isn't an interview, and if they weeded out everyone who'd ever come into their bar for a few drinks, there'd be nobody left in the valley. Teresa Thompson is as laid-back as they come—she'll give you a chance to prove yourself before making any decisions."

"Is it as rough there as everyone says?"

He shrugged.

"It can be, I guess," he said. "But Teresa doesn't take shit off anyone, and she doesn't stand for people messing with the staff. It won't be anything like working at the Breakfast Table. You'll bust ass, but you can make a fortune in tips on a good night."

"How do you know so much about it?" I asked, curious.

"Used to bartend there with Blake," he replied. "Couple years ago."

"Wait, Blake tended bar at the Bitter Moose? Why the hell was he working at the Breakfast Table?"

Joe started laughing, then shook his head.

"You haven't figured that out by now? It's because of Danielle. He's been batshit over her since high school, but she's always blown him off. He used to date her older sister and she fed Danielle all kinds of crap about him. He finally took that job so he could actually spend some time with her, start to wear her down."

"Really?" I asked, fascinated. "But he seems so . . . casual toward her. I mean, he was flirting with me tonight like crazy. I know they're fucking around but I never got the impression he was looking for a relationship."

"Think about it—have you ever seen Danielle get with someone for longer than a week? She's not into the whole relationship thing, never has been. He's going under her radar. It's a setup."

Wow. That really did make sense in a twisted way.

"That's a lot of work."

He shrugged.

"Blake's just killing time until he finishes his degree anyway," he said. "He's got big plans. Doesn't really matter where he works while he pulls it all together, so why not take a job close to Danielle? Of course now he's got her where he wants her."

I wanted to ask him more, but that's when we pulled up to the bar, which was hopping even though it was a Wednesday night. The Moose was a rough-looking two-story building about twenty miles downriver from Callup. It had a big, double-decker porch on the front and looked like something straight out of the 1880s, which wasn't entirely inaccurate. That's when it was first built.

Originally it'd overlooked the river. The north fork had jumped its banks a while back, though, and now the building was half a mile away. Joe turned off the truck and looked in the rearview mirror, a shocked expression coming over his face. Then he made a disgusted, choking noise.

"Oh my God. Are they naked back there?" I asked, my voice a horrified whisper.

Joe burst out laughing and shook his head with a wink.

"Naw, just messin' with you," he said. "It's all good. Let's go inside and have some fun."

An hour later I had to give Joe credit, because he knew how to show a girl a good time. First up, he'd introduced me to Teresa Thompson, declaring, "This is Blake's friend. She's scared because she's a little drunk, and doesn't want you to think she'll be a shitty employee because of it."

I'd started stammering, wondering what the hell I'd ever done to piss him off. Teresa just smiled and told me to sober up before I showed for work the next day and we'd be fine. I floundered some more, talking about school and wanting to do a good job. She told the bartender to give me drinks on the house, saying, "Welcome her to the Moose family right, Connor."

Now I found myself dancing with Danielle in the center of a small dance floor while a local band played classics, wondering why the hell I'd been so dead set against bars. Were there a bunch of rough, tough guys in here? Definitely. But I had Blake and Joe watching my back, and while they weren't quite as scary as Puck, they were more than enough to ward off any unwelcome attention.

Not that I got a lot.

Even dressed in my best, I was nothing compared to Danielle. Don't get me wrong—I know I'm a pretty girl. But she has something going for her that I couldn't beat. Boobs, specifically. Her plentiful cleavage was well and truly on display. Even wearing my lowest-cut V-neck T-shirt, I had nothing but mosquito bites on her.

Usually I liked that—I was all about keeping a low profile.

Tonight I was feeling a little needy, though . . . Fortunately Joe came up behind me, sliding his hands around my waist and down to my hips. I felt damned good about myself after that, because there were lots of women scoping him out. He still only looked at me.

The band started playing some slow, soulful song that Regina loved—"The House of the Rising Sun." I swayed back into him, closing my eyes and leaning my head back against his shoulder. The room swirled around me, but I didn't care because his arms were strong and I felt safe.

That's when it struck me.

I was in the middle of a bar. Drunk. A big, powerful man was holding me close to his body and for the first time in my life I didn't feel scared. Except that wasn't entirely true, because when Puck Redhouse had held me like this I hadn't felt scared, either. I still remembered sitting in front of him out by the bonfire, realizing that so long as he had me, no other man could claim me for the night. I didn't mind that later on I'd be getting naked with him.

Of course, that was before he'd nearly destroyed me by saying I was a bad lay. Then he'd saved my recently abused ass, so I guess after that we were even? Either way, in Joe's arms I felt better than I'd felt in a long time so it was a good night.

Maybe losing my job wasn't such a bad thing after all.

I opened my eyes to find Puck himself staring at me from across the room, eyes burning like coals. I shivered, going liquid instantly. God, seeing him did it every time. What was wrong with me? Puck wasn't even handsome—not like Joe. He was too imperfect, with a ragged scar that cut across his face and a nose that had obviously been broken more than once. Everything about him was rough, almost brutal, and while I knew he wasn't that much older than me, there were ten lifetimes reflected in his gaze.

Puck was taller than Joe, although he wasn't quite as bulky. That didn't mean he was small, just that he didn't make his living

hauling ore in a mine. Joe's skin was darkened slightly by the
ground-in dust and dirt of the deep earth, while Puck's was deeply
bronzed from the sun and the wind, and maybe a hint of some
ancestry that wasn't on the white side.

I felt my nipples tighten as he stared me down, drinking deeply
from his brown beer bottle. What did he think of me cradled in Joe's
arms, leaning back against another man almost dreamily? I couldn't
quite read Puck's expression. It wasn't friendly. Nope, not even a
little. For a second I almost wondered if he'd challenge Joe. I shook
my head, wondering where *that* particular thought had come from.

When I blinked he was gone and I wondered if I'd imagined the
whole thing.

"Hey, bitch," Danielle said, breaking the spell. "You ready for
a bathroom break? I gotta pee like a Russian racehorse. Come with
me or I'll get all sad and lonely and then I'll have to cry by myself
in the ladies' room . . . and you know what that does to my mascara. We can't go there."

"You're drunk off your ass," I told her, wondering how Russian
racehorses peed.

"And?"

Hard to argue with that.

When I finished washing my hands, Danielle had disappeared,
faithless slut. I took a few minutes to primp myself back to respect-
ability, then pushed through the door into the darkened hallway.

Puck stood there, eyes all dark fire and stone.

Shit.

Not a happy look. Not happy at all. I took a split second to
consider my situation, then decided to make a run for it. Just as
fast, Puck stepped forward into my space, blocking the way.
What does he want? Best to just play it through, my fuzzy brain
decided.

"Hey," I said.

He didn't respond, but his eyes trailed down me slowly, taking in every inch of my body. They lingered on my breasts, and I shuddered, remembering the night that he'd done more than just look. Why was he back here? There was absolutely no possible reason for him to be here that ended well for me. None.

Finally he spoke.

"Having a good time?"

I nodded quickly, wondering if I could avoid talking to him entirely. Hell, I wasn't sure I could make a noise if my life depended on it. Couldn't move, either, although my inner ancestral monkey screamed that I should start running for the hills and never stop until I was safely hidden deep inside a cave or something.

"You and that guy a thing?"

I shook my head automatically, then cursed myself because I should've said yes. Should've told him we were together and very happy, and that I planned to marry Joe in a big puffy pastry of a dress in front of five hundred of our closest friends without inviting him. Puck licked his lips, a mixture of frustration and anticipation written across his face.

"You dance like that with a lot of men?"

I shook my head quickly. His eyes grew hot, smothering me, and I had the feeling that we were an instant away from something I couldn't handle. Puck stepped forward. I shifted back, bumping into the wall. His body wasn't touching mine, but I felt him all the same, a pressure washing up against me and pinning me until I couldn't breathe.

"You could dance with me."

I nearly stroked out, eyes darting to either side. Hadn't Joe and Blake missed me by now? Why wasn't anyone saving me? Puck leaned closer until his nose all but touched my cheek, and inhaled, scenting me. I clenched between my legs and then gasped, because even that tiny movement was enough to make it so much worse.

Holy *shit*, I wanted this man.

"I'm going to start working here tomorrow," I managed to whisper. "I got fired from the Breakfast Table, remember?"

"Busy, aren't we?" he whispered, reaching up to catch a chunk of my hair, wrapping it around his hand. "Saw you on the roof earlier. Thought you weren't that kind of girl."

I tried to breathe.

"What kind of girl?"

"My kind."

Holy shit. He was too close, way too in my face and I could smell him all around me, a faint mixture of alcohol, sweat, and the hint of exhaust from his bike. It shouldn't have worked for me but it did. He'd smelled like that five years ago, too, and my traitorous bitch of a body recognized him. Recognized him and wanted him.

Closing my eyes, I tried to think.

"I'm just me," I told him, swallowing. His hand rose, cradling my throat for a second, fingers stroking my jaw. I felt tears welling up in my eyes and my voice broke when I continued. "I don't know what that means, but tonight I'm just trying to have some fun with my friends. Please don't ruin it."

He flinched and pulled back.

"I didn't mean to hurt you."

"I know that."

"Had no fucking clue you were that young, or that you didn't want to be there."

"I know that, too."

Puck looked away, the strained guilt on his face almost more than I could stand. I had to do something, even though I didn't feel strong enough. Reaching up, I cradled the side of his face with my hand, turning it toward me so I could meet his eyes. Then I spoke, putting everything I had into the words, willing him to believe me.

"Meeting you was the best thing that ever happened to me, Puck. Things were fucked up and wrong, but you saved my life. Do you have any idea where I'd be right now if you hadn't come to that party?"

"Becca, you okay?" Joe asked, his voice cutting through the tension. Puck stepped back, although he still kept himself between me and the other man, his stance weirdly protective like always.

So sexy . . .

"I'm fine. Puck is an old friend. We were just talking."

"Danielle and Blake want to go swim down at the river," Joe said slowly, taking in our body language. "Was thinking we'd head out. Unless you want to stay?"

Yeah, I wanted to stay. I wanted to drop to my knees, suck Puck off in front of everyone, and then ride away into the night on his bike. I'd do whatever twisted, fucked-up things he asked me, too, because I was my mother's daughter.

Slut . . .

"No. I want to go with you, Joe."

Puck stiffened, but he stepped to the side, letting me pass as I walked over to Joe. He tugged me into his side, wrapping an arm around my shoulders. Puck didn't move as he and Blake's friend stared each other down, wordlessly sharing an entire conversation I couldn't begin to follow.

"Let's go," I said, turning into Joe and spreading a hand on his chest. He nodded, and we walked out of the bar.

Later that night I lay back on an old blanket under the stars. We'd settled on the river bar just past the bridge, and a small campfire glowed not far away. Danielle and Blake were off in the bushes laughing and wrestling around, which should've been awkward but wasn't somehow.

Joe was great. Super. Exactly the kind of man I needed.

We'd made out for a while, and while he didn't gross me out, he didn't do much for me, either. But when I asked him to stop, he agreed easily enough. Not that he wasn't interested—I'd felt enough action down below to know he was definitely into me—but I liked the way he respected my boundaries.

"It's gorgeous out here," I murmured, one of the greatest understatements of the century. The stars were a million jewels painted across the sky and the burble of the shallow river over the rocks could've soothed Charles Manson, it was so ridiculously peaceful.

"I love this place," Joe said. "Been coming out here since I was a kid."

"How old are you?"

"Twenty-two. Born just a couple miles down the valley. I know a lot of people can't wait to get out of here, but I can't imagine living anywhere else. What about you?"

God, I hated that question.

"I'm from California," I said slowly. "Moved up here about five years ago."

"We didn't go to high school together," he said. "I would've remembered. You're kind of a mystery girl, aren't you?"

I shrugged, not liking the idea of being "mysterious." I wanted to be normal. Boring. Under the radar . . .

"Not really. Family life wasn't so good down south, so when I got the chance to leave, I took it. Regina and Earl Murray took me in, helped me get on my feet. Now I wait tables and go to beauty school."

"Got a feeling that's not the whole story, but I don't want to push," he said. "I had fun tonight. You think you'd be interested in seeing each other again?"

I considered the question.

"Yeah, I might be interested," I said finally, wondering why I didn't get the same thrill from Joe that I got from Puck. Mom always went for the dangerous ones, too, and guess who paid the price? Fuck that. I needed to pull my head out of my ass and appreciate the man I was with. "I want to take things nice and slow, though. If that's a problem, we should probably let it go . . ."

He kissed the top of my head.

"Not a problem," he said. "Not a problem at all. But I've got a question for you."

"What's that?" I asked, my stomach sinking. *Please don't let him ask about Puck . . .*

"You have history with Puck Redhouse," he stated. "That's obvious. That something I should be worrying about?"

Yes! Everyone should worry about Puck—he's dangerous!

"No. No problem there—Puck and I knew each other for a while, once. That's all. There's no history. Nothing that matters now."

My stomach twisted as I said it, because that was a big fucking lie. Puck definitely mattered. There was Life Before Puck and Life After Puck, and those two lives had nothing in common.

But the first life was firmly in the past and I needed it to stay there. Maybe Joe could be part of the second. Snuggling deeper into his arm, I savored his warmth and for the first time in years considered what it might be like to have a decent man in my life.

This is what we want, my brain said firmly. *Now enjoy it.*

THREE

PUCK

The sound of the phone woke me. Carlie groaned.

"Make it stop," she murmured, although I could tell she wasn't really awake. "Don't wanna get up."

Rolling to the side of the bed, I sat up and reached for the handset, wondering for the thousandth time when we'd finally get some fucking cell towers here in the north valley. Should've stayed at her house. Wouldn't have been able to track me down there.

"Puck, it's Boonie," my president said. Scratch that—he'd have found me at her place, too. Carlie was good people, and she knew how things were with the club. More than one church meeting had happened in her living room over the past couple of years. I kept thinking Deep would claim her, but she didn't seem quite ready to settle down with one man. For now, she drifted through different beds, which seemed to work for her.

Worked for me, too.

I'd been horny as fuck last night, no pun intended. It'd been six months since I'd seen Becca—the woman was more beautiful now than she'd ever been. She'd turned twenty-one three months ago . . . Three months I'd spent reminding myself of all the reasons I should stay away from her—the same reasons that'd kept me away the last five years. She'd been abused by bikers. In her eyes I was probably the best of the lot, which was a fucking shameful thought to tolerate. She was terrified of motorcycle clubs and me and just about everything, and whenever I tried to talk to her, she flinched. Oh, and she was too goddamn young.

Except she wasn't too young anymore.

That's what really messed with my head. If I wanted her, I could take her. Nobody would stop me—not even Becca. She was hot for it, which was painfully obvious despite her best efforts to stay distant.

I'd be flattered if her response wasn't to pretend I didn't exist.

So instead of opening my window, walking over, and staking a claim to what my dick asserted (strongly) was my rightful property, I'd fucked Carlie instead. She wasn't the one I wanted but the woman was a yoga teacher. What kind of dumbass turns that down?

"What's up?" I asked Boonie, rubbing the back of my neck.

"You sound like crap," he said, laughing. "Hungover?"

"No, just stayed out too late. You need something, or you just determined to make my life a living hell for shits and grins?"

"Wow, someone needs his beauty sleep. I've got a job for you. Need you to make a run into town, connect with our friends there. Bring your truck."

"Got it."

Hanging up the phone, I reached over and smacked Carlie's butt.

"Suck your own dick," she moaned. "Wanna sleep some more."

"At the moment I'd take sleep over you sucking my dick, too," I replied, rubbing my face and yawning. "But I need you up and out. That was Boonie—he's got business for me."

She moaned again, but she sat up and rolled out of the bed. I watched as she leaned over, boobs jiggling. They were nice, but Becca's were better. Remembered them vividly. She'd filled out since then, which I'd bet my left nut just made them better.

Oh yeah. That was enough to wake my cock up.

Suddenly I wasn't so interested in going back to sleep, but when the president says move, tapping ass ceases to be a priority. I stumbled toward the shower, ducking under long enough to rinse off the sweat and by the time I'd come out Carlie was dressed.

"You need a ride?"

"Nope, I'm going over to Darcy's shop," she said. "Got an appointment in an hour and a half to get my highlights done. Figure I'll stop off and grab her some coffee on the way. Assuming they're open after your little bust-up yesterday."

I grunted.

"So what was that really all about?" she asked, obviously not ready to let it go. "Never seen you get that worked up about a waitress before. Something I should know about?"

Something about her voice sounded off . . . Wait.

"What do you think we have here?" I asked, frowning.

She shrugged, but I caught the hurt look on her face. Fuck. Hadn't seen that coming. Carlie was a nice girl but no fucking way I planned to get involved with her.

"It's just sex, babe," I told her. "You know that, right?"

She didn't look at me. Double fuck. Okay, probably shouldn't hit that again, not if she was going to get all clingy and shit. Not that it was my problem if she did, but Deep was into her and I didn't need complications like this in my life. Hopefully she'd catch the hint. I threw my shit together as she dug around for her purse. The woman wasn't stupid—less than a minute later and she was ready to go.

"You want me to call you?" she asked as I opened the door for her. I shrugged.

"No, I'll probably be busy. Don't wait on me, okay?"

"I hear you," she said softly, then started down the stairs, moving fast to get away from me. I closed the door behind me and locked the dead bolt, wondering how I could be so goddamned stupid. She was already out in the alley as I reached the bottom and stepped outside.

Out in the alley talking to someone.

Joe Collins.

Holy motherfucking, cocksucking shit.

Joe Collins was coming out of Becca's building. Something dark and hateful boiled through me and I considered whether I had enough time to kill him and dump the body before meeting up with Picnic Hayes.

Then reality caught up with me and I had to bite back a humorless laugh. Instant karma, right?

Carlie got the shaft and apparently so did Becca. Just not from me.

Half an hour later I was just shy of the I-90 turnoff when I saw a car pulled off on the side of the road, emergency lights flashing. That was Becca's little Subaru. Fucking perfect, because I didn't have time for this and I *really* didn't want to talk to her—not after watching that asshole leaving her place.

When I'd seen them together at the bar last night I'd nearly lost my shit. Nothing less than instant hatred toward the bastard holding her. For years now I'd been keeping an eye on Becca, my club brothers standing in for me when I wasn't around. So far as I knew, she hadn't really dated anyone seriously. This one, though . . . I'd asked around, and apparently Collins was a decent guy who could hold his own. Exactly the kind of man she should probably be with, which made me hate him even more. Cocksucker.

The whole thing had messed with me, especially after seeing her rolling around with Blake on the roof.

Not that I took the apartment to be close to her. Wasn't a factor. Sure, there were other places to rent. Cheaper places. Nicer. But the downtown location was perfect, close to all the . . . well, Callup didn't have anything downtown. Fuck. Didn't know what I was hoping to accomplish here—she was beyond off-limits. But then I'd seen her last night and the limits shifted . . .

Now here she was, stuck on the side of the road.

I really, really didn't want to see her. Didn't want to see her pretty tits, which looked exceptionally nice this morning, all pushed up with her arms crossed under them. Had no interest in her hair, or how it would look wrapped around my cock. Speaking of things that should've been wrapped around my cock, her lips were nice and puffy.

Bruised from sucking Collins' dick last night?

"What the fuck happened here?" I growled, stepping out of my truck. At least she'd found a decent pullout, one of those wide spaces overlooking the river, shaded by the cottonwoods.

"It made a clanking noise and stopped running," Becca said, eyes darting toward me. "Earl will help me fix it—he always does . . . Is there any chance you could call him for me up at the gas station?"

Yeah. I'd get right on that.

"Grab your shit and get into the truck," I told her, wondering when I'd turned into such a fucking masochist. "Where were you going?"

"Coeur d'Alene," she replied, looking nervous as hell. "I don't want to bother you. I can just wait here—"

"I don't have time to fuck around. Just get in the truck," I told her. She flinched at my tone. *Watch your mouth, asshole.* Wished she wouldn't look at me like a goddamn ax murderer. Of course, that might not be entirely off base given my current mission—God only knew what Hayes needed from me . . . I frowned at the thought, and she made a startled little squeaking noise.

"Have I ever hurt you?" I asked her, abruptly. "Aside from that one night, have I ever done a goddamned thing to make you think I would even *dream* of hurting you?"

Becca shook her head quickly.

"No."

"Then stop looking at me like I'm a serial killer and get in the fucking truck already. I really don't have time for this and I can't leave you here. Move your ass."

Becca ducked into her car through the passenger-side door, flashing me a nice view of said ass in the process. Didn't exactly help my mood. She dug around and came back out with a leather messenger bag. I watched as she locked up and then we climbed into my truck, doors slamming.

Becca looked even more scared than usual, which I guess made sense because I was being a dick—but that was only because she fucked Joe instead of me. If Joe was so great, why the hell wasn't he rescuing her?

You're a fucking idiot, asshole. You wanna sleep with her? Stop scaring her!

"So what's in Coeur d'Alene?" I asked, pulling back out onto the road.

"I've got school there," she replied. "But I think you should just drop me off at the gas station. I'm starting work tonight at the Moose, so I'm going to call in and let them know I can't get into town today."

"That gonna fuck things up for you?"

"It should be okay . . ." she said, her voice trailing off. I glanced over at her but she wouldn't meet my eyes. God, that frustrated me. I bet she looked Collins in the eyes. Sure as hell wasn't scared of Blake.

"I'll give you a ride," I decided. "Got shit to do in town, so I'll bring you back out tonight, drop you at the Moose. You can catch a lift home afterward with your girl."

"You don't need to do that."

"I know I don't need to do it," I snapped, annoyed. Jesus, what was wrong with me? *You're jealous, dickwad* . . . "But I'm going to, so just accept it and move on. You call Earl when we hit cell service. He'll go out and pick up your car, tow it back to his shop. You need a ride tomorrow, I'll take you where you need to go."

Shit, at this rate, I'd be offering to run her out to Joe's for a quickie after she got off shift. Silence fell as we drove, my fingers tapping on the steering wheel as she stared silently out the window. Ten minutes later we reached the Kingston junction and I pulled out onto the interstate.

"So how are you?" she finally asked, breaking the silence. "I haven't seen you around for a while. Then yesterday I saw you twice."

I heard her voice catch, and smiled cynically.

"Three times," I reminded her.

"What?"

"You saw me three times. The diner, the bar, and through my window from the roof."

She choked and I bit back a laugh. Thought she'd gotten away with that, did she?

"Okay, I saw you three times," she admitted. "What were you doing in that apartment?"

"That seems a little obvious. Blow job," I said, feeling a little better. Becca might be skittish, but she was still interested. Last night proved it. She coughed and I decided to show her some mercy. "I'm moving in. Got the keys yesterday—going to be back in town for a while, needed a place to stay. It's cheap and convenient. That a problem for you?"

"No, of course not," she said quickly. I glanced over at her, but she still wouldn't look at me. Well, fuck . . . I needed to calm down, give the girl a break. She'd been the victim all those years ago, not me. Needed to start thinking with the big head.

"Seriously, if it's going to be a problem, now's the time to say something. Didn't think too much of it—it's a small town. Not a ton of places to rent and the price was right."

"It's not a problem."

"Good."

Silence. Five minutes later she was still staring out the window. Now I couldn't tell what the hell was going on. "I do something to piss you off?"

Becca shook her head, then she finally raised her eyes to mine.

"No," she said.

"Then why won't you look at me or talk to me?"

"I'm talking to you right now."

"Don't give me that—you've been doing your best to ignore me on the whole ride. If we've got an issue, let's get it out there."

"You made me lose my job," she replied suddenly.

"McDougal was flipping you shit. I don't care how big Blake is, he couldn't take on that whole crew by himself. You lost your job because your boss is a bitch who blames other people for her own mistakes, the first of which was allowing an asshole like that inside in the first place."

"You seriously believe that?"

"Yeah, I seriously fucking believe that. You're better off without her, and you'll make more money at the Moose anyway."

"That's the other reason I'm mad at you."

"What?"

"The Moose! I don't want to work there."

"Because you'll make more money? Gee, that's truly a fate worse than death."

"Don't be like this," she replied, her voice almost a sigh. "Let's not play games, okay? We have history and that makes me uncomfortable. I don't want you throwing it in my face."

"You're the one who spied on me in my own apartment, not the other way around, Becs. Like I said, you got a problem with me living there, now's the time to speak out. Otherwise I'm moving past this."

"Don't call me Becs."

"Why not, *Becs?*"

She glared at me, practically vibrated with frustration. Fair enough, because I was pretty frustrated myself. Not just about our verbal sparring, either. Hearing her pissed-off little voice made my dick harder, which shouldn't have surprised me because everything about her made my dick harder. Now instead of focusing on what the Reapers might need from me, my mind was torn between two images. One was her naked, spread wide and screaming in pleasure while I pounded her.

The second was that exact same picture, only this time it was Collins fucking her.

I squeezed the steering wheel tighter, then shot her another look. Her fingers tapped against her thigh, full of suppressed energy. Guess Joey-boy wasn't man enough to tire her out. The deep breaths she took made her tits rise and fall underneath a T-shirt thin enough to show the outlines of her nipples.

Little Becca was all kinds of bothered.

God*damn*, but I wanted to fuck her.

Right, like that was a surprise—I'd wanted to fuck her every minute of every day since that night five years ago. Hell, she'd wrapped herself around me all the way from Southern California to Callup, hands clutching at my stomach. The only time I'd lost my boner the whole trip was when the bike numbed me out, and even then I was still hard. Just couldn't feel it anymore.

"I want us to get along," she said suddenly, eyes darting toward me. "I know it's no secret I'm uncomfortable around you. But we live in the same town and it's time to move forward with my life. Part of that is letting this go. Maybe we can be friends."

Friends? Un-fucking-likely.

"And what do you mean by 'friends'?" I asked, keeping my voice neutral.

"Well, you're giving me a ride to school," she replied. "That's very . . . friendly . . . of you. We're going to be neighbors now. Why can't we just get along, you know? That seems less weird than what we are now."

"What are we now?"

"Nothing," she said, and my gut clenched. "We aren't anything. But maybe we can be friends. We're neighbors, so maybe we can act like neighbors. I can cook you dinner or something, thank you for fixing my car."

That startled me, but I didn't react. At least, not by saying anything. My dick was trying to punch its way through my pants, which wasn't particularly helpful under the circumstances.

"You dating Collins?"

She shrugged.

"We went out last night. I'm probably going to see him again. Are you dating Carlie?"

I snorted.

"I don't date."

"Okay . . ."

Silence fell again, and this time I didn't feel like breaking it. Not if she wanted to talk about Carlie—that wouldn't end well for me. I sure as fuck didn't want to talk about Collins. I reached over and turned on some music, catching the way she visibly relaxed out of the corner of my eyes. Funny, but despite the tension, having her in my truck like this felt good.

Half an hour later I dropped her off in front of her school, promising to come back and pick her up after five. Hopefully I'd be able to keep that promise, despite whatever shittastic job Picnic Hayes probably had waiting for me. Knowing my luck, it'd be a body to bury.

Guess I'd keep my fingers crossed that body would belong to Joe Collins. Unlikely, but a man can hope.

BECCA

When we hit cell service, my phone lit up with a missed call from my mom. Like always, her name sent a thrill of perverse hope through me. Maybe this time she was calling to say she'd done it—she'd actually left Teeny. For years now I'd been trying to convince her to walk out and come live with me. Twice she'd said she was doing it, then backed out at the last minute. This devastated me, which is hard to explain, given how terrible she was as a mother. Hell, as a person. But that's the thing about parents—you love them despite everything, because they're yours.

I stole a look at Batma . . . Puck and wondered how stupid it would be to call her back in front of him.

Probably pretty stupid.

We'd never talked about my mom, but it wasn't a stretch to assume he wasn't her biggest fan. Hopefully the call wasn't urgent—I'd have to wait until my break at school to get back to her. Generally our conversations fell into three categories:

1) "I'm leaving Teeny for real this time, Becca. I just need some money for a bus ticket and I'll come up."

2) "I love you, baby," drunken slurring. "I'm so sorry for what I did. You'll see. We can fix it. Be a family." Barfing noise.

3) "I need money, sweetheart. Just this once. We can't pay the (insert bill here) and they're going to (insert consequence here)."

I'd love to say I never sent her any money, but that would be a lie. I loved her. I wanted her back. I wanted to be a whole person again and some small part of me insisted that nobody can be a whole person without their mommy.

Fortunately I rarely let that small part make the decisions, and I definitely didn't give it access to my checking account. Nope, if I sent her something, it was just tips. Those didn't count.

(Right.)

So instead of returning the call, I used the time to check my email, which I couldn't get at home. There wasn't much in my in-box. Several ads for "enhancement" products. A quick note from Danielle saying she'd run into Joe, and that he'd left her makeup bag hanging on my doorknob because she'd forgotten it in his truck last night—could I bring it in to work with me?

Hmmm . . . That was going to be complicated. I hadn't figured out the whole ride/home/work situation in my head. I wrote her a quick note saying I'd try, then put the phone in my purse.

By the time we pulled up to the school, I'd managed to relax despite Puck's oh-so-friendly presence.

"I'll see you at five," he grunted as I hopped out. I wanted to tell him not to worry about it, but I couldn't justify making Danielle drive all that way just because I was scared of one biker. One big, tough biker who just happened to be the only man I'd ever really wanted to—

"Thanks for the ride," I said, my smile bright and plastic.

What the hell was wrong with me?

"Hi, Mom."

"Becca baby! I'm so glad you called. It's been awful, I don't even know what to say, it's so bad."

"What's going on?" I asked, wondering if I really wanted to know. It always ended the same anyway . . .

"Teeny's finally lost his shit," she replied, and for once her voice was sober and somewhat focused. "I think he's going to hurt me."

"Mom, he's been beating the crap out of you for years. What's changed?"

"No, those were just little arguments," she said, brushing me off. "Marriage is hard. You'll learn that someday, if you ever manage to find yourself a man. No, this is different. He's been really angry and upset, and he pulled out his gun last night and held it to my head for an hour. His eyes were awful, Becca. Like a devil's eyes. He says I've been cheating on him and now I'm going to pay."

My chest tightened.

"Mom, you need to get out of there."

"I know," she replied, her voice a tense whisper. "He just got home. I'll try to call later. I need money, baby. Money to leave him. If I don't get out I'm dead."

Then she hung up the phone.

My head started to sway and I felt dizzy.

"You okay?" asked Caitlyn, one my classmates. Apparently she'd caught the tail end of my phone call. I looked up to find her face full of exaggerated concern, a newly lit cigarette dangling forgotten in her fingers.

"I'm fine," I said quickly. Great. Now everyone would be up in my shit, because Caitlyn was the biggest gossip in the whole damned school.

"Do you want to talk?" she asked, her voice oozing sympathy. "People say I'm great at listening."

And repeating.

"It's okay, really," I told her. "Don't worry about it. I need to get back inside."

It wasn't okay, though.

My brain was too restless. I decided to bug out of school early, so I gathered my stuff and walked over to the coffee hut. Caffeine might not solve my problems, but it probably wouldn't make them any worse. I bought a drink and a muffin for dinner, because I'm healthy like that, then found a place to sit on the side of the building.

Teeny. God, I hated that man. He'd gone after Mom with a bat once—I'd been little enough to hide behind the couch that time. Another time she'd turned the bat on him, which was great right up to the point where he pulled his gun and made her beg him not to shoot her.

I'd watched that one from underneath the table.

Now I couldn't get the image out of my head. For years I'd been terrified of him, but I'd learned from Regina and Earl not to let fear rule my life. Would he really do it?

Impossible to know.

She needed to get out of there. Maybe I should call her back . . .

"There's a hot guy out here looking for you," Caitlyn gasped, running around the corner. "He's all dark and scary and fuckable. There's this amazing scar on his face. It looks exactly like the kind of scar you'd get fighting pirates. Please tell me you're screwing that beautiful man—I'll lose all respect for you if you aren't."

"No, he's just my ride," I said, rising to my feet. I swatted my butt to get any dirt or sticks off. Caitlyn scowled at me, then smiled suddenly. Poor dear, she really wasn't very bright. Her little brain moved slowly, telegraphing every thought right onto her face.

"Introduce us?"

"I really have to go," I replied, trying not to roll my eyes as I walked around the corner. Sure enough, Puck was waiting, looking grumpy as ever.

For an instant I considered just turning around and taking off. I'd hide behind the school, make Danielle come and get me.

Get over yourself.

Okay, so I was going to pull my shit together and act like a grown-up, starting with an apology for being rude to him this morning. Did he make me uncomfortable? Yes. Had he been rude? Definitely. But he'd also rescued me on the side of the road and traditionally that calls for graceful tolerance and a pleasant thank-you.

Not like he had to stop in the first place, right?

Moving quickly, I crossed the lot to his truck before the girls standing around smoking had the chance to start with the questions about him. They'd try to get his information out of me tomorrow—we did enjoy our gossip at the school—but I'd worry about that when it happened.

"Thanks for the ride," I said, climbing up into the truck. My eyes took him in and I felt a wave of lust hit me. Beautiful. That's what Caitlyn called him, and I was tempted to agree, but it wasn't really the truth. He was too rugged and scarred to be beautiful. She'd hit it just right with "fuckable," though.

He grunted, turning up the radio in the universal signal to shut up, so shut up I did. We merged onto the freeway and started out of town in silence. Not a pleasant, comfortable silence. This was strange and uncomfortable, with every line of his body radiating tension that made me nervous. Was he about to snap?

I'd grown up around bikers so I knew better than to ask him about his day or why he was so obviously not a happy camper. He wouldn't tell me and I didn't want to know anyway. Okay, I *did* want to know but I shouldn't. Even so, by the time we'd turned off and started up along the river I couldn't take the silent treatment any longer. I had to say something.

Keep it friendly. Break the tension and let him know you're ready to move on.

"Do you want to come over for dinner tomorrow?"

He didn't respond, and I bit my lip, stealing a look at him. God, he was good-looking. Not traditionally handsome—nope, between the scar and the broken nose, that ship had sailed. And he wasn't cute, either. Way too terrifying to be cute.

But there was just something so compelling about his face, the way he held himself, the controlled power in every move he made . . . Drove me crazy every time I thought of it. Drove me crazy, heated me up, and scared the crap out of me—the situation was utterly ridiculous and completely inescapable.

I had to remember that Puck was a biker, and not one of the nice ones. There was a *reason* the Silver Bastards protected Callup and all its inhabitants. Not out of the goodness of their hearts—I didn't believe that for a minute. Nope, their protection was all about territory, kind of like a dog with a bone.

The Silver Bastards might not shit where they ate, but they had to shit somewhere.

Since leaving California, I'd lived my life according to one basic rule—I called it the Mom Principle. When in doubt, think about what Mom would do. Then do the exact opposite. It'd never failed me. Mom loved bikers, which meant I needed to stay the hell away from them. Hold out for a nice guy.

Nice. Normal. Boring . . .

Joe.

Ugh.

When Joe kissed me I just sort of checked out. There was no burning need, no heated desire . . . Puck turned me on just by existing. With him actively existing right next to me, it was almost more than I could handle. To this day, I blame my hormones for my actions, because my brain certainly didn't get a vote. I should've let it die, made a clean escape. Instead I had to open my big fat mouth and make things worse.

"You didn't answer my question earlier."

"What question?"

"Do you want to come over for dinner tomorrow?"

Puck ignored me, but I swear—his hands were suddenly squeezing the steering wheel so hard it should've snapped in half. The truck abruptly slowed and he swerved off the next turnoff to the river, brakes slamming hard. For a minute I thought we might go over the embankment into the water. I froze as he opened his door and got out, slamming it behind him. Then Puck walked away from the truck, kicking a rock hard as he looked out over the water.

Long minutes passed.

I fidgeted, wondering what was going on. Finally my idiotic, self-destructive curiosity got the best of me and I undid my seat belt, stepping out and moving toward him. He had to hear the crunch of the gravel under my feet but he didn't say anything.

"Why did you get out of the truck?"

Silence. Had he heard me? Then slowly Puck turned, radiating a restrained intensity. His eyes flared as he started stalking toward me. Not walking—*stalking*. Like a predator in slow, inevitable pursuit of its dinner. Crap. Puck liked to play with his food, too. I remembered that from California.

What the hell kind of mistake had I just made? I needed to run away, but it was too late—he already had me backed against the truck, although I couldn't remember exactly how I'd gotten there.

"What exactly do you think we have here?" Puck demanded, his voice harsh. My knees threatened to let go so I grabbed the truck behind me with both hands.

"I don't understand."

"You just invited me over for *dinner*," he sneered, like it was a dirty word. "Who do you think I am? One of your girlfriends?"

Um, no danger of that. *Crap.* Damn, but Puck was big. He loomed over me, pinning me with the sheer force of his presence. My heart pounded, utterly convinced that Batman was going to eat me if I didn't *do something right now.*

"I think you're the guy who pulled over this morning and gave me a ride so I wouldn't miss school," I said breathlessly. Puck's mouth twisted into a snarl. Jesus Christ, he'd gone from scary sexy to flat-out scary as fuck faster than Danielle could down a shot. And Danielle was *fast.* "You didn't have to, but you did. You're my new neighbor, too. Things have always been weird and uncomfortable between us. Maybe they don't need to be."

He leaned into me, slamming a hand down against the metal on either side of my body.

"Things are uncomfortable between us because I fucked you at a party after your daddy pimped you out," he said bluntly. "That was a problem for me, given that I was on parole and the powers that be tend to frown upon statutory rape. That was a problem for you because getting raped is a fucking shameful violation, no matter how it goes down. But here's the really shitty part—fucking you was *good*, Becca. Damned good. Believe me, I *remember* how you felt wrapped around my cock. But not even you're good enough to risk going back to prison, so I'm sure you can understand why I was pissed off about the whole situation. I still did the right thing, and helped you out."

I blinked rapidly, trying not to faint. I remembered being wrapped around his cock, too. The memories were twisted and confusing as hell, but they were good. Not just good—fucking amazing. Right up to the point where he'd *hurt* me. *Why is this turning me on?*

Shit. This had to be Mom's fault somehow. She'd somehow passed on her only superpower—the ability to seek out and fall for the worst possible man in any given area code. Only possible explanation.

Puck hadn't finished.

"Dragging your ass out of there seems to have given you the wrong impression about me, *Becs*. Do not think for one minute that I'm the kind of guy who does the right thing. That's not my style. I'm the guy who does what he wants when he wants, and trust me when I say I didn't do nearly enough to you that night to get you out of my system."

Holy. Crap. I couldn't process this. Then his body pressed into mine and it got worse. I could feel him against me. Not just all of

him, but one specific part of him, digging into my stomach. He
lowered his head.

"Let me tell you how this plays out," Puck continued, his voice
going deep and rough as his lips grazed my ear. If I'd turned my
head half an inch, I'd be kissing his cheek.

What the ever-loving fuck is wrong with me?

Why would I even *think* about kissing him?

Because you want him, my body shouted from somewhere deep
inside my gut. No, not gut. This was definitely the va-jay-jay show.
*He's strong, he'll protect you. He'll make you scream and feel good
because he's the baddest motherfucker on this mountain and that's
the only kind of man you want!*

His teeth caught my ear, tugging on it and sucking it into his
mouth. Then his tongue traced me and if I hadn't been pinned
against the truck, I'd have fallen right to the ground. Puck let my
ear go and spoke again.

"I'm not going to fuck you here on the side of the road today,
Becca, despite the fact that it sounds like a hell of a good idea at the
moment. And the next time I see you out with your precious boy
toy, Collins? I'm not going to beat him half to death because he's
touched you. But here's the thing . . . you've pushed me about as far
as I'm willing to go with this friend bullshit. I'm not your friend,
Becca. I've never been your friend and I never will be. I can be the
man who fucks you and owns you, or I can be the man who keeps
an eye on you to make sure your stepdad doesn't come and steal
you back. I can even be the man who watches while you find a nice
little boyfriend you can control and settle down to make babies
together like normal people. But don't you fucking *dare* issue any
more invitations unless you're ready to handle me and don't pretend
for one second you aren't fully aware what that means."

Before I could breathe, think, or start to process his words, Puck
caught my face in both hands and kissed me hard, tongue pushing
deep inside even as he shoved one of his solid thighs between my

legs. Desperate, mind-numbing painful need exploded through me. Five years ago he'd been strong, but now? Puck had filled out and bulked up with age and I knew that there was absolutely nothing I could do to stop him, even if I wanted to.

I'd never wanted anything less.

Suddenly it ended.

I dropped to the ground with a thump, shaking as I raised a hand to my swollen lips, stunned. Puck stepped back, eyes flaring with suppressed need. Then he fumbled in his pocket for something only to find it empty.

"Fuck!" he shouted, turning and pacing toward the river. "Get back in the goddamn truck."

Yeah, wasn't going to argue with that.

Five minutes later he ripped the driver's door open, rocking the vehicle as he got in. We pulled out onto the road with a skid of gravel and then started driving toward Callup again.

This time when he turned up the radio, I kept my mouth shut.

Puck dropped me off in front of the Moose about an hour before my shift was supposed to start. That afternoon I'd decided to catch a ride all the way home—that way I could shower and change, not to mention grabbing Danielle's makeup bag. It was probably still hanging on my door . . .

After our little confrontation, though, I'd been far too busy dealing with all that extra adrenaline exploding through my body to ask for favors. When he'd pulled up to the bar I'd all but jumped out, desperate to get away. He seemed to share the sentiment, hardly waiting for the door to close before taking off again.

Now I sat on a battered picnic table in a patch of grass across the road, staring down into the river as I tried to collect my thoughts. A partially deflated inner tube had been left behind from someone's float earlier that day. I kicked it, feeling wistful. Like always, watching the water run over the rocks soothed me. No matter what else went wrong, at least I lived somewhere beautiful. That had to count for something, right?

"Did you bring my makeup?" Danielle asked cheerfully, plopping down beside me. I shook my head.

"Nope, I didn't get a chance to go home," I told her. "Car trouble. I had to catch a ride from Puck."

"Really . . ." she drawled, her voice full of questions.

"Really," I answered, the word final.

Danielle studied me thoughtfully for a minute, then shrugged. That was one of the things I loved about her—she knew when to let shit go.

"I'll borrow yours, then," she announced, reaching for my purse. She dug through it, pulling out a brightly colored little bag that held my makeup. I'd made it last month out of an old silk kimono I'd found at the Kingston thrift store.

"You know, you could be selling these. Did you ever talk to Regina about putting some in the tea shop?"

"Not yet," I replied. "Been too busy with school. Sewing purses won't pay the bills—I need to stay focused."

"You might be surprised." Danielle popped open my compact mirror and studied her face. "Fuck, I've got so many freckles that I want to scream. Raelene Korgee told me they've got this amazing new foundation at Ulta, up on ninety-five. I want to try some, but it costs a fucking fortune. I don't suppose they'll give you samples, seeing as you're a professional?"

I shook my head, feeling some of my tension release. Danielle always had that effect on me—she was just so down-to-earth. Grounding.

"I wish. I'm getting low on all kinds of stuff. They say the tips are good here. Maybe I can buy some new fall colors," I replied. *Seriously?* my conscience hissed. *You're going to buy makeup while your mom is trapped with Teeny and his guns?*

Danielle smoothed on my dark red lipstick, smacking thought-fully.

"Is this too much for me?"

Glancing at her, I shook my head.

"No, you can pull it off."

I heard a squawking, and looked up to see a line of geese flying overhead. Summer was ending too fast . . . Soon the snow would fall, bringing a slow commute and winter power bills. Despite its charms, living in a hundred-plus-year-old building had some down-sides, and heating was one of them. How much money would Mom need to get away, realistically? Could I afford to help her?

"Blake promises the tips are good. I'll bet they'll be better if we show some skin. If not, there's always the fallback position."

"What's the fallback position?"

"We'll work up at Shanda Reed's place, of course."

My eyes widened, and I turned to her, scandalized.

"Isn't that . . . ? I mean, I've heard rumors, but . . ."

"It's a bordello, all right," she said, sounding pleased with her-self. "Or so they say. Girls can make a lot of money that way."

"You are so fucking full of shit. You'd never work there!"

Danielle burst out laughing, shaking her head.

"You should see your face!"

"God, you freaked me out," I replied, smacking her shoulder. She smacked me back and suddenly we were pushing each other so hard I fell off the bench. Danielle came after me, and we rolled to our backs, still laughing.

"It really *is* a whorehouse," she said. "Blake told me all about it last night—he was super drunk. He said they never take local girls, though. It's an old hotel up past Quincy, way back in the woods on an old lake. Used to be a little resort or something, back before the interstate went through. He told me that Shanda Reed has it set up as a bordello, and that the women working there make a shit ton of money. Guys from the mines, and coming in from Montana."

"Why doesn't the sheriff shut it down?"

"Oh, like that'll happen. When's the last time the sheriff sent anyone up here? Quincy is another fifteen miles past Callup, he's probably forgotten it exists. Hell, Shanda would shoot him if he stuck his nose in her business. She's a total bitch—my mom went to school with her. Hates her. Nope, I'll bet Shanda pays them off and they stay away. Win-win. So that's my new fallback plan—if all else fails, we can start whoring."

I sobered abruptly.

I'd already been a whore. Maybe not one who got paid, but I knew all about servicing men. So did my mom.

"Being a prostitute isn't a good thing," I said abruptly. I sat up and started gathering the makeup that'd spilled out across the grass. Danielle stared at me, her face startled.

"Are you okay? I was just joking, you know. I'd never do that. If I ever get desperate, I'll just go work at a strip club. No need to go full whore when you can just wiggle your ass and collect money."

I shrugged, forcing a fake smile.

"Sure, I'm great. It's about time to start work, though. Let's hit the bathroom and then go get ourselves started, sound good?"

FOUR

My first night at the Moose started out well, which was a damned good thing given my afternoon. It was busy, too, which I appreciated. The more I worked, the less I had to think about the Mom Situation. This was good, because the Mom Situation made me think of California, leading to memories of my extraordinary night with Puck.

Sexy Puck. Scary Puck. Puck pushing me against his truck and shoving his cock into my stomach, growling in my ear . . . It's a particularly fucked-up twist of fate, having your best sexual memories tied together with the kind of pain, suffering, and fear I'd felt the night we met. One of those gifts that keeps on giving, you know?

Maybe that's why Joe did nothing for me—he'd never hurt me.

So you're fucked up, I reminded myself. *You aren't the first and you won't be the last. Let it go.*

Teresa started out by giving us each a navy blue apron, which was the closest thing they had to a uniform. The first few hours were a whirlwind of trying to learn the new menu and computer system. Blake clocked in an hour later, and the fact that he knew most of it already helped a lot. Not only that, Danielle could turn any job fun. Good thing, too, because we had a full house.

The shift didn't start to go south until around ten that night. By then, the dinner crowd was gone and the kitchen had shut down. Now we were settling in for the long haul with the night's serious drinkers. That's when a group of students from the Northwoods Academy showed up, obviously slumming.

I knew a little bit about the school because Earl had worked there as a groundskeeper for the last year. None of it was good. It'd been founded in the late '90s, and the place was full of rich, spoiled brats who should've been in high school and college. They'd been sent "back to nature" by their wealthy parents as an alternative to jail time—nothing like paying off a judge to keep your record clean.

Of course, some just had families who wanted rid of them because they weren't convenient. A few even had movie stars for parents, at least according to Earl. Whatever their reason for landing in Idaho, they were almost all unpleasant and entitled as fuck.

They'd gained a bad reputation around Callup for taking advantage of locals, too. Earl always told me to stay the hell away from them. I'd even heard stories of girls getting lured up there and raped. Were they true? No idea . . . I didn't want to find out, either.

"They can't be legal," I said to Blake, eyeing the group. Thankfully they'd settled in Danielle's section, so it wasn't my job to card them. They looked like the kind of people who would bitch long and hard if their waitress asked for ID. "Why can't we just throw them out?"

"We don't know they aren't legal," he said, shrugging. "Think they take students through twenty-two up there. Online classes and shit—just depends on how desperate they are to avoid doing time. I'd take boarding school over a jail cell, too."

"Are you going to card them?"

"Hell no. They have lots of money to spend and nowhere else to spend it. If we ever get questioned, we'll just say we thought we checked them all. At least a few of them must have fakes. That'll cover our asses. Remember, those little shits are rolling in it—tuition is a fuckload. We'll make good tips and pretend we never saw them. Everyone wins."

I nodded slowly, watching as they scoped out the dim interior, pointing out tables made from polished, split logs and the old mine safety signs ranging along the walls. Danielle seemed comfortable dealing with them, so I decided to watch my tables and mind my business.

Around ten thirty Joe showed up.

He sat his ass down by the bar, smiling at me as he exchanged greetings with Blake. Danielle threw me a knowing wink. Great, that's just what I needed—my best friend in matchmaking mode.

Of course, if I ever wanted to be normal, I'd have to get over this weird obsession with Puck somehow. Maybe I could fake it with Joe, fake it until it turned real. Couldn't hurt to try.

When I took my break at eleven, Joe caught my eye. I smiled, and he took my hand, leading me outside. We walked across the parking lot to the same unruly patch of grass overlooking the river I'd visited earlier. He climbed up onto the picnic table, then patted the spot next to him. We sat like that for a while, looking out across the darkened water, surrounded by the sound of crickets and frogs. It should've felt awkward but it didn't. Being with Joe was relaxing. Comfortable. Pleasantly normal.

"You seem to be doing okay," Joe said finally. "Like the new job?"

"Better than I thought I would. The tips are okay and the people are nice. I guess I expected it to be a lot crazier." I considered my next words carefully, then decided it wouldn't kill me to try opening up a little. "I grew up in a rough situation—lots of fighting and such. I thought it would be more like that, but so far it's nowhere close."

"The Moose can get ugly sometimes, but the bartenders keep an eye on things and Teresa's got a shotgun she's not afraid to pull out as needed. Mostly just the occasional dumbass getting stupid. I guess things turned ugly a few years back, during the contract disputes down at the Evans mine. They asked the Silver Bastards to come out and control things. Settled everyone down. The Moose is the heart of the community in some ways. It was before our time, but when they had the big fire at the Laughing Tess this was where everyone gathered to wait for news. Whole families slept right in the bar."

I shuddered, thinking of the men who'd lost their lives deep underground.

"I could never do that—work in a mine," I said softly. "Hate the idea of being trapped under all that dirt and rock. Does it ever scare you?"

"It's not as bad as you'd think," he replied. "Good money, enough to support a family. But I want out—no future underground, not with the way the business has been going. God knows how long the Tess will stay open."

More silence, then he reached over and pulled me into his side.

"You have plans tomorrow?"

"School in the morning," I replied. "Blake is giving me a ride."

"Want to do something for dinner?"

I thought about my conversation with Puck earlier and shivered. Joe was obviously interested in me, and he was sexy, in a wholesome, mountain kind of way. *Puck is sexier*, my traitorous thoughts whispered.

Yeah, but Joe is normal, I reminded myself firmly.

"Why don't you come over to my place," I said abruptly. "I'll cook for us. Maybe I can bum a ride to the grocery store if my car isn't fixed yet."

"Sure," he said. "What happened to your car?"

"Broke down this morning on the way to school. Earl is fixing it for me."

"That sucks."

"Yeah."

"Did you miss class?"

Pausing, I listened to the rustle of the water over the rocks and considered how to answer. "No, Puck Redhouse gave me a ride."

Joe didn't respond, and I stole a peek at him. He seemed pensive. "Thought you said there wasn't anything between you."

"There isn't," I insisted, wishing it was true. Why couldn't I get Puck out of my head?

Like mother, like daughter.

No. I wouldn't be that woman. I *refused.*

"Once upon a time there was something between us," I said slowly, wishing I could just lie. Mom lied all the time. "It wasn't anything real, though. Not many people know this, but before I came up here I lived down in California. My stepdad was a biker— a hangaround with a club down there. They weren't particularly nice people. That's where I met Puck."

Joe had stiffened next to me. "So you followed him up here?"

"I guess you could say he rescued me. My situation wasn't so good. He saw that and helped me get out."

"Wouldn't peg him as the knight-in-shining-armor type."

A snort of surprised, startled laughter escaped me.

"No, that's not really him," I said. "He still saved me, though."

"So that's the past. What's between you now?"

"Nothing," I said. "I mean, he keeps an eye on me, I guess. In a weird way, I feel safer because he's around. But he makes me uncomfortable, too—when we first met I got hurt, and he was part of that."

"Sounds complicated."

"Definitely," I admitted. *Complicated.* That was a good word.

And Joe was a good guy . . . a guy who deserved better than fake. What the hell had I been thinking? I wasn't my mom—I didn't use men. At least, not on purpose. "If you'd asked me two days ago whether there was anything between us I would've said no way. There's still not anything real . . . I like you a lot, Joe, so I'm going to be honest—he messes with my head and I don't know where to put that."

Joe nodded slowly, then gave me a pained smile.

"You know, I've spent years wondering why the hell I couldn't meet a woman who wouldn't play games. Now here we are and you aren't playing games. Kind of sucks."

I shoved against his shoulder, wishing I was a little less fucked up as a person. His arm tightened around me in a friendly squeeze.

"Tell you what," he said. "Let's make a deal—you figure your stuff out, and if I'm still around and you're interested, you let me know. But I'm looking for something real and I don't think you're in a place where that can happen just yet. You need to work through whatever hang-ups you have about Redhouse first."

"Is this the 'let's just be friends' speech?" I asked, my voice wry. "I hear that's the kiss of death."

Joe laughed.

"No, I'd like to be more than friends—but I'm not an idiot. If you aren't ready to date, I can't change that. I'd rather you figure things out with Puck now."

"There really isn't anything to figure out," I replied, my voice melancholy. "He and I don't have a relationship and we never will. I think you're right, though—I need to get my head straight. Until then we could still hang out and have fun, though."

"Maybe."

The sound of bikes cut through the air, their single headlights flashing across us as they pulled into the parking lot. Growing up in Teeny's house had taught me a lot of things. By the time I was fifteen, I could take a hit, give a blow job, and cook for thirty men on a moment's notice . . . I'd also learned to recognize the sound of certain motorcycles, particularly if they belonged to someone important. Things had been bad for me back home, but they'd have been worse if I hadn't known to hide when the worst of them pulled in for the night.

Puck and his Silver Bastard brothers had just arrived. I knew it for a certainty, even though I hadn't seen their faces over the glare of the lights. Guess old habits die hard.

"Your break is about over," Joe said quietly. "I'll walk you back."

He stepped off the table and turned to me, lifting me down. We walked back over the road and crunched across the gravel as the Bastards backed their Harleys into line. I refused to let myself look for Puck. So what if I was weirdly hung up on him? Life is full of things we want that we shouldn't have.

Cheesecake. Chocolate lava brownies with ice cream for breakfast. That last beer you have after the other beers . . . you know which one I'm talking about—the one that turns a little headache into the hangover to end all hangovers.

Maybe that was a problem. I had a giant, five-year Puck hangover.

Puck was dangerous in a decadent, indecent, cheesecake-at-midnight kind of way. That night in my room, he'd stopped when he'd realized he was hurting me—and believe me, I'd appreciated the gesture—but we'd only scratched the surface of what a man like him would expect from a woman. It had been too much for me, but that didn't mean it wasn't his norm. My attraction to him was a dead end. For the first time in my life I had things to lose if I didn't pull my head out of my ass, so it was time to start pulling.

By now, the Bastards had finished parking their bikes and started walking toward the bar, meeting us halfway there. They were like a pack of wolves, falling in and surrounding us, and I felt myself tensing up. I didn't like being surrounded by big men wearing leather.

Just one more reason to avoid Puck.

Of course, avoiding him would be hard, seeing as how he was right next to me. Joe on my right, Puck on my left. This was a whole new level of awkward, and that horrible tension between me and Puck flared back to life in an instant. I stole a glance at him, but the darkness hid his expression. Probably just as well.

Joe reached over and caught my hand in his, surprising me. Puck made a low, growly noise. I shivered. Despite everything I knew was wrong with him, he could still get me going without even trying. Joe squeezed my fingers—a gesture of comfort—and I had to bite back a nervous giggle. Not a "this is funny" kind of giggle. More of a "I'm going to laugh now because otherwise I may fall apart completely" sound.

So. Now I had Joe on my right and Puck on my left, which you'd think would be awkward. In reality, it was actually super-duper extra awkward, which was significantly more awkward than I'd realized was possible. Tension grew and swirled among the three of us, tangible and pungent. Through it all, Joe kept hold of my hand—he might never be my lover, but he'd be a hell of a good friend. One who apparently wasn't scared of bikers, which was a big plus. I tried to sneak a peek at Puck but still couldn't make out anything in the dark.

Probably just as well.

Not counting Puck, there were four other Silver Bastards giving us a friendly escort, and they'd left a prospect with the bikes. He'd stand out there in the night—watching—for however many hours they were inside, all for the chance to become part of the club.

Brought back memories.

It felt strange sometimes, knowing so much about the MC world without being part of it. I'd grown up in motorcycle clubs, plural. Mom was always moving, right up to the day she met Teeny. When I was little, I'd loved the big, loud machines that ran fast. Now hearing them was like Russian roulette—sometimes they brought bad memories, sometimes they made me feel protected. I used to dream about Teeny every night, Teeny and the men he'd given me to. I didn't anymore, thank God. At least not often. Much as I hated to admit it, the Silver Bastards had created my safe zone. They were close, they scared Teeny, and they would protect me.

How's that for fucked up?

"You like the new job?" Boonie asked me, as if none of this was bizarre and uncomfortable. Hell, maybe it wasn't for him. "Get in any fights yet? You handled yourself well yesterday morning. I was impressed."

"Um, thanks. It's fine so far," I said, edging closer to Joe. He threw a casual arm over my shoulders and I could've kissed him. Clearly he wasn't afraid of the Bastards—a definite point in his favor. Boonie snorted, obviously seeing right through me and finding it entertaining.

Puck seemed less entertained . . . If he'd been menacing before, now he'd moved back into full predator mode. My stupid body thought that was sexy as hell.

After what had to be the longest walk in history, we reached the wide half flight of stairs leading up to the bar's front porch. It was a double-decker, and once upon a time there'd been a hotel upstairs. Well, either a hotel or a brothel—the answer depended on who you asked. The door opened and bright light hit us. Then I was inside. Joe gave me one last squeeze, then let me go. I turned toward the bar and nearly ran into Puck, who was standing way, way too close.

"Careful," he said.

Danielle—God, I loved that woman—came over and grabbed my arm, jerking me away from the men toward the service bar.

"Those academy fuckers are a pain in my ass," she hissed, oblivious to my drama. (That's how good a friend she was—she actually sensed my problems and fixed them *without conscious effort*.) "Blake wants to kill them, but I'm holding him back. D'you think you can take them over for a few before I lose my shit?"

"Sure," I said, ducking behind the bar to snag my apron.

"You good?" Joe asked, grabbing a stool. Not ten feet behind him was Puck, watching us with narrowed eyes, arms crossed over his muscular chest. I had a sudden urge to grab Joe's shirt, pull him down, and kiss him hard. Just to piss off Puck. *Real classy there, Becca.* I forced myself to give Joe all my attention, ignoring the grumpy biker glaring at us.

"Sorry," I said, and he cocked his head.

"For what?"

"For being fucked up," I answered, ducking my head. He reached forward and chucked me under the chin, grinning.

"Well, as your *friend*, I'm sure I'll learn to live with it," he said. "You know, this is good in a way."

"How's that?"

"Now I can burp and fart around you."

I wrinkled my nose and Joe laughed. "Should get back home. I have to be up early."

"Take care," I told him.

"You, too."

Joe winked at me, then turned and walked out the door. Puck still stood there, watching it all, and the darkness in his expression made me shiver.

It wasn't a shiver of fear.

PUCK

"You're pathetic," Boonie declared, smirking at me. We'd taken one of the high tables in the back of the Moose, which made it easy to keep an eye on the whole place. Collins was gone. Good thing, too. When he'd put his arm around Becca my blood pressure exploded. Found myself fingering the gun in my pocket. Boonie seemed to think this was funny, the cocksucker. "You want her, take her."

"Yeah, 'cause it's that simple."

He snorted, exchanging looks with Deep and Demon. Deep shrugged.

"If you're a real man, you'll do what needs to be done," he muttered, reaching for his beer.

"Sort of like what you're doing with Carlie?" I asked him, raising a brow. "Couldn't help but notice whose bed she wasn't in last night."

Deep's eyes narrowed and he leaned forward, but Demon elbowed him in the ribs. Hard. The two were Irish twins—born ten months apart—and I'd never seen brothers who enjoyed fighting with each other more.

"He's right," Demon said. "Shut your fuckin' mouth."

"This is nice," Boonie announced. "We should do this more often, don't you think?"

Ignoring him, I settled back on my stool and surveyed the room. We sat in Becca's section, and what I saw wasn't making me happy. I knew she was a good waitress, but she'd just started here and it showed. Not only had she fucked up several orders, she didn't quite seem to get the rhythm of the bar. That wasn't my problem, though.

My problem was that despite these fuckups, nobody seemed to mind. I had a nasty suspicion this was due to her perky tits, friendly smile, and tight little ass that seriously just needed a bite taken right out of it.

She really, really needed to get a new job—every man in the place wanted her. Including me. Especially me. I hated them. All of them. I shifted uncomfortably, because just like every time I shared a room with her, my pants had gotten tight.

Torture. Becca was just so fucking fine on every level, and not just her looks. There was something about the way she carried herself . . . I couldn't put my finger on it. Like she was dancing through life to some song nobody else could hear. Never met another woman like her—she wasn't just sexy, she was a survivor and I admired that.

She'd grown up so much since the first time I'd met her. Bigger boobs, a nice fullness to her ass that was nowhere close to fat but would be perfect to hold tight while I fucked her. Her lips had plumped, too, and over the years she'd gained a sparkle in her eyes that turned her from pretty to 100 percent spectacular.

Not to mention how she'd tasted.

Nearly blew in my pants when I'd taken that mouth. Just the memory got me hard. Make that harder. Fucking basket case.

When I'd pulled up to find her sitting outside with Collins, a thousand murder scenarios ran through my mind. And yeah, I know I covered that already, but if anything ever deserved emphasis, this was it. Collins needed to *die*. I didn't care how nice he was. After that I'd throw Becca on the back of my bike and make a run for the hills . . .

Okay, so there were a few problems with the plan, the top one being she hated me. Or she should—I'd certainly given her cause. Boonie nudged me.

"Did I mention you're pathetic? You want her, take her. Otherwise let it go because you're an embarrassment to all men in general and to the Silver Bastards in particular."

"She's scared shitless of me," I pointed out.

"She used to be," he acknowledged. "But yesterday she threw herself into a fight when she thought you needed help. When shit got real, she didn't run. She got *pissed*—I admire that. Stop being a fucking pussy."

I didn't respond, because this wasn't a conversation I wanted to continue. Nosy fucker that he was, Boonie couldn't let it go. Instead he caught her eye and waved her over.

"What can I do for you?" she asked brightly. Not to me. Of course not to me. If she ignored me any harder, she'd strain something.

"A round for the table," Boonie replied. "Then we're gonna want some privacy."

"Sure thing," she replied, understanding flickering in her eyes, reminding me just how well Becca knew the life. Or at least, how well she knew one fucked-up, sick little corner of our world . . . She started back to the bar, detouring when the group of students started yelling at her for service. I tensed, but Boonie caught my arm.

"You can't be around to protect her all the time," he said. "They're just being little pricks. Won't be the first or last time she'll have to handle that type. Unless you plan to claim her and take her away from all this?"

I flipped him off and he laughed. One of the students stood up and lurched toward the bathrooms, pulling a blonde girl behind him. He was tall, with the smooth look of a spoiled preppy twat. All dark, floppy hair and standard-issue tribal tattoos because clearly he couldn't think of anything better to put on his skin.

Fucking pussy. His little girlfriend giggled and shot glances back toward the rest of the kids, clearly scandalized and full of excitement that they were sneaking off together. He probably had a new one every night, or he would if he wasn't trapped up at that school for cockwads too rich to wipe their own assholes.

The diamonds sparkling on the bitch's ears were real. I'd bet my bike on it.

Becca would look real pretty wearing earrings like that . . . Although if I owned her she'd never find out—just one more reason to stay the fuck away.

She came back with our drinks, handing them around the table. When she turned to go, Boonie stuck his leg out and she tripped right into me. I caught her, of course. Her body was soft and she smelled good, like flowers or something. Flowers and mint? Fuck if I knew—made me want to eat her, though. Memories flooded me, everything from the sweet, salty taste of her cunt to the noises she'd made when she came. Heat shot through my cock as she pulled away, glaring at us.

"Thanks, asshole," I muttered at Boonie, but I didn't say it to his face—too busy watching Becca strut off toward the bar. I was so busy perving on her ass that I almost missed what happened next. The blonde girl stumbled out of the back hallway, hair rumpled and lipstick worn off. Thirty seconds later the preppy asshole followed, his shirt pulled loose and a satisfied smirk on his face. None of this would've been noteworthy if he hadn't lurched straight into our table.

"Fuck off," Deep muttered, but the kid straightened and I realized he wasn't drunk at all. He might be carrying himself that way, but his eyes were sharp and speculative. Interesting.

"Brought your money," he murmured. "Shane said you'd have something for me. Outside in ten."

Seconds later he was off again, stumbling and laughing at his friends. Boonie's face stayed completely neutral, but when he reached for his drink and took a long pull, I sensed smug satisfaction.

"What was that about?" Deep asked.

"Little project I've been working on," Boonie said. "We'll cover everything at church. Wasn't sure he'd pull through, consider this something of a test."

"Who? That little prick?" Deep asked.

"That little prick's dad was a contract killer for the Irish mob," Boonie said. I raised an eyebrow.

"No shit?" I asked. "What the fuck is he doing here?"

"Trying to stay alive," Boonie answered. "Or rather, he's protecting the one trying to stay alive. Shane McDonogh, who used to be a genuine mob prince. His mom, Christina, married Jamie Callaghan. Raised him down in Vegas. Nobody knows for sure who his father was."

Interesting. Even I knew the McDonoghs had owned the Laughing Tess for five generations. Five violent, angry generations where the miners, the union, and the McDonoghs had fought with one another for control of the valley.

Not long after I'd gotten out of prison, the old man had died.

Hadn't left the mine to his daughter, though. Went straight to the grandson.

"Doesn't that make him about the richest kid in Idaho?" I asked. Boonie snorted.

"Might make him the richest kid in North America," he replied. "Not that it's doing him any good. They've been fighting the will for years. Mommy wants her mine back."

"What's he want with us? Drugs? Gotta be boring as fuck up at that school."

"Protection," Boonie said, his voice satisfied. "He knows we run the valley. He's rich on paper, but funds are limited and he has no manpower. Now he's cooling his heels at the academy."

"Nice family," I said. "If he's worth so much, why doesn't he just find a lawyer to take them out? You hang that mine out as bait, they'll be swarming to help him."

"Don't know the whole story," Boonie said. "Don't really care. All that matters is that in ten minutes we're going to get paid a fuck-load of money for a few guns so the young prince can sleep a little easier at night. Our discretion justifies a slight markup, of course . . ."

I grinned, because Boonie had a gift for finding money-making opportunities.

"That goes through, told him we could talk about a more long-term solution," he added. "He's got big plans. Blackthorne thinks he could be good for the valley. Hard to say."

Deep raised his beer bottle, silently saluting him as my eyes drifted back toward Becca. She was leaning over a table, ass twitching as she wiped off the spilled beer. Mentally I was already shoving her down face-first before fucking her right the hell into oblivion.

"Might want to close your mouth," Boonie said, nudging me. "Don't want to drool in your beer. Now bottoms up, because we've got a meeting outside. Deep, you take the porch—maybe have your-self a smoke and keep an eye out. Puck, you're with me, unless you'd rather have the smoke?"

I dropped my hand from inside my cut, where I'd reached for my cigs automatically. Boonie gave a snort of laughter, which I deserved for being so fucking predictable. I'd stopped smoking six months back, yet I still caught myself going for them at least ten times a day.

The dark-haired kid met us back behind the bar, his giggling girl-friend nowhere to be seen. I studied him in the darkness, trying to place his age. Twenty, twenty-one? He had a hard look to his eyes, and his body language had changed. Inside I'd pegged him for a pussy, but now?

I could see him as a contract killer's kid.

"You still want all six?" Boonie asked, hefting a leather saddle-bag. "They're clean."

"Yeah," he said, his voice quiet. "Shane said it's a done deal?"

Boonie nodded. The boy pulled out an envelope and tossed it to me. I opened it, flipping through a very nice wad of cash. A quick mental tally confirmed the amount, and I gave my president a nod. He opened the saddlebag and pulled out one of those cloth grocery bags, all rolled tight around a hard ball of what I knew were handguns.

The kid took them.

"Want to check them over?" Boonie asked. The kid shook his head, flashing a grin at us.

"Your reputation is good," he said. "We respect that. Otherwise we wouldn't be looking to work with you more. Send me a message when you've made your decision."

"And if we want to talk to your boss?"

He shrugged.

"That's trickier. Electronic tether up at the campus, for one thing. And it's not our way to expose him. We'll see."

That struck me as off, but I held my tongue. Had to trust that

Boonie knew what he was doing, save my questions for church. You don't undermine a brother in front of outsiders. No fucking way.

The kid took the guns and put them into the trunk of a very sporty little BMW convertible that'd been parked in the shadows on the side of the building. It had "princess" written all over it, and I sincerely hoped it belonged to his girlfriend.

Then he turned back to us.

"Looking forward to doing more business," he said, holding out his hand to me. Interesting. His shake was firm and strong. "I'm Rourke Malloy."

"Puck."

He nodded, clearly committing me to memory, then walked away, his body casual confidence. I glanced at Boonie.

"We done?"

"Yup," he replied. "Let's get Deep and head back to the club-house. We'll go over everything at church tomorrow. You want to go back inside, maybe say good night to your girlfriend?"

The question annoyed me, because I'd planned on doing something very much like that. Not saying good night—of course not. But I'd figured I'd check her out at least one more time, maybe make sure she was doing okay.

Now I couldn't, and Boonie knew it.

Christ I needed a smoke. Couldn't have one of those, either.

"I hate you."

"Stop being a little bitch and take care of business," he said, laughing. "Claim her or get over it."

Fuck, I wished it was that easy.

BECCA

"Hold up, I'll walk you out," Blake said. "Just have to grab something out of the back room first."

I pulled out a chair and collapsed, because my feet were killing me. I appreciated the fact that he didn't want us girls wandering around a dark parking lot at three a.m. on our own, but standing and waiting for him simply wasn't an option.

"So how did you do?" Danielle asked, grabbing the seat next to me. "I made out better than I expected—not half bad for a first night. Says something good about the place. Of course that table of little fuckwads stiffed me on the tip, but no surprise there. I knew they would, from the minute they came in. Think they're the shit, don't they?"

I shrugged, because she wasn't really expecting an answer.

"You ladies ready?" Blake asked.

"Yeah," I said. He laughed and reached out to catch our hands, dragging us to our feet.

"Don't you ever get tired?" I muttered.

"Nope," he replied, his voice disgustingly fresh and smug. "Endless energy. Be afraid."

"I live in fear."

Danielle giggled and popped up on her toes to kiss him. When he tried to catch her and kiss her back, she ducked around and jumped on his back without warning.

"Jesus!" Blake muttered, staggering, but he looked happy. Joe had been right—Blake was into Danielle for real. Shit. I hoped she didn't destroy him . . .

"Take me to my car," she announced, bouncing up and down. "If you're a good boy, you'll get a reward."

He started toward the door and I followed, feeling like the third wheel. Usually that wasn't a problem with these two, but it was late and obviously Blake wanted her at home and in his bed. The fact that I needed a ride complicated that, seeing as it took her in the wrong direction.

"I'm sorry my car's not here," I told her.

"Don't worry about it," she said as we passed through the back door, locking it behind us. Teresa was still in her office but she had an apartment upstairs so we didn't need to wait around for her. Blake trotted down the steps, me trailing behind like a puppy. We were halfway across the lot when I saw someone move in the darkness.

"Shit," I hissed. "There's someone back here."

"If you're a murderer, you can back the fuck off!" Danielle shouted. "I have a gun and Blake killed someone with his bare hands once, asshole!"

Blake stopped cold.

"What the hell?"

"It's all about creating an atmosphere of fear," Danielle said confidently. "We'll just scare him off. It's probably just some dumbass kid having fun with us."

He—whoever he was—wasn't exactly radiating fear. I guessed this from the way he started walking toward us, each step crunching the gravel. I felt like there should be menacing music in the background. Maybe the lone call of a loon . . . Blake lowered Danielle and took on that menacing aura he'd had during the fight yesterday morning.

I was very, very glad to have him on my side.

Then the figure stepped into the ring of light surrounding the porch. Puck. I felt an innapropriate thrill, remembering all too well how he'd kissed me earlier . . . Hard hands cupping my face. Raw need in his eyes and the frustration written across his every move.

Now he waited for me in the darkness.

I wasn't sure whether I should be relieved that we weren't about to get murdered, or scared, because whatever Puck's intentions were, they wouldn't be pure and innocent. *Meet him head-on*, I decided. *Never show a biker weakness.*

"What are you doing here?" I asked, challenging him. "Not enough that Boonie trips me while I'm trying to work? And don't deny it—I saw the look on his face."

"Thought you might need a ride home," he replied, his voice soft and deep. "And I happened to be passing by. Figured I'd wait."

"What are you, some kind of fucking stalker?" Danielle demanded bluntly.

"Danielle, I can handle this," I protested.

"So handle it," she muttered. "I'm ready to go home and he's in my way."

Puck's face hardened and I realized we were headed down a dark path here. Danielle was brave and loyal, but her sense of preservation was lacking. Throw in the fact that Blake was always ready to throw down, and Puck . . . Well, best not to go there.

"Danielle, he saved my ass today," I said quickly, shifting out of tough girl mode. "It's all good. He just caught me off guard and I'm tired. And Puck, it's really nice of you to offer, but—"

I stopped talking abruptly. Danielle and Blake obviously wanted some time together, but she was such a good friend she'd run me home first. That meant close to an extra forty minutes of driving for her in the dead of night, all so I wouldn't have to spend time with Puck.

She'd do it without a second thought, too—that's the kind of person she was. But should I really be asking her to just because he sort of scared me?

"You know what? A ride would be great," I told him, forcing myself to smile. Blake shot me a quick glance as Danielle started protesting again.

"You don't need—"

"Let's go," Puck replied, reaching out and catching my hand. Then I was tagging along after him across the parking lot. Danielle squawked and Blake grabbed her. I heard them arguing in loud whispers and figured she was about ten seconds away from launching a one-woman jihad against Puck.

Fortunately we'd almost reached his bike. He paused, looking at me, his face thoughtful.

"If you want out, now's the time," he said in a low voice, and I wondered if he meant more than just a ride. What did I want? I was tired, my feet hurt, and Puck smelled good.

I glanced back at my best friend—still arguing with Blake. I needed to shut this down.

"Danielle, it's fine," I said, projecting my voice across the parking lot. "Puck can give me a ride and you can go to Blake's place. Don't worry."

She stilled and Blake wrapped his arm around her neck, pulling her body into his. He didn't say anything, just waited for her to make the decision to back down. She narrowed her eyes and crossed her arms.

"If you do anything to her I'll get you, Redhouse," she threatened. Damn. Danielle was *fierce*.

"Take your woman home," Puck told Blake. Danielle sputtered but Puck ignored her, pulling me toward the Harley parked around the side of the building. Then he was on it, kicking it to life as I stood there, frozen, because I'd made a serious miscalculation. For some reason, I'd assumed he had his truck.

I hadn't been on a bike for five years.

They'd been a huge part of my life, growing up. Hell, Mom had a picture of me on one when I was a baby. For all I knew, the man holding me had been my father—she'd never said either way, and the one time I'd asked, she'd told me to shut my fucking mouth. Maybe he was just another in my string of "daddies." Impossible to know.

Now Puck wanted me on the back of his bike. I remembered my arms wrapped tight around his stomach that day we'd left California, face buried in his back, trembling in pain and fear. I'd cried for hours, not that it mattered. We started riding and kept riding, stopping only for gas and the occasional smoke. They'd wanted to get the hell out of Longnecks territory before someone decided to come after me.

Not that the Silver Bastards were running scared.

Never.

But they'd had better things to do than get into a war over a random girl they'd picked up at a party.

"Get on," Puck said, turning to look at me. His face was shadowed, but I swore his eyes burned like coals. What had I been thinking, agreeing to go anywhere with him? Had I lost my mind?

Maybe.

But maybe I was just being a giant wuss. Danielle and Blake deserved some time together.

"Okay," I said, throwing my leg over the bike. I took a deep breath and wrapped my arms around his stomach, trying not to think about how tight and hard it still was. No beer gut here. Puck pulled out of the parking lot and onto the blacktop.

Then we were flying through the night.

It's funny how you build the things that scare you up in your mind.

I'd been flinching every time I heard a bike for years. They represented everything bad about my childhood—the pain, the fear . . . Sometimes they represented the good. The Silver Bastards. Puck watching over me.

But good or bad, I'd completely blocked out one critical reality— flying down the highway on a bike is fucking *amazing*.

The night air was still warm, although in a week or two that would change. Puck smelled good and he handled the big machine like a master. I closed my eyes, focusing on the feeling of his back against my chest, his bulky strength in front of me.

Damn, he was sexy.

Of course, the fact that a powerful Harley engine roared between my legs like the world's biggest vibrator didn't exactly hurt. Whatever the reason, by the time we'd gone that first mile I'd forgotten all about being afraid. There's something completely liberating about riding behind a man, because they control everything. You can only hold on and follow their lead. Trust they know what they're doing. That they'll bring you home safe.

That's what fucked me up.

I forgot I shouldn't trust Puck.

When we started out, I'd held him as impersonally as possible. Granted, any time you're on a bike it's pretty personal, but that's no excuse for what I did next. Gradually I let my fingers spread out, widening across his stomach. I found the ridges of muscles, savoring the gentle play of them under his skin when he leaned into a curve.

My body leaned with his, following his lead perfectly.

That gave me the excuse to tighten my arms around him, one hand slipping up just a little higher, the other dropping until I felt the metal of his belt buckle under my fingers.

Doesn't mean a thing, I told myself. *Anyone would hold him like that. Just part of riding the bike together.*

But it wasn't.

All I could think about was dropping my hand lower, exploring the length of his cock through his pants. Would he be hard? A thrill ran through me at the thought, and my nipples perked up. I knew I had to be growing wet down below, but somehow it didn't feel real. Not here in the darkness, with the wind roaring around us and his face safely turned away from mine. I could just hide my face against his back and pretend none of it was happening, right? By the time we reached Callup and he slowed, I was squirming. Why the hell couldn't I feel this way around Joe?

Puck drove down the empty main street, slowing as we reached my corner building. He turned around the side and pulled into the alley, stopping gradually. Then he turned off the engine, the sudden silence hitting me like a slap in the face. What was I doing? I'd plastered myself against his back, I had one hand halfway up his chest and the other across his belt buckle.

"Thanks," I said abruptly. His hands clamped down over mine before I could escape, silently calling bullshit.

"You still like riding bikes," he said slowly, his voice a low growl. I tried to shrug, which was impossible given our position.

"I guess it can be fun," I admitted.

He didn't respond, at least not with words. Instead he slowly pushed my hand lower.

"What are you doing?" I whispered.

"You wanted to touch me," he replied. "But you're too scared."

My hand found the hard ridge of his erection, tight against the worn fabric of his jeans. Need and desire hit me like a blow, curling up along my spine, pooling between my legs.

Puck wanted me. Bad.

My fingers clutched him. It wasn't planned but oh, it was good . . . Puck stiffened, his head leaning back with a sigh. My other hand dug into the hard, firm muscle of his pec. His fingers wrapped around mine, squeezing himself with my hand harder than I would've had the nerve to do.

My body had turned into a quivering mass of pure lust, and when he started jacking my hand up and down across his length I nearly died. Not like I *should* have almost died. You know, from shock and horror? Nope. The emptiness between my legs screamed out for more because despite the fact that I was spread wide around him, there wasn't a hint of friction for me to get off on.

Puck shuddered and I felt a rush of power mixed with my own aching need. Here was this big, strong man at my mercy, all because I was rubbing his cock through a layer of denim in the dark.

Then he spoke, and I remembered that Puck was never at anyone's mercy.

"I think about you," he said, his voice agonized. "I've jacked off a thousand times, remembering that night. I've fucked a shitload of women, too. Tried to find one to replace you. I swear to fuck, Becca, if you were anyone else I'd just take you and be done with it. You're lodged in my brain like a bullet and it's poisoning me."

I froze, reality washing back in. My hand stopped moving, but he tightened his fingers around mine, forcing me to start again. He was harder now—bigger—and I wondered how much it had to hurt, keeping that monster all penned up in his pants.

He wanted to fuck me. Bad. I wanted him, too, but his words were like cold water, reminding me this wasn't a game.

"So," Puck continued, his tone so intense it scared me. "I think it's time we cleared this shit up. I like your hand on my dick. I'd like your mouth on it better. I want your cunt, your ass—everything. No more games, Becca. You know who and what I am, and you know that when I fuck you, it won't be pretty. I don't do pretty. I've held off because of what happened and I felt guilty but that shit is in the past. I'm done. You got thirty seconds to say no, then I'm taking you upstairs and all bets are off."

The words hit me like a physical blow. My hands tightened reflexively and I shuddered, because I've never wanted anything more than I wanted to go upstairs with him. I managed to break through the fog of lust for an instant, asking him the million-dollar question.

"What do you mean, all bets are off?"

Puck gave a harsh, humorless laugh. "I mean I'm done dancing around you. You got hurt, I felt bad. But tonight you grabbed me and now I'm out of patience. We didn't have history between us, you'd be under me already, Becca. And I won't pretend to be something I'm not. I want a woman, I take her. I keep her until we're finished and I call the shots while we're together. No games. This is your last out."

My thighs clenched and I knew what I wanted to say. Then my mother's voice cut through my head.

Little slut.

Had she felt this way about Teeny? How many times had she let her body do the thinking for her?

"I call the shots while we're together."

Puck let my hand go and I stilled, clutching him for an instant longer. Then I let go and pulled back.

"Thanks for the ride home," I managed to say, my voice unsteady. "And thank you for clearing things up. I've got to get to sleep. It's been a long day and I have school tomorrow afternoon."

He froze, a cold and frustrated statue. I clambered off the bike, forced to lean a hand against Puck's shoulder to steady myself because my legs had turned to rubber. Then I made for my door. I kept expecting him to say something, or maybe come after me.

A part of me wanted him to.

Wanted him to take away the decision, to force me so I wouldn't have to own up to the fact that I needed him so badly it hurt. Life would be so much easier if I wasn't responsible . . . But who am I kidding? My life has never been easy. Puck stayed silent until I reached the stairwell door, then spoke one last time.

"I took your choice away five years ago. Tonight I gave it back to you. Consider us even."

FIVE

My bed felt like a pile of rocks.

No matter how I twisted and turned, I couldn't get comfortable. Puck's words ran through my brain, twisting around and fucking with my nerves. Mom's phone call echoed through me, too. She hadn't called back, but I knew better than to try and call her myself. Not if Teeny was on a tear. Part of me almost wished she wouldn't call, and I know that makes me sound like a shit person. But she destroyed everything she touched. I hated how talking to her made me feel, then hated myself for picking up the phone when she called again. Most of all, I hated all the hope and excitement I felt every time I thought she might actually leave him—it always led to disappointment.

By five I realized the whole thing was pointless. Might as well just get up.

Coffee couldn't replace sleep, but it helped. So did my favorite playlist. By the time I fired up my Singer sewing machine the first light of dawn was streaking across the sky. I still had some silk from the kimono I'd used to make my makeup bag. Danielle's words came back to me—maybe I really could sell some of them? They were certainly unique . . .

Two hours later I put the finishing touches on an entirely new bag design. The sun was up and my eyes were heavy, but I stumbled back toward my bed feeling satisfied and settled. I'd catch an hour of sleep before school—that should tide me over. Maybe I couldn't control Puck or my job or my mom . . . but when I sat down in front of that machine, beautiful things came out. Things nobody else could make—things straight from my heart.

That had to count for something, right?

Usually I only heard from my mom every couple of months.

Her phone was deactivated half the time because she was always behind on her bills. She'd disappear for five or six weeks, then I'd get a call out of nowhere from a strange new number. Other times she'd email me from a public computer, or give me a quick call using someone else's phone.

Like so many things about our lives, I grew up without realizing there was another way to exist. Most people would find it strange or uncomfortable, going without a reliable connection to the outside world. With me and Mom, that's just the way things were. When the bills got paid, life was good. The rest of the time we made due.

Mom had always been a motorcycle club groupie, so I couldn't remember a time when I wasn't surrounded by big men and loud bikes. It sounds bad, but I wasn't entirely unhappy growing up. Before Teeny I remembered traveling and doing fun things with other kids.

Then everything changed.

Before she met him things were good, even though we'd been

living in our car for a while after the last man she'd hooked up with dumped her. We'd slept in the car lots of times over the years, so I wasn't scared. She used to make a game of it and that was fun. Then one day Mom dropped me with a friend and disappeared for a week. When she came back, she told me I had a new daddy, his name was Teeny, and that we were all going to be a family together. That's when we moved into his house.

I loved it at first—I had my own room and everything.

When school started that year, I'd gotten to ride on a big yellow school bus with a bunch of other kids, and I even made some friends. At eight years old, kids tend not to notice the fact that a girl in their class hasn't had a bath in three days, or that her clothes are too small. The teachers were onto us, of course—I remember strange people in suits coming to the house, checking our cabinets for food, and asking my mom a lot of questions—but I still felt like I fit in.

Then slowly I realized something wasn't right.

For one thing, I didn't get invited to play with other kids after school, or to their birthday parties. For my tenth birthday I had a party and only one girl came. Her mom didn't drop her off. She just stood around, watching nervously while my mom fussed with my cake, and then they left before we even had a chance to play games. Slowly I learned that I was biker trash, and even if the kids didn't know it, their parents did.

By the time I hit middle school, all the kids knew it, too.

There was *normal* and then there was us.

But when I left California, I left Biker Trash Becca behind. Regina and Earl looked at me and saw who I really was—a young girl who needed help. They opened their home and their hearts to me, and the rest of Callup followed suit. For the first time in my life I really belonged. Not only that, I was safe, surrounded by layers of protection. First Regina and Earl, then my new friends at the school. Their families adopted me, too, and standing guard over all of us were the Silver Bastards, who considered the town and its inhabitants their own.

Even now, despite the weirdness with Puck, my life was good. Almost normal. I had a job, I had school, and I was still in control.

Funny how one phone call can completely fuck up everything.

My cell phone started blowing up around two that afternoon, but I was just starting an evaluation, so I ignored it after a quick check to see who was calling. Mom. Shit. I'd have to call her back after school . . . Then she called me four more times in ten minutes and I started to freak out. Another hour passed before I could get away and check my messages. The first was calm enough, at least on the Mom Scale.

"Baby, you need to call me right now. It's important."

By the second message she sounded upset. Not that my mother getting upset was anything new—she was always either in a great mood or ten seconds from losing it, not much left in between.

"Becca, I just tried calling your apartment. I don't know why you can't live somewhere that has better service. You really need to call me. Now."

It was the third message that really worried me, though. This time she sounded scared. Like, scared for real. Combine that with the repeated calls and warning sirens started going off in my head.

"It's important, Becca. Please call me. I need to get away from Teeny—it's not safe here anymore. I know we've had our differences, but I really need your help now."

My breath caught, then I forced myself to calm down. She'd said she was ready to leave him half a dozen times. Then she'd change her mind . . . Would she really go through with it? When I was younger, I'd always wondered if Teeny was a wizard, because he seemed to have a near-magical hold over my mother.

I called her back, fingers trembling. She didn't answer and I didn't leave a message. For all I knew Teeny would steal her phone and listen to it, so I sent her a vague text instead.

ME: Mom—ill be at school until five and then home for the evening. Call me.

I was useless after that. All I could think about was Mom and Teeny and whether she was serious this time. Well, that's all I could think about until four thirty.

That's when distraction arrived in hot-guy form.

News spread through the school in a flash, of course, and all the girls were whispering and giggling about him. Nothing unusual there. Stressed out or not, I was still a functioning human woman so I decided to do a discreet walk-by to the bathroom to check him out. My breath caught.

Tall. Built, with strong arms and spiky blond hair.

Fuckballs.

That was Painter, Puck's friend. I'd recognize him anywhere, even if he wasn't wearing his Reaper colors. Not that I *knew* him— not really. But he'd been in jail with Puck. The welcome-home party that changed my whole life had been half for Painter, half for Puck. We'd all ridden back to Idaho together and I'd caught Painter's eyes following me a time or two. Speculative and assessing, like I was some kind of strange creature he couldn't quite identify.

Now he was chatting up Anna, who was working reception, so I ducked back down the hallway and into the bathroom. Why? I have no idea. Painter's arrival had nothing to do with me. Probably. Didn't mean I wanted to talk to him.

But seeing him reminded me of Puck and things went downhill from there. Specifically, I pondered all the reasons I absolutely shouldn't ever talk to or even look at him again. Biker? Check. Dangerous? Check. Scary sexy? Check.

Scary, period.

I amended my mental "fuckballs" to "flying fuckballs with caramel sauce on top."

He's not Teeny, but he's still part of Teeny's world, I lectured myself, trying to focus on the combs I was sanitizing. *And in his world, sometimes they give teenage girls to men as "welcome home from prison" presents, dumbass. Did you forget that part of the story? Puck Redhouse saved you to cover his own ass. This is not a romance and it won't end happily ever after.*

No. That wasn't fair. Puck had been doing more than covering his ass when he dragged me out of California. He'd never been in real danger—wasn't like the SWAT team had been poised and ready to bust him for screwing a minor. Nobody at that party had cared what happened to me at all. Not until him. He'd saved me because somewhere deep inside he was a decent human being.

The romance bit, though . . . That was dead-on. If I wanted happily ever after, Joe Collins was my guy.

I didn't share any of this with Blake, who gave me a ride home after school. He had classes down at North Idaho College on Mondays, Wednesdays, and Fridays, so when our schedules aligned, he drove. The system worked, although I wished he'd let me give him gas money. Fortunately, Earl had left a message earlier in the day saying that my car was ready and he'd left it parked in the alley behind my apartment. Over the weekend I'd have to go and pick some huckleberries to make him a pie, I decided. Earl loved his huckleberry pie, and we were at the tail end of the season so it was now or never.

"You got time to give me a haircut tonight?" Blake asked about a mile outside Callup.

"Sure," I told him. I'd been cutting his hair for a while now. I might not have a license yet, but a simple trim like his was easy enough to do.

"That'd be great. I'm on at seven at the Moose, but I'm hoping to pick up Danielle in time for us to grab some dinner before our shifts start."

"Sounds good to me."

"You got plans for tonight?"

"Nope, just going to relax at home. Maybe drink some wine and sit out on the roof with a book or something."

"What about Joe? You could give him a call."

"It's been a busy week," I said, dodging the question. "Lots of things happening. I'm ready for some time alone."

Usually I spent my Friday nights hanging out with friends. Tonight I was really looking forward to doing nothing. I knew that eventually I'd be working most weekends, but until Danielle and I were up to speed Teresa didn't want us both on shift during the busiest nights.

Maybe I'd use the time to count and roll all my coins. I threw all my change from tips into a big glass jug that I broke into whenever I truly hit bottom. If Mom finally left Teeny, I'd need it. Not that it would be enough . . . money was going to be a big problem.

Don't get too excited, I warned myself firmly. *She never leaves him. Maybe she never will.*

Thankfully, Blake dropped the conversation about Joe, parking behind my place in comfortable silence. We went upstairs and I pulled one of my mismatched wooden chairs into the center of the living room. The floor was faded, scuffed hardwood and I loved every inch of it—the easy sweep-up after haircuts was just one of many advantages.

"Okay," I told him. "Get your ass over to the sink and let's get you washed up."

"I'm going to grab a beer, that okay?"

"Sure, get one for me," I told him as I ducked into the bathroom to grab some shampoo.

"Just one," he warned. "Don't want you cutting off my ear."

I heard the pop of a beer cap coming off. Then he handed me a brown bottle. Taking a deep swig, I flipped on the hot water, which always took forever.

Blake pulled off his shirt and leaned over the basin, pretending to flinch when I started rinsing his hair.

"You're such a baby," I told him. "Stop whining, or I really will snip your ears."

"Were you always a bitch like this? I remember you being nicer."

"I'm taking lessons from Danielle."

Blake laughed, and minutes later I had him washed and ready to go, wrapping a towel around his head to sop up the water. He flipped it expertly into a girl-style wrap around his head, then struck a "sexy" pose for me.

"How do I look?" he asked. "Fabulous?"

I shook my head and took another drink of beer.

"Sit your fabulous ass down in the chair. Otherwise you won't have enough time for dinner."

While he made himself comfortable, I turned on my little stereo. I'd bought it the day after Thanksgiving last year in Coeur d'Alene with Regina, when it was marked down to forty bucks. It had pretty good sound, though. Way better than you'd expect for the price.

"Okay, we doing the usual?" I asked, coming over to stand behind him, draping a second towel around his shoulders. It didn't cover as much as a cape would, but I didn't charge like a salon, either. Outside I heard the roar of bike pipes. Puck. Great. Why did he have to move in next to me?

"Yeah," Blake said. "You know me—keep it simple."

Simple it was. He liked his hair short, so short that he didn't have to worry about it at all, which made my life easy. A few snips to shape the top, then the trimmer did most of the work for me. Ten minutes later we'd finished our beers and the cut, and Blake was back on his feet, brushing the loose hairs off his chest.

He stretched and looked at me, smiling.

"You know, if I wasn't batshit crazy over Danielle I'd be all over you, Becca," he said. I blinked, startled.

"What?"

"I think sometimes you don't realize how special you are," he said, casually grabbing his shirt and pulling it over his head. "Joe's a decent guy, and he'd take good care of you. Maybe he's not your one and only, but don't ever settle, okay? You're better than that."

I gaped at him as he gave me a quick hug, opening his wallet to pull out a ten-dollar bill. It wasn't much, but he always liked to leave me something. It'd be a big help, too. My power bill was due soon and I was still short.

"You don't need to pay me," I reminded him. "You always drive. I should be paying you for the gas."

Blake rolled his eyes.

"I can't let you drive," he said, his voice soft with a hint of humor. "You know how I feel about women drivers. Not only that, you're cheap. Costs me twice that much in town."

"Wow, you almost got out the door without fucking up," I said, flipping him off. He laughed and threw me a little salute as the door closed behind him.

Huh.

I'd been friends with Blake for close to a year now, but he still managed to surprise me.

I drank another beer as I swept up hair trimmings, then took a shower to wash off the day's grime. I followed the shower with a pair of loose cotton pants and a tank top. I hadn't been kidding about wanting to relax. Not even my Singer tempted me at this point . . .

Hungry, I opened my fridge to figure out food and had to laugh because it was full of beer. It always was, despite my poverty—another sign that I had good friends. My place was the most convenient for all of us to get together and I'd learned long ago that a few

seed beers tended to replicate themselves as time went on. I couldn't
remember the last time I'd had to actually buy alcohol, which was
a damned good thing because I also couldn't remember the last
time I could afford it.

Twenty minutes later, I finished off my dinner of generic maca-
roni and cheese (nothing but the best in my house!) feeling pleasantly
relaxed. It was nearly eight thirty and the sun had faded behind the
hills. There would still be light for a long time but when you lived in
the bottom of a valley, direct sun exposure is sadly limited . . .

Like most nights, I decided to climb out on the roof next door.
I grabbed a blanket and threw it down, lying back and closing my
eyes to ponder the situation with my mom.

Would she really leave him?

The thought excited and terrified me. For years I'd been furious
over all she'd done to ruin my life. I couldn't count how many times
I'd cried, Regina's strong, work-hardened arms wrapped tight
around me. Slowly that had changed . . . I wouldn't say I'd *forgiven*
Mom, but holding on to anger gets old. Last year I'd made a conscious decision to start letting it go. Sometimes I managed to pull
that off, sometimes I didn't.

But maybe this time things might really be different. Could I let
myself hope? Just a little?

"So which one is it?"

I jerked upright with a squawk. Puck Redhouse was sitting on
the false front of the building directly in front of me, arms crossed
and eyes hard.

"Excuse me?"

"Which guy are you fucking?" he asked, the words clipped.
"First I see you playing grabass with Blake Carver. Then you're
with Collins. Now Blake's back at your place half naked. Your girl
Danielle know what kind of 'friend' you are?"

My eyes narrowed as his meaning sank in. I opened my mouth

to insist that there was nothing between me and Blake, then snapped it shut because why the hell should I have to defend myself to Puck Redhouse?

"What, can't think of an excuse?" he asked, voice tight.

"Exactly what should I say? That I'm a slut who'll sleep with anything that moves? Hypocrite much?"

That startled him. Fair enough—I'd startled myself. *This is the problem with alcohol*, my sense of self-preservation pointed out. *Don't piss off the scary guy, you fuckwit!*

"Guess I had that coming," he acknowledged reluctantly after a long pause. "It's none of my business who you sleep with."

One word from me and he'd make it his business, though. He'd made that clear last night, and now it hung between us so thick I could hardly breathe. Awkward silence fell. I shot a glance at my open window, wondering if I could make a run for it. That's when I realized Puck must've seen me with Blake—all of my curtains were wide open.

I'd gotten too used to his place being empty.

"Feel free to go hide if you're scared of me," Puck commented.

"Very mature," I pointed out, narrowing my eyes. "Daring me not to leave? What is this, kindergarten?"

Puck gave a laugh and pushed off the facade, lowering himself to my side on the blanket.

"Seems to be working," he answered, his words light but his voice still strained. "Maybe I should dare you again."

I stared out across the roof, refusing to meet his eyes. Then something cold touched my hand. I accepted the bottle of beer Puck offered, taking a deep drink.

"Thanks," I told him, ignoring the internal voice telling me very firmly to shut the fuck up. "What did you have in mind?"

"I dare you to stay out here with me for a while," he said slowly. "I dare you to tell me the truth."

"Why should I do that?"

"You probably shouldn't," he said. "In fact, you definitely shouldn't. I can't be trusted and I don't have good intentions. You should go inside right now, little girl. Go sew yourself a doll or something."

"That is truly shitty," I said, lying back down on the blanket. "How the hell am I supposed to go back inside now?"

"All part of my evil plan," he acknowledged, propping up his head with one arm.

"I'm not a little girl," I pointed out. "I'm an adult."

"Yeah, there's nothing like pointing out that you're all grown up to prove you really are."

"Why do you always have to be a total asshat?"

"It's my way."

I closed my eyes, wondering if I'd lost my mind. Almost certainly. I should go back inside right now—but I could *feel* him next to me. Smell him. It all came flooding back to me, the way he'd taken my hand and led me back behind the house that night. When he'd pulled me down between his legs, leaning me into his strength . . . When his hands ran across my body, touching me and learning me in the firelight . . .

I'd loved it.

And last night? Best not to think about *that*.

So incredibly fucked up. Everything. I hadn't chosen him and I felt guilty sometimes for how good it'd been before it went bad. I shouldn't have enjoyed Puck's touch, because it wasn't right and only a slut gets off on some guy who's abusing her.

I wasn't a slut. I was *normal*.

But that didn't change the reality that I'd most definitely gotten off with Puck. He was nothing like the others. Not even close. When I dreamed about him and woke up screaming, those weren't screams of fear. Even now I felt my breasts tightening and I knew if he looked at me, he'd see my nipples under my tank top.

Shit, I wasn't even wearing a bra.

"So tell me," he said, his voice soft and compelling.

"Tell you what?"

"Who are you fucking?"

"That's none of your business," I said, digging in my heels. "I don't owe you any answers."

"You cut hair for anyone?" he asked. The change of subject took me off guard and I didn't consider my answer before speaking.

"That's sort of the goal," I replied. "But I'm not licensed yet, so I only do it for friends. I'm not allowed to take money for it, either."

"But you do. I saw him pay you. Or was that for other services?"

Douche.

"You tell me," I snapped. "You were spying on us, right? Do you get off on watching, Puck?"

"No. I hate it when other men touch you. Haven't you figured that out yet?"

The admission stunned me into silence. Around us the crickets had come out in force, singing their soft music through the cooling air. I loved summer nights like this, all mild and warm and still . . . Minutes passed without any more snide comments and I felt myself slowly relax. It shouldn't always have to be a fight.

"Can I ask you something?"

"Sure," Puck replied, his voice a low, sexy rumble that sent chills through me. I took a deep breath, wondering if I was making a huge mistake. I'd always wanted to know, though—to understand what'd really happened that morning in California.

"Why did you do it?"

"Do what?"

"Why did you tell Teeny I was shitty in the sack, then rescue me? I mean, if you didn't like sex with me, why did you even care? Nobody ever helped me before then . . . You weren't the first one he gave me to, you know. None of them gave a damn. What made you do it?"

He sighed heavily, and I heard the soft clinking of his bottle as he took a drink and then set it back down.

"Fuck . . . well first up, I never said you weren't a good lay. You were a fuckin' great lay, best I ever had. I told one of my brothers I'd scared you, that's all. Teeny was listening in because he's a cock-sucking weasel, and I guess he put his own spin on it. I never meant for you to get hurt. Christ. Felt guilty as fuck."

Wow. All these years I thought I'd disappointed him. Crazy how one casual comment had the power to change my life. Destroy it and save it, all in one swoop. Didn't seem right.

"But it wasn't just guilt—the situation pissed me off. All of it. Realizing I'd been played . . . I guess I was worried about going back to jail, too, but mostly I was just fucking pissed off that I'd been out less than a day and already things were fucked to hell and back. Not that I blamed you—I mean, you were the victim, not me. Once I figured it out, I couldn't just leave you there."

That wasn't the whole truth, though. He totally could've just left me there. Everyone else had.

"I know all about motorcycle clubs," I said slowly. "Nobody talks about it, but the Silver Bastards aren't exactly shiny and bright and legal. That's reality. Teeny's house was a regular pit stop for all types of bikers and none of them ever gave a flying fuck about me before that. You can't tell me you've never seen a woman in trouble before, or that you've tried to save all of them."

A bright streak flared across the sky, burning out as suddenly as it appeared. Falling star. What should I wish? Probably for my mom to leave Teeny. What I really wanted, though, was to lean over and kiss Puck.

I was the best he ever had.

"Not all clubs are the same," Puck said slowly. "Some are better than others. I'm not saying the Bastards are innocent and perfect, but your stepdad is scum and he'd never make it in our territory.

We'd take him out. The Longnecks aren't much of a club, either. Technically they're still our allies, but we've lost all respect for them and they know it. It's not an excuse for what happened, but I can tell you this—it wouldn't have gone down like that in Callup. The Silver Bastards don't rape little girls."

"You telling me your brothers never share their women?"

"Old ladies and family?" he asked. "Nope, not really our thing. Some club whore wants to fuck five guys, that's her call. Nobody gonna force her, though. And Boonie wouldn't put up with some kid being pimped out like you were—no fucking way. We'd end that shit straight up, and we'd end it permanently."

"I can see that," I admitted. "I like Darcy. I mean, I don't know her that well, but when I was trying to decide about beauty school, she took me out for coffee and we talked some. She said if I did a good job, sooner or later she'd make room for me at her day spa."

"Yeah, Darcy is like that. She's a good woman. God, this is so fucked up, but you need to know that what your mom and Teeny have? That's not normal, not for a real club. We like to keep our shit tight. We have to be able to trust our women—when the cops come, they gotta take our backs. You can't beat someone into loyalty. Doesn't work that way."

"It does with the Longnecks."

"That'll destroy them, sooner or later. Fear is great, so long as it's outsiders. Inside the club, we're about respect, not fear. Otherwise things fall apart. That shit's a fucking cancer."

I considered his words. What he said was so different from what I'd experienced for myself, but I could see the truth in it, too. I'd been watching the Bastards for five years now, and he was right. Totally different from the Longnecks, at least so far as I could tell.

"Something to think about," I murmured, feeling sleepy. A yawn hit me, but I managed to smother it.

"I could use a haircut," Puck said casually.

"I thought we couldn't be friends."

"Sometimes I get pissed and say stupid things."

I wish I could blame the beer for my answer, but that wouldn't be fair. The blame for what happened next was squarely on me.

"Okay, then. I guess I could give you a haircut."

SIX

PUCK

Of the many, many idiotic moves I'd made in my life, this was probably the worst.

I blamed my cock for the decision—I'd spent the night telling myself all the reasons I should ditch her ass, because life is too fucking short. Then I'd jerk off. Then I'd fantasize about killing Collins until I got horny again.

(Yeah, it doesn't make sense to me, either.)

Now I stood in the center of Becca's kitchen, studying the tiny apartment I'd last seen right after she moved in. Two years ago, I'd picked the lock and checked it out. Creepy? Probably, but I wanted to be sure she was somewhere safe and decent. The memory of her little girl's bedroom down in California still haunted me, from the spilled booze on the floor to the sight of my colors hanging next to her school clothes . . .

So fucking wrong.

Not that I'd grown up anywhere decent. Couldn't even remember my mom, but I'd trailed after Dad and his Silver Bastard brothers like a happy puppy. Hell, there'd always been a woman with open arms and a big heart to feed me. Hanging out in bars wasn't a conventional childhood but Dad had loved me. No matter what else he fucked up, no matter where we landed, he always had enough extra time for me when I needed him. Things worked out fine so long as we stayed two steps ahead of the law.

I blinked, bringing myself back to reality. Becca's place was nice—kind of small, with garage sale furniture and secondhand everything. Obviously she'd made all these pillows and throws and shit. Curtains. Hell, I didn't know how to describe it but it worked. My place felt like somewhere you crashed for the night. Her place felt like a home.

In the corner of the front room was the curved little turret area with her weird, old-fashioned sewing machine. I'd heard all about her sewing from Darcy. Becca was good. Like, really good. Good enough that Darcy hired her to make new "window treatments" (whatever the hell those were) for her business last year, which was really saying something. You could buy those fuckers at Walmart for almost nothing.

Of course, Darcy had a whole explanation about why Becca's curtains were better than Walmart's, which I couldn't follow but totally believed. The shop looked fantastic. Like a magazine.

Becca's apartment was just about perfect now that she'd had a chance to fix it up. Of course, I'd be happier if the downstairs door locked, but even I had to admit that probably wasn't a big deal. Nobody in Callup locked their doors, not unless they had things to hide.

My own place had three locks.

"How much do you want taken off?" Becca asked, bustling around and gathering her scissors and shit. What the hell had I been thinking? My hair grew until it got annoying and then I cut it off. It wasn't annoying right now so it didn't need a cut. Simple.

But watching her fuss over Blake earlier nearly killed me—
Christ, but she needs to start shutting her fucking shades—and I
wanted her to touch me like that. To give me what she'd given him.
The rational part of my brain knew there probably wasn't anything
between them. That hardly mattered, though, because every time I
saw them together I wanted to beat him to a fucking pulp.

My cock got hard just thinking about it. Right. Nothing fucked
up about *that*. Time to dial back the homicidal urges a bit . . .

"Okay, come over here so I can wash your hair."

I reached for my shirt, pulling it up and over my head. Becca's
mouth twisted like she'd been eating lemons.

"What?"

"Why did you take off your shirt?"

"Blake wasn't wearing his."

"He didn't want to get it wet."

"You really want to talk about getting things wet?"

She flushed and my cock throbbed. Now there was a dark path
if ever one existed . . . I held my shirt in front of my pants. Camou-
flage. If Becca had any fucking clue how horny I was, she'd kick me
out on my ass. I could control myself, though, if it meant getting
close to her.

Pussy. I practically heard Painter's voice mocking me in my
head. Right, like he should talk.

"Okay, lean over the sink," she said quietly. Following her
direction, I leaned. She unhooked the faucet, revealing a surprisingly modern hose connection. "Earl put this in for me. Regina has
one just like it that I like to use on her hair, up at their place. He
installed it for a Christmas present last year after I started school."

I ignored her words as warm water sluiced over me, because I
could give two shits about Earl. She leaned in, smelling all clean
and fresh, with a hint of orange. Not perfume or anything like that.
Must just be the soap she used. Her tits brushed my side as she
turned off the water and reached for the shampoo.

Were her nipples hard?

Then Becca's fingers dug into my hair, which had to be the sweetest torture in history. I remembered those same fingers stretched tight around my cock, squeezing and working me until I'd lost the ability to think. Been drunk off my ass that night but I hadn't blacked out, thank fuck. The only thing worse than waking up and discovering what I'd done would've been losing those memories—if you're gonna do the time, goddamn shame to forget a crime that sweet. Still jerked off to the thought at least once a week because I'm a fucking masochist.

"How's that?" Becca asked, her voice soft and husky.

"It's good," I managed to croak out. She leaned in closer and I felt her boobs push into me—had she washed Blake's hair like this?

Wasn't down with that. Not even a little.

The scalp massage lasted a long time, way longer than it needed to. Did she want to touch me as bad as I wanted to touch her? Was she thinking about the taste of my come, or how she'd grabbed my hair and screamed when I ate her pussy? Over and over her fingers ran across my skin, smoothing and releasing . . .

"Okay, time to rinse," she whispered, shifting her legs restlessly. I bit back a groan. Fuck. This was physical pain. Warm water washed over my head. If Becca had any sense, she'd turn cold spray on my crotch.

She reached for the conditioner—tits brushing my side again—and I felt her shiver. Christ. She felt it, too. My dick screamed for relief. I reached down as quietly as possible, pushing the heel of my hand down along the length, trying to make it better somehow.

The mixture of pressure and pain felt good in a sick way.

Becca's hands dug in again and I started cataloging bike parts in my head. Wasn't sure how much more I could take. Was she doing it on purpose?

Fuck, I hoped so.

"Almost finished," she whispered and I swear, I heard the same agonized need in her tone that I felt running through my whole goddamn body. *Take her*, my mind whispered. *Throw Becca down across that table and fuck her 'til she screams. When Blake and Collins come running to the rescue, you can shoot them and carry her off into the mountains. Do it.*

Jesus. I needed to pull my shit together. Fast.

Becca rinsed one more time, and then she was wrapping a towel around my hair. I stood—knees shaking—and walked into the living room where Blake's chair sat, taunting me.

"Shut the shades," I gritted from between clenched teeth. "People can see every move you make in here if you don't. Fucking fishbowl."

"I'd be a lot more worried about that if anyone went outside after dark in Callup," she replied quietly. "Sidewalks are rolled up for the night, Puck."

"Shut the fucking shades," I repeated, the words catching in my throat. Becca shrugged and obeyed, and my eyes followed her graceful form as she moved around the open area. The woman was perfect. Like a dancer. Christ, what I'd give to see her work a pole. I'd lied to her the other day when I said I could be the man who watched when she got married and had a family and lived a normal life . . .

I wasn't that man.

I'd been playing a game with myself, pretending to be something I wasn't because it was the right thing to do. Told her the truth about one thing, though—I definitely wasn't the guy who did the right thing. Never had been. Everything was so fucking clear now, because I knew exactly what I should do next.

Leave Becca alone.

Let her live a nice, normal life with a nice, normal man who worked a regular job and came home on time when he clocked out. Last night I'd even done it. I'd let her walk away from me instead of hauling her up to my bed, where she belonged.

Tonight I was fresh out of self-control.

"Okay," she said, coming to stand behind me. She rubbed the towel then pulled it free, fingers running lightly through my hair. "How do you want it cut?"

"What?"

"Your hair? How do you want it cut?"

"Um, I don't care," I managed to say, mind spinning. "Whatever you think looks good."

Becca stilled.

"You didn't really want a haircut, did you?"

"Oh, I wanted this," I muttered, the words 100 percent true. "You got no fucking clue."

"I think this might be a bad idea," she replied hesitantly. "You know, I've had four beers tonight. Maybe we should just go to bed."

The words fell heavy between us.

"Bed works."

She giggled nervously. "I can't believe I just said that."

"C'mere," I told her, catching her hand and pulling her around in front of me. Becca came to stand between my spread legs, reaching up to play with my hair again. Her gaze was a little glassy and her nipples were hard as rocks, which was all too visible since the front of her tank top was soaking wet.

A decent man would've pointed that out.

Instead I wrapped my hands around her waist, tugging her closer.

"How do you think I should cut my hair?"

"You shouldn't. It's perfect just like this—free and loose. Suits you."

Holding her gaze, I ran my hands up her sides until my thumbs rested on the underside of her boobs. She swayed and I caught the fabric, inching it up. The soft pants she wore hung loose on her hips, leaving the expanse of her stomach visible. The little dent in the center called to me.

"This isn't a good idea."

"Probably shouldn't think about it then," I replied. Her stomach smelled like baby powder and it tasted like heaven. Need burned in my stomach, pulsing up into my cock. I kissed my way toward her breasts without hurrying, which wasn't like me. Part of the reason I'd stayed away wasn't just because of how we'd met—it was because of who I am. I don't say sweet things and make love and all that bullshit. I like sex hard and rough, no holding back. Over the years I'd scared women off, which never bothered me in the slightest. If they couldn't give me what I wanted, they were useless.

Becca needed soft. Now I was the useless one.

I could pretend, though. At least for a little while. Moving upward, I nudged at her tank with my nose, finding the underside of her breast and sucking at it. One hand drifted down to her ass, cupping and massaging until she sighed and leaned into me. I found her nipple and licked it.

Becca gasped, her hands clutching my hair tight.

Pulling the nipple deep into my mouth I tasted her, mind playing back over the last time we'd done this. I'd hurt her, but Jesus, it'd been good. Felt guilty every time I thought about it, which was often. Daily. My cock was solid as a core sample, every heartbeat throbbing painfully. Becca moaned, the sound soft and sweet.

That did it—the monster inside me broke free, killing the lie.

Fuck this nice shit.

She squealed as I stood abruptly, her legs wrapping around my waist instinctively, which suited me just fine. My fingers dug deep into her ass as I shoved my hard-on into Becca's softness. The painful, tight grip of my jeans was fucking horrible and amazing all at once, because we were finally making some progress toward what I really wanted.

Rocking into her with my hips, one hand reached up and caught her hair, jerking her head back roughly. My mouth went for her throat, biting and sucking and licking as she started thrashing.

Trying to get away?

Too late.

I finally had Becca at my mercy after years of thinking about

her, imagining her, jacking off with her face in my head while I
twisted and burned in frustration. Her innocence and age had been
the ultimate cock-block . . .

She was all grown up now.

I took six steps across the floor, dropping us both into the couch,
covering and pinning her with my body. Then I had her hands
caught up and over her head, trapping her exactly like she was in
my sick fantasies.

"Puck," she moaned. I cut her off with my mouth before she had
the chance to say more. My tongue dove deep, claiming her and
branding her like I'd be doing with my come just as soon as I got
our clothes off. The logistics of that were still up in the air . . . The
laws of physics implied that I'd have to back away to get my jeans
off, but every time my hips ground into hers I was more determined
than ever to stay well and fucking put until I came.

Eventually I pulled my mouth free, dragging it back down to her
tits, sucking them in hard, desperate to taste more of her.

"Puck," she said again, her voice full of need and surrender. I
ignored her, reaching down between us, finding the top of her pants
and pushing them down. Oh *fuck*, she was wet. My fingers slid in,
opening her fast and hard. Becca shrieked, her back arching up and
off the couch. My thumb found her clit and started playing with it
as her hands fought for freedom.

Sweet Jesus.

So wet, so deep, so amazing . . . I couldn't wait to get inside.
Ladies first and all that shit, so I kept my fingers moving when
Becca gasped and called out my name again. We moved fast—
probably too fast—but the thought of slowing down was beyond
my ability to comprehend. She cried out, whimpering.

Close. So *fucking* close.

She'd come soon. Then it'd be my turn and fuck if I could imagine anything on earth I'd ever wanted more. Becca exploded around

my hand, pulsing and shuddering, clutching my fingers hard enough to remind me just how tight she'd been around my cock.

"Holy shit," she whispered as she came back down. "Holy *shit*. Puck, what the hell was that? What *was* that?"

"You know damned well what it was," I told her roughly, reaching down to unzip my pants. Condom. Needed a condom. Fuck, I didn't have my wallet with me, it was back at my apartment. Okay, two options. I could go grab it or see if she had one . . . Both bad choices. Very bad choices. If I left, she might get away. And no fucking way I wanted to know if she had condoms.

That's when the phone rang.

"Mom," Becca said, her eyes growing wide. Damn. I might be fucked up, but even I knew that girls shouldn't say "Mom" right after they come.

It's like a rule.

The phone rang again. Becca pushed against my chest urgently.

"I have to get that," she muttered, eyes wide. I stayed put, wondering how the hell we'd gone from her screaming my name to talking about her mother. "She's been trying to get hold of me. Something's really wrong."

The phone kept ringing as it sank in. Becca had every intention of not finishing what we'd started. My cock throbbed, balls tight, and suddenly I was *not* a happy camper.

"Call her back," I growled. Becca punched my chest, face growing angry.

"Get the fuck off me. I need to get the phone. Now."

BECCA

Puck stared down at me, his eyes dark and his breath coming hard. I felt how much he wanted me—no way I could miss that dick of his shoved up between my legs—and I remembered exactly how it'd felt deep inside my body.

Beautiful. Painful. Terrifying.

The phone rang again.

"I have to answer," I whispered. "It's important."

He growled at me and then rolled off, the sudden absence of his heat and weight painful. I jumped up and ran for the phone just as the answering machine kicked in. Mom's voice filled the air.

"Becca, where the hell are you?" she asked, her voice breathless. "You said to call you at home. I really need to talk to you, baby."

I caught the handset and hit the button before she could say any more. Behind me I sensed Puck radiating hostility and frustration. Nothing I could do about him right now, so I focused on the phone.

"Mom, I'm here."

"Becca!" she replied, her voice full of relief. "I'm so glad you answered. Honey, I have to make this fast. Teeny is downstairs and he's drunk again. I think he's going to hurt me if I stay here. I need you to send me money so I can get away."

Her words slammed into me, shattering my emotions along different, conflicting trajectories. Fear, of course. And anger. Toward Teeny . . . toward *her*, because something about this sounded off, despite all my hopes. With Mom it always came back to money. Why would this time be any different?

"Mom, I don't have any extra money," I said quietly. Behind me I heard Puck still, then he muttered something. Sticking a finger in my ear, I focused on my mother, ignoring him.

"Baby, I get that you aren't rolling in it," she said. "But this is for real. This isn't a late phone bill or the electricity or even a fucking car payment. That man is off his rocker and he says he's going to kill me. I need to get away, and I need to get away soon. You have to send me money right now."

Her words chilled me. *Kill her?*

"How much?"

"Two thousand dollars."

I froze.

"Mom, I don't have that much."

"You've got a car, right?"

"Not one that's worth two grand," I said bluntly. "I could sell everything I own and not have that much."

"Figure something out," she replied desperately. "Baby, I can't get away without your help and I can't stay here. I know I've been a crappy parent—I realize that. But I love you, I've always loved you, and I know you love me."

"Mom, this isn't about whether I love you. I don't have the money and I can't just make it appear out of the air."

"Can you borrow it from someone?" she pressed. "Make some guy feel good, then hit him up for a loan?"

My stomach twisted.

"No."

"You're pretty, always have been," she wheedled. "Why don't you go to a strip club? You could earn that money in a night or two, send it down to me. I'd do it myself, but they'd never take me. Not like I am now. I'm too old, baby."

I closed my eyes, trying to picture taking off my clothes in front of a crowd of staring men. No. No way. How dare she even consider asking me that?

"I can empty my tip jar," I said. "But it's not much, maybe fifteen or twenty bucks. I'll send it to you tomorrow. It's the best I can do."

Her voice turned hard.

"He's going to kill me," she snapped. "What kind of girl lets her mother die because she's too good to take off her clothes? You did a lot more than that down here, and don't think I've forgotten how you cried when you left. You didn't want to ride off with that boy— I forced you to go, to save your life. Now you won't do the same for me?"

My stomach heaved, and I swayed. Why? Why did she have to do this?

"I'll send you my tip money," I repeated slowly. "There must be someone else you can ask, Mom. Can you steal some money from Teeny while he's sleeping?"

"You're ungrateful," she hissed, hanging up on me. I ran my fingers through my hair, trying to steady myself, setting the phone on the table. What the hell was that all about? Should I believe her?

No.

It couldn't be that bad. Mom was a survivor. If she really wanted to leave her husband she could just climb in her car and leave—I knew Teeny. He'd get mad, maybe smack her around a bit. Then he'd pass out and she could run away.

"Why would you send that woman anything?"

I jumped, turning to face Puck. He loomed over me, anger written all over his face, and my breath caught.

"I forgot you were here."

His face darkened.

"Got what you want from me?" he asked, his voice mocking. Then he reached down and grabbed his dick through his jeans, squeezing it lewdly. "Because you left me hanging."

Seriously? My eyes narrowed.

"My mom says Teeny is going to kill her," I said, emphasizing each word carefully. "She needs two grand to get away and come up here. Your dick is not a priority, under the circumstances."

"Bullshit," he replied, snorting. "She needs two grand to buy drugs, or pay someone off so they don't plant your stepdad in the ground, where he belongs."

I shrugged awkwardly, because he wasn't necessarily wrong. Not that I wanted to concede the point.

"She sounded different this time," I said, and I hated the hint of weakness that crept in my voice. He probably thought I was a gullible fool. Maybe I was. Or maybe she'd finally had enough and wanted to get out. Could I ever forgive myself if Teeny hurt her seriously? "I want to save her from him."

"Come here."

"Why?" I asked. Puck raised a brow.

"We weren't finished."

"My mom just called and told me her husband was going to *kill her*," I told him desperately. "And you still want to have sex? What kind of asshole says that?"

He stepped forward and caught my hand, pressing it down against the front of his jeans. His fingers wrapped around mine, squeezing his cock. Dark red stained his cheek, the white of his scar standing out. Sometimes I forgot just how scary Puck could be.

"The kind of asshole who knows she's playing you. And yeah, I still want to have sex," he said. "Been thinkin' about it for five years, ever since I took you away from that hellhole. Remember? Because it *was* a hellhole and she's the fucking devil. That bitch pimped you out and now you're going to send her money? What the fuck are you smoking?"

I stiffened. *Jerk.* Of course, he wasn't the only one I was angry at, but he was here.

"She's my mom," I told him. "And despite everything, I love her. I don't know why, but I do and you have no right to judge me for that. I'm not planning to send her a bunch of money. I don't *have* a bunch of money. But if I did, it wouldn't be any of your damned business."

Puck leaned down, his face right in mine, a muscle in his jaw flexing.

"It's my business now."

"Since when?"

"I'm thinkin' right about the time you came all over me, screaming my name."

I gasped, pulling my hand away from him. Or rather, trying to pull my hand away, because he wasn't exactly letting it go. Then his other hand came around the back of my neck, jerking me forward into him. His lips covered mine and his tongue tried to push inside. But I still heard my mom's voice in my head. *"He's going to kill me."*

I bit Puck's lip, and it wasn't a love bite.

"Jesus," he said, jerking back. His tongue flicked out, exploring the small cut, which was starting to bleed.

"We made a mistake," I said, trying not to look at him. This was hard, considering he was still gripping the back of my neck. I tried to break free, but his fingers tightened, reminding me how much stronger than me he was.

That's when the reality of the situation hit.

I might be worked up about my mom, but there was a big, strong man holding me who was worked up over the fact that he hadn't gotten his happy ending.

A scary biker man.

I licked my lips, suddenly worried for a different reason.

"I don't want to have sex," I blurted out.

"You did five minutes ago."

My eyes searched his, looking for a hint of softness or compassion. All I saw was blazing need tempered with anger. Puck's hands tightened. I raised my free arm and touched his chest, wishing I could reach in there and find whatever compassion he might keep hiding deep inside.

There certainly wasn't any visible on the surface.

I swallowed. "I really want to go to sleep. Alone. Tonight wasn't what I planned and I have a lot to think about."

"So now you're telling me you didn't want it? Because my fingers are still sopping wet from your cunt. Call me crazy, but that usually means a bitch is into it."

Bitch? Oh, I didn't like that. Not one bit. I forgot my momentary fear, defaulting back to pissed off. This was better—anger worked for me.

"Let. Me. Go," I gritted out. Puck glared at me, then let go so abruptly I almost fell over.

"You're crazy," he said, stepping back. "I've done nothing but take care of you, yet one phone call from that cunt and you forget all about me. Don't fucking pretend you weren't as into this as I was—now you've got what you wanted and it's all over."

"Yeah, I guess I'm guilty," I hissed. "I'm attracted to you, asshole, so when you started pushing I didn't say no, because it felt good. Is that a crime? Maybe you think I'm a slut, so fuck you for that. But even sluts get a *vote* in who they sleep with. There's something scary in you, Puck. I know what you really are, and I don't want anything to do with it. You're strong and you hit people and I want to talk to someone about my mom, but all you care about is sex!"

"Bullshit," he said, shaking his head. "I could've fucked you years ago if I only cared about sex, *Becs*. But I actually give a shit about you, so I left you alone. But don't worry—I'm not a complete moron. I can smell crazy from a mile away and it's startin' to stink in here, so let's lay this out. Your bitch mother made you fuck strange men. I saved your ass. Why the hell should either of us waste one more second of our lives on the cunt?"

I gritted my teeth, my hands trembling from way too many feelings exploding all at once.

"Because you were one of those men," I told him, my voice cold and hard. "In case you don't remember? *Teeny made me fuck you.* I got my orders and I followed them. I'm glad you saved me afterward, but don't think for one minute that made it any easier when you pushed me down on that bed and *shoved your cock up my ass*. That hurt, Puck. A lot. So much I could hardly sit on that fucking bike of yours when she forced me onto it. Do you remember that part? Mom saw a chance to get me out and she took it—and don't you think for a minute that was easy for her. For all she knew, he'd kill her for it and she did it anyway. So you keep telling yourself that you're a big fucking hero and my mom's evil for what she did to me, but I'm not stupid enough to fall for it. There weren't any good guys at that party. You were all bad. All of you. Now get the fuck out of my apartment."

He stared at me, and for once he didn't have a damned thing to say.

Nope.

Puck Redhouse just blinked at me like a big, dumb idiot.

"The door's over there," I reminded him coolly.

"You're a real fuckin' bitch."

I shrugged.

"Better a bitch than a rapist. Get out."

SEVEN

SATURDAY
BECCA

What the fuck is wrong with me?

I studied my reflection, looking for some clue as to how or why I was such a head case. The mirror showed nothing new, nothing interesting to indicate that I'd had one of the best orgasms of my life last night, followed by a complete emotional meltdown.

Oh, and there was ripping apart the man who probably saved my life. That was nice, too. A woman should really look a little different after something like that, yet here I was. Just the usual plain brown hair, boring eyes, and mouth that could probably do with a hint of lip gloss if I wanted to go out anywhere. At least my teeth were clean . . . I couldn't brush away the memories, but I had damned fresh breath. That should count for something, right?

Of course a good night's sleep would've counted for more, but I'd fucked that up, too. Instead I'd spent hours sewing furiously, my

Singer's hum filling the apartment as I shredded the salvaged materials filling my fabric bin. Nothing turned out right, no matter what I tried to create. They were all hideous and wrong, just like me.

I'd collapsed on the floor at five that morning, passing out from exhaustion.

The phone rang, and I grabbed it, expecting to hear Danielle's voice. She'd promised to call me this morning once she woke up. We had a date to do our nails at eleven, a weekly ritual I'd come to treasure for a variety of reasons, not least of which was the opportunity to experiment on a willing victim who never complained when my design innovations failed to translate.

"Becca?"

"Mom?" I asked, startled. She'd been so angry last night. My argument with Puck kept replaying in my head. He'd been right—she'd hurt me so many times. Why should I be giving her any more of my soul?

Because you love her, my heart whispered. This sucked, because it was true.

"I'm sorry, baby," she said, her voice subdued. "I couldn't sleep all night. I shouldn't have talked to you like that. You need to take care of yourself. I understand."

"Are you okay?"

She didn't respond, then she coughed, her voice sounding rough.

"I'm fine," she whispered, and I knew she wasn't.

"What did he do?"

"Nothing. I'm fine. You don't worry about me. I'm sure it'll be okay."

"Did he hurt you last night?"

She hesitated again. "You know how he gets. I think he broke my arm. It's all swollen, but I can't go to the doctor. I'll get one shot to leave, baby. I can't waste it."

A giant, vicious hand caught my gut and squeezed it hard.

"I'm going to count up the change in my tip jar," I whispered. "I'll send it to you. Maybe I can sell something."

"It won't be enough. Don't bother."

"Mom . . ."

"Baby, it's over. You have to live your life. I love you."

Then she hung up the phone. I stared down at it, stunned, then ran for the bathroom. I barely reached the toilet in time, and then I was heaving and throwing up until my stomach ached and throat burned.

I had to figure something out. I couldn't let Teeny kill my mother.

Unfortunately, I had no idea how to stop him.

Nothing felt real after that.

I didn't know what to do with myself, so I cleaned up the mess of shredded fabric and loose threads I'd created the night before. Then Danielle called, reminding me to bring over my laundry for our manicure date. I carried all of it down to my car, lost in thought.

What a crazy week.

First the job, now my mom . . . Oh, and Puck. What the hell was I supposed to do about Puck? Maybe I wouldn't have to do anything about him—if he had half a brain he'd never talk to me again. Not after I exploded my crazy all over him like some kind of swollen, bloated tomato left to rot in the sun.

I glanced over at the doorway to Puck's building, wondering if he was home.

I owed him an apology.

He'd been a dick, no question. But calling him a rapist went too far because it flat-out wasn't true. He'd had no idea what was really happening that strange, life-changing night. He thought I was some girl he met at a party, some normal girl who wanted to sleep with him and I'd encouraged that impression. When he'd figured it out, he did the right thing even though leaving me would've been a thousand times easier.

He'd called me a bitch last night, and he'd been right.

Now I needed to act like an adult and own what I'd done. Would my temper ever stop getting me into trouble?

Walking down the alley, I felt caught between conflicting emotions. I hoped he'd be there so I could say I was sorry and get it over with. I also hoped he wouldn't answer the door, because facing him was going to suck and I didn't want to do it. What happened next was completely anticlimactic. I reached for the stairwell door only to find it locked. No buzzer, no intercom, no way of signaling someone upstairs that they had company. I looked around for his bike but couldn't see it anywhere. Wherever Puck was, I had no way of contacting him.

Okay, then. So much for that plan.

Trudging back to the car, everything swirled through my head as I tried to figure it out. So many things fucked up in my life, but at least there was one problem I knew how to fix.

Every pair of jeans I owned was dirty.

So were my panties, sheets, bras, and everything else. I got in my car and drove over to Danielle's place for our weekly manicure/laundry party because no matter how shitty life gets, you still have to wash your clothes.

"I got this new pink polish yesterday afternoon," Danielle announced when we finally got settled at her table, looking pleased with herself. My whites hummed in the background, her washing machine whirling and swirling from a closet in the hall. "Think I might color my hair to match. Yay or nay?"

"What?" I asked, trying to focus. My whole world had changed, yet here we were, talking about nail colors.

So weird.

"The pink?" she prompted. I blinked, collecting myself.

"Oh, it's cute," I told her. "Sorry, I had a strange morning."

"How's that?"

I took a deep breath, wondering where to begin.

"So, my mom called last night. She says Teeny lost his shit. She asked me for money to leave him."

Danielle's eyes widened as she set down the nail polish. She didn't know the full story about my life back in California, but she knew enough to realize this was a Big Fucking Deal.

"Seriously? After all this time she's actually considering it for real?" she whispered. "What did you tell her about the money?"

I shrugged. "I told her no. She wants two grand and I don't have it. Then she said I was a horrible daughter and if he kills her, it's my fault."

"What. The. Fuck." Danielle said, her face turning fierce.

"Puck said she's just trying to get money out of me. He's probably right—she's always trying to get money out of me."

"Wait." She held up a hand. "Rewind that thought. Why is Puck part of this story? Oh my God, was he at your place?"

Puck. Last night came flooding back to me and I shivered. I'd been trying very hard not to think about him or the apology I still owed him. God, why did it all have to happen at once? My past was crashing down around me like a tidal wave. I couldn't catch my breath.

"That's a loaded question. It's complicated," I told her, closing my eyes. Complicated? Now that was a fucking understatement. "I did something stupid last night."

"What?" she demanded. I didn't answer. "Holy shit, did you sleep with Puck?"

"No!" I insisted.

"You're lying," she sad flatly. "You're a really crappy liar, Becca—you need to work on that, because it's an important life skill. So how was he? I've always wanted to get him naked . . ."

"Danielle!"

"No, no. I won't go there, obviously," she insisted. "But I'm your friend, Becca. Talk to me. Maybe I can help."

"It's really messed up," I said slowly. "I never told you this, but Puck and I had sex down in California."

Her brows raised and her mouth dropped. Literally. Just like a cartoon character.

"Wow. But weren't you like twelve or something?"

"I'd just turned sixteen. He was twenty-one."

"That's fucked up, Becca."

I shrugged. "Where I come from, it's not a big deal. I mean, it *is* a big deal, but it wasn't his fault. He had no idea how young I was, and if anything he got set up. My stepdad arranged it."

Danielle swallowed.

"What do you mean?"

"Teeny gave me to Puck. He'd just gotten out of prison. Like, gotten out of prison *that day*. They were having a party for him, and I caught his eye. That's when Teeny told me to make him happy or I'd pay. You come from a nice family, Danielle—mine was different. Shit like this happens all the time, especially in motorcycle clubs like the Longnecks. The world is full of evil people. And it's not like I'm the only one, you know—all kinds of girls end up following bikers home. Sometimes they're underage. Sometimes they want to leave and they can't . . ."

"That's disgusting."

"It is what it is," I replied quietly. "And Puck wasn't the first. The others were . . . awful. I actually enjoyed it with Puck, at least until things got rough."

"I've heard he's wild," she murmured. "Did he hurt you?"

"Yeah, but he stopped when I asked him to. It was sweet in a fucked-up way. Then things got ugly. Puck told one of his friends that I wasn't good enough and Teeny heard about it. He beat me up the next morning."

Danielle swallowed.

"You don't have to tell me this. I mean, I know I told you to spill and I'm here for you, but I wasn't trying to force you to open up if you don't want to."

"No, it feels good to talk about it," I admitted. "The only other person who knows it all is Regina. Anyway, Puck found out what happened and he was pissed. Like, *really* pissed. He was on parole—could've gone back to jail. So he kicked the shit out of Teeny and took me home with him. Like, I got on his bike and we left. I've never been back and I haven't even seen my mom since then . . . He brought me to Callup and the club asked Regina and Earl to take me in. They did and you know the rest. So that's me and Puck. It's a clusterfuck."

"Damn," she replied, frowning. "And now he lives across the roof from you. Are you okay with that?"

"I think so," I answered. "I have such weird feelings about him. He scares me—they all scare me. Sometimes when I see a biker, the bottom of my stomach twists and I want to throw up a little. At the same time, I'm probably only alive because he stepped up and saved me. The Silver Bastards were good to me, Danielle. Really good. They were outnumbered, you know. Rescuing me was a big risk. On the ride home, Boonie promised that they'd protect me as long as I needed them, and they have. Last year—when I told Regina I wanted to start beauty school—she talked to Darcy about it. We went to coffee and she told me all about what to expect. Did you know she's got both her massage and cosmetology licenses? Darcy can even do permanent cosmetics. She also told me she'd help me find a place when I'm done, either at her place or through one of her contacts."

"I always wondered what it was between you and the club," Danielle said softly. "I mean, I knew shit was complicated—usually people gossip when someone new moves to town. But nobody gossiped about you. The club shut it down."

"Yeah . . ."

"So what's going on now?"

"Things changed after my ride home with him the other night. Probably won't surprise you, but there's tension between us. Always has been, but I'm an adult now. I tried to talk to him about being friends and he made it clear that when it comes to us, it's all or nothing. I told him no. Then he saw me with Blake."

"Blake?" she asked, sitting up straight. I flapped my hand at her.

"Settle down, big girl. He wanted a haircut after school. I didn't think about closing my shades, so Puck watched us and Blake took off his shirt like he always does, you know? Puck saw me with Joe the other night, too—you know, at the Moose—and I guess it's been bothering him. We talked for a while on the roof, then he asked for a haircut. I said yes and he came inside. Long story short, we made out and he got me off on the couch. Then my mom called before we could do anything more."

Danielle didn't say anything for a minute. Then she stood and walked quietly over to her fridge and pulled a bottle of Fireball out of the freezer. Opening it, she handed it over without a word.

I drank straight from the bottle, cinnamon burning my throat. I managed not to drop it as I coughed. Danielle took it back and sucked down some for herself before setting it on the table between us.

"That's officially the most fucked-up thing I've ever heard. How are things between you and Puck now?"

"Well, he told me Mom was just playing me and I got mad at him. So I called him a rapist and kicked him out of my apartment." Silence.

"He didn't rape me," I added. "He saved me."

"You win," she said after a pause.

"Win what?"

"The fucked-up prize," she replied. "I thought I would, because Blake and I—never mind, doesn't matter anyway. So you called him a rapist and kicked him out because he said your mom might be trying to play you?"

"Pretty much. He also wanted me to have sex with him after, said I left him hanging. I tried to apologize to him this morning but I couldn't seen any signs of life in his apartment. Of course, he might've been ignoring me. Probably not his favorite person right now. What the hell am I going to do, Danielle?"

She cocked her head, thinking.

"What do you want to do?"

"I want to be happy."

"Give me more to work with. Do you want Puck?"

"No," I said slowly. "I mean, yes. I totally want Puck, as in having sex with him would kick ass. But it's more than I can handle—he's so intense, you know? And I have no idea what to do about my mom, either. When she called this morning she said she'd been wrong, that she needs to find her own way out, and that I'm a good daughter. Up to that point I was pissed at her, but now I just feel guilty. I want to help her but I don't have two grand. And what if she does leave him? I mean, where is she going to live? With me? I love her and I want her to get away, but having her in my place would be really hard. I'm not sure her brain is even right—she's gotten beat so much over the years and she's done a lot of drugs. Realistically, I'd be way too busy taking care of her to have a relationship with anyone. I'm just too fucked up for this."

"Then don't do it."

"Don't do what?"

"Any of it," she said. "Let's assume your mom is serious and actually leaves him. You can find somewhere else for her to live. Taking care of someone and living with them are two different things. I'll even help you—women leave men all the time, and there are shelters and stuff. You don't have to do this all by yourself."

"No, I want her with me," I insisted, and it wasn't a lie. "She's a shittastic mom, but she's still mine and I love her."

"Okay, so that means you need to get rid of Puck," she said. "Sounds like after last night it won't be too hard."

"I still need to apologize to him."

"Yeah, although he was being a douche, so don't whip yourself too much. Just tell him you're sorry and walk away. Short and sweet."

"All right."

"Now, about your mom. You say she needs two grand?"

"That's what she told me."

"She's full of shit. She can go to a women's shelter, hide out for a week or two, and then get a bus ticket up here. That's reasonable."

"Still costs money," I told her. "And I'm not sure she'll go to a shelter. She's stubborn."

Danielle sighed. "If she won't go to a shelter, then she doesn't really want to leave him and two grand won't change anything. You need enough money to get her up here, but she has to take the first step. You can't do it for her."

I nodded slowly, because she was right.

"You're going to be okay, Becca," Danielle said, leaning forward to catch my shoulders. Her eyes met mine, full of love and support. *God, I'm lucky to have a friend like this.* "We all love you. This shit with Puck will blow over—he'll find someone else and it'll all be history. Don't worry, okay?"

I nodded again, refusing to acknowledge the tiny twinge of pain I felt. Just another symptom of how fucked up I'd gotten, because the thought of Puck with another woman didn't exactly make me feel better.

Nope.

If anything, I felt like barfing.

Hopefully that was just the Fireball.

My day got better after my visit with Danielle.

Usually I don't buy into the whole talking-things-through school of thought but this time it worked for me. My best friend was just so matter-of-fact and full of common sense that by the time we'd finished our nails, I felt almost human again because she was right.

I didn't *have* to do this.

Mom made her own bed a long time ago—nobody expected me to rescue or save her. Whatever I decided to do, it was entirely my choice.

Rejecting Puck was my choice, too. If I couldn't handle a relationship, I couldn't handle a relationship and it wasn't against the law to stay single. I definitely owed him an apology, though. Would talking to him be hard? Yes. But I'd survived worse.

Ultimately, the Mom Situation was the tough one to figure out. In some ways it would've been so much easier if she hadn't called back. Our talk that morning threw me off in a big way—my mom didn't apologize. Ever. This was way different from any of her normal tricks, and that scared me.

What if I didn't send her the money and he actually killed her? But how could I send it even if I wanted to? It wasn't like two grand would just fall out of the sky.

The thought haunted me as I drove home with my clean clothes. I stopped by Puck's apartment again, hoping he'd be there so I could get it over with. Sometimes you just have to rip the Band-Aid off, you know? Naturally he was nowhere to be found. Instead of letting myself fester and worry, I decided to follow my original plan for the day and went huckleberry picking.

Three hours later I had enough of the tiny purple berries to make a pie for Earl. With luck I'd get a bonus batch of muffins out of it, too. Just accomplishing something so simple made me feel better, and I even found myself singing along to my music when I showered before my shift. So what if I owed a scary biker an apology and my mom might get murdered any minute?

I'd have muffins for breakfast.

By nine that night, not even the thought of muffins helped, because the dickwads (and dickwaddettes) from the Northwoods

Academy had plopped their asses down in my section at the Moose. So far as I could tell, the school was one big asshole factory.

"I thought they weren't allowed off campus," I hissed at Danielle, slamming my tray down on the bar next to her. She wasn't on tonight, but she'd come in to give me moral support. Probably planned to give Blake more than that during his break, lucky boy. "Why the hell are they here again?"

"Hell if I know," she replied, shrugging. "Just watch out for that blonde bitch with the diamonds. I busted ass keeping up with all their fucking orders the other night. One of the guys left a damned good tip, a fifty. She swapped it out for a twenty, pocketed the difference."

I raised my brows. The "blonde bitch" looked like she was maybe eighteen years old, and the clothing she wore probably cost more than my car.

"You think she needs money?" I asked, intrigued.

"I could give a fuck—I earned that tip. If you get a chance, spit in her drink, will you?"

Laughing, I shrugged off her suggestion. I couldn't afford to lose another job. That didn't mean I wouldn't spit in the bitch's drink, of course. I would, first chance I got. Nobody fucks with my friends. I just didn't want to risk anyone overhearing me agreeing with the suggestion. Good to know about the tip, too—I'd keep an eye on blondie.

Thirty bucks was half a tank of gas.

An hour later I'd decided spitting in the drinks wasn't bad enough. I'd never met more entitled, wretched excuses for human beings. All of them. Well, almost all of them . . . Of the ten or so taking up two tables along the back wall, there was one who seemed aloof from the bullshit. He was the clear leader of the group, the obvious alpha. They were all trying to catch his attention, but he ignored them.

The guy was about my age, with darkish, floppy hair. I didn't quite know just what made him different, aside from the aura of untouchability. He laughed and talked just like the others. He wore the same uniform of overpriced, designer clothes that looked like a movie star's version of going country for the night, and he obviously took his wealth for granted.

I almost dismissed him with the rest . . .

His eyes scanned the room, though, always searching. I caught them on me more than once. Like he was studying what made me work, deep inside. I couldn't tell if he was truly a rich boy out slumming or very cleverly disguised predator.

Something about him reminded me of Puck.

Just what we needed around here—more scary people.

Things got busier as the night progressed. Teresa had brought in a live band for the night, and by eleven Danielle had grabbed her apron and started pitching in. When Teresa saw her I wondered if we'd get in trouble, but she just said, "Don't forget to write down your hours . . ."

That's about the time Boonie and Darcy showed up. Ten minutes later Puck arrived, along with Deep, Demon, and Carlie. I'd been looking for him all day, determined to apologize for what I'd said the night before. Now that he was really here, though, the thought of talking to him terrified me. Still, I had to do it, and the sooner the better. I set down my tray and intercepted the group as they crossed the room.

"Puck, do you have a minute?"

Puck ignored me completely. It was like I didn't even exist. I wanted to hate him for that but I couldn't really blame him—I'd called him a rapist, and that's a pretty big deal no matter how you look at it. Deep and Demon followed Puck's lead and walked past without a word. The worst, though, Carlie. She didn't ignore me. Nope. She smiled at me, and in her eyes I saw pity.

She fucking *pitied* me.

Bitch.

Because God obviously hates me, Boonie and Darcy had already taken a table in my section, which meant I had to trail after Puck and his MC brothers like a fucking puppy to take their orders. Just how I was supposed to accomplish that confused me, what with the silent treatment and all. Boonie solved the problem by ordering a round for the entire table, and I found myself retreating back toward the bar.

"Bummer," Danielle whispered as she passed by, having obviously watched our little show (along with everyone else in the bar, because the situation wasn't awkward enough already, right?). "That's harsh."

"What should I do?"

"You find a way to apologize and hope he finds a new place to go drinking," she replied. "Not much else you can do."

"*Find a way to apologize.*" Easy for her to say—she wasn't the one being ignored. I stalled for a few minutes at the bar, but then the drinks were ready and waiting for me.

Showtime.

I carried them back over to the bikers' table, trying to catch Puck's eye. Carlie sat between him and Deep, and I wondered which man she'd come with. She'd clearly been with Puck the other morning at breakfast . . . I forced myself to smile at her brightly despite the fact that I wanted to poison her. Puck was mine.

Wait. Where did *that* come from? Puck wasn't mine. Not even a little bit. I didn't *want* him, either.

Liar.

Over the next half hour I caught myself checking them out, trying to determine whether or not they were a couple. Puck wasn't paying much attention to Carlie, though. If anything she seemed attached to Deep. Good. I hoped they got married and had fifty babies until she got fat. Still, she was sitting next to Puck and she'd been with him the other morning, too. As if to rub salt in my wounds, Carlie was annoyingly friendly and nice to me when I came back to collect the empties.

"You're Becca, right?" she asked. "We didn't get a chance to talk the other day—"

"She's nobody," Puck said, cutting her off. Carlie gaped, glancing between us. The others watched silently as my heart clenched. I wanted to run away. Hide. Pretend none of it had ever happened.

No.

Time to end it.

I set my tray down on the table and stood straight, looking directly into Puck's face.

"I have something to say to you," I told him, pitching my voice loud enough to be heard over the music. "What I said last night was wrong. I'm sorry about that. It wasn't true. You aren't a rapist."

Carlie gasped and Darcy blinked. The men just watched silently. I closed my eyes briefly, wishing I could open them and find myself somewhere else. Anywhere else. No such luck—when I opened them again, Puck was staring at me, his eyes boring through me like two hot coals.

Well. Guess I'd caught his attention.

"I think I need to make something very clear," I continued. "Five years ago, when I met you in California, I did everything I could to make you think I wanted to be with you. Teeny set it all up and I played along, and you were as much a victim as I was. You didn't rape me, and once you figured it all out you could have just left. Instead you saved me and I'll appreciate that for the rest of my life. I called you a rapist last night because you were telling me things I didn't want to hear and I got angry. In fact, I get angry a lot. It's sort of a problem for me, so I apologize. Thank you again for bringing me to Idaho and saving my life."

With that I grabbed the tray and walked away, feeling my hands shake. Danielle waited for me by the bar, searching my face.

"You did it?"

"Yup."

"Seriously? Right there in front of all of them?"

"Yup."

"You okay?"

I considered the question. "No, I think I'm about to freak out."

"Go back into the kitchen and sit in the walk-in," she said quickly. "I'll cover for you. Stay in there until you calm down."

"Can you see him?"

"Puck?"

"Of course," I hissed. "Is he looking at me? He didn't say anything. None of them did."

"Yes, he's watching us," she replied, eyes darting. "But he's not getting up or coming over. He's just drinking his beer and watching. The look on his face is kind of scary. Go sit in the walk-in. The cold air will make you feel better. No matter what happens, remember that I'm here. Blake, too. We've got your back."

I nodded and ducked around the bar, slipping past Blake as I darted into the kitchen. Gordon—the short-order cook—had shut everything down hours ago, although the faint smell of fried food hung in the air. I opened the big cooler door, flipping on the light as I stepped inside. The door closed behind me, cutting out the sound of the bar, and I grabbed the little stool next to the wall shelf to sit on.

There's something wonderful about a walk-in cooler.

It's cold, of course. In a commercial kitchen that's a very good thing, because it's always hot when you're working over a massive grill. In the summer it's even hotter, which made the walk-in an oasis. Tonight it was my sanctuary, although I already felt the light sweat I'd built up in the bar chilling on my skin. The faint goose bumps grounded me. I inhaled deeply, savoring the silence.

I could do this. I could go out there and look at Puck and smile and serve him and his friends. I'd hold my head high while I did it, too—I didn't have a choice. Callup was a small town and unless I decided to leave, I'd run into them.

Of course, I *could* leave Callup.

Like every other time I'd considered moving, my mind instantly rejected the idea. I loved Callup and I felt safe here—that hadn't changed.

The cooler door opened.

"You okay?" Blake asked. "Anyone I need to kill?"

I smiled, because I knew he wasn't entirely joking. He was the reason I needed to pull myself together and go back out there. Him and Danielle and Regina and Earl and everyone else who made up my world. So what if Puck hated me?

I'd been hated before.

"Yeah, I'm okay," I told him. He reached out and caught my hand, pulling me to my feet.

"Teresa's asking where you are," he told me. "I said you were grabbing fresh lemons."

I glanced around, finding the clear plastic container of sliced lemons on the shelf and grabbing it. Blake smiled at me, his face reassuring.

Holding his hand, I walked back out into the bar.

EIGHT

PUCK

My hand gripped my pint glass so hard it was a miracle the damned thing didn't break.

"Thank you for bringing me to Idaho and saving my life."

Becca's words kept running through my head. For a while last night—the first hour after she called me a rapist—I'd wanted to kill her. After all I'd done for her, all I'd given . . . Then I'd finally had her right where she needed to be and she pulled that shit on me.

Crazy bitch.

It worked, too, because deep down inside I still felt guilty as fuck about that night. I felt even guiltier because I'd spent the last five years trying to figure out ways to make it happen again. I'd watched her over in her apartment after our fight—*close your god-damned shades, Becca*—working away on her fucking sewing machine. There I was, my soul ripped right the fuck apart, and Becca was making some bullshit craft project.

That's when I'd grabbed my keys and took my bike out along the river until I hit the highway. I'd stopped there, looking east toward Montana, wondering if I should just start riding in that direction. I could leave all of it behind. The club, Becca, everything. I'd take my bike and fly with the wind until life made sense again.

I didn't, of course.

I still wasn't sure why.

Becca walked by carrying a heavy tray, ass twitching in a way that cried out for a smack. Christ, but I *still* wanted to fuck her. She was serving those academy fucks, all crowded around two tables along the wall. The girls acted like self-centered little twats, playing at being grown-up. I saw one flipping Becca shit, which pissed me off.

This made no sense—I was still pissed at her myself, so why I would care about someone else treating her right I couldn't imagine. I guess deep down inside there'd always be a part of me that considered her mine?

Fuck if I knew.

While the girls gave her crap and whined about their drinks, the boys were checking her out like she was a stripper working a pole. I half expected one to tuck a dollar bill into the front of her low-cut T-shirt.

Hmm . . . If that happened, I'd have to take the little cocksucker out. No help for it.

"Think you should handle things with Malloy," Boonie said, startling me. "He wants to talk. Can't make it too obvious."

I glanced over at him. Deep had pulled Carlie into his lap, and was making a show of feeling her up. She eyed me, maybe wondering if it'd make me jealous? I ignored the look, because Deep had plans for her, even if she hadn't figured it out yet.

"Let's go to the restroom," Darcy said, catching Carlie's arm. Carlie nodded, slipping out from behind the table. Then the two women disappeared down the back hallway, leaving us free to talk business.

"So why do you want me handling it?" I asked Boonie quietly, leaning forward.

"Makes more sense, you're closer in age," Boonie said. "Kid like that steps out to talk with an old man, people will be more likely to notice. Want you to feel him out, tell me what you think."

I shrugged. I didn't quite buy the excuse, but Boonie obviously had his reasons. Hell, anything that got me away from Becca for the moment had to be good, right?

"Okay."

Ten minutes later, Rourke stood and worked his way toward the front of the bar, pulling a pack of cigarettes from his pocket.

Fucking great.

Now I had to go out there and pretend to smoke. Deep smirked at me, and for a moment I wondered if they were setting me up just to fuck with my head. Then Boonie nudged me with his boot, and I caught his gaze again. The man was all business—nope, he wasn't fucking with me.

"Gonna grab a smoke," I announced, then stood and walked toward the front of the bar. I opened the door and looked around, spotting Rourke on the corner of the porch, casually lighting up.

"You got an extra?" I asked him.

"Sure," he said, holding out his pack. I pulled one out. It felt so good in my fingers that it hurt. Fuck, I wanted that smoke. Almost as much as I wanted Becca.

Both would kill me.

"Light?" he asked. I considered it, then shook my head. If someone came out I'd light it, but we were alone for now. I'd talk to him, save the smoke for when I actually needed the cover.

That's me. Regular fucking saint.

"So what's up?" I asked him. "Boonie said you wanted to meet."

"I think we've got a situation the club can help us with," he said slowly. "The Vegas Belles—that new strip club that opened near the

Washington-Idaho border. I hear they're pulling business from the Reapers' strip club."

I shrugged, wondering where he was headed with this. I'd heard from Painter a few days ago, and Malloy was right. Profits at The Line had been suffering ever since the new place opened just down the street. So far they hadn't taken action, but that wouldn't last forever. Sooner or later the Vegas Belles would either get pulled into the Reapers' fold or shut down—that's the way things worked in north Idaho.

"Haven't heard much about it," I said.

"They're a front for the Callaghans," Roake said, leaning forward against the rail. "Jamie Callaghan is moving in, getting ready for Shane McDonogh's twenty-first birthday. That's when everything comes to a head for us. If Jamie wins, they'll put Shane away and control of the Laughing Tess will move out of the valley forever. You don't want Jamie in charge. Trust me on that."

"Why do you care?" I asked. "Lay it out for me—a show of faith would go a long way here."

"They sent me to Northwoods to keep Shane in the fold," he replied. "He's supposed to be one of us, you know. The Callaghans always planned to bring him in but he's never been very good at following orders. I guess I'm not, either."

"What about your dad?" I asked bluntly. "He's not a man to cross. What will he think?"

"He's not a Callaghan, either," Rourke replied, shrugging. "They may think he is, but Dad cares about himself and nobody else. Not me, not my mother. None of it. I could give two fucks about that asshole."

Interesting. That didn't match our intel.

"So what's the plan?"

He eyed me speculatively.

"Is the MC in or out?"

"I don't speak for the club," I said. "The brothers vote. You want me to bring something to the table, you need to give it to me first."

"Fair enough," he said, stubbing out his smoke. He'd hardly touched it and I wondered if he was even a smoker. Fucking waste. Christ, I wanted to light up. My fingers literally itched for it. "Shane needs to hold on until he's twenty-one. That's when his court-ordered house arrest ends and he takes control of the Laughing Tess. Sounds simple enough, but they throw new shit at us constantly, trying to wiggle out of his grandfather's will. Bullshit legal filings, mental competency hearings, you name it. We think they tried to poison him last week, although it's hard to know for sure."

"Thought they needed him alive?"

"Define 'alive,'" he muttered. "They find a way to turn him into a vegetable, that'd suit their needs just fine. His mom will file for permanent guardianship and take over the Laughing Tess. That's a win for the Callaghans—when Christina's mouth moves, Jamie's voice comes out. I'm here to tell you that it's time to take sides, and the club needs to back Shane. Otherwise the valley is fucked."

I nodded, thinking he was probably right. They'd siphon off everything until there was nothing left. Hell, they'd already managed to fuck the miners in the ass. The local union had been screaming about safety equipment for years, but the nationals pretended not to hear. We had the Callaghans to thank for that.

"So what do you want?"

"Shane wants to meet you," he said. "We'll sneak you into the school tonight. We've set up a party—lots of local kids coming. That'll be your cover if anyone sees you around. Just another ass-hole looking to get drunk up at the academy, chasing after a girl or a fight or whatever."

Explained why Boonie picked me, I decided. At twenty-six I wasn't exactly a kid, but I was the youngest full member of the club.

"Okay," I said. "I'll come talk to him. But I want something to give my president for now."

"We're natural allies. You want the valley safe, Shane wants the valley safe. Short term, your club and the Reapers MC need the Vegas Belles out of commission. Jamie Callaghan will be coming up this week to look things over—might be the best shot we ever have to get him. We'll provide the intel on his visit, you provide the muscle. Everyone wins."

I considered it, then nodded.

"I'll talk to Boonie," I told him. "Then I'll head up to the school. Just remember, we're not playing games here. You get that?"

Rourke laughed, sounding older and more cynical than any kid his age had a right to be.

"We already have a long list of people who want to take us out," he said. "Trust me, we aren't looking to add to it."

"Fair enough."

I rolled the unlit cigarette in my fingers. I should crush it, throw it off the porch. Tucked it into my pocket instead.

Fuck smoking and fuck Becca.

Maybe a good fight with the Callaghans would clear the air. Not like I had much to lose, no matter how it played out. Rourke Malloy was right about one thing, though. We definitely didn't want Jamie Callaghan taking over the Laughing Tess.

BECCA

After my little time-out in the cooler, things got better. Puck still didn't talk to me, but all things considered, that was a lesser evil. I felt his eyes following me but I forced myself not to pay attention.

It helped that the bar was hopping and the students were running me ragged, bitching about their drinks and insisting I was fucking things up. By the third time Blake had to remake a Sex on the Beach—*"It's just not quite right, you know? What kind of vodka did he use? And is that pineapple juice? I wanted pineapple juice"*—I was about ready to poison them.

Just keeping up with their shit was a full-time job. I had to watch them constantly. That's why I noticed that when the scary-looking one strolled outside the bar for a smoke, Puck followed him.

"You see that?" I asked Danielle quietly as we passed each other at the service bar. "Puck went after that guy. You think there's something going on there?"

"Nope," she said firmly. "And if there was, you wouldn't want to know about it anyway so let it go."

Good point.

Unfortunately, the rest of the students were still thirsty and when I hit their table again, a guy with muddy brown hair tried to cop a feel. I dodged him, my smile hardening. He offered a drunken smirk, which pissed off the very tipsy redheaded girl sitting next to him.

"Could you move any slower?" she sniped.

"Sorry," I managed to grit out, but when I hit the service bar again I leaned across toward Danielle, who had taken a break serving drinks to wash glasses.

"I've had it with those fuckers," I hissed. "One just went for my ass."

"Let me handle it. What did they order?"

"Couple more pitchers."

With a wink, she grabbed a pitcher and dunked it quickly in the soapy water, capturing about three inches of the liquid. Then she started filling it with beer.

"You're gonna get fired!" I hissed, looking around to see if anyone noticed. Nobody was paying attention except for Blake, who raised a brow but said nothing.

"I'm not even officially on the clock," she replied, grabbing a second pitcher and doing the same. "Just doing my part to help some friends. Not my fault if Teresa hasn't taught me the proper procedure for washing dishes yet. Go bring those assholes their beer—it's your job to provide excellent service, regardless of whether you like them."

I grinned at her.

"I love you."

"I know," she replied, using her best Han Solo voice.

Two minutes later I was setting the pitchers in the center of their table, biting my lip to keep from giggling. Did this make me a bad person? Absolutely, but when the asshole caught my leg again and groped the inside of my thigh, any lingering guilt disappeared. That douche deserved whatever he got and then some. Fucker.

Ten minutes later Puck and his new friend came back inside. He spoke to Boonie, then caught my eye. We stared at each other across the bar, and I'd have given my sewing machine to know what he was thinking.

He shook his head and walked out again.

That's when I caught a break, because the alpha-type student waved at me. I walked over to him, startled to realize how big he was. He wasn't quite as young as I'd thought, either. Probably my age.

"Can you close everyone out?" he asked. "We're headed back to the school for a party."

Like I cared what they were doing? I just wanted them gone.

"Sure thing." I ran the credit cards and brought their checks, forcing myself to smile even though I wanted to flip all of them off. Then I grabbed their empties in a not-so-subtle move designed to hint that they should get the fuck out. Hopefully they wouldn't short me on the tip but I wasn't willing to stick around to see.

That's when Handsy Boy snapped his fingers at me like a dog.

I spun on him, fully intending to hit his head with my tray, dirty glasses and all.

"Let me handle this," Danielle said, her voice grim. "Take a minute to calm down out back—if Teresa has a problem, I'll let her know. Now give me the tray and get your ass out of here."

Handing it over, I made tracks for the back, passing by the bathrooms and through the "Staff Only" door to the porch. As soon as the door swung shut behind me, my chest loosened. God, I hated jerks like that. The sounds of the bar were muffled out here. I sat on the steps, wrapping my arms around my knees and breathing deep, trying to settle myself down.

The world was full of assholes. Pissed me off.

I heard a motorcycle engine roar to life out front—sounded like Puck's. I couldn't tell for sure from here . . . Maybe not—he was probably gone already. Why did I feel so weak around him, yet some stranger groping me in a bar just made me mad?

Probably because the little prick inside couldn't have been a real threat if he tried. He wasn't a biker or a badass or even a real man. Just a spoiled brat who thought having rich parents made him better than other people. Five minutes later I'd managed to calm down, so I stood and dusted off my butt before stepping back inside. I passed Teresa's office and then pushed back through the "Staff Only" door into the bathroom hallway.

Prince Handsy was waiting for me, a shit-eating grin splitting his face.

"How about a kiss?"

Oh, no fucking way.

No. Fucking. Way.

He lunged for me and I lifted my knee, catching him in the balls with the fury of an avenging angel. He screamed like a baby. Darcy burst out of the women's bathroom, eyes wide.

"You okay?" she demanded, taking in the scene.

"I'm great," I announced, wishing I'd taken him down an hour earlier. Prick.

"What the fuck is going on back here?" Teresa demanded,

crowding into the hallway. Behind her were Danielle and Blake and a whole bunch of other people, including the drunken redhead. She squealed and dropped to her knees next to her writhing boyfriend.

"She attacked him! Call the cops—have that little bitch arrested!"

That's when the black-haired alpha-type student pushed his way through and grabbed her arm, jerking her back.

"Go wait by the car," he ordered. She started to protest, but a death glare from him silenced her like a switch. Damn.

"We'll talk in my office," Teresa said to me firmly. "I'll handle this."

"Sure," I said, the adrenaline of the attack fading just enough that I realized what I'd done. I was about to lose my second job in a week for fighting. How was that even possible? Every day for the last five years, I'd asked myself the same question—what would my mom do? Then I'd do the opposite . . . yet here I was. Fighting. Again.

"Everyone back off," Darcy announced, her voice loud and full of authority. "This is none of your business, so get back to drinking."

"He's drunk and he's been eyeing her all night," the black-haired guy said to Teresa. "He's already groped her at least once. I'm sure she was just defending herself."

"I know," Teresa said, meeting his eyes head-on. "I'm done with your shit. You can take your friends and get the hell out."

Handsy moaned and sat up.

"Call the cops. I want to press charges."

"You can talk to my shotgun," Teresa replied flatly.

"No need," Alpha Guy said smoothly. "He's sorry for his behavior, and he'd like to leave a generous tip to apologize. He won't be back. Get your ass up, fuckwad."

He gave his friend a kick to emphasize the point, and we all watched as the asshole stood up slowly. To my astonishment, he reached into his pocket and pulled out his wallet, sorting through the bills inside before he took out a fifty and held it out toward me.

"Try again," Dark Hair snapped.

The asshole opened his wallet again, finding a second fifty.

"Now say you're sorry."

"I'm sorry," he hissed.

"Go wait in the fucking car."

With that, he gave me a nasty glare and started walking away painfully.

"I'm very sorry about that," Dark Hair said. Strangely enough, he seemed to be directing the words toward Darcy, which didn't make any sense but then again, none of it did.

"I'll talk to Boonie," she replied. "He'll be in touch."

"Thanks."

I met Danielle's gaze, my eyes wide. *What the hell was that?* she mouthed at me. I shrugged, because I had no clue.

"In my office," Teresa repeated. The sinking feeling hit my stomach again. At least I'd made enough to keep my phone on before I got fired . . . "Everyone else, get back to drinking. It's over."

"Okay, tell it to me straight," she said when we were inside, the door shut behind us. "What the fuck happened out there?"

"He's been grabbing at me all night," I said slowly, trying not to sound defensive. "The last time it happened, he stuck his hand between my legs. Danielle sent me outside to calm down, and when I came back he was waiting and made another grab at me. I had to defend myself."

Teresa stared me down, her face thoughtful. Shit. This was it—she'd figured me out and now it would come . . .

"Okay," she said finally. "So can you finish your shift? We can cover if you need to go home."

What?

"I attacked one of the customers," I reminded her, confused.

"No, a customer attacked you," she replied, eyes hard. "I know we've got a reputation as a tough bar, but nobody fucks with my people. That boy's lucky you got to him before I did."

"Oh . . ." Wow. Hadn't seen that coming. "Well, uh . . . I guess I can go back to work? I mean, I'm okay. He didn't hurt me."

"Great," she said. "Get yourself a shot to smooth out the rough edges and then back at it. And don't worry about that shithead bothering you again. Darcy will take care of it."

"Why . . . ?" I closed my mouth, cutting off the question, realizing I didn't need or want to know the answer. Nope. Best to let it go, so I left her office and got my shot.

Then I started waiting my tables again.

Darcy and Boonie were still there, and Darcy offered me a concerned look. I decided to pretend nothing had happened. Danielle came over to me, wrapping an arm around my shoulders. "You okay?"

"Fine," I replied. "No big deal. I think I like this place, though."

Danielle smiled, nudging me with her shoulder.

"Me, too."

Thankfully, we were only a few minutes from last call, and the rest of the night had slipped by without any more drama. I dragged into my apartment at three in the morning, exhausted but satisfied. I put on some music, grabbed a glass of water, and sat down at my table to count my tips. It wasn't a fortune, but I'd be able to pay the power bill and eat for another week if I was careful.

Working at the Moose might be okay after all.

I glanced over at my Singer, feeling hopeful for the first time that day. The sleek, black machine with its gold filigree and etching called to me, and I laughed. Maybe tomorrow I'd start that quilt I'd been thinking about. I knew just the pattern, too. Jacob's Ladder.

So what if Puck hated me? I'd fucked up but I'd done my best to fix it. I had no idea what might happen with my mom, but if she pulled herself together and left Teeny, I'd be ready for her. If she didn't, at least I'd proven I could take care of myself.

SUNDAY
PUCK

"You should've fucking called me," I told Boonie, wishing I could hit him. We'd gathered at the clubhouse for the club's weekly meeting. Darcy had been cooking pancakes, eggs, and bacon for us when we'd pulled up, so I'd offered her a hand because I'm a giver like that.

Also wanted to know if Becca had mentioned me after I left last night.

Not that I'd cop to it. Hell no . . . yet there I found myself in the kitchen, helping cook breakfast on the off chance that Darcy might take pity on me, throw me some information. That's when she told me about Becca, the prick in the hallway, and Roarke Malloy's response.

Thirty seconds later I was in Boonie's face, demanding some answers.

"Why would I call you?" he asked, his voice taunting. "You've said more than once that you're not claiming her. She handled the situation just fine on her own—tough little thing."

"We've always protected her," I protested. "We need to send a fucking message."

Boonie's eyes hardened.

"We've kept an eye on her, sure," he said. "But she's not club property. You want us to treat her like an old lady, claim her. Shit or get off the pot."

I wanted to protest. Punch him, or argue, or even just tell him to fuck off. My president stared at me blandly, because he was right and we both knew it. She wasn't mine. Would the club still protect

Becca? Absolutely. We'd protect anyone in Callup if we had to . . . But she'd protected herself last night and there'd been no direct insult to the Bastards.

"Claim her or let her go," Boonie added, his voice deadly serious. "This halfway shit doesn't cut it. We all heard her at the Moose. Either what she said works for you or it doesn't. Ball's in your court."

I glared at him, because he was right. I was still frustrated with her, though. She fucked with my head, something I'd had ample time to consider while savoring my scrounged cigarette last night before pulling out of the parking lot.

Yeah. That's how pathetic things had gotten. I'd actually sat alone in the darkness lusting after a girl like some fucking Robert Pattinson wannabe.

At least I smoked instead of sparkled.

Boonie shrugged.

"It's time for church. C'mon."

I took my place around the battered old table we'd set up in the back room. Twelve of the brothers joined us, while five more hadn't been able to come. Two were retired, although they still held their colors. Another had to work, and the final two were in Montana visiting another chapter.

I'd never actually planned to stay in Callup. I was a Montana boy, born and bred . . . But somehow I never got around to leaving after I got back from prison. Becca was part of it. The Reapers were an element, too—Painter and I were tight, usually got together at least once a week. Less lately, since shit went down with him and Melanie, but that's the way of the world.

"So we're here to discuss the Shane McDonogh situation," Boonie announced. "There are new developments. Puck, you want to share?"

"So I talked to Rourke Malloy last night, outside the Moose," I said, forcing myself to focus. "It was an eye-opening conversation. We know that McDonogh has been in some sort of power struggle with his stepdad, Jamie Callaghan. We didn't have the details but I learned a lot last night. Seriously fucked-up shit. Malloy told me that they're determined to keep McDonogh from claiming his inheritance—he's supposed to take control of the Laughing Tess next year, when he turns twenty-one. Malloy says the local union supports him."

"True," Deep said quietly. "Although it goes against the grain to back a McDonogh. We've been hanging on, hoping he'll take after his daddy, not his granddad. Kade Blackthorne insists that blood will run true. Until then, most of us are carrying our own rescue equipment. I don't trust the shit underground. Needs replacing."

I frowned.

"What blood?"

"Blackthorne's," Deep said. "Rumor is, Shane's dad was Bull Blackthorne. He was president of the local back when Christine McDonogh decided she wanted to piss off her daddy—she ran around with him for a while. Then Bull found himself dead and Christine found herself knocked up. Suddenly she's marrying Jamie Callaghan and moving to Vegas. Hasn't been back since, unless she needed money."

"It's just a rumor," Boonie said, frowning. "Hell, doesn't matter who the kid's dad was. All that matters is whether he'll be better for the valley than his mom and her husband."

"He'll be better," Deep said. "Can't be worse."

"We're hoping the safety equipment will get replaced when Shane takes over," Demon added quietly. "At least, that's the party line down at the local. The national guys could give two fucks. I bought my own self rescuer. If there's another fire I don't want to die down there because the McDonogh corporation won't pay for upgrades."

"The national guys are controlled by the Callaghans," Boonie said.

"Well, Malloy says that Callaghan and his bitch wife are trying to get Shane declared crazy, lock him up long term," I continued. "I guess there's a loophole—if that happens, his mom would be taking over."

"They've got the money and lawyers to do it," Boonie said.

"He wants an alliance," I continued. "After I talked to Malloy, I went up to the academy. The students had some party going on back in the woods. Malloy used it as an excuse to sneak me in and I met with McDonogh himself."

Deep perked up.

"He look as much like Bull as they say?"

I shrugged.

"Hell if I know—I'm not from around here, remember?"

"Christ," Deep muttered. "Fucking useless."

"He backed up what Malloy had to say," I continued, flipping him off. "According to them, the Vegas Belles strip club is a Callaghan front. Not a huge surprise—Painter tells me the Reapers have suspected as much all along, so that's a point in McDonogh's favor. He said that they're using the club to launder money taken from the mine, and that when they have full control they'll suck the valley dry."

"I believe it," Demon said. "They're feeding us bullshit over there already—things don't add up. Word is, the corporate trustees are on the Callaghan payroll."

"So what do they want from us?"

"McDonogh says that his stepdaddy will be visiting next week. He doesn't have a time yet, but he'll be at the strip club, which means we can get to him. McDonogh and his people will provide the intel, the Bastards and the Reapers are the muscle. With one raid, we slap down the Callaghans and take out the strip club. Win-win."

I fell silent.

"What do you think?" Boonie asked. "Is it a setup?"

"I don't see what McDonogh's motivation would be," I answered, running scenarios through my head. "The kid has an ankle monitor and can't leave the campus grounds. Some sort of fancy computerized system, never seen anything like it. There's no question he's pissed off—scared, too, probably. If what he says is right, there's about a thousand different ways he can lose at this game."

"We should do it," Demon said, his voice final. "That new strip joint is causing trouble for the Reapers. Reason enough right there. If there's a way to save McDonogh and retake control of the Tess, the miners stand behind us."

"One thing throws me off," Boonie said, his voice thoughtful. "Why is Rourke Malloy double-crossing his family? I understood the guns—that's just self-preservation, and I'm sure they've got plenty of enemies. Malloy pulls this and they find out, they'll put a hit on him no matter who his father is. In fact, that might make it worse. The dad's been with the Callaghans for decades. It's a serious betrayal."

"Malloy says his dad's no good," I replied. "Family shit."

"He seems like a smart kid," Boonie said. "You really think anyone with half a brain turns on the Irish mob just because he's got daddy issues? Sounds like suicide."

"Only if he loses," I pointed out. "Sometimes you have to choose a side and fight. Malloy's obviously picked his."

The words hung over the room.

"We know which side we should be on, too," Deep said. "Not everyone in this room has worked underground, but this is our community. The Laughing Tess is what keeps us alive. If we've got a chance to protect it, we need to take it. Otherwise we aren't the men I thought we were."

"Guess that sums it up," Boonie said slowly. "Anyone else want to talk?"

Nobody spoke.

"All right, then. All in favor?"

I voiced my "Aye" with the others, then we moved on to new business. Something about a missing keg pump. I zoned out, wondering why the hell I had to fall for a chick who hated me.

Penance, maybe.

Touching the scar on my face, I considered how my life might've been different if I'd been a girl. Both me and Becca were born to the life . . . I'd grown up surrounded by hard men and instability, just like her. Now I was one of them. My dad always watched out for me but I'd had to stand my ground and had paid the price in blood. Blood and time.

Becca never got that opportunity.

If I ever had kids, they damned well better be boys. Yeah, like I'd be that lucky. I pictured a little girl with Becca's big eyes, smiling up at me. Then I pictured her the same age Becca was when we'd met. Young. Way the fuck too young, yet I'd lusted after Becca like some kind of sick asshole.

Some guy messed with my daughter like that, I'd kill him.

That's when it hit me. Someday I wanted to have kids, and in my head they looked like Becca. Why the hell was I still pissed at her, anyway? We'd both fucked up plenty over the years, yet I'd sat alone in the dark last night like a creeper—smoking—instead of accepting reality. What the hell was I waiting for?

Fuck this shit.

"Anything else?" Boonie asked. "I think we're about done here."

"Hey, I've got something," I said, the words surprising me.

"What's that?"

"I'm claiming Becca Jones."

Boonie snorted.

"Think you claimed her five years ago, dumbass," Demon said. "This isn't news."

"No, I mean I'm claiming her for real. Now. I'm done fucking around. Gonna make her my old lady."

"'Bout time," Boonie said, all but rolling his eyes. "Any more moping around and I'll shoot you myself. Anyone got a problem with Puck taking Becca?"

I looked around the table, meeting my brothers' eyes one by one. They damned well better not have a problem.

"She knows how to keep her mouth shut," Miner said. "Can handle herself when shit goes down. She'll do fine."

The others nodded, and just like that I had an old lady.

Supposed I should go tell her. Would she fight with me? Maybe a little, but that was okay. I'd always liked it rough.

NINE

BECCA

Things are always better after a good night's sleep, and last night I'd finally gotten one. I hadn't rolled out of bed until early afternoon and still hadn't showered.

Fortunately the only job I had for the day was baking Earl's pie. Teresa had been happy with the work I'd done the night before—happy enough that she put me on evenings, Tuesday through Saturday. Not the best schedule for my social life, but exactly what I needed to make money.

Between that and school, Sunday was my only full day off and I planned to enjoy it.

I'd just finished drinking my coffee when I heard the sound of Puck's motorcycle out in the alley. The night before kept running through my mind. He'd never responded to my apology. Was he still mad? Did it matter? I'd already decided I didn't want anything to do with him, so why should I even care?

I totally cared.

The bike died, and then I heard the sound of footsteps in the stairwell. *Crap.* It couldn't be him. And if it was? What did he want? What should I say? Then he knocked on the door and I couldn't think anymore at all. I stood slowly, wishing I'd bothered to comb my hair, or at the very least change out of my jammie pants.

It doesn't matter what you look like, I reminded myself firmly. *You aren't getting involved with him. Snap out of it.*

Easier said than done.

I walked over to the door and unlocked it, opening it slowly. Puck stood outside, his face impossible to read. He looked good. Really good. He wore his standard uniform of faded jeans, leather boots, and T-shirt that exposed the partial sleeves of his tattoos. He had on his club colors, too, the dark leather and stark patches reminded me once again just how dangerous he was.

"Puck," I said. He stepped inside, eyes tracing my face. It wasn't exactly comfortable, the way he pinned me down with his gaze. Definitely a predator sizing up his prey. Puck was handsome but never pretty and the scar crossing his face was brutal. His entire life was brutal. I knew better than to trust him, yet now that he stood before me, it took everything I had not to touch him. Hold him. Run my fingers through his hair to see if it was still as soft as I remembered it.

He wanted the same thing from me, too. It raged through his eyes. Puck wrapped a hand around the back of my neck, then spoke my name in a hungry growl. "Becca."

Suddenly his mouth covered mine. My lips parted for his tongue as the world tilted beneath me. I felt his hand slide down the back of my jammies, burrowing deep to cup my ass. My arms went around his neck and any foolish doubts I had disappeared.

This was exactly where I needed to be.

My heart might not be ready for a real relationship with Puck, but my body was 100 percent on board with screwing him. Preferably right now, up against the wall. This was good, because I couldn't have moved my head if I tried—his fingers held my hair too tight. His hardness pressed into me and when he started walking me backward toward my bedroom, it never occurred to me to protest.

Nothing occurred to me, actually.

Full brain shutdown.

All I felt was him, all I wanted was him. In me, on me, surrounding me. The backs of my knees hit the bed and he pushed me down. Not gently. Nope. Puck covered me with his body, pulling back just enough to study my face. His eyes burned through my soul like coals.

"You want out, say something now," he gritted, pulling off his leather vest. I shook my head rapidly. He caught the edges of my pants, sliding his fingers inside and jerking them down my legs. Then his hands went to his belt and he ripped it loose. He opened his fly and there he was—fully erect and bigger than I remembered.

I stared at him, mesmerized, licking my lips. Puck groaned.

"Don't look at me like that," he growled. "I don't want to hurt you, but you keep that shit up, I might."

Then he had a condom out and on, his cock pushing at the entrance to my body. It happened so fast. Was I ready for him? Would he tear me open, hurt me? My body stiffened.

Puck didn't even pause.

His cock bottomed out in an instant, stretching and filling me as I gasped, a mixture of pain and pleasure so intense it was its own kind of pain. Then his body covered mine, his hips grinding into me hard, like he needed friction but didn't want to risk pulling out even a little.

Given how this pushed his pelvic bone into my clit, I wasn't exactly complaining.

"More," I gasped, clutching at his biceps with my fingers. Puck slammed into me, shoving me down into my worn, springy mattress, grunting with every stroke as if his life hung in the balance.

Mine certainly seemed to hang suspended, desperate for the release only he could give me. Desire and need and tension spiraled through me like wild lightning, carrying me toward the finish line faster than should've been possible.

Puck caught my ankles, jerking them up onto his shoulders. The new angle changed everything, creating a leverage that sent him impossibly deeper into my body.

"Touch yourself," he demanded tightly. "Get yourself off while I'm fucking you. I own this body now—show me what it can do."

I obeyed breathlessly, rubbing my clit frantically. Never felt anything this good in my life. Puck's eyes caught mine, holding my gaze captive as his cock tortured me. My orgasm hit with a rush and I screamed, body convulsing. He grinned savagely, then started pounding me so hard I knew walking might be a problem afterward.

I didn't care.

Every stroke hit deep inside, my body flushed and sensitized until he felt twice his size. God in heaven . . . He'd said he owned me, and he did. My body recognized its master even if I didn't. It wanted to please him, to obey and satisfy. Suddenly Puck came, body shuddering as I felt the throb of his cock deep within.

His hand caught my hair again, tilting my head for another savage kiss as the last of his seed filled me.

The sound of our panting filled the air.

Eventually he pulled free, tugging off the condom as he lowered his body across mine. I sighed. I'd never felt anything like this—not even close. Not even when he'd gone down on me in California, making me come for the first time.

"Nice," he finally managed to say. "'Bout fucking time, too."

I didn't respond, because what the hell does a girl say after something like that? "Thanks a bunch" doesn't quite cover this kind of situation. Instead of speaking, I wrapped my arms around him and pulled him into my embrace. His weight covered me and we lay there, catching our breath.

"That was unexpected," I finally said. Puck didn't respond, just rolled to the side to lie next to me. I studied him, mesmerized by the lines of his face.

"I accept your apology," he said finally. "Just in case you hadn't picked up on that."

I laughed.

"Yeah, I sort of figured."

"We've played around long enough," he continued. "Not a secret that I want you—seems to go both ways. It's time."

Time? I wondered that that meant. Oh God, I hope he meant time for more sex . . .

"I seem to remember you make fast recoveries," I said, reaching down between us. His cock had never fully softened. The skin was silky and smooth between my fingers, and I felt the harder ridges beneath tighten.

"Let's clear things up," he said, his tone catching me off guard. "This isn't a onetime thing. I'm claiming you, Becca. Already talked to the club about it—they know you're mine."

I stilled.

"I don't remember agreeing to that," I said slowly. "In fact, I've been thinking things through and decided I'm nowhere near ready for a relationship. The whole thing with my mom, and school—"

"We've been in a relationship for five years now," Puck said, his voice hard. "It wasn't normal, it wasn't exclusive . . . Hell, I don't know what the fuck it was, but we both know that's the truth. Whatever's between us, it's been there since the first night we met."

I studied his face, trying to decide if I bought into that theory. He'd been a constant in my life, that was for damned sure. But this relationship thing seemed a little overwhelming.

"Last night you weren't even talking to me," I replied, trying not to panic. "Then you show up here, fuck me, and say we're in a relationship? I feel like I'm missing a chunk of the story."

"You're not a normal girl," he said, his face softening. He

reached over, catching a chunk of my hair and rubbing it between his fingers. "You grew up wrong and bad shit happened. I'm a part of that. I grew up wrong, too, although less bad shit happened to me. Here's the thing—people like me don't follow the same rules that everyone else does. I make my own rules, and I live life fast and hard enough that I don't have time to fuck around once I find a good thing. And whatever else is going on here, you're a good thing."

"I want to be normal," I whispered. "I'm not like you."

"Sucks, but that's reality," he replied, leaning over to kiss me softly. The sensation of his lips brushing mine was distracting, and I felt him start to surround me again. His cock grew harder in my hand. My fingers traced his length longingly.

Then he pulled back.

"Becs, you're my woman now. That's the way it is."

Hmm . . . Suddenly Puck was less sexy.

"Don't I get a choice?"

"You already made the choice. You let me in here, you took me into your body. We've been dancing around it for too long now."

"Choosing to fuck someone is not the same as agreeing to a relationship with them," I informed him, my voice tight. "And don't call me Becs. My name is Becca."

"Okay, we'll compromise," he replied. "We'll just fuck around for a while, how's that? Just tell me you won't screw anyone else along the way and we'll let things grow naturally."

I narrowed my eyes.

"I'm not an idiot," I said. "And I'm not one of these stupid little girls you can manipulate with a smile. I know exactly what it means when a man like you goes to a party or on a run. You'll fuck anything that moves while I sit at home, waiting."

Puck gave a laugh.

"You sure like the word 'fuck' a lot, don't you?"

"It's a good word."

"Well, let me put it like this." He said. "I've *fucked* a lot of women—in the end, every pussy is pretty much the same. You're not the same, though. You're special and I'm not a kid who can't go ten minutes without getting my dick wet. I'm ready for more than sex."

"Since when?"

A strange look came over his face.

"This morning," he replied. "Couple hours ago."

"That doesn't make any sense," I insisted. Puck laughed again, then flopped on his back, catching me and carrying me with him.

"Life doesn't make sense, Becs. You just gotta roll with it."

"I said don't call me that."

"I'll make you a deal. Admit we're a couple and I'll start calling you Becca."

I frowned, trapped.

"That's what I thought. *Becs*. Now get your clothes on and let's make a picnic lunch. I want to take you for a ride."

PUCK

An hour later, Becca stood at the end of the second highest rock ledge, staring down into the water. I'd taken her up along the north fork of the Coeur d'Alene River, savoring the feel of her arms wrapped tight around my stomach and her boobs pressed into my back the entire time. Now we were at the Big Rock, which was exactly what it sounded like—a giant granite rock formation sticking out and over the water.

"I can't believe how clear it is," she said, her voice hardly more than a whisper. I followed her gaze. Below us was a deep, wide pool of utterly clear water. I could see every colored rock littering the bottom. A fish swam by lazily, completely unaware of the danger hovering above.

Still couldn't believe she was really here, that we'd finally managed to cut through the bullshit and get together. Okay, so she wasn't totally on board yet, but she would be. She wasn't the kind of girl to fuck around, despite her history. Maybe because of it.

Christ, just being with her made me feel good.

"Wait until you jump off," I told her. "It's cold but it fucking kicks ass, too. Makes your heart pound. Total adrenaline rush. Can't believe you've never been here before."

Becca looked up at me, delight written all over her face.

"I can't believe it, either," she said. "If I find out Danielle kept this from me, I'll strangle her."

"She's got to know about it," I told her. "Every kid who grows up around here comes and parties at this place. It's a thing."

I pointed behind us toward the graffiti covering one of the rocks, declaring that the class of 2002 would rule the world.

Wonder how that worked out for them?

I wouldn't know—I'd never graduated from high school. Got my GED in juvie, though. So far it hadn't held me back. Of course, the Bastards tended not to worry too much about diplomas. They were more interested in the fact that I'd turned down three different plea bargains.

"I'm just surprised there aren't more people here," I continued. "On a Sunday afternoon this place should be packed."

"I think you scared them off with your bike," Becca said, her voice dry. "Or it might have been the way you growled at them."

I laughed, because she made a good point. There'd been a group of teens here when we first pulled up, but they'd disappeared fast enough when they saw my colors. That worked out well for me, because I'd been dreaming about Becca naked and swimming around in that water for a long time now. Speaking of . . .

"Okay, strip down," I told her, reaching for my shirt. I had it up and over my head, then I caught her staring at me. Not a "you're incredibly sexy" stare, but a "what the fuck are you thinking?" stare.

"What?"

"You want to go skinny-dipping?" she asked, her voice a startled squeak.

"Water's cold, Becca. You jump in wearing your clothes, you'll freeze your ass off on the ride home. Strip down."

"What if someone comes?"

I shrugged.

"You're gorgeous, babe, but you don't have anything new to this world. You've got the same parts as everyone else, so I doubt they'll be too shocked."

She blushed, which was cute. Funny, too, given she'd grown up around bikers. We weren't exactly a shy people. I reached for my boots, pulling them off and then shoving down my pants. My dick was hard again, which was impressive considering I'd already fucked her twice that afternoon—once on her bed and once up against the kitchen wall halfway through making lunch. For some reason I'd expected the second time to be slower, less urgent, but seeing her naked just set me off. Couldn't be helped.

"Okay," Becca said, giggling and glancing around. She didn't need to worry. We were on the old river road, well back from the main route to Callup. The only signs of civilization were some old bridge girders peeking out from above the trees in the distance.

Then Becca pulled her shirt off and I forgot all about swimming.

Damn, but she had nice tits. All round and perky, with tight pink nipples that just really, really needed to be sucked on for a while. I reached for her, but she darted away and suddenly we were in a race to get off our clothes.

We weren't on the highest section of the rock, but we were high enough that when Becca turned and jumped off without a hint of hesitation, it surprised me. I watched as she cannonballed into the water, then kicked her way up and popped out, gasping and laughing.

"Oh my God, it's so fucking cold!" she shouted. "You didn't warn me. It's colder than the regular river."

"It's deep and in the shade," I yelled back, grinning. Then I dove in, flooded with exhilaration. I sliced through the icy cold water. I surfaced a good ten feet from her and lunged.

I wanted to feel those tight nipples all slippery and wet.

Becca laughed and splashed at me, then my arms caught her and pulled her tight into my body, our slick bodies sliding and rubbing against each other.

"It's really, really fucking cold," she whispered. "But it gets better after you start to go numb."

She had a point—I couldn't even feel my dick and I had a feeling my balls had crawled right up into my body.

"You know, I'd love to fuck you in the water, but I'm not sure it's happening," I admitted. She giggled, then leaned forward and kissed me. I savored the sensation. Even with my dick out of commission, this was the best date I'd ever had. And yeah, it was a date. I didn't even care. I'd been a complete fucking idiot to wait this long.

She needed that time, dumbass.

Kicking my legs powerfully, I lay back in the water with her on top of me, sucking on her lips as my hands roamed free across her body. I found the crack of her ass, then slid my fingers lower. Now *there* was a nice way to warm my fingers . . .

Becca shivered, and I liked to think it wasn't just from the cold. Her arms came around my shoulders, clutching me tight. Loved holding her like that.

Then she reared up and shoved me under the water.

I came up with a sputtering roar to find her swimming away as fast as she could, laughing hysterically the whole time.

"You'll pay for that shit!" I shouted, starting after her.

"Whatcha gonna do? Spank me?"

"That's a great idea, babe. I'm all over it." Thirty seconds later I had her again, and we wrestled in the water and splashed each other until her lips started turning blue.

Fortunately I had a plan for warming her up.

Course, I'd have to thaw out my dick first.

An hour later we lay in the grass on the side of the river, dry and happy. I'd eaten her out, she'd sucked me off, and then we fucked again just for the hell of it.

Life was good.

Unfortunately the sun was starting to set. The river valley was narrow enough that the light tended to fade fast. Becca climbed up and over me, straddling my lap as she leaned her hands against my chest. I caught her by the waist and considered my woman.

She was braless under her tank top—somehow I'd managed to lose it when I got our clothes off the rock. Shit happens, and all that. Now she wore the tank and her jeans, and I swear to God, she was a biker's dream come true. Her hair hung down in water-kissed locks and she had just a hint of pink burn across her nose.

"You get that I'm keeping you, right?" I asked. "We can call it whatever you want, but it's real. Admit it."

Becca cocked her head, and gave a soft smile.

"Yeah, I guess it's real," she whispered, then she leaned down and kissed me.

Biker heaven, right there. Too bad I couldn't get another rise out of my cock if my life depended on it—straight-up fucked out, more's the shame.

Still, it was a great problem to have, all things considered.

BECCA

Puck snored. Not a whole lot, just enough to be really cute.

"Cute" wasn't really a word I'd ever associated with him, but when he fell asleep there was something soft and almost gentle in his face. The scar was still there, of course, but now he was totally relaxed—happy—and it showed. I still wasn't sure about the whole "I'm keeping you" thing, but I figured it would work itself out because he was right. Whatever this was, it was real and it made me happy, too.

What time was it? The clock said five in the morning . . . I wanted some water. Slipping out of bed, I padded softly into my kitchen to grab a drink of water.

We'd decided to stay at my place because it was nicer overall— homey and comfortable.

The blink of the message machine caught my eye after I got my drink. Someone had called—maybe while we were taking a shower together? I grabbed the handset and pushed the button.

"Becca baby, it's Mom. I told you that it was okay and I'd be fine. I'm not fine, honey. I'm beat up real bad. My arm is definitely broken and I'm pretty sure I have a concussion. Some of the girls tried to take me to the hospital but I'm afraid to go. If the cops come after Teeny, they'll only lock him up for a few hours and when he makes bail things will be worse. I really need you to send me money. A lot of money. Otherwise I'll never get out alive. I hate to do this to you, baby, but this is for real. I don't want to die."

My stomach crawled up into my throat—she'd never sounded like this before. Like she'd been strangled. I knew how that felt.

He'd strangled me once, too.

I had to do something, I realized. Puck had been right—the woman was a con artist, no question. But she was my mom, and she truly believed she was going to die. I heard it in her voice.

You can't fake something like that.

I walked over to my Singer and sat down in front of it, fingers running over the black enamel and gold leaf. It was more than a hundred years old . . . The most valuable thing I owned. How much was it worth? Should I try to sell it?

I thought of Regina's kind, loving face, the wrinkles around her eyes . . . the way she'd held me while I cried.

Priceless.

The Singer was priceless and I had no right to sell it—it wasn't really mine. I was just using it until it went to its next owner, because a thing like that can't be bought or sold.

Instead I went over to my tip jar counting the piles of quarters, dimes, and nickels. Twenty minutes later I'd determined that I had $122.16, counting the hundred bucks I'd gotten from Prince Handsy. Combined with my checking account that made $144.79—my entire cash value as a human being, and that was before I paid my power bill or filled my gas tank.

It would have to be enough. I'd call her in the morning.

"You okay?" Puck asked as I slipped into bed.

"Yeah, it's all good," I whispered, hoping it would be. He grunted and pulled me into his arms protectively. Not even the memory of Mom's voice could keep me up after that.

There's something wonderful about waking up in bed with a sexy man. Well, lots of wonderful things, not least of which was the way he flipped me on my stomach and fucked me from behind.

Yeah, that part was good.

Even better, though, was the big breakfast he helped me cook. I didn't have any ingredients, a problem he solved by walking across the roof and raiding his own kitchen. Together we made eggs, bacon, and coffee, then sat down to each together like a real couple.

"So what's your work schedule like?" he asked. "I know you have school during the day . . ."

"I go to school about twenty to thirty hours a week," I told him. "It's usually a full-time program, but they made an exception for me. For now, Teresa has me on nights, Tuesday through Saturday."

He frowned.

"Doesn't leave a whole lot of extra time."

"I'm a busy girl," I said, realizing this could be an issue. "There's nobody but me, Puck. If I don't pay the tuition bills, nobody else will. I'm not afraid to work hard."

"How much longer until you graduate?"

"Probably six months, if things go well. Longer if they don't. I knew it was a tough schedule when I started, but I don't want to wait tables forever. Don't want to move away from Callup, either. The options are limited."

He nodded, still looking less than thrilled.

"So you have school today?"

"Yeah, I'll need to start getting ready soon," I said. "I want to get there by ten. That way I can leave around three, which gives me time to bake a pie for Earl before I go out to their place for dinner."

He sat back in his chair, crossing his arms. "So you're telling me I've been beaten out by school and a pie?"

I smiled apologetically.

"In my defense, it's a huckleberry pie—last berries of the season," I said. "I'd invite you to come with me, but I think I'll need some time to explain this to them. This is a big turnaround for me . . . being with you, I mean."

"I think they'll be less surprised than you think. But I'm guessing they go to bed pretty early. I'll come over after that."

"That's a pretty big assumption," I murmured, sipping my coffee. He raised his brows and I had to laugh. "Okay, it's not that big of an assumption."

"I've got shit to do today," he said. "So it looks like maybe I should get started. If I'm lucky, I'll make it back in time to steal a slice of your pie."

"That sounds really dirty."

"That's why I said it," he replied, then leaned forward across the table, catching me by the back of the neck for a coffee-flavored kiss.

There was something so controlling and possessive about the way he always did that. It should bother me. Instead it turned me on.

Fucked up.

Right on cue, my phone buzzed to life not long after I reached the main highway. Usually I'd wait to check my messages. Today I wanted to call Mom and let her know that I had money for her.

"Becca?" she asked, her voice a harsh and broken whisper. "Becca, is that you?"

"Yeah, Mama," I said, whatever leftover glow I'd had from my morning with Puck well and truly gone. "I got your message. How are you doing?"

"Not so good," she whispered. "You have to get me out of here."

"I've got a hundred and forty-four dollars," I told her. "I can send it today. It's not enough for a bus ticket, but it should get you to a shelter."

Silence.

"Baby, I told you I needed two grand," she said. "I mean, I definitely want you to send whatever you've got, but it won't be enough. Not even close."

I closed my eyes and rubbed the bridge of my nose.

"Mom, that doesn't make any sense. You can go to a women's shelter. They'll hide you until you're healed up and can travel. We'll save up for a ticket to Spokane and I'll pick you up, take you home with me."

More silence, then she sighed heavily.

"There's something I haven't told you," she said. "It's not just about bus tickets. I need the money to pay off some of the club girls."

"Mom, if your life is in danger, I don't care about whatever the hell you owe those women. They were idiots to lend you money in the first place. This is reality—I have a hundred and forty-four bucks.

That's all there is. If I send it, I won't even be able to pay my power bill or buy gas."

She gave a harsh, humorless laugh. It turned into a terrible, racking cough that didn't stop for a good thirty seconds—sounded like she was gacking out a lung.

"I wish it was that easy," she said. "They're watching over me. Teeny's convinced I'm going to run away, so he's got them watching me all the time. I need to pay them off. I do that, they'll let me leave and I can come up to you. Things are different down here than they used to be, Becca. I need that money or I'm going to die in this house. Please, I'm begging you . . . Shit, he's coming. I have to go."

The call ended.

I sat in my car, hands trembling, trying to think of what to do. I had to save her, of course. I couldn't just let her die because I was too squeamish about how I made money. Maybe I should go check out that strip club after all? I knew girls could earn a lot fast stripping—Mom always had.

Puck flickered through my thoughts and I pushed his image away. I couldn't worry about him *and* my mom, and I'd be damned if I'd ask him for money. He could talk about "keeping" me all he wanted but I was my own woman. I'd fought too hard for that independence to just give it away. Mom was a kept woman and look how that turned out.

So. Money. I needed to get money, and I needed to get it fast.

First things first—I called the school and told them I wouldn't be in.

Then I searched for the strip club's address, which wasn't hard to find. There were only two clubs in the area—zoning restrictions were harsh, something I'd always assumed was heavily influenced by the Reapers MC. How a second club had managed to open up right down the road from theirs was a mystery, but I didn't doubt for a minute that someone had been paid very well for that particular privilege.

There it was. Vegas Belles. They opened at eleven, which gave me just enough time to stop off and fix myself up a bit before going in.

Hopefully they were hiring.

I'd like to say that I'd never been in a strip club. That'd be just peachy. Even better, I'd love to say I'd never worked a stripper's pole, but I actually had a real talent for it.

How did I get so good?

Well, it goes back to all the time I'd spent in strip clubs years ago. When I was a kid, stripping was one of Mom's fallback income sources, ranking above outright prostitution (plan C) and finding herself a man stupid enough to support her (plan A). I'd grown up around them, in them, you name it. Hell, I'd spent more than one night sleeping under a dressing table or on a pile of discarded clothing.

Most strippers have big hearts, at least when it comes to little girls. They'd give me candies between snorting lines, and one even taught me how to do my stage makeup. By the time I was ten, I had that shit down cold. I'd never actually worked in a club myself, but I had no doubt I would've if I'd stayed in California.

One or two nights wouldn't kill me.

I'd stopped off at Walmart to invest in a cheap but sexy G-string and demi bra from the clearance rack, which I'd changed into in the store bathroom. Then I'd driven to Post Falls and parked outside the Vegas Belles building, waiting for them to open.

Unfortunately, they were located just down the street from The Line, which was run by the Reapers MC, so I felt like I had to duck down every time a car or bike drove past. I didn't know any of the members well, but we'd traveled together five years ago. Painter and Puck still hung together a lot—I'd seen them out riding together. I couldn't risk one of them seeing me and reporting to Puck. (Yeah,

I know I'd said it wasn't any of his business, but I wasn't stupid. Puck would shit bricks if he knew what I was doing.)

The doors opened at eleven. I straightened my hair, slapped on some fresh lipstick, and walked into the building, trying to radiate confidence.

A bouncer met me at the door, looking me over with raised brows.

"You guys hiring?" I asked brightly.

"Sometimes," he said. "Depends on what the boss needs and how good you are. He's not here yet. You can wait over by the bar."

Well, crap.

"Okay, thanks," I said, smiling brightly. Never piss off the bouncers—Mom taught me that early on. An angry bouncer can cause a girl all kinds of trouble. I walked over to the bar and sat down. A woman wearing a bustier was setting up for the day—she looked like she was about thirty. Blonde hair teased high and heavy makeup.

"Dancing or waiting tables?" she asked, her voice friendly enough.

"I've already got a job waiting tables," I said, shrugging. "Don't really need another one of those."

She nodded.

"Have you danced around here before?" she asked casually. I found her phrasing interesting . . . She hadn't come right out and asked me if I'd worked at The Line, but there weren't any other options.

"No, but I've had some experience," I said, deciding to keep things ambiguous. She nodded thoughtfully, leaning forward on the bar.

"You look like a nice kid, so I'm going to be straight with you. You go in there, they'll probably expect a blow job. You up for that?"

My eyes widened, although I shouldn't have been surprised. I'd heard of that happening, of course, and I was pretty sure my mom had done it a time or two. But The Line had a reputation for not forcing girls to do anything . . . I'd assumed this place would be the same, given the direct competition between them for dancers. Stupid of me.

"Seriously?"

She nodded, her face sour.

"Yeah," she said. "It's bullshit. I mean, I've got no problem with anyone who chooses to do it, but if you're looking for quick cash, you'd probably do better turning a couple tricks."

I sat back, stomach churning.

"Or you could go over to The Line and get a real job," she added. "They'll treat you better."

I frowned. "Why are you working here if The Line is better?"

"It's complicated."

"Yeah, my life is complicated, too. The Line isn't an option."

Curiosity sparked in her eyes, and she bit her lip. Something felt off here. What was her angle?

"You want some water or something?" she asked. "It'll be a while before Mr. McGraine gets here. He's the manager."

"Sure, thanks," I said absently, then pulled a dollar out of my purse to tip her. She waved it off, setting a glass in front of me. I sat drinking it, looking around the club. They'd taken the Vegas theme all the way. There were neon signs covering the walls, along with big murals of various casinos and attractions. Along one wall was a row of slot machines and video poker, although they were clearly labeled as being "For Novelty Purposes Only."

Right.

Tubes of tiny white lights lined the stages, and the poles were each lit up with different colors. The whole place was tacky as hell, but somehow still smooth and polished.

Slick.

Like Vegas.

Everything was obviously set up for the day, but nobody was

dancing yet. This was probably because the place was empty. Apparently most of the area's hornier men weren't up and about just yet.

"They did a good job decorating in here," I said, nodding toward the stage. The bartender shrugged, then turned away pointedly as another woman strolled up to the bar. She was young and pretty, but I could see the faint hint of a bruise on her face, covered by makeup. She was dressed like a showgirl.

"Hey," she said, her voice low.

"Hi," I replied, wondering if I was going to get another warning.

"You looking to dance?" she asked. I nodded. "You should leave. Get out now. This isn't a good place."

"Lisa—don't you have somewhere you should be right now?" a man asked, his voice firm. Lisa stiffened, then nodded her head quickly and scurried off. I turned to look at the man, who wore a suit and had a broad, friendly smile on his face.

"Hi, I'm Lachlan McGraine. I'm the manager here. I hear you're interested in becoming one of our dancers?"

He looked so nice, so normal. Utterly harmless in every way to a degree that it creeped me out. Something about him made the little hairs stand up on the back of my head . . . His smile was just a little too bland, his eyes a little too flat.

Or maybe I was just losing my mind. That bartender had me all paranoid, I decided. And God only knew what Lisa had been talking about.

"Let's talk in my office," he said. I stood and started in the direction he pointed. His hand came around and touched the small of my back just a little too firmly. It wasn't just a touch designed to guide me—it felt controlling.

We went through a door down a long, black hallway that ended in an emergency exit door. A big man stood in front of it, and as I walked toward him, his eyes slowly and deliberately crawled up and down my figure.

I didn't like this place. I really, really didn't like it.

"Here's my office," McGraine said, opening a door on one side of the hallway. It was a good-sized room, with a broad desk, a couch, coffee table, and two comfortable leather chairs. At the far end a pole had been installed on top of a low-rise section of dance floor.

McGraine closed the door and leaned against the front of his desk. He didn't invite me to sit.

"So, have you danced before?"

"My mom taught me," I said. "I grew up in California. She worked in a lot of clubs down there."

"Why do you want to work here?"

I smiled, thinking the answer should be obvious.

"I want to earn better money than I get waiting tables. I'm in school and I don't have a lot of employment options right now."

"And why did you choose Vegas Belles?"

To avoid the Reapers.

"Because you're new, and I heard the girls here make good money."

"You try out at The Line?"

"No."

He raised a brow.

"You have a problem with the Reapers MC?"

I shook my head quickly. Too quickly, I realized, because he smirked. Sheesh.

"Okay, take off your clothes and dance for me," he said. "We'll see what you can do."

I swallowed, because this was it. I caught the edges of my shirt, then looked down, thinking. The last time I'd done this had been in my stepfather's house. He'd been watching. With his friends.

I promised myself I'd never do it again—not like this.

"What kind of shifts do you have open?" I asked suddenly, feeling desperate. "I mean, if you like what I can do."

"Right now we have weekdays."

"No evenings?"

"Not for someone new, no," he said. "We've got new girls in from Vegas all the time. Locals get day shifts unless they work their way up."

Something like relief flooded me. I couldn't work day shifts—I'd lose my spot at school. They'd already been great about working around my schedule, but the reality was that I had to be there in the afternoons. Otherwise I'd never graduate.

I couldn't do this. I couldn't give up the future I'd worked so hard to create to earn money for Mom—I didn't even know for sure whether she was telling me the truth . . . She'd always lied to get money. That's how she lived.

"I'm sorry, I made a mistake," I said quickly. "I can't work weekdays. I should go."

He nodded his head slowly, pushing to his feet.

"Sure," he replied. "If you change your mind, come back. I haven't seen your moves yet, but you're my type. We can probably find something for you."

His eyes flickered across my boobs when he said "my type" and I thought I might throw up. Thankfully he opened the door and I was able to leave quickly. The bartender winked at me as I walked by, feeling icky and disgusted with myself. Outside the air was fresh and the sun was bright—the strip club had felt like being trapped in a crazy, alternate-world pit. Or course, that was mostly in my mind. The building itself was nice.

Being inside just felt so wrong. Guess I wasn't as tough as I used to be. Of course, in my new life—my *sane* life—I didn't need to be.

Now I had to figure out some other way to save my mom. I climbed into my car and drove to the library, figuring that was as good a place to start as any—if nothing else, I could use their computers. I might not be able to send her as much money, but there had to be resources for women in her situation . . .

Two hours later I had everything I needed.

There was a women's center right in my old hometown, and I'd even talked to the manager on the phone. She promised me that when Mom was ready to go, they could send out a squad car with a trained counselor to pick her up.

They just needed a time and location.

I clutched the phone numbers in my hand and stood outside in the green grass. There was a nice spot under a tree across the parking lot. I walked over and lowered myself to the ground, determined to get it over with. Then I dialed my mom's number.

"Are you getting the money?" she asked. I braced myself, my face flushing with emotion.

"No. I wasn't able to get any more money. But I have something better—I've found some people who can help you. Rescue you. All you have to do is call them and they'll come out with the police to pick you up. They do this kind of thing all the time. One phone call—that's all it takes. They'll even help us buy a bus ticket so you can come stay with me in Callup."

She didn't speak for a minute. Then she screeched so loud it nearly broke my eardrum.

"You ungrateful little shit! If I thought some bitch with the police could help me, I'd have called her already. I have a goddamned phone. You're so fucking high and mighty that you've forgotten what it means to take care of your family. I don't care how you get that money—steal it, fuck someone, do whatever it takes. Otherwise—"

I turned off the phone and dropped it into the grass.

Holy. Shit.

I felt tears well up in my eyes, and then I wiped them away, because *fuck her.*

Puck was right.

Mom was playing me. Again. I'd offered her a way out and she wouldn't even consider it, which meant that she'd never been serious about coming up here at all. Why the hell did I even take her phone calls, anyway? I was done. *Done.* No more. She could fuck right off, and I wasn't sending her what was left of my money, either. I'd use it to pay my damned bills like a responsible person.

I grabbed my phone and stood, walking toward my car. I'd drop off my utility payment before driving home and baking pie for Earl. Then I'd go have dinner with him and Regina—my real family—and forget all about that hateful bitch down in California.

Just because she'd given birth to me didn't mean I had to take her shit.

During the drive home I played all my favorite music loud, singing and rocking out along the way because for the first time in my life I felt truly free.

I had my own life now and it was good. Maybe Puck would spend the night again. The thought put a smile on my face.

She didn't get to ruin it—I wouldn't let her.

TEN.

Two hours later smoke filled the kitchen and the smoke alarm was screaming. It was loud, too. Earl didn't believe in fucking around when it came to alarms. I'd smelled the pie burning just seconds ago, yet now it was like a bomb had gone off in my kitchen.

Crap.

I opened the oven to discover I'd put in too much filling. It'd bubbled out and over the sides of the crust, dripping down onto the bottom of the oven. Grabbing a couple of towels, I pulled the pie out and set it on a cooling rack, then slammed the oven shut and ran to open the windows.

That's when someone knocked on the door. My heart raced . . . Puck? He'd mentioned coming over for a slice of pie, but I hadn't seen his bike when I got home. I'd tried calling his place. No answer. I assumed he had a cell phone but even if I'd had the number it would've been useless here in the valley.

"Hey there," I said, opening the door wide. Puck did that thing of his, catching me by the back of the neck and pulling me in for a long, hot kiss that left me breathless. Finally he ended it, resting his forehead against mine.

"Is there a particular reason your kitchen is on fire?"

I shook my head slowly, loving how his head moved with mine. It was cute—the kind of thing girls did with their boyfriends on TV.

"The pie boiled over," I said. He drew back, frowning.

"That mean I won't get a piece?"

"What if I told you we'd have really great sex instead?"

Still frowning, he raised a brow.

"You didn't answer the question."

I smacked his shoulder and he smirked, pulling me into his side before dropping a kiss on my head.

"I'll take the sex," he said. "But I gotta admit, I'm disappointed about the pie."

"It's fine. Some burned on the bottom of the oven. It's not the prettiest, but it'll still taste good. I'm taking it out to Earl and Regina's, though."

"They're old, so they won't be able to eat all of it. Bring me leftovers and I'll survive. Now let's move on to the sex option."

I glanced at the clock.

"We've got about half an hour before I leave," I said. "But I need to clean up first."

"Not a problem."

Ten minutes later he had me up against the wall of my tiny shower, one leg cocked up and over his hip, mouth attached to my neck as his fingers plunged deep inside. It was cramped and awkward and beautiful all at once.

"Holy crap," I moaned. "I can't believe how good that feels."

"About to get better," Puck said. Suddenly his hands caught my thighs, lifting me enough to slip his dick inside. He filled me, hips crushing into mine as I squished back into the shower wall. It should've hurt but it didn't. Not at all.

Somehow the moment was perfect in every way.

Then he started moving and I realized "perfect" was more of a state of being than one particular position, because I swear it felt better every second.

"Damn, that's good," he muttered, starting to move more quickly. I felt the tension build, faster than usual. This felt different, better than before. Slicker, hotter . . . harder.

My fingers dug into his muscles. Then he hit that special spot deep inside and my back arched, dragging my nails across his skin. If he noticed, he didn't show it. Now my entire body was wound tight and I felt that sweet relief hovering just out of reach.

"Harder," I moaned. "Fuck me harder."

"Keep talking," he grunted. "It's hot as hell."

"Your cock feels better than . . ."

"Do *not* say some other guy's name."

A snort of laughter escaped me.

"No," I gasped. "I wasn't thinking that."

"What were you thinking about?" he asked, giving his hips a hard swivel.

"My vibrator," I managed to gasp out. "Sometimes at night I imagine it's your dick."

"Jesus Christ."

Impossibly, he found his way deeper inside and I realized walking afterward might be a bit of a problem. Not that I cared. I was about ten seconds away from coming.

Five . . . four . . . three . . .

Boom.

My world exploded. I clenched him so hard it should've hurt, but he just stiffened and I felt the hot spurts deep inside. Water poured over us as we clung to each other, trying not to collapse under the weight of our shared pleasure.

Then Puck was pulling free, lowering me gently to the floor.

"I think you tore strips out of my back," he said. I turned him around in the tiny space.

"Crap." Sure enough, my nails had left bright red trails of blood dripping across his skin. "That's a little gruesome. I'm really sorry."

"I'm not," he said. "I like playing rough, Becca. You push as hard as you want."

I wasn't sure what to think about that, so I decided to ignore it in favor of cupping water in my hands to rinse between my legs . . .

Oh. Fuck.

"We didn't use a condom," I whispered, horrified. "We didn't use a fucking condom!"

Puck stilled.

"Didn't even think of it," he admitted. "I just wanted inside you. You aren't on anything?"

"No," I said.

We stared at each other, stunned.

"Huh," he said finally. "You have any idea where you are in your cycle?"

"You know about that stuff?"

"I'm a grown man, Becca," he said. "Not a twelve-year-old. Of course I know about that stuff. What are the odds we just knocked you up?"

I shook my head and shrugged.

"No idea," I admitted. "I've never been very regular."

"Then we're probably just fine," he said. "I don't have anything, in case you're worried."

I blinked, trying to process what he said.

"Okay."

"Okay."

"Um, I think I need to wash my hair before I leave," I said finally.

"That your hint you want me out of the shower?" he asked, a touch of humor in his voice.

"Yeah, I think so."

Puck caught me close, one hand on each side of my head as he searched my eyes.

"It's gonna be just fine, all right? You get ready, then go out and enjoy your dinner. Don't worry about it."

Yeah, right. No worries at all.

Earl's huckleberry pie was still steaming when I left the apartment at five thirty p.m.—Regina served dinner at six, sharp, and she didn't have a lot of patience for people who found themselves running late.

The rush was worth it, though, because I loved Regina's cooking almost as much as I loved sex with Puck.

It wasn't anything fancy but it was always good because Regina didn't like to do things halfway. Nope. When she served mashed potatoes she boiled them herself, then used real butter, real cream, and a hint of salt to create something that bore no resemblance whatsoever to that shit you buy in the store.

After Earl's heart attack, I'd talked to her about changing her ways. She'd looked at me like I'd lost my mind, declaring she'd stop using real butter just as soon as he stopped drinking and smoking. If he didn't care enough about his own health to change, no reason she should have to eat food that tasted like Elmer's glue.

Needless to say, real butter still sat on her table.

Tonight's dinner was just as good as always—roast venison (compliments of Earl), veggies, potatoes and gravy, followed by the pie served warm with ice cream.

Regina and Earl never pushed me to confide in them, and I hadn't intended to bring up my mom at all. Something about sitting at the table together always got me talking, though, and tonight was no exception. As I watched Earl cut the roast, I found myself sharing the phone calls and my afternoon visit to the Vegas Belles Gentlemen's Club.

"I can't believe I fell for her bullshit again," I said, poking at my potatoes with a fork. "You'd think I'd be smarter by now."

"We're hardwired to love our parents," Regina said. "It's part of being human. Something went wrong in your mama's wiring, otherwise she'd treat you better. That doesn't mean you should beat yourself up for having a heart."

"What did you think of that strip club?" Earl asked, his eyes bright. I choked.

"Nice try," Regina said, smacking him with a serving spoon. "Our girl nearly found herself taking off her clothes for strange men. You really want a club description?"

Regina continued to mutter as Earl caught my eye and winked. I bit back a giggle—the man had always been a joker, and he loved messing with his wife's head. She never saw it coming, no matter how many times he did it.

"Should I go get the pie?"

"Damned straight," Earl said. "Ice cream, too?"

"Would I let you eat huckleberry pie without ice cream?" Regina asked sternly. "You may be a forgetful old fool, but I'm still playing with a full deck. Becca, come to the kitchen with me."

I shot an eye roll at Earl, then followed her out of the dining room. Their house was nothing special—just a little two-story that was nearly a hundred years old and showed every minute of its age. Nothing felt as safe and warm as this place, though. I never had a home with my mom, but I definitely had one here.

"You do the honors," she said grandly, gesturing toward the pie. This was a Big Deal—usually she served the pie, pawning ice cream duty off on me. "I'm proud of you. You drew a line and stopped that woman from taking advantage of you. I know it wasn't easy."

"It wasn't," I admitted, pulling out the pie server and a sharp knife. "I'm glad I did it, too. She's already caused enough damage."

"Damned straight."

Regina let me lead the way out of the kitchen, carrying my pie proudly. I set it down in the center of the table, wishing it didn't have a ring of bright purple juice and ooze leaking from the side.

"Looks great," Earl said.

"It looks like a two-year-old made it," I replied, my tone rueful.

"Doesn't matter what it looks like," Regina said. "Taste is what matters. Don't just stand there—serve the dessert before we all starve to death."

Earl and I started laughing, because nobody could ever starve in Regina's house. The real danger would be waking up one day weighing five hundred pounds. I sliced through the flaky crust, the still-warm filling welling up. Regina handed me a plate and I lifted it out, going back a second time to scoop up the tiny berries that spilled out the sides.

"So," I said casually. "I have some more news. I'm seeing someone. At least, sort of seeing someone."

"Really?" Regina asked, deftly plopping ice cream on the plate and handing it off to Earl as I scooped a second piece. "Is it that Collins boy? He's a good sort."

"Union boys say he's got potential," Earl added. "You could do worse."

I swallowed. "I'm seeing Puck Redhouse."

Silence.

Looking up, I found both of them staring at me.

"I know things were strange between me and him . . ."

"That's an understatement," Regina said. "Now just because you dropped a bomb on us doesn't mean you can stop scooping the pie. Maybe you're not ready yet."

"To date Puck?"

"No, to be in charge of huckleberry pie," she replied, biting back a smile. "Can't say I'm surprised about Redhouse. I saw him watching you at the Breakfast Table the other day. He's always had it bad for you. I just didn't realize you felt the same way."

"I'm not sure it's a good idea," I admitted. "It's kind of scary—but he makes me happy, too."

"You're stepping out of your comfort zone," she replied. "That's always scary. Doesn't mean you shouldn't do it. You make sure he treats you right and it'll all work out fine."

Ten minutes later I sat back in my chair, stuffed nearly to the point of popping.

"You want another piece?" Regina asked. I shook my head—I'd be able to go without eating for a week after that meal. Thank God I didn't have to work afterward, either, because just standing up to clear the table almost killed me.

"Can you do the dishes?" Earl asked Regina, startling me. "I've got that thing for our girl out in the garage. Probably even more important now, all things considered."

Regina glanced at him, an entire conversation taking place silently between them.

"Sure thing—you two take care of your business."

He winked at her, then stood and stretched, looking pleased with himself.

"So what's going on?" I asked once we were outside.

"This business with your mom—it's bad news," he said. "And you still don't know how it'll play out. Say she really did decide to leave him, come up here. Would you be safe?"

"She's not coming," I said flatly. "You didn't hear her. She's just playing me for money. Again."

"If that's the case, she's obviously desperate," he replied. "And desperate people are dangerous. I've got a bad feeling about all of this. Proud of you for standing up to her, but I don't think it's over. Got something I want you to start carrying."

My eyes widened as he walked over to the huge, custom-welded sheet metal cabinet he kept his tools and guns in. It'd come from the Laughing Tess back in the day, where he'd spent close to thirty years underground before McDonogh Corp. laid him off two years back. Working for the school had been a big step down for him, but he'd handled it with grace.

Earl fiddled with the padlock, something that'd always seemed out of place to me because they didn't even lock their front door. Then he opened it and pulled an old cigar box off one of the shelves, carrying it back over to his workbench.

He lifted the lid, revealing a small revolver inlaid with mother-of-pearl on the stock.

"This belonged to my mother," he said, his voice strong and plain. "My dad gave it to her when he left for World War II. She'd married him the day before. I'd like you to have it."

My eyes widened.

"I can't take that," I whispered.

"Yes, you can," he said. "This is a great weapon, and still in beautiful condition. It's small and light, designed for a woman's hand. Not only that, it's completely untraceable. I hope you never have to use it, but if Teeny Patchel ever shows his face up here, I want you to take this and put a bullet in his brain. Then you call me and we'll figure out what to do with the body. You keep Puck Redhouse in line, too."

My mouth dropped.

"You can't be serious."

"You know me better, little girl. I never joke about guns."

This was true. Earl had hunted his entire life. He'd shot the deer we'd eaten for dinner, and he'd taught me how to dress and butcher a kill the first year I lived with them, because *anyone who owns a gun should know exactly what a bullet can do to a living creature.*

"I don't think I'll need to shoot anyone."

"Good," he replied, smiling. "Let's hope it never happens. But know this—we're here for you. No matter what. You're like our own flesh and blood, and there's nothing you could do that'll make us stop loving you."

Tears welled up in my eyes and he coughed uncomfortably.

"Let's go out and put her through her paces," he said gruffly. I smiled and followed him out of the garage. They lived ten miles outside of town, straight up a mountainside, so Earl had his own little target range set up in the meadow.

He and I spent the next hour shooting, him telling corny jokes and me laughing as the light slowly faded. We'd spent so many evenings like this over the years. I'd never be a hunter and I could care less about guns, but I loved shooting with Earl.

Eventually it got dark enough that we couldn't see the targets, so we called it quits. We strolled back to the house, where I saw Puck's motorcycle parked right next to my little Subaru. That slowed me down. What was he doing here?

He was eating pie.

I discovered this when I walked into the kitchen, cigar box in my hand.

"Hey, Becca," he said, nodding at me. Regina sat next to him drinking coffee like they'd been best friends for years. "Sorry to crash your dinner, but I had no idea what time you'd be back and I was in the area."

I opened my mouth to call bullshit on him, then realized it might actually be true. Boonie and Darcy lived a couple miles down the mountain from here.

"He didn't just barge in," Regina chimed in. "He drove by and saw your car, and I found him tucking a note under the windshield wiper. Of course I invited him in."

Puck smiled at me, then finished off his pie and stood up. "You ready to leave?"

"Yes," Earl said. "I'm ready for bed. Remember what I told you, Becca. I may be an old man, but I mean what I say."

Puck cocked a brow at me and I shrugged, because no way was I going to tell him that Earl had sort of offered to dispose of his body if he got on my bad side. Instead I gathered my things, and then Regina was handing me a plate full of leftovers, along with stern instructions to come again as soon as I could.

"So Earl didn't break out the shotgun. That's a good sign," Puck said as we walked out. *Oh, Puck, if you only knew . . .* "I'll follow you back to town on the bike. We'll sleep at your place again."

"You seem awful sure of yourself."

"Yup," he replied, and I had to laugh.

It'd been a crazy, fucked-up emotional roller coaster of a week, I thought as I pulled out of the driveway, but at least I still had Regina and Earl. The motorcycle roared to life behind me, and I glanced back to see Puck's headlight in my mirror.

So now I had Regina and Earl and Puck. Well, I had Puck so long as I didn't have to shoot him. If I did, I had no doubt that Earl would come through for me.

He always had.

Puck's hand slid between my legs, pushing them apart. I didn't know what time it was—felt like five in the morning. Cracking an eye I looked at the clock. Eight a.m. Impossible, it couldn't be later than six . . . I moaned because I was tired and wanted to sleep longer. Then a mouth covered my clit and I started moaning for a better reason. An hour later I rolled off Puck and flopped down next to him, pleasantly awake and alert for the day.

"You're a pretty good alarm clock."

"I like to make myself useful," he said. "What time do you need to be at school?"

"Not until eleven today." I glanced over at the clock. Nine in the morning—I still had an hour to get ready before I had to leave. Time for breakfast and a shower, and I should probably pack a dinner, too. My shift didn't start until seven, but Teresa had left a message asking if I could come in early. I could definitely use the money.

Between my shopping trip to Walmart and paying the electric, I was down to fourteen dollars. Just enough to get me through, so long as I caught rides with Blake and didn't eat too much. I started to sit up, but Puck caught my arm and pulled me back down.

"Just a minute," he said. "Wanted to talk to you about something."

"What's that?"

"You work tomorrow night?"

"It's Wednesday, so yeah," I replied, curious. "Why?"

"We're having a thing at the clubhouse," he said. I wrapped my arm around him, snuggling down into his side. I had a feeling I knew what direction this was headed. I didn't like it.

"I have to work," I said again, firmly.

"If I talked to Teresa and got you the night off, would that be all right? She owes me a favor or two. Wouldn't be a regular thing, but we've got guests coming in from out of town. I'd like them to see you."

His words struck me as odd.

"I'd like them to see you." Not *"I'd like them to meet you."* Puck wanted them to look at me, like I was a thing to be owned and used . . . That brought up memories, and they weren't all pleasant ones.

"I don't like biker parties," I said. "I should probably just work—I haven't been there long enough to be asking for favors. I can't really afford it anyway."

He fell silent, tracing a small circle on my shoulder.

"You are aware I'm in a motorcycle club, right?" he finally asked, a touch of humor in his voice. "Biker parties are a big part of my life, and they'll be a big part of yours, too, if you're my old lady."

I pushed up and glared at him.

"I am not your old lady. We're sort of hooking up in an undefined way. That's it."

"Hooking up exclusively," he pointed out. "You're on the back of my bike and you're under my protection. That's pretty damned close to old lady territory."

"No," I said, shaking my head hard. "I'm serious, Puck. I don't want to go there. We can date, have sex, whatever. I'll never be anyone's old lady. Been there, done that."

His eyes snapped up from my boobs. "The fuck? Did you just say you'd been someone's old lady?"

I sighed, flopping down next to him. "Sorry, I was talking about my mom. I've seen what it is to be an old lady, not just with her but with other women. It's all fun and games until someone smacks you across the face for not fetching a beer fast enough. Pass."

"You're being a bitch again."

"Fuck off," I said, rolling out of bed. I walked toward the bathroom, grabbing clothes as I went. I didn't need this shit, not from Puck. Not from anyone.

"You're essentially saying I'm gonna start hitting you, but when I call you on it, I'm the dick?" he asked, his voice hard. "Christ, Becca. Got that head shoved pretty far up your ass. I haven't done shit to you and I'm getting tired of pointing that out."

I spun around, opening my mouth to tear into him when it hit me. Puck was right.

I'd insulted the hell out of him. Again. I closed my mouth and blinked.

"You make a good point," I finally said slowly. "I'm not ready to make a commitment, but that wasn't a very nice thing to say, either."

"I call it like I see it."

We considered each other, then I shook my head. "I don't think this is going to work. My life is busy. Crazy. I don't have the mental energy for a relationship."

Puck stood and walked toward me, all loose-limbed and predatory. Then he leaned in close, catching my head and whispering in my ear. "You're making this harder than it needs to be. I asked you to a party. I want to show you off because you're beautiful, and I'm proud that someone like you would put up with someone like me. Is that such a terrible thing for a man to feel about his woman?"

I shivered, because he still smelled like sex. I wanted more.

"All right," I replied softly. "But only if it's okay with Teresa. And no crazy shit."

"You don't have to do anything," he said. "You show me respect, I'll show you respect and we'll have a good time."

I reached down and caught his hardening cock in my hand, squeezing it lightly.

"We'll have a good time," I agreed, hoping it was true. Worth a shot, and I was sure he could get me out of work. The club was as deeply embedded in valley life as the mine or the union—when they asked a favor, people said yes. Not out of fear. Out of respect.

That was the difference, I realized suddenly. The difference between the club I'd grown up around and this one.

Respect.

Maybe we could work this out after all . . .

"Hey Puck?"

"Yeah, Becs?"

"I'm sorry I blew up at you. It's not an excuse, but sometimes my temper gets away from me," I admitted.

"I'm startin' to figure that out," he replied. Then he kissed me and I forgot why I'd gotten upset in the first place.

WEDNESDAY MORNING
PUCK

Painter gave me a half hug, thumping my back in greeting. I stepped back, looking him over. The years had treated both of us well, although I couldn't say the same about prison. It'd made us harder.

Also made me appreciate life more. Painter had gone the other direction—I couldn't remember the last time I'd seen him smile, let alone laugh.

I guess there was the time we took his kid Izzy to the park?

After he landed back inside the state pen, things got worse. At least he'd been in Idaho, so I was able to go see him regularly. He'd served the club in prison and did what he had to. It changed him, though, in a way our time in California didn't.

One thing hadn't changed, though. The bond we'd forged in that cell together? Stronger than blood and utterly unbreakable. He was my brother, now and always.

"Good to see you," I said lightly, as if there weren't more than six years of history hanging heavy between us.

"Same here," he replied. The rest of the Reapers were inside the clubhouse already, but we always took a few minutes for ourselves to check in. Went back to prison—never knew where you'd find yourself, so you had to be ready at all times.

"Anything I should know about?" I asked him. He shrugged, his face closed off. Fair enough.

"So you been to the new strip club?" he asked. "I hear that's what we're talking about today."

"Yeah," I said. "Went last week to check it out. The Callaghans sure aren't afraid to spend money, are they?"

"We had a few girls jump ship," he replied. "I'm not too involved, but I guess they're coming back now. Apparently it isn't all love and sunshine at the Vegas Belles. We put some people in place, too. Their reports back up your information."

"Not a huge surprise," I replied, reaching for my cigarettes. "Fuck. Forgot I quit."

Painter snorted.

"So, I heard a rumor."

I bit back a dumbass smile, because I knew where he was going and I felt like one of those idiots we always made fun of when they shuffled off to the visitors' room to see their girlfriends. But hell, just thinking about Becs made me happy.

"Oh?"

"You got an old lady now?" he said. "That pretty little thing we brought up from Cali? How'd that happen?"

"I guess I just got tired of waiting."

"Didn't know you were waiting."

"Wasn't entirely sure myself," I replied. "Now I know. Ever since that night, it's been there."

"If you start writing poetry about her, I'll slit your throat myself."

"Were you always such a dick?"

"Yes."

"Funny, don't remember that part. Guess I was too busy saving your ass."

"Tell yourself whatever you have to. Let's go inside. I want to finish this shit up and have a beer. You got any good pussy around here?"

"You never change, do you?"

"Got no reason to," he replied.

"Probably shouldn't give you shit about that, under the circumstances."

"Don't worry—I'll get you back. Can't wait to see your girl again. All kinds of things I should probably tell her about you. Nothing quite like honesty in a relationship."

"You do, I'll shoot you," I warned him, and he grinned.

"Get in line. Mel's got first dibs."

"Thanks for the hospitality," Picnic Hayes said, looking around the room. The Reapers' president caught my eye, giving a brief nod. Hayes was a father and when shit went down with Becca, he'd taken my back in a big way. Since then he'd treated me like a true brother. People noticed, too. I owed him for that.

"Glad to have you here," Boonie replied. "You know we always got your back. You want me to start?"

Picnic grunted his agreement, although we'd all known Boonie would be the first to speak. Like so many things in our world, this was a show of respect. Respect governed us and held us together, and God help the man stupid enough to misunderstand.

Fortunately, Shane McDonogh seemed to get it just fine, something that had come through loud and clear in his dealings with us.

"I've already shared this with Pic," Boonie said. "But we've talked to McDonogh and Malloy again this morning. According to their sources, Jamie Callaghan will be visiting the Vegas Belles Gentlemen's Club"—he said the title with a hint of mockery—"tomorrow afternoon. That's why we called this for midweek. They don't know how long he'll be there, but he's flying in at ten a.m. and plans to go straight to the club after a business lunch."

"You all know receipts are down at The Line," said another of the Reapers, a big man named Gage. "We've lost some girls, too. Not that big of a deal, but the loss of customers complicates things. Cops like to watch how many cars come and go. The more traffic we have, the more money we can push through without setting off alarms. Obviously the Callaghans are looking to do the same thing. That's a problem for all of us."

Deep raised a hand, and Boonie nodded at him.

"Management just shot down another union request for safety upgrades at the Tess. Not sure how much everyone knows about the situation there, but this is bigger than just our clubs. The Tess provides more than two-thirds of the valley's income—well, documented income . . ." Several guys laughed at that. Deep continued, "The Callaghans run the national union and it's pretty obvious by now that they're poised to take over the mine. We have to shut them out. Otherwise—sooner or later—we'll have another major accident of some kind. The last one almost took Callup with it. We got a good thing here. Don't want to lose it."

The room sobered, because it was true. It might've been nearly twenty years ago, but the horror of that fire still hung over the valley. It didn't matter that I was still a kid in Montana. You couldn't breathe the air here without feeling the memories press down.

"How confident are you in this kid's intel?" Hayes asked. "I agree that something needs to be done, both for the valley and to protect The Line. But we're only going to get one shot. We go in and miss Jamie Callaghan, they'll tighten things up and we might not get another chance."

"Puck's talked to McDonogh in person," Boonie said. "Tell us your thoughts."

I considered my words carefully before speaking. Lives hung on what I said next, and the responsibility weighed on me.

"He's young," I said finally. "But he's not stupid. He's fighting for his life and he knows it. They may not be able to kill him outright, but they'll turn him into a vegetable and lock him away forever if they can. He knows we're his best shot for help locally . . . us and the union, but the ties are close enough at this point that you don't get one without the other. I can't see any reason for him to lie to us about this. He has more to lose than we do."

Hayes and Boonie shared a look, and I felt tension tightening around the room. Sure, we'd talk about it some more and vote in the end, but the issue was settled in that instant.

"So tomorrow we fight?" Gage asked. "If that's the case, I should get my people ready. Don't want them caught in the cross fire if we can help it."

"Who all do you have inside?" Boonie asked.

"Bartender," he said. "Maryse. One waitress, Lisa. Milasy and Renee are dancing—both scheduled for tomorrow afternoon. I know we'll need intel tomorrow but I want them out of the line of fire. They've put themselves on the line for the club in a big way."

"Let's send men in early," Deep said. "Pretend to be customers. Figure out who's loyal to Callaghan, and who's just bystanders. We have five or six inside before we make our move, that'll even the odds quite a bit."

"Okay," Hayes said. "Who hasn't been over there yet?"

Several men raised their hands, including Painter. That surprised me. I shot him a look and he raised a brow, challenging me.

The Prince of Pussy wasn't getting out quite as much these days . . . interesting.

Hayes pointed to eight men in turn, including my best friend. "We'll start sending you in around noon, one at a time. Drink slow. Don't sit together, talk, nothing. If they spot one of you, the others ignore it unless you get a sign, got me? We'll coordinate from outside using your reports, send a text right before we go in. That work?"

The room filled with grunts of agreement.

"We'll have those selected stick around for a few, make sure we've got it figured out," Boonie said. "The rest of you can go back out and enjoy some of our hospitality. Some of the local ladies have been working hard to provide you with food and entertainment, so don't be afraid to take advantage. Anyone needs a place to stay tonight, let me know. We'll get you fixed up."

Just like that it was over. I walked out of the room, down the hall, and out into the main room. We'd taken over an old bar a few years back after it went under. Real estate was cheap in the valley and the place made a hell of a clubhouse. We'd fenced in the back with six-foot chain-link topped with razor wire. Throw in a fire pit, music, and Darcy's flare for smacking down drama? The place was almost perfect.

The only thing missing was Becca.

I passed through the door and nodded at the prospect watching over the bikes, throwing a leg over my Harley. It was time to go grab my woman.

ELEVEN

BECCA

It was nearly nine before Puck knocked at the door. He'd told me
he might be a little late, but for some reason around eight I'd
become convinced that he'd changed his mind—that this whole
thing had been some sort of weird, crazy dream.

Given how unsure I was of things between us, you'd think that
would have made me feel better. Instead it felt like a cancer eating
at my gut. I wanted him. Bad. Not just in the sack, either. I just
liked the thought of his big frame standing in my door, all solid and
sexy and mine.

I'd long since finished getting ready and was sitting in front of
my Singer when he finally showed up. I'd had a couple drinks by
then, because despite the whole "want bad" thing, I was still a little
nervous about my first biker party in five years. I decided that
uncertainty was a good enough excuse to throw myself at him
through the open door. Puck didn't blink, just caught me and

started kissing me, letting me know powerfully and without words that he was happy to see me, too.

By the time we came up to breathe, I'd forgotten all about the party. I just wanted to drag Puck back into the bedroom and go at it like a couple of animals.

"Settle down," he murmured, cupping my cheeks with his palms. "You know I'm all about the thrust and repeat, but tonight I want to show you off. You're special, babe. Want them to see it for themselves."

His words warmed me all the way through, so I didn't protest too much. Instead I grabbed a lightweight jacket and followed him out the door, hoping he was right about me. I'd been torn about what to wear—I knew we'd be riding his bike, so that limited my options. Still wanted to look good for his friends, though.

Thank God for Danielle.

I'd gotten home from school at five to find her waiting for me inside (she had a key of course). Spread out across my couch were seven different options, ranging from "biker whore fantasy" to "Sunday school teacher visits the club." I'd gone for a middle option—"biker slut dresses for church." Or maybe it was "church lady wants to get laid"?

It's a fine line.

Thus I found myself wearing tightly fitted skinny jeans low on my hips, with dark black boots that were stylish but functional. They had a nice heel and black lacing up the back. Combined with the jeans, they made my legs look long and slender, but also promised to protect me from the Harley pipes. They had the additional benefit of covering a lot of skin while still screaming sex. Anyone trying to cop a feel would get a handful of denim.

Up top we took a different approach. Danielle put me in a black tank top with a scooped neck that showed off my boobs. She'd wanted me to tug it down to show the top of my bra, which I decided was too much. We compromised by putting me into a beautiful red bra with black lace, just in case the shirt dipped on its own. It was sexy as hell but still decent. My shoulders were bare and she braided my hair back.

Then I threw on some smoky eye makeup and dark plum lipstick. Shazam. Now I felt sexy and comfortable without being half naked.

Puck obviously agreed, because when we stepped out into the alley, he turned and pushed me up against the wall, kissing me again. My arms went around his neck and I felt his cock grinding into me through our clothes. When we broke free, gasping for air, I found myself pleading with him. "Let's blow off the party and go back upstairs. Just you and me."

Puck stilled, then pulled back to frown at me.

"You don't have to be scared, Becca," he said. "Hell, you know most of the club already. Darcy will be there, and probably Carlie. We've got some of the Reapers over, too, and Painter. These aren't scary strangers, babe."

Unfortunately, the first thing that popped out of my mouth was a little too revealing.

"Carlie is *not* one of my friends."

"Jealous?" Puck whispered, kissing the side of my neck. Hell yes, I was jealous.

"Like I care who you've been with."

Puck's face darkened. "I care who you've been with. I used to lie in bed thinking about it. Whether you were fucking someone, how he made you feel. If he'd hurt you. I didn't want you falling for anyone and I hated the thought of anyone bothering you. Couldn't make up my mind which idea I hated most—you alone and unhappy or with some asshole enjoying life."

"I might've been a little jealous of Carlie," I admitted.

"We keep this crap up, we'll miss the party."

"It's not that late," I protested, surprised.

"Yeah, but it's a Wednesday night and I've got shit to deal with tomorrow," he said. "Club business. We usually get together on Wednesdays, but a lot of the guys have to work on Thursday. It's over by midnight."

As he pulled me toward his bike, something he said stuck in my head. Something I'd been wondering about.

"Puck, what do you do for a living?"

He stilled, then turned to me.

"Why would you ask that?" His voice was soft, but his tone was harsh. Suddenly Scary Puck was back—so different from the man I'd seen over the past couple of days. How did he switch off modes so fast, and which was the real man?

"Everyone has to pay the bills," I continued, my voice quiet. "I wait tables. Blake tends bar. Joe works in the mine. What am I getting into with you?"

"You know I can't answer that," he said, his tone still harsh but a hint of compassion in his eyes. "You grew up around a club. I've never pretended to be something I'm not."

"You said the Silver Bastards were different."

His lips twitched in what was supposed to be a smile.

"Not that different. C'mon. Let's go."

The clubhouse was only ten minutes away—an old bar just outside of town. I'd driven by a thousand times, of course, but I'd never been inside. It was known for wild parties. Once or twice before every election, the sheriff would raid it—I'd always wondered why nobody got arrested. Then one day Blake filled me in.

The sheriff did the least he could to appease the county commissioners, and not one thing more. According to Blake, the commissioners didn't care for the club one bit. At the sheriff's department they were a little more pragmatic. With the club in charge, the "criminal element" was somewhat contained and self-policed. That kept down crime overall, which was what really mattered.

I suspected there were strategic payoffs in place, too. Seemed like there'd been some hefty anonymous donations to the law enforcement benefit fund each year that nobody wanted to talk about.

The system worked.

I hopped off Puck's bike and helped him back it into the line of Harleys. Things were so familiar and so foreign at the same time. Three prospects lingered outside, two Silver Bastards and one Reaper. They avoided staring at me. I'd gone to high school with one of them.

There had always been prospects hanging around the Long-necks, too.

Suddenly I wished I'd had a little more to drink, because I was alarmingly sober. Loud music poured from the bar, and when Puck wrapped an arm around my neck and started toward the building my feet didn't want to move.

"It's okay," he whispered, giving me a squeeze. "Remember, these are my brothers. They're the same people who saved you. They'll protect you and so will I. This should be easy—you already know all the rules. I've seen how hard it is for girls coming into the life. You're way ahead of them."

I nodded, hoping it was true. Closing my eyes, I took in his scent with the predictable response. My nipples tightened, my thighs felt restless, and when he slid a hand down to my ass for a quick squeeze, suddenly my world was full of color.

"I'm ready," I whispered.

The party wasn't what I'd expected—for one thing, it wasn't nearly crazy enough. When I thought of MC parties, I thought of strippers hanging from the ceiling, rivers of booze, and people shooting up everywhere. The Longnecks were trashy, loud, and always fucked up on something. Make that fucked up on *everything*.

Intellectually I knew the Reapers and Silver Bastards were somewhat different. The Bastards partied, of course—that's how it all started—but they were also more functional and less brutish. Less of a gang and more of a unit.

I couldn't miss the difference tonight.

Were people drinking? Yes, no question. And there were girls wandering around showing plenty of skin. It wasn't a free-for-all, though. There was an air of purpose, and the men weren't getting particularly drunk. They formed small clumps, Reapers and Silver Bastards talking quietly. What the hell kind of party was this?

Fuck. Something big was up.

I wrapped my arms around Puck, and squeezed in close to whisper in his ear.

"You sure you're busy tomorrow? I'm thinking of going in to school late . . ."

"Sorry, babe," he replied absently. "I've got shit to do."

Crap crap *crappity.*

They were planning something, probably something bad. I'd felt this kind of tension in a club too many times not to spot it. Puck would be in danger tomorrow and I couldn't know any of the details. He might die. That was the way of this world and I'd sworn I'd never let myself get drawn back into it, yet here I was.

And I was here, no question. If I'd doubted that before, I couldn't deny the truth any longer. If something bad happened to Puck tomorrow, it might kill me.

I'd fallen for the asshole—like mother, like daughter.

"Painter, you know Becca," Puck said, snapping me out of my dark thoughts. I looked up to see the tall, lean biker with the chiseled face and spiky blond hair that I'd first met at Teeny's house. I knew he'd spent more than a year in jail with Puck. Now they were best friends. The man gave of an aura of scariness that couldn't be denied, so I forced myself to ignore it.

All the men in Puck's world were scary. Time to pull myself together and deal with it.

"Good to see you again," I said, deciding to face my history head-on. "I don't think I ever thanked you for California. Hope you won't hold it against me."

He nodded his head, eyes assessing. I hadn't been able to read him back then and I couldn't read him now. He didn't seem overtly hostile. That had to be a good sign.

"So you're Puck's property now?" he asked. "Interesting. You'll take good care of him."

I smiled nervously, because his words weren't exactly comforting. One, I'd never agreed to be Puck's property, yet obviously he'd told the clubs otherwise. Two, the *"you'll take good care of him"* hadn't been a question or an encouragement. More like a threat. I'd take care of Puck or Painter would take care of me. Obviously he didn't fuck around when it came to his friends.

That was a good thing, I decided. Tomorrow they'd be in danger—I wanted someone strong at Puck's back.

"You'll take good care of him, too," I said, smiling at Painter. "That's what brothers are for, right?"

His eyes widened, and I got the impression I'd surprised him. Good. I wasn't the same little girl he'd met five years ago, and he needed to know it.

Puck gave a laugh, smacking my butt again.

"You want a drink?" he asked. I nodded, wishing Painter would stop staring at me. "Over here."

We moved toward the bar, which was manned by yet another prospect. How many of those guys did they have, anyway? I'd never really learned how many Silver Bastards there were in Callup. They seemed to sort of rotate in and out, which made keeping track of them harder.

Probably not an accident.

A minute later I held a beer as I followed Puck across the room toward Boonie and the man I recognized as the Reapers' president.

He was old enough to be my father, but still strong and sort of sexy in a weird way. He'd had a funny name . . .

"Pic, this is Becca," Puck said. "She's with me now."

Picnic Hayes. That was it. I smiled at him, wishing I'd chugged the beer already. Seeing him made me think of the Longnecks and our crazy ride north.

"Good to see you again," he said. "I heard Puck had finally claimed you. Hope it works out for you."

"She's tough," Boonie commented. "Shoulda seen her at the Breakfast Table last week. Some asshole jumped Puck and she went after him with a coffeepot. Lost her job over it."

Picnic raised a brow, clearly surprised, and I felt a small smile curling my lips. I *had* jumped right in and it felt good. I'd been a small, weak victim when he'd met me before. Now I was strong. Holding my own.

"Good for you," Picnic said. "Puck, you got a minute? I wanted to go over a couple things with you."

"Sure," Puck said. "Let me get Becs settled."

My new confidence disappeared. We'd never said anything about him leaving me alone at the party. I surveyed the party again, everything looking more sinister and scary this time. The girls skittered around like they might get smacked if they weren't careful. The men seemed larger. Angrier.

I gulped my beer, forcing myself to calm down. The real menace was in my head.

"Hey, would I leave you?" Puck asked softly as we walked away.

"I think you read my mind," I said nervously. "I don't want to be alone."

"We're going to find Darcy. You can stay with her until I'm done, then I'll come back for you. Remember, when you hooked up with me, you hooked up with the whole club. We're all here for you, Becs. This might not seem like a safe place, but it really is. Nobody can hurt you as long as we're together. Every man in here is my brother and someday the women will be your sisters. Darcy's probably in the kitchen."

Puck started toward the back, threading through clumps of men and women littering the room. Quite a few of them were old ladies, I realized. Some wore vests and others just gave off the aura of confidence that came from belonging. I saw some of the men I'd met down in Cali, too. A great big Reaper whose name I still remembered. Horse. He had a short, bubbly little brunette woman glued to his arm. She laughed at something, the sound friendly and happy.

There was another one I remembered, too. Rooper? Booger? Shit, his name wouldn't come to me. He was alone, but when a girl came up to him with a drink and tried to worm her way into his side, he blew her off.

Toward the back of the bar was a hallway, off to the right. The music got louder as we followed it through the building. Along the left wall were a series of doors, two of which were labeled as bathrooms. Then we passed an open door. I shot a glance inside to find a big room with a heavy wooden table. On one wall hung several obviously old sets of Silver Bastard colors. Puck frowned and shut the door.

Okay, that must be the chapel.

The hallway opened up into a kitchen area. Along the back wall was a grill, and several women hovered around a big center counter, fixing platters of food. Directing them was Darcy. She saw me and a huge smile took over her face.

"Becca!" she called, sauntering over with a sexy sway of her hips. She had to be nearly fifteen years older than me, maybe more, but the woman still knew how to work it.

"I need to talk to Boonie and Picnic," Puck said. "Will you keep an eye on Becca, make her feel welcome? I don't want to leave her alone yet. Not until she's more comfortable."

Darcy nodded, a flash of understanding passing across her face. Over the years I'd wondered how much she knew about me. In the Longnecks, women never learned any of the secrets. I'd suspected Darcy knew most of what happened with the Bastards, including where and how they'd found me. Now I had confirmation.

"Can you give me a hand?" she asked. "We've got food set up out back, and the first wave has eaten. Now we're refilling and getting ready for dessert. Just cold cuts tonight, nothing fancy. Ladies, this is Becca."

Women smiled at me, murmuring their hellos as I washed my hands at the sink. I had just settled in to separate and lay out slices of cheese when Carlie came in through the back door.

"That keg will need changing out soon," she announced. Then she saw me. My breath caught—obviously there had once been something between her and Puck. Just as obviously it was over. Now what?

"Hey, Becca," she said brightly. Too brightly? "Deep said you might be here tonight. I hear you and Puck are together now. Good for you."

Yup, way too bright. She still had a thing for him. That didn't stop her from walking over and offering me a hug that felt genuine enough. To my surprise, she took the opportunity to whisper something in my ear.

"We're both big girls, here," she said. "I'm happy for you and Puck and I've got no problem with you. But these bitches are waiting for me to start crying or something, and I'll be damned if I'll do it. It would mean a lot to me if you'd treat me like we've been friends for a while. Let me save face?"

Then she pulled back, meeting my gaze, and I saw a hint of desperation in her eyes.

"I didn't realize you knew each other," someone commented, her voice sly and nasty. I looked over to find Darcy glaring at a girl wearing short shorts and a bikini top. I knew her, of course. Bridget

Marks—she'd been a bitch in high school and obviously nothing had changed since then.

I felt sudden compassion for Carlie.

"We go way back," I said loudly. "Carlie and I haven't been able to hang out as much recently. Between work and school I've been so busy lately, you know? I haven't seen you forever, either, Bridget. How are you doing? You finish your degree yet?"

Just like that, the power in the room shifted from Bridget to me, because she'd flunked out and everyone knew it. She hadn't done much else, either, other than getting knocked up twice by two different guys. Not that she was raising the kids—nope, she'd dropped them at her mom's place and kept right on partying.

Carlie wrapped an arm around my shoulder and laughed. "I've missed you, Becca."

The statement was so ridiculous that I found myself laughing, too. Outmanuevered, Bridget stomped down the hall. I actually liked Carlie, I decided. What a surprise. I polished off my beer with a gulp, thinking maybe things might work out after all.

"Becca, do you have a minute?" Darcy asked.

"Sure," I said, wondering if she would call us on our little game. *Ruh roh.* Following her out the door, I found myself in a large, fenced area. There was a bonfire inside a stone ring and big speakers blasted music.

"Over here," she said, grabbing one side of a trash can next to a table full of food. There was a good-sized crowd out here, although not huge. Maybe thirty people? "Can you help me carry this out?"

I grabbed a handle and we hauled it toward a gate on one side of the fence. A man wearing a Silver Bastards cut opened it for us, frowning.

"You want help with that, Darce?"

"We got it," she said cheerfully. Then we were out of the fence and walking down the side of the building, cutting down on the noise considerably. "Appreciate the help. I wanted to talk to you, and figured we might as well take care of this at the same time. Only way to get any privacy around this place, you know?"

"Yeah, I can see that," I replied, hoping I wasn't about to get in trouble. "What's up?"

"Just wanted to check on you," she said. "You and Puck have known each other a long time, but this still happened pretty fast. These guys don't fuck around when they decide they want a girl. You okay with everything?"

I stumbled on a rock in the darkness and nearly dropped my side of the big plastic bin. We stopped for a minute, catching our breath.

"I think I'm okay," I said finally. "You know how I wound up in Callup?"

"I know everything Boonie knows, at least when it comes to you," she admitted. "And I heard what you said the other night at the bar, of course."

Oops. I'd forgotten about my public confession.

"I'll bet Carlie's curious as hell about that one."

"Carlie's a good girl," Darcy replied. "She had a thing for Puck, you know how that goes in a club. He's not into her and when he realized there was an emotional tie, he cut her loose. Best he could do. You saved her in there. Some of those bitches can't wait to cut a girl if she falls."

"Women will do that," I said slowly. Darcy frowned.

"Not all women," she replied, her voice hard. "These girls drag in here, fuck one of the guys, and think they're one of us. I don't care how many of the brothers you screw—you fuck over the sisters, it's not gonna end well. We have to stick together. Carlie's not an old lady yet, but she's still a sister in my book."

"Can I ask you something?"

"Sure. Can't promise I'll answer, but I will if I can."

"The Longnecks—they're the MC my stepdad hung around with—they kept a lot of club whores around. Do the Silver Bastards do that, too?"

"Yup," she replied. "It's a free country and the brothers bring guests here all the time. Some of them stick around, some of them don't. Some find they aren't as welcome as they thought."

"Doesn't that bother you?"

"Boonie's dick is the only one that matters to me," she replied, her voice matter-of-fact. "As for the women, I care less about who they're sleeping with than how they act the rest of the time. Like I said, fuck with the sisters and you won't last. Bridget won't be back if she keeps this shit up."

"Old ladies didn't get to make those decisions in the Longnecks."

Darcy smiled sweetly. "We don't get to make those decisions in the Silver Bastards, either. Yet the right decisions still magically happen. Nobody knows how, really. Guess it's just all our good karma coming back to us."

My mouth dropped. Darcy winked.

"You think those men don't need us?" she asked. "Boonie likes sleeping next to me. Gets cold and lonely when all the old ladies take a girls' weekend in Seattle. Would be even colder and lonelier if we didn't come back, and one time we forgot to for nearly a week. Fortunately things worked out and we found our way home again. Now things tend to work out faster."

My eyes went wide.

"You serious?"

"Do I look like a woman who will eat shit?"

Point taken.

"Let's get this trash out. I'm sure Puck will be looking for you soon, and I want to make sure all the girls meet you first. That boy's crazy about you—it's cute. Like a pit bull crushing on a kitten."

Laughing, I grabbed my side of the can and we hauled it around to the front. One of the prospects came running, pulling out the bag and tying it off. Then he tossed it into the back of an old pickup at the end of the parking lot. We started back.

"So how's school going?" Darcy asked. "Morgan's pregnant, and she said she wants to take some time off when the baby comes. I could sure use your help at the shop."

"I won't have my license for another six months," I admitted. "I can't go full-time and still work until three every morning."

Darcy nodded, looking thoughtful. Then we were at the gate again. I passed inside to find Puck and Painter filling paper plates at the food table.

"Go play with your boy," Darcy told me. "Enjoy your night off together."

Nodding eagerly I walked toward him, noting that the party was starting to pick up outside. Several girls were dancing and one had pulled off her shirt. Puck saw me and grinned, handing over a cup of beer.

"Are you trying to get me drunk?"

"Only way the poor bastard gets laid," Painter pointed out. "You should throw him a pity fuck later. Otherwise he'll whine like a little bitch all night. Gets old."

"Fuck off," Puck told him, pulling me in for a kiss. He tasted good, like whiskey. I never did figure out what happened to the beer I was holding, because five seconds later my legs were around his waist and he was walking across the grass toward the back of the lot. His hard cock pressed between my legs and my fingers dug into his hair desperately.

I heard a few whoops and catcalls, and for a second I flashed on a memory of a party years ago. One where another biker had hauled me off into the darkness. Hauled me off and hurt me.

Then we reached the back and Puck set me on a wooden table.

"Fuck, I'm crazy about you," he muttered, and the memory faded. He stepped into me, leaving no doubt just how much he meant his words. "I know you were nervous about tonight, but you're doing great. Tell me to stop. Otherwise I'm fucking you right here, Becca. Don't think I can wait any longer."

Music still filled the air, but back here darkness cradled us. It felt strangely private, despite the crowd, and a screen of low bushes blocked us off for the most part. I felt like I should protest . . . I just couldn't remember why. Puck tugged down my tank and scooped my breast up out of my bra. Then his mouth covered it and lust took over. I fell back across the table as he followed me down, hands roaming.

That's when I realized I'd made a very serious tactical error.

"Jesus Christ, these jeans are tight," he grunted when he came up for air. I felt his fingers at my waist, trying to slip inside and failing. "Like a goddamned chastity belt."

I bit back a giggle, then pushed at his chest.

"Let me up and I'll fix it." He growled but pulled back to give me space. I scooted down and hopped off the table, reaching for my fly. Unfortunately, that made me think of his fly and I got distracted. Seconds later I had his cock out, jacking it hard with my hand as he groaned.

The sound reminded me of our first night together—it'd been good at first. Real good.

Dropping to my knees, I decided I'd make it good again.

"Becca . . ."

I laughed as I drew him in deep, letting the sound's vibrations surround him. I tasted a hint of salty pre-come as my fingers found his balls. Puck swayed, then his hand caught my head and he started guiding me.

"I could watch you like this for hours," he said. "Kneeling in front of me. Lips all wet and shiny from sucking my cock. Just needs one more thing."

Suddenly his fingers were tugging at my hair, pulling out the braid as my hair fell around my shoulders. I opened my mouth and took him back inside, savoring the taste. No matter what else happened tomorrow, in that moment Puck Redhouse belonged to me, and me alone.

PUCK

Mouth or cunt? Fuck, I couldn't decide which I loved more. I'd learned something, though—no matter where I found myself inside Becca's body, I wanted to stay there forever. Was definitely throwing out those fuckin' jeans of hers tomorrow, though. Doesn't matter how fuckable a woman looks in a pair of pants if you can't get them off when it's time to tap ass.

Becca's tongue traced the bottom of my cock as her fingers worked my nuts. She kept that up I'd be coming soon. Just like that, I made my decision.

Cunt.

Tugging on her hair I pulled free, then pulled her to stand in front of me. A satisfied smile curved that sweet mouth of hers. My hands dropped to her waist, fumbling with her jeans.

"Get those things down," I growled, full of frustrated need. Her eyes widened.

"I thought . . . ?"

"Pull down your fucking pants," I repeated, reaching down to grab my cock. "I want in. Now."

Desire darkened her expression. In the distance I heard shouting, but I didn't give a flying fuck what might be happening at the party. Becca reached for her pants, unzipping them and shimmying them to her hips with a twitch of her butt.

"Shit, I have these boots on . . ."

I caught her shoulders and turned her, pushing her down across the table. Her hands went out as she caught her weight. Then my cock was poking her ass. Memories hit me—how hot she'd been, how tight. I really, really wanted to get back inside there. Her body stiffened, and I rubbed her hip then reached between us to find her cunt, slick and sweet.

Yeah, she was ready.

Somehow I managed to hold off long enough to slide on a condom. Needed to get her on the Pill ASAP—riding her bareback the other night had been incredible. Wanted her like that all the time. The condom snapped into place and then I slid home, filling her with one hard thrust of my hips. Becca squealed and I caught her shoulders, controlling every move of her body.

It belonged to me now.

I started out with strong, steady strokes, although I couldn't go as deep as usual. Her pants pinned her legs together awkwardly. Somehow it still worked—she actually squeezed me harder this way. Every movement carried me closer, come pooling in my balls. I tensed, stopping for a second because I wasn't ready to blow just yet.

"Puck . . ." Becca whispered as her body clenched hard on me. I think my heart stopped until she released me, then she did it again, wiggling her hips back at me. "Fuck me, babe. I'm really close."

I wrapped a handful of hair around one wrist and jerked her head back, slamming home. My other hand caught her waist, holding her tight enough I'd probably leave marks. Becca twisted, gasping every time I filled her and whimpering when I pulled out again.

That's when I really let go.

In the distance music played. People shouted and laughed and I'm sure some of them were watching us. I didn't care. My entire world had narrowed down to the sight of her ass bucking against my dick, her arms braced on the table as I plowed her harder and harder. Then she squealed and exploded around me, pussy clenching so fucking hard it hurt. I pushed through, impossibly close to my own release.

It hit. Molten lava blew out of my balls as my vision blacked and faded. I was floating in space for an instant, waiting for reality to come back into focus.

Damn. *Damn.*

Reaching down to catch the condom, I pulled slowly free, wishing I could just stay planted there forever. Becca had collapsed across the table, her back heaving as she panted. Her ass taunted me, and despite the fact that I'd just come hard I wanted her again, right there.

I'd hurt her the first time. Now I had to teach her how much it didn't have to hurt. Not tonight, unfortunately . . . I also wanted to come all over her face. Into that hair, too. Rub it in and mark her forever.

Christ, I needed a list or something.

Slowly Becca pushed herself up, turning to look at me. Beautiful girl. Bright cheeks, eyes at half-mast. Hair flying everywhere . . .

I wanted to tattoo my name on her forehead. I'd kill any man who tried to touch her. No joke.

"Not bad," she managed to say. Then she giggled and I knew I was well and truly fucked. I'd never recover from this. Hell, I didn't even want to.

Becca Jones might be my property in the eyes of the club, but the reality was that she owned me and there wasn't a damned thing I could do about it.

TWELVE

BECCA

Way too many thoughts raced through my head as we returned to the party. I kept waiting for the fear to crash back in. I should be worrying about Puck sharing me. Who I'd go with next. How much they'd make me drink, or whether I'd have to do any drugs . . .

Instead my pants felt a little twitchy, and I had a couple scrapes on my stomach. Possibly a sliver. Otherwise I was good.

Great.

Happy.

I kept breaking out in more giggles every time I thought about what we'd just done. Puck must've thought I was super drunk, but I wasn't drunk at all. Hardly even buzzed. Nope, all I could think about was the fact that I'd won.

Becca Jones had grown into someone who could have fun with her cute boyfriend—okay, probably not the right word for Puck, but you get the picture—at a party.

Not only that, nobody bothered to stare at me, despite being rumpled and obviously well laid. They were too busy watching a couple of half-naked girls making out. That's right—not one person cared what I'd just been doing out in the darkness. Felt liberating as hell.

Then I saw the food tables and hunger hit me. I was starving. Clearly I'd worked up an appetite.

"Let's grab something to eat," I said. "I think I interrupted your dinner earlier."

"For the record, feel free to do that any time you want," Puck told me. "I'll die a happy man."

"Melodramatic, much?"

He swatted my butt affectionately (I was sensing a pattern there) and we grabbed a couple of paper plates, filling them. Then we found a spot to sit at another table, one closer to the fire.

"Puck," a man said. "Tell us about your girl."

The brothers who looked almost like twins, Demon and Deep, came to sit facing us across the table. I'd seen them around town and served them before, but we'd never really talked.

"You know Becca," Puck said. "Works at the Moose, remember?"

"Hey," I said, hoping I didn't have anything disgusting in my teeth.

"Heard you had a run-in the other night," Demon said. "You doin' okay?"

Run-in? Oh yeah, the handsy student. Ugh.

"It wasn't a big deal," I replied. "One of the assholes from the academy tried to cop a feel. I took care of him."

The memory of him screaming and rolling on the floor brought a smile to my face. Puck gave a frustrated snarl, and Deep burst out laughing.

"Darcy said she nearly took his balls off," he said. "You'd best hold yours tight, Puck. Hate for you to have an unfortunate accident."

"Fuckin' hysterical, both of you. Seriously, that guy ever shows his face there again, you call me. I'll kill him."

Puck wasn't joking.

"Teresa kicked him out permanently," I said. "Even if she hadn't, I don't think I'd have to worry. There was another kid there—he has dark hair. I think you've met him." Puck stiffened. "He seemed pretty pissed off about it. He even apologized for his friend's behavior. To Darcy. Isn't that interesting?"

"Fascinating," Puck growled.

"Good thing your woman had someone there to protect her," Deep said companionably. "But don't worry—she'll be okay. Probably. The Moose might be rough, and the guys who come in there like to fight, but . . . Nope, it's just like that. You got a gun, Becca?"

"Fuck off," Puck said, standing abruptly. "Becca, you want another drink?"

"Yeah," I said, wondering if I'd get in trouble for kicking Deep under the table. Might be worth it.

"I'll be right back," Puck said. "Deep and Demon will make sure you're fine out here, won't they?"

Demon nodded, smirking as Puck walked away.

"You scared him off," I accused.

"Yup," Deep said. "Wanted to ask you about Carlie."

I shook my head. "I don't have anything to tell you."

"You know she used to fuck him, right?"

"This isn't a conversation I need to have."

"I think you do," he replied, "Because I hear you're BFFs now, and that's weird. Girls don't do that. What the fuck is going on?"

Was this really happening? I'd forgotten how fast gossip spreads in clubs . . . and since when did bikers call people BFFs? Common wisdom said it was women who liked to talk, but it'd been my experience that the guys were even worse.

Case in point.

"Is it so odd that two women would exchange a friendly hug?"

"Yes, especially when one of them's fucking the guy the other one used to fuck."

"Why do you care?"

"Carlie is mine. I want to figure out what's in her head. Maybe you can tell me."

That stopped me, and I frowned.

"What?" I asked.

"She's mine."

"But she was sleeping with Puck."

"I've banged half the women here tonight, even some of the old ladies. Doesn't change the fact that Carlie's mine. I want to know if she's over Puck. What did she say to you?"

This was possibly the strangest conversation I'd ever had. I knew one thing for sure, though. Sharing what Carlie had said to me violated the Code.

"She just wanted to say hello."

Deep stared at me and I stared back, neither of us blinking. That's when Demon started laughing. "You're fucked, bro. Get over it."

The moment broke and I decided to focus very carefully on my sandwich. This discussion needed to end. Fortunately, another man came and sat at the table, joining the brothers. He didn't bother talking to me, which was fine. Those potato chips weren't going to eat themselves. I needed to focus.

"You hear the news?" the new guy asked.

"What's that?"

"Bozeman chapter—president's old lady kicked him out. Caught him screwing around on her."

"She's a bitch," Demon said. "Always has been. He's better off without her. Not sure why they were still together anyway."

"Money," Deep chimed in. "You know her family's loaded,

right? He shoulda left a long time ago—she's been trying to lock his balls up for years. Man can't live that way."

Great. Not only had Puck left me alone, he'd left me in a nest of sexists. Of course, most of the guys here probably fell into that category . . .

"Women should stay home," the stranger declared. "Money gives them ideas. Bitch has her own money, she talks too much. Thinks she's the boss."

"Excuse me," I said abruptly, standing. "I need the restroom."

"Puck said to wait," Deep told me, reaching out and catching my arm. His voice was serious, and while he wasn't squeezing my arm, I realized he wasn't playing around, either. "So you wait."

The fear I'd thought was gone hit me in a rush. I was surrounded by big men. Scary men. They could do whatever they wanted, and I couldn't stop them. Puck wasn't here.

"Okay," I whispered, swallowing.

"Jesus, don't be a dick about it," Demon said to his brother. He looked at me, face serious. "Not everyone knows who you are yet, Becca. Puck just wants you safe. That's why he asked you to stay with us. Deep's just pissy because you won't tell him what Carlie said."

I swallowed, trying to convince myself that Deep might be big and tough, but on some level he was still a whiny little boy who wanted a toy. Not that it changed anything. Boys broke toys all the time.

"Here's your beer," Puck said, settling down next to me. "Everything okay?"

Locking eyes with Deep, I nodded.

"Peachy."

I hadn't been drunk earlier, but now? Yeah, the room was definitely swaying. I was in a ridiculously tiny bathroom, furiously washing my hands. I'd been stupid enough to touch the toilet seat, and while

I had no doubt it had started out cleanish (Darcy didn't strike me as a woman who tolerated filth), I wished I'd just peed outside. Some of those guys weren't so great about their aim . . .

Puck waited for me in the hallway. I'd just finished wiping my hands on my jeans (the paper towels were out—should I mention that to someone?) when I heard the shouting. Opening the door, I peeked out cautiously. Puck was gone. More shouting, coming from the main room, then a loud crashing noise.

Shit.

I crept out, trying to make myself small. I didn't want to get in the middle of a fight, but if Puck had left it was for something serious. Hiding in the bathroom just wasn't an option.

A group of girls stood at the end of the hallway, watching and chattering in excitement.

"What's going on?" I asked before realizing one of the girls was Bridget. She was too excited to play bitch, thankfully.

"One of the Reapers is fighting with Clay Allen," she said. "He's a hangaround. He showed up with some girl and the guy went crazy."

"Is Puck out there?"

"Oh yeah . . ." she replied, her tone somehow dirty.

Great.

"Excuse me," I said, pushing through. A wall of big, beefy backs covered in leather blocked my view so I ran over to the bar and climbed up to see if my man was fighting. I really hoped not. I hadn't scoped out any coffeepots around here to rescue him with.

I saw Puck right away. He wasn't fighting. He just stood in the center of the ring of bikers, watching Painter beat the shit out of the unfortunate Clay Allen, whose name was new to me. Not a Callup man.

A woman shrieked, and I realized that the Reapers MC president was holding someone prisoner in his big arms. She kicked and screamed, obviously enraged.

"You asshole!" she shouted. I couldn't tell if she was shouting at
Painter or Picnic or the guy on the ground. The big man just held
her tighter, his face grim.

Painter kept punching Allen viciously, the blows sending painful, wet smacking noises echoing through the room. After what felt
like an eternity, Puck waded in, grabbing Painter and pulling him
back. He shrugged him off, ready to go at it again, but when Puck
said something the big blond man stopped, panting heavily.

"Get him out of here," Painter ordered. Nobody moved. "Get
him the fuck out of here before I kill him!"

"Fuck," Horse said, stepping forward to grab Allen under the
arms. A path cleared for him to drag the man out of the clubhouse.
Painter turned on the girl, stalking toward her purposefully with
an air of menace. Picnic abruptly swung her around behind his
body. Then he turned to face down Painter, arms crossed.

"Not happening, son."

"It's none of your business," Painter snarled. "She's the one who
came here."

"I didn't even know where we were going!" she yelled from
behind the other Reaper. "It was just a date, you asshole."

"He's a fucking biker. You broke the rules, Mel. Get your ass
over here."

"Not happening," Picnic repeated, his voice firm. "I am not
dealing with this shit tonight. Painter, get your ass home. Melanie,
you're with me."

Painter growled and then the girl shoved Picnic out of the way,
stunning me. How the hell had she done that? In an instant she was
in Painter's face, shouting at him so loud it hurt my ears.

"You need to get the fuck out of my life! What I do is none of
your goddamned business."

"Fuck it," Picnic announced. "I'm done with both of you."

With that he turned and walked away. It took an instant to sink in, then the girl got a strange look on her face. Painter started to smile—not a nice smile.

"I'll give you a ride home, Mel," he said, his voice full of soft menace. "We can talk when we get there. Privacy, you know?"

The unfortunate Melanie looked around, then realized she was surrounded by men who took their lead from the Reapers president.

"Fuck . . ."

"Maybe we'll do that, too," Painter said. Then he caught her arms and started dragging her toward the door. She screamed again, this time in fear. I saw Darcy push forward, face determined. Boonie caught her. Melanie started slapping at Painter and he laughed. Then he picked her up in a firefighter's carry and walked out the door.

Silence filled the room. After an eternity, Darcy spun and glared at Boonie until he let her go, then she glared at the rest of us, too.

"The kitchen is fucking closed," she announced. "I'm going home."

Then she stalked out the front door without looking back. Boonie shook his head and I heard several of the guys laugh.

Jesus. What had just happened?

"Becca?" Puck stood below me, his expression serious. "You need a hand down?"

"No," I said quickly. What I needed was to get the hell out of this clubhouse. I had no idea who that woman was or why Painter had been fighting, but I knew a bad thing when I saw it. I dropped to my butt and slid off the bar. "Can we go home?"

"Yeah," Puck said. "Night didn't quite go the way I expected."
No shit.

He took my hand, stopped off to say good-bye to Boonie, Picnic, and a few others. I didn't look at anyone—I was way too busy trying not to freak the hell out. Then we were on Puck's bike and he kicked it to life, roaring off down the road. I held him tight, burying my head in his back, wondering what I should say to him when we got home.

PUCK

"I think you should go back to your place tonight," Becca told me. We stood outside her apartment, which she had taken care not to unlock. Message received. "I need to think about what happened."

"Let's talk about it," I replied, knowing I was fucked here. Becca was all kinds of screwed up in her head. That little show Painter put on with Melanie obviously set her emotions spinning.

"I think I saw everything pretty clearly." Her face had closed off and she wouldn't look at me.

"No, I think you saw something so far out of fucking context you couldn't possibly understand it," I argued. "Just tell me this— before the fight, were you having a good time?"

She glanced away, then nodded.

"You know I was."

"Don't judge what you don't understand. That's between them, and believe me—it's complicated and it's nobody's business but theirs. Not yours, not mine, not the club's."

"Doesn't it bother you that he just hauled her out of there? It's kidnapping!"

Becca turned on me, eyes full of fire again. Excellent—I could handle her anger. That creepy, silent indifference was a thousand times worse.

"Picnic Hayes is practically that girl's stepdad."

She froze. Fuck. Stepdads weren't the good guys in her world.

"Make that her foster dad," I explained. "More like you and Earl. Shit. He's married to the woman who helped raise her. London. Look, this is all coming out wrong. Just believe me when I say he wouldn't let her get hurt. He's just tired of getting caught in the middle because they're determined to fight with each other. They have shit they need to work out—a lot of shit. Maybe now they'll do it. That's what was really happening last night. Painter would die before he hurt her."

"He sure as hell hurt the guy she was with. What was that all about?"

"Like I said—complicated," I said, rubbing a hand through my hair. "Let's go inside."

"No," Becca said, but she didn't sound angry anymore. Just tired. "I need some time to think. This has all happened way too fast."

Bullshit. So what if we'd gotten together fast—we had five years of history between us, the kind of history that accelerated things.

"Are you blowing me off?"

"No." She shook her head. "I mean, kind of. Just for tonight. I need a break, Puck. Think how much my life has changed this past week. I want some time alone."

More bullshit. I wanted to grab her like Painter had grabbed Mel, throw her over my shoulder and teach her who she belonged to. Me. Now and forever. But Becca wasn't Mel, and she needed space. I could do that for a night. One night. Then I'd set her straight.

"I probably won't see you again until you get off shift tomorrow night," I said, thinking of our raid on the Vegas Belles. "Got shit going on all day."

Her face twisted, and for an instant I thought she might cry. Then she shook her head again, even as she leaned into me, wrapping her arms around my body.

"I'm just really tired," she said. "I want to sleep by myself. Why don't we meet for dinner on Friday, talk things through then. Or maybe—if you aren't busy tomorrow night—you could stop by the Moose?"

I hugged her, kissing the top of her head.

"Go to bed," I said, hating the words. "If I can't make the Moose, we'll talk on Friday."

There was another problem. At some point we'd need to figure out a better schedule. Between work and school, she hardly had anything left for me. Maybe she'd let me help her out a little? Becca nodded, then turned and dug a key out of her pocket. I'd have to get her a better lock, I decided. This piece of shit was way too easy to pick.

"Night," she said quietly. Then she stepped inside and closed the door.

God damn it.

Painter needed his ass kicked. Maybe I'd have time tomorrow after the raid, because this was fucking bullshit.

BECCA

Strangely enough, I actually slept really well that night.

I couldn't chalk it up to peace of mind or feeling like I'd figured things out. Not at all. But the combination of alcohol, sex, and an adrenaline crash were enough to knock me out, which was a very good thing.

The next morning I woke up early enough to take a shower and sew for a while before heading out to school. Sewing had always been my therapy—now it calmed me down. Unfortunately it was way too early to talk to Danielle about the Puck situation. She'd still be asleep.

As for Puck, he was probably gone already. Would he come back safe from whatever the club was doing today? It was a valid question, which said something scary about our relationship. Suppose we stayed together, turned into a couple like Boonie and Darcy. Did I really want to know the details of his life?

How could I be with someone if I couldn't face the reality of who he was?

I wrestled with all of these thoughts while carefully guiding a strip of bright red silk through the Singer. The tension was off, and I couldn't quite find the sweet spot. The machine kept crumpling and twisting the delicate fabric.

Fucking metaphor for my life.

Ten minutes later I nailed it, right as the phone rang. I stopped the machine and stretched my neck as I walked over to answer it. That was the only thing I didn't like about sewing—sometimes I got so caught up in what I was doing that I forgot to move.

I answered the phone and my world cracked wide open.

"Becca?"

Teeny. I hadn't heard his voice in years, but just that one word— my name—threw me right back. My back hunched and I melted into myself. God, but I hated this man. Wait. *No.* I refused to let him do this to me. Never again.

"What the hell do you want?" *Nice.* I'd never had the nerve to talk to him like that before. I gave myself a mental shoulder pat.

"I have some bad news, honey," he replied, his tone touched with what I suspected was supposed to be sorrow. It sounded smug, though. Smug and self-satisfied. I could almost see the expression to match the voice on his pointy, ferretlike face. "It's about your mother."

"What about her?" I asked, stiffening.

"She left me," he said, his tone hardening. "And then she had an accident. Two nights ago. Drove right off the side of a cliff. She'd been drinking of course, and now she's gone. It's very sad."

His words hit me like physical blows. No, knives. Knives slicing through my stomach, sending my intestines falling to the kitchen floor in a quivering, bleeding heap.

"You're lying."

"No, honey, I'm not lying. She's been getting wilder, more irra- tional. Telling crazy stories, can you imagine? I tried to stop her but she just wouldn't listen. You know how she is when she's drunk. When the cops showed up at the house I didn't believe them at first, either. I had to go identify her body yesterday morning. It's definitely her."

"Fuck you," I growled. "She said you were beating her up. What did you do to her?"

"Nothing, Becca. She did it to herself."

I hung up the phone, looking around my apartment. Tears filled my eyes. I didn't want to believe him—could he be lying? Oh, God. *Please*. The phone rang again. Teeny.

"Don't hang up," he said quickly.

"You're lying," I said, my voice flat. "You're lying like you always lie. What's your game, Teeny?"

"You're in denial, Becca. But don't worry, I took a picture of her at the morgue, so that you could see for yourself. Perhaps you shouldn't look—such a disturbing image . . . But you do what you think is right."

Then he laughed and I knew it was true. She was really dead. Teeny was way too proud of himself and I knew in that instant he'd killed her.

Murdered her, just like she'd said he would.

And I let it happen.

A sudden vision of her came to me. I'd been five years old, maybe six. It was Halloween, and she dressed me up like a little princess. She was dressed like a queen, and we'd gone trick-or-treating for hours, followed by a sleepover in the living room.

I couldn't remember the town or where we'd been living or anything like that . . . but I remembered the crowns we'd made together. She'd used wire to build the frames, then we'd covered them with tinfoil and glued on bright glitter.

She'd been the most beautiful thing I'd ever seen.

"She's really dead, isn't she?" I whispered, my voice small.

"Yes," he replied. "She's really dead. Here's the reality, sweetheart—she was a bad wife and she got what she deserved."

I threw the phone across the room.

That. Evil. Bastard.

It started ringing again. Not the headset I'd thrown, but the one in my bedroom. He was there, waiting for me like some sort of hideous troll determined to destroy everything I loved. I shouldn't answer. I knew I shouldn't answer.

"Hello," I said, my voice dull.

"It's really sad about your mom," Teeny said. "I'm devastated, naturally. Losing your wife is a terrible thing. Fortunately I've met someone else already and now that she's gone, it simplifies my life. That's why I thought it would be best to put this final decision in your hands."

"Decision?"

"She's already been cremated, of course," he said. "Can't have a body lying around forever. It's up to you what happens next, Becca. There are final expenses—these things aren't cheap."

Numbness had taken over my body. I stared across my room, trying to wrap my head around the reality that my mother was actually dead. Then his words sank in.

"These things aren't cheap."

Suddenly I understood. I understood all of it.

"What do you want?" I asked, the emotion draining from my voice because I already knew the answer. Teeny wanted money. Teeny always wanted money.

I felt his triumph through the phone, hateful toad.

"Three thousand dollars," he said. "You send me that and I'll send your mother's ashes. I'll text the photo of her body and a picture of the death certificate as soon as we hang up. You have three days to send the money. Otherwise I'm dumping her out."

The phone call ended.

God, not even Teeny could be this evil. But he could. He was capable of anything, and we both knew it. I walked out to my kitchen and slumped down into a chair, bumping the table. The vase of wildflowers I'd picked last weekend tipped over, spilling water across everything. *Goddammit*. I reached over and grabbed it, throwing it at the wall with all my strength.

The shattering sound it made was sweet in my ears. Crisp. Clean.

Liberating.

I looked around the apartment for something else to throw. What I saw sickened me, it was so pathetic. A thousand little touches over the years had turned my place into a home. Some of them were my own creations—pillows and curtains. Throws. I'd taken cheap art posters and hung them on the walls, as if that could ever give me a hint of class.

Who the hell did I think I was fooling?

It didn't matter what I did or where I lived, because one thing would never change. Becca Jones was trash. My mom had been trash. Now she was dead and the same evil bastard was *still* calling the shots, like a poisonous spider I'd never be able escape from.

Everything I'd done was a lie.

Time to destroy it. All of it.

I pushed myself up and out of the chair so hard it crashed over backward. Then I stomped into the kitchen and grabbed the chef's knife Regina had given me when I first moved out. It was sharp. Maybe too sharp, because I'd cut myself on it more than once. It stayed sharp, too, because Earl had given me a whetstone to go with it, and the crazy man wasn't above doing spot checks to make sure I cared for my tools, kitchen and otherwise.

Lifting the knife, I tested the edge with my finger, a line of red fire appearing.

The pain felt good.

Simple and easy to understand, unlike the pain still ripping through me every time I pictured my mom's face. Had he beaten her to death? Shot her? Maybe he just got her drunk and pushed the car over the edge—that would be simple enough.

Why the fuck hadn't I found a way to get her the money?

I grabbed the couch cushion I'd made from Earl's old shirts and sank the knife deep inside, pretending it was Teeny's face. Then I ripped it open and pulled out the stuffing, throwing it on the ground. Next was a wall hanging I'd made from strips of cloth sewn together in a sunburst pattern. Didn't take long. After that I went after the posters. They ripped almost too easily, making a beautiful tearing noise that failed to satisfy.

Spinning, I looked for something else to destroy.

The curtains. Tearing *them* would be better . . . They were more work, which was good. The red fabric was heavier and I had to drag a chair over to reach, because when I tried to yank them down they were too strong for me.

Earl had hung the rods, and Earl didn't do shit halfway.

First I cut them into strips, savoring the sound of the knife ripping through the threads. Then I pulled the rods down, throwing each of them across the room in a different direction. In my mind they were spears, punching holes through Teeny's chest.

Strips of fabric puddled like blood across the floor.

I eyed my couch. I wanted to kill it. I wanted to kill *everything*. I started toward it, figuring I'd start with the cushions before I attacked the frame. I could use my hammer on that part.

Fuck you, Teeny!

A glint of reflected sunlight caught my eye.

My Singer.

She sat there in the turret window, bathed in light, calling to me. The machine was a work of art. Smooth, black lines. Perfectly oiled, ready and waiting to create something beautiful. They'd painted it with real gold leaf, and not even the electric motor could tarnish its glory.

That Singer was a thing of beauty.

Too bad that beauty was a *fucking lie*.

Regina had given it to me, and I'd been so proud because she'd trusted me with it. Idiot. She told me to use it to create, to design a new life for myself. This was the kind of machine that a mother gave to her daughter as a sign of her love, but only in a real family. A normal family.

It sat there in the sunshine, pointing at the ceiling like a middle finger.

Putting me in my place.

Fuck this. Fuck *all* of it. I bypassed the couch with grim purpose, my decision made. Of course, I flubbed the grand gesture by tripping over the bin holding my fabrics, falling on my face. The knife went flying. Somewhere in the back of my brain I realized that my nose was hurting.

I wiped it with the back of my hand, then stared at my skin, mesmerized by the sight of bright red blood.

The blood between my legs had been red. After Teeny got me that first time, Mom took me into the bathroom and hosed me down in the shower. I remembered watching the stained water swirl around and around before it disappeared down the drain. I don't know what I expected after that.

No, that's a lie.

I expected her to save me.

I expected her to put me in the car and start driving far far away.

Instead, she cried and I cried but when it was all over, nothing changed except Teeny visiting my room at night. Then he'd started sharing me with his friends and there'd been more blood.

Catching the edge of the Singer's wooden cabinet, I steadied myself. The legs were wrought iron—stunningly beautiful in their own right. The whole fucking machine was art and it was perfect and creative and it had no fucking place in my life.

None.

I staggered to my feet, then reached down to lift the entire thing up. It was heavy, but not too heavy for me. I wasn't some useless, delicate little girl who'd been spoiled and fussed over. Nope. I was strong. I'd survived rape, I'd survived Teeny, and I'd damned well survive losing my mom.

It took two tries to raise the Singer high enough, but I managed it.

Then I turned to the window. The sun was shining down across the mountains, bathing me in light just like it'd illuminated the Singer earlier.

Mom would never see that sun again.

Hoisting the machine, I threw it through the curved glass with a scream. The shattering sound broke the air and it was more beautiful than I could've imagined. Vaguely I realized there were shards of glass in my hair and my clothing but I didn't give a shit.

Nope.

My work wasn't done yet.

I reached for the fabric bin, hoisting it next. On top were the squares I'd started cutting for the Jacob's Ladder quilt. Stupid, stupid, *stupid* little fuckers . . . I dumped out the plastic tub through the window, then tossed it through to join the shattered machine on the street.

"What the hell is going on?" someone shouted. I looked down to find three very startled people staring up at me.

One of them was my former boss, Eva. Her eyes were wide and her mouth was open. Combined with her heavy makeup and fake red hair, she looked just like a clown. A nasty, hateful clown. I flipped the bitch off, then reached for the plastic chest holding all my craft sundries and bobbins. The lid flew free as I chucked it, sending threads and ribbons flying out into the air like an explosion of colorful textile fireworks.

Suddenly my stomach rebelled.

Too much pain, too much anger, too much adrenaline. Breakfast was coming back up, and it was coming up fast. I ran for the bathroom and missed, crashing into my kitchen table in the process.

That's where I threw up the first time, a disgusting mixture of half-digested food and fresh blood from my nose. The second time I made it to the sink.

I stood there, panting and crying. People were still yelling outside, then I heard someone pounding on my apartment door.

The enormity of what I'd done hit.

I'd destroyed Regina's sewing machine.

The same machine I hadn't been willing to sell to save my mother's life. What the hell was wrong with me? How could I ignore my mother's suffering to protect a fucking machine?

Dear God, how was I going to explain it Regina?

I stood slowly, ignoring the pounding on my door as reality crashed around me. Teeny had murdered my mom and he was going to get away with it. I'd never even get her ashes unless I paid him off.

No.

Just . . . No.

The thumping on my door continued, but I didn't pay any attention, because suddenly things were so incredibly clear. How come I hadn't figured it out earlier? I felt a hysterical laugh trying to force its way out as I ran into my bedroom and grabbed a backpack. I had to work fast—any minute someone would call Regina and Earl, tell them that I'd lost my mind. That I'd thrown their precious family heirloom into the street.

Maybe they'd forgive me for that. Probably. That's the kind of people they were. Now wasn't the time to find out, though. I had way too much to do and I couldn't risk them stopping me—the last thing I needed was to drag them down with me as accomplices. I started grabbing clothes and stuffing them into the bag. Leaning across my bed, I picked up the cigar case on my bedside table and shoved it in, too.

Bathroom.

Brushing my teeth with one hand, I grabbed my toiletries with the other. Shampoo, conditioner, razor. Makeup. All of it went into the backpack, which I threw over my shoulder. My purse still hung from the little hook on the wall next to my door. It had my money inside—fourteen dollars. Pathetic. That wouldn't even fill my gas tank.

But I knew where I could get more.

Flinging open the door, I nearly ran Eva down as I pushed past her. She shouted something at me, which I ignored. Eva didn't matter anymore. None of it mattered. My little blue car sat waiting for me out in the alley. She'd been good to me, and now I needed her to be better—we had a long drive ahead of us.

All the way to California.

And when I got there? Well, then I'd use my other family heirloom from Regina and Earl to kill Teeny Patchel. End this shit once and for all.

I couldn't wait.

THIRTEEN

An hour later I pulled up to the Vegas Belles Gentlemen's Club. The adrenaline and initial explosion of anger had faded, leaving me tired but determined. My phone had been blowing up the entire drive. Regina. Earl. Danielle. Blake. Even Darcy tried to get in touch. Apparently my tantrum was the biggest thing to hit Callup since . . . Well, since my fight at the Breakfast Table last week.

Oops.

Not that it mattered—I had a job to do, and I'd worry about Callup afterward. Odds were good I'd never come back here anyway. I couldn't risk making Puck an accomplice any more than I'd risk Regina and Earl—he'd already spent enough time in prison. The thought of leaving hurt, but the thought of Teeny continuing to live hurt even more.

I had to end it. End him. Maybe I'd get lucky and find my mother's ashes at his place, but that wasn't the part that mattered.

What mattered was killing him.

To do that I needed money, enough money to get down to California and then hopefully get away once I finished. I could try to borrow it, of course. But anyone who helped me would become an accomplice to murder. We couldn't have that. Nope. This one was on me, no one else. I might not be much better than my mother, but at least I wouldn't take anyone else down with me.

I'd work at the Vegas Belles for a day, get as much cash as I could, and then start driving. If I ran out of money on the way, I'd stop at another club and do it again.

Too bad I hadn't gotten over my precious dignity in time to save my mom.

The bouncer at the door recognized me. I'd stopped to clean up, of course, and change into something more suitable. I remembered the bartender's words and wondered if she'd been serious about the blow job.

Probably.

Oh well. I'd had to do worse.

"Welcome back," he said, opening the door for me. "Decide you want to work after all?"

"Yeah," I said, putting on my friendliest, least crazy face. "I got cold feet last time—now I'm ready to go."

"It's your lucky day," he said, winking. God, men were stupid. "We've got the big boss coming in from out of town, and three of the girls called in sick. Don't fall on your face and you'll get hired, no hassle."

That was lucky. About time something went my way.

The same bartender was inside again. She frowned when she saw me and I wondered what her problem was. Then I realized it really didn't matter, because I wasn't here to impress her. I just needed to convince them to let me work long enough to collect a couple hundred bucks.

Then I'd never see them again anyway.

She walked over to me.

"You should leave," she said in a low voice. "Not a good day to start here."

"I need the money. Is the manager around?" She nodded tightly, then pointed toward the door leading to the hallway.

"Go down to his office," she said. "We got VIPs coming in soon. He's busy, so go fast."

"Thanks."

"Don't thank me," she muttered. "Fucking stupid to come back here."

Stupid? She didn't know the half of it. I walked across the room, noting that only one waitress was working the floor. There were two men sitting near the stage, where a girl danced slowly. Her heart really wasn't in it, and I couldn't blame her. Two customers weren't enough to make any money.

Shit.

What would I do if I couldn't earn enough? Crossing my fingers, I walked over to the door leading to the office. Three big men stood out in the hallway wearing "Security" shirts. More bouncers.

"I'm supposed to talk to Mr. McGraine about a job," I said, looking between them. "The bartender sent me. I already talked to him once this week—he said I could come back if I changed my mind."

One of the guys nodded.

"He's on the phone. Give it a minute, and then I'll ask him."

"Okay."

We stood there for long seconds, me trying to look like I knew what I was doing. One of the men checked me out blatantly the entire time. A second was checking his phone while the third—the one who'd talked to me—stood still and blank as a statue.

Kind of creepy.

I felt a nervous giggle building in my stomach, and I swallowed

it down ruthlessly. I couldn't afford to blow this by doing something stupid. Finally the big blank guy knocked on the door, as if
in response to some secret signal only he could hear.

"Yeah?"

"You got a girl here to see you, boss," he said. "Says she talked
to you earlier this week. Looking for work."

"Send her in."

He nodded at me as he opened the door. This was it. Taking a
deep breath, I stepped through. Inside I found three men, McGraine
and two I didn't recognize. All of them wore suits and an air of
nervous tension filled the room.

"Hi," I said, trying to radiate confidence. "I don't know if you
remember, but—"

McGraine cut me off.

"You still looking to dance?"

"Um, yeah, I am."

"Great, you can start right now," he told me. "Half the staff
called in sick. You can do lap dances. Don't want you on the stage
until I've had a chance to see you perform. In a while we've got some
guests coming in—you do whatever the hell they say. We'll make it
right with you afterward, got me? Don't worry about collecting
money up front. You'll get whatever you're owed and a cash bonus."

That sounded shady. My eyes narrowed.

"Do you have any paperwork . . . ?"

"Later," he snapped. "Get your ass into the dressing room and
get ready. They'll be here in twenty minutes."

McGraine strode over to the door and opened it. "Crouse—you
take her back. Have one of the other girls fill her in on the house
rules."

Then he shoved me out the door—and it was a real shove, as in
his hand on my lower back, propelling me through—and I found
myself staring up at the bouncer who'd been checking me out.

Of course Crouse would be the creeper. Just my luck. He smiled at me.

"Follow me."

The "dressing room" was more like a locker room—obviously the budget for fixing up the interior hadn't stretched to give the girls more than the bare essentials. There was a row of metal cabinets along one wall, two big mirrors, and a counter with a utility sink.

Three girls were getting ready—one of them was obviously a waitress. She wore a black corset top, a short black skirt, and black fishnet tights. Her shoes were a good five inches tall, and they made my feet hurt just looking at them.

"New dancer," Crouse announced, looking over the women. One wore a bra and G-string, and the second was dressed like a slutty cowgirl, complete with a lariat. All of them jumped when Crouse spoke and I got the sense that employee morale wasn't very high at the Vegas Belles.

Didn't matter to me. This was all about the money.

"Hi, I'm Venus," the cowgirl said. "When did you start?"

"Right now," I replied, feeling a little nervous. "Mr. McGraine just hired me."

They exchanged looks.

"Lucky you," the waitress said. "It's not always that easy. They're fucked today—bunch of people didn't show up."

"They said I can't dance on the stage until they have a chance to audition me," I explained, feeling almost apologetic. If the bartender had been telling the truth, these women had done more than just show up to earn their spots. "I'm supposed to stick to lap dances."

"Try to get them in the champagne room," said the half-naked girl. She leaned forward into the mirror, carefully layering her lashes with mascara. "Get the right guy in there and it won't matter that you aren't up on the stage. Just don't forget to tip the waitresses."

"Thanks, Claire," said the one in black. She tied a little apron around her waist, then smiled at me. "You'll do great."

Then she turned and walked out of the room.

"What are you going to wear?" asked Venus the Cowgirl.

"Um, I have some lingerie," I said, looking around awkwardly.

"Grab a locker," Claire said. "Doesn't matter which one. Put your shit in there and pull out the key. The bartenders will hold on to it for you while you dance."

That didn't seem like the best of systems, but I figured it didn't really matter if someone cleaned me out. I'd only be here one day anyway. I'd left my purse and a spare set of keys hidden in the car. Earl had built a secret compartment into the trunk, so I should be safe even if someone broke into it, unless the entire car got stolen.

I supposed if that happened I was fucked anyway.

"Let's see what you've got," the cowgirl said.

I pulled off my shirt, showing them the black and red bra I'd bought the other day at Walmart. It wasn't perfect, but it would do. Then I unzipped my pants and pulled them down. Underneath I wore a matching thong.

They exchanged unimpressed glances—apparently stripping at the Vegas Belles was more sophisticated than at an MC clubhouse. Noted.

"I'll take you shopping after the shift ends," Claire said. "You'll make more with something else. It'll have to do for today."

"Thanks," I replied. "How naked do you get for the lap dances?"

"On the main floor, keep your bra on," Claire said. "We do full contact here, but if they want your boobs they can buy a room. You take a waitress with you . . . Oh fuck."

"What?" I asked anxiously.

"We don't have enough waitresses." She frowned at me. "Okay, here's the situation. You're not supposed to go into a room without a waitress. They bring the drinks, but they're also in there to keep an eye on you, make sure you stay safe. Sometimes guys don't listen

to the rules, you know? The waitress can get a bouncer for you . . .
Except today we only have two, which means you'll be on your own."

"I guess we'll just have to let the security guys know they should
stay close," Venus said. "If we need them, we can always scream."

"I want to go back to The Line," Claire announced. "This is
fucking ridiculous. I shouldn't have come over here. They give all
the good shifts to the Vegas dancers anyway."

A man stuck his head in.

"You're on in two minutes," he told her, then disappeared again.

"That's Trey. He does the music and announcements," Claire
explained. "Okay, let's get out there. If you have any questions,
don't be afraid to ask. There's hardly anyone in the club right now,
but we should have more at noon. Lots of guys come over from the
tech park on their lunch breaks for a quickie."

"Quickie?" I asked.

"Whatever happens in the champagne room is up to you,"
Claire said, winking. "Just remember, the house gets a cut. Lisa—
she's another dancer—held out on them and someone beat her up
in the parking lot. You figure it out."

"Shit."

"Yeah. Okay, let's go."

It's one thing to bravely determine you'll make enough money to
fund a road-trip-slash-killing-spree by selling lap dances. It's
another to actually do it. Close to fifteen men were in the club now.
I knew they had money and that I wanted to get the money from
them. I even knew what to do to them to make it happen. I just
wasn't sure how to get started.

"Walk over and ask him if he wants a dance," the friendly waitress said, coming to stand next to me. "Look at that guy in the
corner. He's just been sitting there for half an hour. I'm sure he'd
buy a dance from you—he's hardly even watching the stage, which

means he's here for something else. He's a big tipper, too. Gotta love that in a man."

She nodded toward a figure sitting in the shadows.

"Okay, I can do this," I said, then started walking toward him. They really needed better lighting in here, I decided. Dim light might be a stripper's friend, but this particular corner was like a black hole.

I glanced at the ceiling and realized the bulb was out—that's why I couldn't really see him until it was too late.

"Hi, would you like to buy a dance?" I asked. A hand shot out, catching my wrist. "Hey, you can't do that . . ."

My words trailed off as he leaned forward. Oh fuck. Then he stood up and I decided I must've done something truly horrible in a past life. It was Painter. The same Painter who'd dragged an unwilling woman out of the clubhouse last night.

Worst. Luck. Ever.

"Let's go to the champagne room," he said in a low, menacing growl.

"Um, I don't think that's a good idea," I replied, trying to back away. He didn't give an inch, something dark and predatory in his gaze. I'd seen that look before. On Puck. Painter was hunting. I needed to get the hell out of here. Immediately.

"I've made a mistake," I babbled. "I'll leave now. You can tell Puck I'm going home. He can talk to me there."

"Too late," he said. "Champagne room. Now. Get your ass in there."

My chest tightened.

"What are you going to do to me?" I asked, my voice a whisper.

"We got a problem?" a man asked. I looked up to see Crouse looming over us. Painter's hand tightened, and I considered saying yes. Then he'd fight with Crouse and I'd have a chance to get away. There must be a thousand strip clubs between here and California—I'd go to one of those instead.

Yeah. Perfect solution.

I'd just opened my mouth when someone caught my eye. Behind the bouncer.

Demon.

Oh double fuck, I thought. Everything fell together in my head. The meet last night. Puck having "shit to do" all day. The clubs were up to something and if two of the brothers were in here right now, odds were good that I'd found myself right in the middle of it.

The Vegas Belles *had* opened up right down the street from The Line . . . This was bad. Real bad.

"Everything is okay," I squeaked. "He's an old friend—I was just startled to see him here. We're going to the champagne room now."

With that I grabbed his hand and started dragging Painter across the room toward the hallway housing the champagne rooms. Along the way I saw one, two . . . three other men from the clubhouse. None of them wearing their colors.

Definitely a major operation. Painter followed me, his face grim, as Crouse opened up the last door on the right for us.

"You need a waitress," the big man told me.

"The other girls told me we'd be working without them today," I replied. "Because so many didn't show up to work."

Jesus. They must've had an idea what's going on . . . More pieces fell together. The bartender saying it was a bad day to start. Half the staff gone.

"I'll be outside," Crouse said, glaring at Painter. "She's new and I like her. Don't fuck her up or you'll pay."

Giving a high, nervous laugh I shut the door and turned on Painter.

"What the hell did I walk into?" I asked.

He stepped toward me, darkness written all over him.

"If you needed to know that, we would've told you. See how that works? Why the fuck are you here, Becca? Puck thinks you're safe at school. I don't like bitches who lie to my brothers."

I swallowed, noticing how he stood between me and the door. For the first time I realized that maybe bringing him in here wasn't such a great idea. No witnesses. Crouse might be outside, but there was a lot of music in the club, too. Would he be able to hear me if I called for help?

"They said some important people were coming into town today. Is that why you're here?" I said, trying to distract him. The room was only about ten feet square. I felt my back hit the wall. Painter stepped into me, his body hard and unforgiving. Then he leaned down and spoke directly into my ear.

"Do you realize what I could do to you in here?" he asked. "How dangerous this is? I could rape you, Becca. Kill you. Blackmail you. Hell, I could even force you to spy on the Silver Bastards, now couldn't I? Or has that happened already? Are you working for the Callaghans? Puck's gonna want to know the details."

He reached up and caught a lock of my hair, combing it out with his finger, then stroking my shoulder.

"I just needed some money," I said, terrified. "This seemed like the best way to get some fast. One shift here, then I was leaving town. Puck never has to know."

"Puck and I don't lie to each other," Painter snapped, stepping back. He ran a hand through his hair, glaring at me. "We did *time* together, do you know what that means? My life was in his hands every day—couldn't lie to him if I tried."

"Not even for his protection?" I whispered. Painter shook his head.

"You don't get a vote, so shut the fuck up," he replied. "Shit's going down soon. I love my brother and for some reason he cares about you, which makes you my problem. I'm assuming they have video monitoring in here, so we're going to have to pretend for a while. I'm gonna sit on that big, comfy chair for a while and you're gonna sit on my lap and wiggle around. Don't get in my face and don't piss me off more than I am already. I'll tell you what to do when the time comes."

With that he turned and sat in a smooth, leather-covered chair in the center of the room. I'd been so focused on him that I'd hardly noticed it.

"Lap."

Then he whipped out his phone and started sending text messages without looking at me. I walked over and dropped my G-string-clad ass into his lap, praying very hard I wouldn't feel a hard-on.

Oh, thank God. Nothing.

I gave a sigh of relief—I'd screwed men to survive before, but I wasn't sure I could handle it again. Not with Puck's friend. I closed my eyes and started wiggling my butt, making sure to stay as far forward as I could.

Had anything ever been more awkward in the history of time? No. No, it hadn't. I wanted to disappear, just completely cease to exist.

"In a few minutes things will start happening," Painter said quietly. "Sure you've figured that much out. Here's something to consider—you fuck things up for us, it won't be *your* head that rolls."

"What do you mean?"

"You're Puck's old lady. That means he's responsible for everything you do. You ruin things today, he's the one who pays. Choose your actions carefully. Right now this is still a private matter between him and you. Not that anyone will be terribly impressed with your shit, but punishing you will be his business, not ours. Once your actions impact the club, retribution moves to a new level."

My stomach roiled and I thought I might throw up.

"I had no idea you'd be here today," I whispered, wondering if he'd ever believe me. Did it even matter? "If I'd known, I never would've come. All I wanted was enough money to get out of town . . . I'm sorry. God, I fucked up everything."

"Save it for Puck. I don't care about your bullshit."

Horrible, awkward silence fell as I continued rubbing against him. I started counting in my head, focusing on each number to keep myself from freaking out, making things worse. Then a loud scream cut through the music drifting in from the club, followed by some thudding noises.

"That's it," Painter said, shoving me off the chair. I landed on my knees and found myself scrambling to get out of his way. "You stay in here, keep your head low, and don't fuck anything up. I'll send Puck to get you after it ends. Do not talk to anyone about this or I will personally hunt you down and kill you. Got it?"

I nodded quickly, eyes wide.

"Got it."

Painter nodded, stepping across the room to open the door. He gave me one final look. "My brother deserves someone better than you."

Nodding my head, I agreed with him. He really did.

PUCK

Boonie and I pulled up behind the club in the van. A prospect sat in the driver's seat—he'd stay there for the duration, ready to take off as soon as we came back out. In less than a minute we'd walk over to the back of the Vegas Belles building, where our plant, Maryse, would let us in through the emergency exit by the champagne rooms. We'd debated quite a while over which route to take—the rest of the club had gone in through the front. The other exit would take us closer to the office, but would be harder for Maryse to reach, too. Not only that, any firepower in the building would be concentrated there.

Another van pulled up near the far exit. Waiting. So far as we knew, the men inside were clueless about the raid. Jamie Callaghan and his entourage had gone inside five minutes earlier. If things went right, he'd spend less than ten minutes total time in the building.

My phone buzzed.

PAINTER: Problem. Beccas in here. I put her in a private room.
She's safe, but we need to pull her out bef leaving

What. The. Fuck.

For a minute I thought my head might explode. *Becca was supposed to be at school.* I started typing a text back, then realized it was pointless. We didn't have time to talk, let alone change the plan. Painter had saved my life more than once, a favor I'd returned. I'd have to trust him.

"Becca is inside," I told Boonie. He nodded sharply, although I knew he had to be curious. A thousand possible scenarios ran through my head, each one worse than the last.

No matter how I looked at it, there was no excuse for her to be here. None. Christ, had she been working for the Callaghans all along? Impossible.

"Time," Boonie said. We started toward the door, which opened on cue. Maryse held it as we entered, then she bolted toward the van. The prospect would protect her until it was time to go. I passed by the champagne rooms, wondering which one held Becca. Didn't matter now—the best way to protect her at this point was to finish out the operation as fast and efficiently as possible.

Then I'd have time to strangle her in comfort.

We passed through the hallway and onto the main club floor. Painter and Gage held two groups of people hostage, already ahead of schedule. Six of them were obviously customers, terrified men who'd been herded back into a corner with several strippers and waitresses.

In the center of the floor stood four more men, hands on their heads. Two wore "Security" shirts while the others had on suits.

Jamie Callaghan's entourage. There'd been three of them total.

If our count was right, that meant six more men were in the building. The bulk of the brothers was out of sight. According to the plan they'd gone for the office, hopefully grabbing Callaghan and McGraine and pulling them out through the back and into the vans.

"You good in here?" Boonie asked.

"Under control," Painter replied. "Other team is already down the other hallway."

"Okay, I'm joining them," Boonie said. "Puck will cover me while I go back. Then he'll do a sweep and hold the fort with you."

"Sounds good," Gage rumbled. One of the customers spoke up hesitantly.

"We don't want any trouble," he said. "This is between you guys—we haven't seen anything. Let us go and we'll never talk about what we saw here. I promise."

"Sit tight and you'll be fine," Boonie said. "You're right—it isn't about you. You keep your mouths shut and in an hour it'll be like this never happened. Of course, you talk, you die. We'll hunt you down no matter where you go. There are hundreds of us, all over the country, so silence is really your best option."

One of the waitresses started sobbing quietly.

"Shouldn't have started working for the competition," Boonie snapped, his voice heartless. "Shut the fuck up."

She shoved her arm across her mouth, muffling the noise. Time for us to move on. I followed Boonie across the room, gun in hand. The door to the second hallway was propped open, with Ruger and Horse standing guard against the far wall. Two more bouncers lay on the floor in front of them, hands folded behind their heads.

"It's clear," Ruger said, nodding at Boonie. "They're in the office."

Boonie started down the hall as I turned back toward the main floor.

"How clear are we?" I asked, moving on to the next phase.

"Double-check the bar, then hit the champagne rooms," Gage

said. "We've kept count—nobody's back there but Becca, unless someone's been hiding since before the club opened. Clear the rooms then come back to help with the hostages."

All according to plan.

I ran back into the hallway and started opening doors. There were six of them, and the first four were empty. Then I opened the fifth. I almost missed Becca at first—she'd tucked herself into the corner behind the door. When she saw me her face turned white.

"I can explain," she whispered. The sight of her—half naked—should've set me off. Instead I went totally cold. Five years. *Five fucking years* I'd waited for this woman, treated her like she was glass. Held back. Now she was waving her tits in a fucking strip club. How long had she been coming here? Had she ever been in school at all?

No, she couldn't have worked here long—someone would have seen her. None of it made sense—not that it mattered right now. I had to get her out of here and finish clearing the rooms. I'd figure out what the hell was really going on after we finished up.

Fucking bitch.

"Get out of here," I said, grabbing her arm and jerking her into the hallway. "Go out the back door. You'll see a van there—get inside and wait for me."

She nodded quickly, stumbling as she ran toward the emergency exit.

I turned to the final door.

That's when shit got real.

FOURTEEN

BECCA

I'll never forget the look on Puck's face when he found me hiding in the champagne room. Not disgust, or anger . . . Not even betrayal.

Much worse.

He'd looked right through me, eyes as dead as Painter's. Up to that point I'd managed not to think about him, not to consider the consequences of my actions on our relationship. It wasn't that I'd expected to take off for California and then come back to pick things up where we left them.

I really hadn't been thinking at all.

Now—as I reached for the bar on the exit door—reality struck. I'd destroyed us. Whatever "us" there had been, I'd killed it because I was fucked in the head.

More evidence that everything I'd fought for in Callup was a lie. Girls like me didn't get happily ever afters. We got dark strip clubs and men with guns, right up to the point where it all ended in an orgy of violence. If we got very lucky, we got to be the murderers and not the victims.

From the look in Puck's eyes, I might've landed on the wrong side of that equation.

I turned to look at him one last time—no way I planned to go sit quietly in that van and wait for him. The MC had a job to do here, and it didn't include chasing me down. If I could reach my car, I still had a fighting chance.

Puck was reaching for the final door when it slammed open between us. Crouse came out swinging, catching Puck under the chin and knocking him across the hallway. The gun flew and then it was in Crouse's hand. He pointed it at Puck, holding him pinned to the floor.

Holy. Shit.

What the hell should I do now?

"Get outside, girlie," Crouse said over his shoulder, his words a growl. "This doesn't have anything to do with you. Get out and run away before shit gets worse."

My eyes darted between him and Puck. This was it. Crouse had given me a shot and I should take it. I couldn't do anything for Puck anyway.

Push through the door and run for the car. You don't have any choice.

Shouting came from the main room, then Painter appeared at the end of the hallway. He had his gun out, pointing at Crouse. The big man kept his own weapon on Puck, hands steady.

Standoff.

"The girl can go," Crouse said, jerking his head toward me. "She's not part of this."

Painter's eyes caught mine, and he nodded sharply. Britney Spears's voice burst out through the sound system, perky and happy and so out of place I wanted to smash my head against the wall.

Smash my head . . .

In brackets right next to the door was a nice big, shiny red fire
extinguisher. Suddenly I knew exactly what to do. I reached for it,
popping it free as I held Painter's gaze. His eyes stayed blank,
revealing nothing. I slid out of my heels silently, lifted the metal
canister over my head and raised it high.

The noise it made when I cracked Crouse over the head was loud
enough that not even the music drowned it out. Puck exploded into
motion, rolling to the side and jumping to his feet. Damned good
thing, too, because Crouse's gun went off, punching a hole right
where he'd been only seconds earlier.

That never happened in the movies.

Of course, in the movies Crouse would have been knocked
instantly unconscious, which also didn't happen. He was pretty
damned wobbly, though, so when Puck tackled him and grabbed
for his gun, it wasn't exactly a fair fight.

Then it was all over.

Crouse stood unsteadily in the center of the hallway, hands
raised.

"Out with the others," Puck growled at him. The big bouncer
glanced at me one last time, and then to my shock he winked.

What the hell was that about?

Apparently Puck wondered the same thing, because I saw him
studying us closely. Great. Just what I needed.

"Get out while you can, girlie," Crouse said again, then he started
lumbering down the hallway. "Men like us are no good for you."

"Take her out to the van," Painter snapped at Puck. "Something's wrong here. Maybe she's in on it."

Puck nodded, catching my arm with hard, unforgiving fingers.
Bright sun hit as we opened the door, stepping out of the dark
underworld of the club into the clean, fresh air.

"You have a lot to explain," he said, shoving me into the van. I fell down hard, and then he was handcuffing me to a rail mounted on the side of the rig.

Well. So much for stripping.

PUCK

We drove in silence, following the van that held Jamie Callaghan and his buddies. Boonie sat up front with the prospect, while Painter and I covered the back. Becca huddled against one side, shivering. I kept expecting her to cry or beg or show some kind of emotion.

She didn't even look at me—totally lost in her own world.

Why the hell had she been in that club? None of it made sense. The worst-case scenario was that she'd been working for the Callaghans, but it didn't add up for a lot of reasons, not least of which was the fact that she'd tried to kill a man to save me.

(Had to admit—the image of Becca in her bra and panties fighting was gonna feature heavily in my future fantasy life. Felt the stir of a hard-on every time I thought about it.)

Sexy wasn't a defense, though. I needed to face reality. If there was the slightest chance she was spying for the Callaghans, blood would flow. Was it possible? No. Becca was a local girl, zero connections to them. Not only that, if she'd been working at the Vegas Belles regularly instead of going to school, I'd have known about it. We didn't have the place under 24/7 surveillance, but we had our spies inside. They'd given us a list of employees.

She wasn't on it.

According to Maryse, she'd only been in there once before. She'd told me right before we dropped her off, and the woman had no reason to lie.

The van swayed as we turned off the highway and onto the gravel road to the Armory. The old National Guard fortress belonged to the Reapers, serving as a clubhouse, flophouse, and makeshift prison. They owned the land for miles around it, too.

Jamie Callaghan was going to have a very unpleasant night.

Thankfully this wasn't my problem—my part of the raid was done. As soon as we unloaded I planned to throw Becca onto my bike and take her home to get some answers. I glanced at her again and revised my plans. Get her some clothes first. *Then* throw her on my bike. Maybe I should fuck her, too. Yeah. That was a plan. After that, though, I'd definitely be getting some answers. The van stopped and we slid the doors open. Painter and I hopped out, slamming the doors behind us.

Boonie walked over to me, frowning.

"You gonna leave her in there?" he asked lightly.

"No, but figured I should check in before taking off," I said. "You feel like this needs to be club business? Otherwise I plan to treat it like a personal issue."

"The bouncer had a thing for her," Painter chimed in. "But I don't think he even knew her name. Just thought she was pretty and Maryse backs that up. Becca was only there to make a quick buck—no reason to get the club involved."

Boonie nodded.

"I'll talk to Pic about it, but I tend to agree," he said. "This is your problem, Puck. Any idea why she'd want to get a job stripping? Can't wrap my head around it."

"Puck, can I talk to you?" a woman's voice called. I looked up to see London, Picnic Hayes's old lady, walking toward me. The others were "escorting" Callaghan and his men out of the other van right in front of her, but she didn't pay any attention. Instead she frowned at me.

Fucking great. Picnic was gearing up to torture a guy, but London wanted to give *me* shit.

"What?" I asked, knowing my tone bordered on rude because

I'd never liked her. Stick up her ass, and she'd betrayed Pic. I'd never quite forgiven her for that.

"I got a call from Darcy earlier," she said.

"What's going on?" Boonie asked. "Everything okay?"

"It's about Puck's old lady," London said. "Darcy didn't call you guys because she knew you were busy, but something bad happened."

I waited. "What?"

"She said that Becca went crazy earlier today. She threw a sewing machine out of her apartment into the street, right through a window. Bunch of other stuff, too. Then she took off in her car and hasn't been answering her cell phone. They've got no idea if she's still in the valley or what happened, but her entire apartment is destroyed. No signs that anyone was in there with her, or that she was attacked—Darcy said she did it by herself."

Jesus. This shit just got weirder.

"Fuck," Boonie muttered. I rubbed my forehead. Whatever had happened to send Becca to that strip club, it was extreme.

"One last thing," London said, digging around in her pocket. "They checked the history on her home phone. Before she left, she got several calls from this number."

She pulled out a piece of paper and handed it over. Southern California area code. All the pieces fell into place and sudden rage filled me. Christ, I wanted to punch something. So obvious.

"It never fucking stops. It was her mother—that bitch is like a disease."

"What's going on?" Boonie asked.

"Cunt's been after her about money," I growled. "Just bullshit games, but Becca falls for it every time. If something went down, she probably wouldn't talk to me, either. We got in a fight over it."

"Darcy's worried," London said. "If you've got any idea where Becca is, you should call and tell her. I guess there are other people who want answers, too."

Fucking great—just what I needed. A committee.

"She's in the van," I said, forcing myself to keep my voice steady. I wanted to shout or kick something. God, I hated that bitch. "Will you call Darce and let her know everything is okay?"

London stared me down. "When you have to haul women to the Armory in the back of vans, everything is not okay."

That caught me short. Fuck.

"Completely different situation than yours was, London," Boonie said. "Believe me. Keep us posted, Puck."

"Sure," I said, turning back to the van. I caught the door and slid it open, climbing in to unlock Becca. Sensing we had more of an audience than we needed, I slid the door shut behind me again.

"What happens now?" she asked, her voice dull. Why did she keep letting her mom do this? I'd hauled her ass out of there five years ago, yet she still danced whenever the woman called. Bullshit.

"You're going to start by telling me why you destroyed your apartment and threw your sewing machine out the window," I said, unsnapping the handcuffs. Becca sat up, rubbing her wrist. "Then we'll move on to the whole stripping thing."

"I wasn't trying to cause trouble for the club," she said, avoiding the first question. "Whatever was going on down there, I wasn't part of it. I don't know anything about the Vegas Belles."

"I know. Just get your ass outside."

I opened the door and she slid out, still barefoot. London glanced between us, then shook her head.

"You want some clothes for her?"

"Yeah, that'd be great."

"Take the room on the second floor," she said flatly. "I'll send Mellie up in a little while with something for her to wear."

"Mellie's here?" Painter asked.

"Yeah, I'm watching Izzy for her tonight," London replied.

"Why?"

"None of your business."

Painter narrowed his eyes. Fuck this. I had enough of my own drama.

"Let's get out of here," I snapped at Becca. She followed me silently, ignoring the curious looks from the Reapers and Silver Bastards still milling around the courtyard.

BECCA

"In here," Puck said. I walked into the room and turned to face him, still feeling numb. I'd had that one burst of energy when he'd been in danger, when everything had gone sharp and clear. Then it faded back into the dull pain of grief and guilt.

Puck shut the door, crossing his arms over his chest as he leaned back against the wall. "Okay, tell me what the fuck is going on."

"My mom is dead," I said, deciding to lay it all out. "I needed enough money to go to California. Figured I'd work for an afternoon at the club, see if I could make some quick cash."

He sighed, rubbing a hand over his chin.

"Sorry about your mom," he said finally. "I'm assuming that's why you lost your shit and threw your sewing machine out the window?"

"In my defense, Eva was walking by outside. I was hoping to hit her."

"This isn't a joke, Becca."

"Oh, I think it's a joke all right," I replied bitterly. "Do you know what I've spent the last five years trying to do?'

"What?"

"Not turn into my mother," I replied. "Yet here I am in an MC clubhouse in nothing but my underwear. What's that bed for?"

He looked at it, puzzled—the thing was old and battered, the blankets so thin they hardly qualified.

"This is one of those rooms the old ladies won't clean, isn't it?"

I asked, raising a brow. "I know what this place is. You run trains in here, don't you? You and all your friends and whatever poor whore is stupid enough to let herself get sucked in. I swore I'd never see one of these rooms again, Puck. Then Teeny called me and I'm right back where I started. I have to fix it."

Puck's face hardened.

"You're not thinking straight," he said coldly. "I'm sorry your mom is dead but you need to shut your mouth."

"Fuck off, Puck."

He started toward me, grim purpose written all over his face.

"If you needed money, you should've come to me," he said. "I'm your old man. Shit like this happens, you're supposed to call me."

Seriously?

"Couple problems with that scenario," I snapped. "One, you're not my old man, yet you keep telling people I'm your old lady. I haven't agreed, Puck. Takes two people, did you know that?"

"Becca—"

"Don't condescend to me," I continued. The anger was pushing through the numbness. It felt good. Really good. "I'm an adult and I've been taking care of myself for years now."

"And a fucking great job you're doing, too. Where are your clothes, Becca? Oh, wait. You lost them during a raid on a strip club. Was that before or after you threw everything you owned out the window?"

"Teeny murdered my mother!"

Puck froze.

"What?"

"He killed her," I said, my throat tightening. Shit. I was going to cry again, and I didn't want to cry. I wanted to be strong and angry. Focused. "She warned me. She said he'd kill her unless I sent money for her to get away, but I didn't have the money. I even went to the strip club earlier this week—figured I'd try to earn it for her. But I couldn't go through with it because I had my precious dignity and school and *you*, asshole. Yeah, that's right. I didn't want to lose you, so I let her go instead. Now she's dead. He killed her."

Puck stepped toward me, but I held up a hand. He ignored it and I fell into his arms, tears breaking free. Then he rubbed my back softly. God, why was he being so nice? It made everything harder.

I wanted to fight, not cry.

"Okay, let's figure some stuff out," he said finally. "First—and I have to ask this—do you have any real proof she's dead? He might be lying to you."

"My cell phone," I whispered. "It's back at my car, but he sent me pictures. From the morgue. Also a death certificate. It's real."

"Okay," he replied. "And how do you know he's the one who killed her?"

"Because she said he would. She begged me to save her and I wouldn't. This is my fault."

"No," he said. Suddenly he was looking me right in the eye, holding my shoulders in both his hands. "You didn't cause any of this. This is *not* your fault—she made her own choices and they included hurting and using you. If you told her no, it was because you were smart enough to save yourself. About fucking time, too."

"You just had to add the last part, didn't you?"

He didn't respond, although I saw his mouth tighten. Good. I'd gotten to him.

Silence fell in the room.

"So why did you need money for California?" he asked finally. "Is he having a funeral?"

I shook my head bitterly. "No, but he said if I wanted her ashes, I had to pay him. A lot."

"You're fucking kidding me."

"Three grand. If I don't send it, he's dumping her out."

Puck's face darkened, and I saw the little muscles in his jaw clench. "So he called to say your mom's dead and then shake you down. You weren't going to earn three grand at that club, Becca.

Not in a day—and you had to know I'd come looking for you when I heard what happened. What's really going on?"

I considered the question. If I stalled him, sooner or later I'd get my car back. I could still go after Teeny.

"Answer the fucking question, Becca."

"I wanted to get her ashes."

"You know I'd help you."

"Your help comes with strings."

"I get it," he said suddenly. "You think if you attack me enough I'll give up. Answer. Now. Why were you going to California?"

"I was going to kill him," I admitted. "I don't feel like I'll ever be free unless he's dead. Maybe it sounds crazy, but he's an evil, evil man and he doesn't deserve to live. That's why I didn't talk to anyone—I didn't want to turn you into my accomplices."

Puck growled, then pushed away from me to stalk toward the window. He leaned forward on it, fingertips turning white as he squeezed hard. I supposed I should be glad he wasn't squeezing my throat.

"Did it occur to you that I could take care of this?" he said, teeth clenched. I looked at him blankly.

"What do you mean?"

"You asked once what I do for the club. I fix problems. Teeny is a problem."

I swallowed.

"You can't do that."

"Yeah, I can," he replied, turning back to look at me. His eyes darkened, and I shivered. I'd only seen him like this once before, the morning he'd stolen me away. All hot anger burning under a surface of cold purpose. So dangerous. "If you want him dead, I'll make it happen. But you have to fucking talk to me about it."

"You sound like a sociopath," I blurted out. *Shit*. "I can't believe I said that."

Puck came over and caught the back of my neck, jerking me into his body. The air had changed between us—there'd been anger before. Now there was more.

"You belong to me," he growled, cupping the side of my face with his other hand. I felt his fingers wrap around my jaw, oh-so-close to my throat. "That means I take care of you. I thought you were safe from your stepdad. He's still hurting you, though, so you're not safe. Now I'll solve that problem so he never hurts you again. That doesn't make me a sociopath—that makes me your old man."

Then his mouth took mine, tongue thrusting inside brutally. The horror of the day, all the adrenaline, everything hit me all at once. I'd been dying slowly inside all afternoon, but now I felt alive again. I reached up and caught his hair in my hands, pulling him into me with a force I'd never used before. Puck groaned, then shoved me down and back onto the bed.

The mattress was spongy and soft. The blankets were old and faded. God only knew the last time they'd changed the sheets.

I didn't care.

All that mattered was the feel of him as he shoved my legs apart. Then his hand was down between us, digging under my thong. His fingers found my center like a target, shoving deep inside.

My back arched and I convulsed against him. It wasn't an instant orgasm, but it was something damned close. Like all the tension I'd been carrying that day was desperate to escape but couldn't quite pull it off without his help.

Puck broke free from my mouth, then dropped his head and grabbed my bra with his teeth. My breast popped free and he sucked it in almost painfully. Need exploded between my legs, a tension that ran from my breast to my clit, where his thumb started working me.

"Puck," I moaned.

He pulled back and gave a harsh laugh.

"Nothing like an angry fuck, huh?"

His words struck me.

Angry fuck. That summed up what I wanted perfectly . . . Something dark and rough and free from any kind of concern for his needs.

I pushed up, catching his chest with my hand and shoving him over. The move caught him off guard and he went down.

Then I was on top of him, straddling his body as I tore at his shirt. Puck was a smart man—didn't take him long before the fabric was up and over his head. I reached behind my back, trying to find my bra hooks but my fingers turned awkward. Finally I just pulled the whole thing up and over my head. Then I was down across his chest, rubbing my nipples into his as I ground my clit against his cock.

"You aren't my old man," I growled, staring into his eyes. Puck bared his teeth at me as his hands caught my ass, fingers digging deep into the flesh. His hips bucked up.

"You're mine. Pretend all you want, but this is my cunt, my ass, and I don't share you with anyone. I'll protect you and you'll take care of me and there's not a goddamned thing you can do about it."

My back arched when his fingers stabbed me again. Then I was flying over and onto my back, legs up and around his body while his hips ground me down into the mattress.

"This," he said, thrusting his fingers again. "This belongs to me."

Puck's other hand started burrowing and I shuddered. He'd found my asshole, wiggling against it with savage pleasure.

"This is mine, too," he added. "And if I want your mouth, I'll fuck you there. You want more. Admit it."

"Fuck off."

"Nope," he said, pulling his hands suddenly free. Then he spread them on either side of my head and pushed up. That pressed his dick down hard into my pussy. Nice.

But why wasn't he moving?

I needed him in motion, pressing against my clit and making me scream. The tension inside me needed to get out. I was going crazy—had been going crazy all day. This was the first thing that made sense, the first thing that didn't hurt my soul.

"Goddammit, Puck!" *I need you.* I couldn't say it, though. Couldn't give him the satisfaction.

"Admit you're my old lady," he growled again. "Just say the words and I'll fuck your brains out."

"No."

Puck took a deep, shuddering breath and started to lift his body off the bed.

"Yes," I gasped, reaching for his butt, pulling him into me desperately. "I'll be your old lady. Whatever. Just fuck me!"

Puck's eyes flared, and then he was reaching between us, ripping open his pants. Seconds later he thrust inside. My entire body shuddered and I screamed, the relief was so intense.

I wasn't there yet, of course. I need more motion, more penetration, more of everything.

Damned good start, though.

Puck's hips drove deep, over and over again. I tried to match his rhythm at first but it was hopeless. He was too heavy, too hard. Too fast. It was all I could do to hang on as he pounded into me.

We were so close now.

Sweat broke out all over my body, a light mist that slicked our flesh and made every touch that much more exquisite. Puck paused. I moaned, digging my fingers into his flesh, and he laughed.

Then he dropped his head and gave me a long, slow kiss.

"I like fucking my old lady," he said, eyes taunting me. I squeezed him deep inside, payback for that little cruelty, and he laughed. "Just keep punishing me like that, babe. I'll suffer through, somehow."

I slapped his ass and he bucked, but it got the job done. He started moving again, long, slow strokes now. The angle was exactly right and his pelvic bone pressed hard against my clit each time, right to the point of pain.

Then he'd pull back, starting the cycle over again.

Each time I got closer, but not close enough. An eternity passed as I twisted beneath him, gasping for breath.

"Please . . ." I moaned, although I wasn't sure who I was moaning at. Did it matter?

Then he changed his pace, pushing inside before pausing for a twist. By the second time it was all over. I blew apart with a gasp of relief, my mind clear for the first time since I'd gotten the phone call about my mom. Puck came with me, groaning and shaking as his seed pulsed into my depths.

Then he collapsed over my body.

"We should fight more often," he managed to say after a long pause. I nodded.

"Yeah, definitely."

"You're still my old lady."

"If I say yes, will you listen to me?"

"Sure."

"I don't want you to kill Teeny."

Puck stilled.

"What do you mean?" he asked, his tone guarded.

"I want to kill him," I whispered. "You have no idea how much he's made me suffer. I need to do it, Puck. I want to see the look in his eyes right before he dies. I want him to feel as much fear as I did. Give him a taste of what he did to my mom. Then I want him to beg for mercy right up to the instant I shoot him in the head."

Puck rolled to the side, throwing an arm across his face.

"And you called me the sociopath," he muttered. "You got no idea what you're talking about, Becca. It doesn't matter how much someone deserves to die—when you take a life, you lose some of yourself, too."

"I'm going to do it," I told him. "Do you really think you could stop me? Sooner or later I'll find a way if you don't help."

He sighed.

"Let me think about it."

That was it. In that instant I knew I'd won. I couldn't wait to see the look in Teeny's eyes when I shoved the gun into his mouth.

Three thousand dollars.

He just had to get greedy.

PUCK

"Boonie, you got a minute?"

I'd found my president downstairs, arms crossed as he leaned against a cement pillar. I'd been down here enough to know it wasn't a pleasant kind of place. This was where the Reapers took their prisoners. Some came back out. Some didn't.

I had no idea which category Jamie Callaghan fell into and I didn't care.

The metal door leading to one of the rooms opened, and Picnic stepped outside.

"We got a problem," he said to Boonie. "Or at least a complication."

"What's that?"

"Callaghan says he's got something on Shane McDonogh. Something big. He's taken precautions—if he disappears, it'll blow up in his face."

"Kill McGraine," Boonie said. "That should settle Jamie down."

Pic shook his head.

"I think there's an opportunity here," he said. "We broker a peace between Callaghan and McDonogh, it could buy all of us the time to find a long term solution."

"The valley can't afford to let Callaghan live."

"He's just one of them," Picnic said. "You kill him, another one will pop up in his place. Changes nothing. If we let him go now, he's willing to shut down the Vegas Belles. Not only does that take out our competition, but it sets him back in terms of ability to siphon cash off the mine."

"We should run it by McDonogh," Boonie said thoughtfully. "I can see the value, but we need his buy-in."

"Why?"

Boonie sighed, looking tired. "Because it's about more than your fucking strip club, Reese. We're playing a long game here and the entire valley's at stake. I want to talk to him before we make a decision."

"Email Malloy," I suggested. "McDonogh's tough to reach, but maybe they can sneak you in like they did me."

"I don't think I'll blend in quite as well," Boonie said, his voice dry. I shook my head.

"Doesn't matter. You meet him in the woods behind his building, nobody will see you anyway. That's where I went before. Anyone could've done it."

"I'll give it a shot." Boonie pulled out his phone and turned it on.

"Hey, I still need a minute," I said, wishing I didn't have to interrupt him. "The situation with Becca. It's serious."

"What's up?" Picnic asked.

"Her mom's dead. That's why she lost her shit earlier today. Becca's convinced her stepdad killed her, and she's decided to hunt him down and put a bullet in his head."

Suddenly I had their full attention.

"What the fuck?"

"She went to the Vegas Belles to try and make some quick cash. Was planning to drive down to California and shoot him. Obviously she's not thinking straight . . . Don't know how the hell she imagined she could pull it off."

"Don't underestimate a desperate woman," Pic said, his voice grim.

"I told her I'd do it," I said. "I don't want her carrying that burden the rest of her life. Not sure she could handle it."

"She's stronger than you think," Boonie said. "But I hear you. What's the plan?"

"Figured I'd start by making sure I won't touch off a war if I put this guy in the ground. He's a hangaround with the Longnecks and his brother's a patch holder."

"They're nothing," Picnic said dismissively. "I'll let Shade know at national, but he won't care. They're weak and they're cowards—we've got no respect for them."

I felt some of my tension lift. One less thing to worry about.

"In that case, I'd like to drive down there and take care of things myself," I said. "Becca wants to come with me and I said she could. Figure I can round up one of the nomads to help keep an eye on her while I finish the job."

"Sounds good," Boonie said. "Keep us posted."

"You got it."

He leaned forward and gave me a rough hug, slapping my back. Picnic followed suit, and then I was heading back upstairs.

I found Becca in the kitchen, talking to London. She wore a loose pair of jeans and a faded Reapers support shirt. It had to be the least sexy outfit I'd ever seen her in, but she still made it work.

Funny, that.

I came to stand behind her, slipping my hands around to feel her stomach. London watched us, sipping a cup of coffee.

"You need anything for the road?" she asked. "Sandwiches? Snacks?"

"How'd you know we're headed on a trip?" Becca asked.

"I smelled drama," London said, her voice dry. "Drive safe."

I pulled Becca close, hoping London was wrong. Taking out Teeny shouldn't be any more dramatic than smashing a bug. He wasn't worth the emotional energy—hopefully I'd get Becca to see that for herself.

FIFTEEN

BECCA

Puck refused to leave until the next morning, despite my begging and pleading. He said it was already too late in the day and he was right.

Still pissed me off.

At first he'd tried to get me back to Callup for the night, which I flatly refused to do. I wasn't ready to face Regina and Earl, not after what I'd done. He didn't trust me to stay by myself, though, so I ended up hanging in the kitchen for a few hours at the Armory with London Hayes, Reese Hayes's wife. Darcy had called over— apparently she wanted to come check on me. After she saw the look of horror on my face, London convinced her to stay home.

I hadn't been brave enough to tell Danielle where I was, although I texted to say I was safe and with Puck. She was a tough girl, and with Blake at her back I had no doubt she'd try to invade the

Armory. Odds were good she'd do it, too. Danielle was many things, but cowardly wasn't one of them.

Regina and Earl also wanted to talk.

I couldn't do it. They had to know what I'd done by now—Callup wasn't a quiet kind of town. I begged Puck to call them and let them know I was all right.

He frowned, but he did it.

Then he drove up to Callup to pack a bag, stopping off at the Moose to let them know my mom had died. Teresa was wonderful about it, making me feel even guiltier that I hadn't called her earlier.

In fact, the longer I sat in bed (and no, not the nasty one on the second floor—once Puck decided to leave me there, he arranged for a real room), the more my guilt grew. There were people who cared about me. People who'd given me everything, yet when things fell apart I didn't reach out.

After this was all over, I'd go to them. I'd make sure they knew how much I loved and appreciated them.

Well, unless I was in prison.

Of course, that was probably less likely now that I had Puck with me. Sure, he'd been caught before—but only once. He had to have learned something about covering his tracks along the way, right?

God, I hoped so. I didn't want him going to prison on my behalf. He didn't seem particularly worried about that happening, though—I knew this because when he finally crawled into bed after returning to the armory, he told me.

"I'm your old man," he said. "You need to trust me. I'll handle it."

"How will you handle it?" I asked, my head tucked against his chest. "I'm part of this—I need to know what the plan is."

"Your job is to follow my lead," he replied. I opened my mouth to protest, but he rolled me over on the bed. Then his fingers were inside me and I totally forgot about the question.

The drive was supposed to take around twenty hours, which we'd do over two days. I'd suggested that if we weren't going to leave right away, we should consider driving straight through on Friday. Puck pointed out that arriving all exhausted wouldn't help our cause, but he was on board with leaving at six the next morning and putting in a long day.

We'd pulled away from a truck stop after dinner when Teeny called Friday night. I stared down at my phone, paralyzed.

"What should I do?"

"Answer it," Puck said. "Tell him that you're getting him the money—you can say you're working me for it. Then ask about your mom's ashes or something. Anything to get him talking. Maybe he'll give us something we can use."

Nodding, I answered. "Hello?"

"Becca, I expected to hear from you by now," my stepfather replied, his voice all smooth and smug. "You make any decisions yet?"

"I'm working on getting the money," I said, parroting Puck. "Um, there's this guy . . . We haven't been together very long. He's not sure he wants to help me out. I need a little more time to convince him."

Teeny gave a knowing laugh.

"Little slut."

I wanted to throw the phone out the truck window. Instead I looked at Puck, all strong and silent next to me. He reached over and gave my leg a squeeze. Just that little touch steadied me.

"I'm doing what it takes," I told Teeny. "How are you handling things? I would imagine this is kind of crazy . . ."

"Call me when you have the money," he said, ending the call.

So much for pumping him for information. I put down the phone, staring ahead at the yellow stripes splitting the road.

"I take it he didn't feel like chatting?"

"Nope. He's all business. Wants his money."

"It's not too late," Puck said.

"Too late for what?"

"To end this," he replied. "Just walk away. I can still take care of him for you."

I considered his words—shit was getting real now. Did I really want to kill a man? Would it actually solve anything? The more I turned it over in my head, the more certain I was of my answer.

"I want to look in his eyes and tell him that he's dying because of me. I want him to beg for mercy and say he's sorry . . . I want him to cry. Then I'll shoot him anyway and it'll be a very good thing."

"Remind me not to piss you off," Puck said lightly. I turned to look at him. His eyes stayed fixed on the road, one hand casually draped across the steering wheel. His hair was rumpled, he wore a faded shirt and even more faded jeans, and every inch of him was hard, strong muscle. An inappropriate tendril of lust wound through me.

"You know, it's really creepy that my mom's dead and I still want to have sex with you."

Puck glanced at me.

"Not really," he said. "When shit falls apart it's a distraction. Adrenaline does it, too. I never want to fuck more than I do after a good fight."

"I remember," I murmured, shivering. He'd been so intense when I'd first met him, tangible hunger in his gaze as he took my hand.

"Don't worry," he continued. "No matter how tired we are, when we hit the hotel I'll find the energy to screw you. You'll get better sleep that way."

"That has to be one of the most arrogant things I've ever heard you say," I sputtered. "God, what am I? A chore?"

Puck laughed.

"Love fuckin' with your head."

I smacked him. Annoyingly, he didn't even flinch. Could've been a gnat for all he noticed. "You'll pay for that. Maybe I'll demand a room with two beds and make you sleep on your own."

"You don't get to pick the room," he said. "I'm paying for it and I want a king-sized bed. But even if you were paying, you'd still be in my bed. That's how it works, babe. You belong to me now."

He wasn't joking.

"When you talk like that it makes me nervous."

"Why?"

"Because I've worked really hard to build my own life. I don't want to hand off control to anyone—and I'm a person, not a thing. You don't get to own me."

Puck nodded his head, but didn't respond. I watched him for long minutes, waiting for something. Finally he flipped on a turn signal. We pulled off the road and he put the truck in park, turning to look at me. His eyes were dead serious, not a hint of smile touching his mouth. Silence filled the truck.

"You need to get this straight, Becca" Puck said slowly. "You're mine. You seem to think that's still up for debate—it's not. I've claimed you and the club agreed. That's how it works in my world. End of story."

The words cut through me and I felt my blood pressure rise.

"That doesn't mean you can tell me what to do."

"I'm driving to California to kill a man for you. Are we really arguing about which bed you're sleeping in?" he asked, leaning toward me. I pulled away but Puck was too fast for me. With a snap, my seat belt came free. Then he caught my neck, jerking me across the seat until our noses all but touched.

"You're mine. I fought for you five years ago and then I let you go. That was your free pass. Now you've invited me back in and I'm here to stay. I'll kill for you. Die for you, too. But I will not fucking let you go, Becca, and I won't let you distance yourself, either. Get that straight."

I shivered, because I could see just how serious he was. It was scary . . . and sexy. That just seemed so wrong—what kind of woman gets off on a threat like that?

Me, apparently.

Puck's lips found mine, his tongue sweeping along the seam. "Open."

When he pushed inside I melted, one hand coming up to twist into his hair. The other slid lower, catching on his thigh and squeezing it. Puck groaned and guided it higher, toward the bulge of his cock. I caught it and squeezed. Puck shifted, lowering his butt so that I could reach more easily.

Sliding my fingers up and down, I started jacking him through the jeans. A part of me was vaguely aware that he was using sex to distract me, but I didn't care. I just loved the way he shuddered under my touch.

Finally Puck pulled away from my mouth, leaning his head back against the headrest. I looked up at him, still working his cock, and he met my gaze. Then I licked my lips. He groaned.

"Suck me off."

Nodding, I held his eyes as my hands fumbled with his fly. Impatiently, he shoved them out of the way, lifting his hips long enough to shift his jeans. Then his hand—still on the back of my neck—pushed me toward him.

This was where I should've stopped to make a spirited, well-thought-out argument about whether a woman could or should be owned. Unfortunately I was way too turned on. My nipples had hardened and the space between my legs clenched.

I pulled out his dick slowly, then leaned over and licked the underside of the head. Puck groaned, raising his other hand to tangle his fingers in my hair.

"Inside."

My mouth opened and I obeyed, pressing the bottom of my tongue against his length. My hand found his shaft, working it as my head started to bob, Puck's hands guiding me and setting the rhythm.

Men had held me this way before—bad men. I knew how easy it was to lose control of the situation. Normally just thinking about it was enough to scare me. Now it turned me on in a big, unhealthy way that I decided I really shouldn't think about. Nothing good could come from facing my own fucked-uppedness.

Puck had been right about one thing—we'd crossed a bridge somewhere along the way and things were different now.

His breathing came faster and I found his hands tightening, growing rougher. He wasn't hurting me, but he wasn't giving me much in the way of control, either. Strangely, there was something liberating about that—I didn't have to debate how I was doing or whether it was a mistake. We were past that point. All that mattered now was the taste of Puck in my mouth, the slick length of his cock between my fingers.

He was close. I could tell from the way the ridges in his cock hardened, and the catch in his breath every time I drew him back into my mouth. My tongue was getting sore but I kept going, mindless in my determination to get him off.

Maybe then he'd get me off.

I certainly wanted it. My legs shifted restlessly under the flowing cotton skirt London had given me that morning. We'd gone and picked up my car, so I had my own clothing in the back, but there hadn't been any reason to change.

Too bad we were twisted across uncomfortable truck seats, because I wanted to reach down under my skirt, touch myself while I touched him.

Not exactly practical under the circumstances.

"Becca, you're so fucking hot," Puck groaned. "When I think of all the shit I'm going to do to you . . ."

That should've scared me. Instead—when his hand pushed my head down just a little harder—I found myself sucking him even deeper. The tip of his cock reached the back of my throat. I started to gag and he loosened his grip immediately.

This caught me off guard.

Not the fact that I'd gagged, but that he'd given me a little too much, realized it, and let me go. He hadn't hurt me for real. I didn't start to panic and I wasn't even scared he'd push it too far. Hell, I was still turned on.

Holy shit.

I started to laugh, which is a damned awkward thing to do while you're giving a blow job. I caught myself and refocused, but a weird kind of giddy glee kept threatening to overtake me.

A man pushed his dick into my mouth until I gagged and it wasn't scary!

More giggles broke free in awkward little bursts. Finally Puck tugged on my hair, pulling my mouth free.

"It's creepy as fuck when you laugh at my dick like that. You wanna share the joke?"

I pushed myself up, looking at his face. Poor Puck. I smiled at him.

"You didn't scare me."

"Huh?"

"Just now—you shoved your dick too hard down my throat, you had your hands on my head and everything. Then I gagged and you let me go."

"Not exactly my goal to kill you," he replied, obviously confused.

"But here's the thing—I wasn't scared when you did it. I knew you wouldn't hurt me. That's a first for me."

Shock covered his face.

"You tellin' me you've been afraid every time we've fucked?"

I shook my head quickly. "No, but it's the first time a man's ever stuck his cock down my throat and held my head that I haven't been afraid I'd die."

Abruptly my smile faded.

"Wow, that sounds so fucked up when I say it out loud."

Puck nodded slowly, his eyes still wary. The truck rocked as a semi blew past.

"Shit," I said, pulling myself up. "I think that guy saw us."

"So?"

"He'll think I was giving you head!"

"You *were* giving me head."

Jesus, the man was impossible. I glared at him and he sighed.

"Okay, the fact that me fucking you isn't scary is great. Having said that, my dick's still stickin' out and I'm starting to wonder if I should put it away."

He said it all tough and badass, but the question in his eyes was real. Poor guy—I'd probably given him blue balls. Fortunately I knew how to fix that . . . Smiling up at him, I licked my lips and leaned back down.

After a few minutes his hands found my head again. Then his breath grew tight and his hips strained upward. Triumph filled me because in that moment one of us definitely owned the other—Puck was mine, pure and simple.

An hour later I still felt triumphant. I couldn't stop smiling, and I found myself babbling about anything and everything until Puck wanted to strangle me. I knew this because he told me. Not that I cared—nothing could kill this mood.

"I still can't believe it," I told him. "I wasn't thinking about Teeny at all!"

Puck scowled.

"Do you usually think about your stepdad while I'm fuckin' you?" he asked.

"No, it's not like that," I explained, rolling my eyes. "It's just that he . . . well, he got off on that. Choking me."

Puck's face grew dark and I saw his finger tighten on the steering wheel. "Why the fuck haven't you told me that before?"

"Um . . . It's not really something I start all my conversations with, Puck. 'Hi, I'm Becca. My favorite color is red and I hate being choked with cock.' Um, no. That's not how it's done."

His death grip on the steering wheel tightened.

"You started laughing in the middle of sex because I wasn't hurting you," he snapped. "If you've got shit that's going to fuck with your head, I should know about it. What if I'd really scared you?"

"You won't," I said, smiling because it was true. "I finally figured it out. That's why I was laughing—it wasn't a bad thing. It's wonderful."

Puck glanced at me with something like pain in his eyes. I reached out to catch his biceps, squeezing it.

"I trust you, Puck. This may sound fucked up, but I just realized that and it's kind of exciting."

He didn't respond for a while, then he dropped his right arm down and caught my hand.

"Not sure what to say," he admitted finally. "I can tell you this, though. You're my woman and I'm not going to hurt you. We can play all the games you like and I won't lie—rough sex gets me off. But I'd never knowingly hurt you, Becca."

"I know. I never thought I'd find someone like you . . . It means Teeny didn't win. He beat my mom, but he hasn't beaten me. I still hate him and I still want him dead, but he didn't win. That means everything."

PUCK

Becca was snoring.

Not loud, annoying snores. More of a soft, snuffling irregular purr. We were a few hours outside Las Vegas in some shithole little hotel that we'd found after sixteen hours of driving. The place was a dump but neither of us cared. We were wiped. Becca had passed right out, but I found myself wide awake, staring at the ceiling.

She'd started laughing because I hadn't choked her with my cock.

I held her hand and said all the right things, but every time I thought about it, killing rage started pouring through me again. Becca's stepdad was garbage—this wasn't a revelation. I'd seen him beating her, known he'd raped her. Known he'd pimped her out to other men . . . I'd even known he still haunted her. I just hadn't realized she thought about him during sex.

I wasn't sure how I should feel about this, but I was pretty sure my actual feelings were wrong, because I felt jealous.

Becca's mind should be on me when I was balls-deep inside her. Only me. Always me. I'd disliked the fucker the minute I met him, a dislike that transformed to hate when I found him beating her. When I'd offered to kill him for her, it'd been sincere. Teeny Patchel was using up valuable air, something that someone should probably fix.

Now, though. Now I had a whole new motivation.

I couldn't wait to see the life drain out of that fucker's eyes.

The burner phone I grabbed before leaving Coeur d'Alene buzzed next to the bed. I reached for it, finding a message from Diesel, one of the nomads I'd reached out to.

DIESEL: You awake?

Typing awkwardly with one hand, I replied.

ME: Yes
DIESEL: Call?
ME: Give me five.

Sliding out from under Becca, I stood and pulled on my jeans. Then I grabbed the phone and stepped out onto the covered walkway outside. The place's glory days had been back in the '60s, and nothing had been updated or repaired since, so far as I could tell. Only two other cars in the parking lot and the office had shut down for the night.

"Hey," Diesel said when he answered.

"Thanks for getting back to me—got a situation I could use some help with. I heard you're in the San Diego area?"

"Yeah, had some business down here," Diesel replied. He was a Reaper and we'd met two or three times at different events. Not a friendly guy, but a solid brother.

"Picnic said you might be the man to talk to," I said. "My old lady's mom died. Now her stepdad wants money or he won't give my girl the ashes. I think we may need to take action."

Diesel grunted.

"What kind of action you thinking?"

"Could be serious."

"I hear you," he replied. "I can be around. When do you get into town?"

"Tomorrow," I replied. "Guy lives in Santa Valeria. We'll hit town around two or three. Figure I'll get Becca settled and then we can go hunting."

"Sounds good."

"One more thing."

"Yeah?"

"She thinks she's coming with us." Diesel gave a startled snort of laughter.

"Uh, no."

"No shit," I replied. "But she won't see it that way. If we've got any allies around, I'd love to have someone keeping an eye on her."

"I'll see who I can drum up," he replied. "Maybe call Shade—I know there's some Devil's Jacks in town. He could reach out to them for me."

"Thanks."

We figured out where to meet and then I hung up the phone,

feeling better. I had no doubt I could handle Teeny on my own, but backup was always our friend. Becca needed a babysitter, too. If I'd learned anything, it was that she never did what I expected.

She was still sleeping when I slipped back into the room. I locked the door behind me and wedged a chair up and under the handle. I climbed into the bed and pulled her over my body like a blanket, soft hair feathering around my chest and under my chin.

Yeah, killing Teeny would feel damned good. Just needed to make sure Becca was protected, both from him and herself. If anyone went down for this hit, it wouldn't be my girl.

Nope. I'd make damned sure of that.

BECCA

We reached Santa Valeria around three in the afternoon. Puck had been quiet for most of the day, his mood almost grim. Made sense to me—I'd never planned out a murder before, but it probably wasn't something to take lightly, all things considered.

It'd seemed so simple up in Idaho. We'd drive down here, find Teeny, and shoot him. Now that we were here, though? All sorts of logistical questions kept bubbling through my brain.

"How are we going to do this?" I asked Puck as we pulled into a gas station. The building hadn't been here five years ago, that much I remembered. Just that one change was enough to throw me off, and I realized how much I didn't know about my hometown, mom, or Teeny these days.

"Don't know yet," he replied, reaching for his wallet. I still had my pathetic fourteen bucks and change in my purse. I'd tried to give it to Puck for expenses but he wouldn't take it.

"I'll go take a look around this afternoon, after I get you settled at a hotel. We'll make plans after that."

He stepped out of the truck, walking toward the station to

prepay, since we'd been using cash for everything. In fact, Puck had been incredibly careful about leaving any traces along the way, to the point of confiscating my cell phone and giving me a burner with only one phone number in it—the disposable cell he now carried. The morning we left the Armory, he'd even handed me a fake driver's license. I assumed he had one, too. He'd also put new plates on his vehicle and when I'd asked him about it, he stared me down silently.

Deciding I wanted to hit the bathroom, I opened my door and stepped out. Looking across to the second set of pumps, my breath caught.

No. *No.*

Holy. Fucking. Shit.

I must be losing my mind because that was my mother standing there, gassing up a battered Camaro.

No. *No way.* This couldn't be happening, could it? I started toward her, wondering if this was another dream. I'd had a couple of them—dreams where Regina told me none of it was real. Mom was fine and she'd left Teeny and we'd all live happily ever after together.

Then I'd wake up and it hurt like I'd just lost her all over again.

"Mom?" I asked, my voice hesitant. The woman froze, then turned slowly toward me. Her eyes widened in shock and . . . horror? "Mom, is that really you?"

She shook her head, eyes wide. I reached for her and she started trembling.

"Becca . . ." she whispered. "I'm so—I mean, I didn't think . . . I'm so sorry, baby. I didn't mean to hurt you."

Her words sank in and realization flooded me. This wasn't some kind of miracle. She knew I'd thought she was dead—her entire body radiated guilt. Holy. Shit.

"Is this about money?" I asked, feeling something break deep inside my soul. "Is this really just another of your cons? It is, isn't it? You thought I'd send you three grand and then what? You'd send up a box of ashes from the fire pit? What the fuck is wrong with you!?"

My voice rose at the end to a shriek. Tears started rolling down her face and she reached for me. I flinched back, realizing I was on the brink of losing it.

"I'm sorry," Mom said, her eyes darting. We were creating a scene. Too bad. "I have to go."

Stunned, I watched as she jerked the gas nozzle free. Then she climbed into her car and pulled out with a screeching of tires, gas cap flying. It rolled across the pavement, coming to a stop about six inches from my foot.

What the fuck had just happened?

"Becca, you okay?"

I looked over to find Puck staring at me, confused. No. I wasn't okay. Tears started to build in my eyes, then I was in his arms, crying.

"Baby, you gotta tell me what's wrong," he said after a few seconds. His entire body was tense—ready for a fight. Shit. I needed to pull myself together.

"It was my mom," I said, forcing myself to stop sniffling. "She's alive."

Puck stilled.

"What?"

"I was getting out of the truck to go to the bathroom. Then I looked over there and saw my mom."

Something crossed his face, a hint of shock tempered with . . . pity?

"Sweetheart, it's not uncommon for someone to think they've seen someone who died."

"No, it was her, Puck," I said, my voice forceful. "I talked to her. She called me by name, said she was sorry. Then she got in her car and drove off. That's her fucking gas cap right there."

"What the hell?"

"It's a con," I said, feeling like the stupidest person on earth. "She'd been calling, begging for money. I kept telling her no so I guess she raised the stakes."

"That fucking cunt," he growled. He let me go, spinning toward his truck in helpless, frustrated anger. For a minute I thought he might punch it. Then—just like that—he pulled it together.

"Get in."

"Puck—"

"Get. In. The. Truck." Rage covered his face, along with that terrible darkness I'd seen from him a few times. Oh fuck. This was bad. Really bad.

Wait. *Mom was alive.* That was good. I didn't want her dead, did I?

Mixed, confused emotions crashed through me as I climbed into my seat. I was vaguely aware of Puck outside, gassing us up. My thoughts flew too fast to catch as I tried to understand what had happened.

Mom was alive. She'd pretended to be dead. Told her daughter that she was dead.

For three thousand fucking dollars.

Pain sliced through me as it fell together. Pain. Relief. Shock. Hurt.

How could she care so little for me, put me through that kind of hell for money? *Because she's a junkie and a crook. She doesn't care about anyone but herself.* Fucking bitch.

The rig swayed as Puck climbed in, looking straight forward. Rage radiated off every square inch of his body.

"This ends now."

"What?" I asked.

"This shit with your mom," he replied. "She's cut off. Today. You're never talking to her again. That woman is fucking toxic and she's out of your life."

"Excuse me?" I asked, turning on him. My head was a swirl of a thousand different emotions—Mom had been *dead* and suddenly she wasn't. She'd tricked me and used me and treated me like I wasn't even a real human being whose feelings mattered. Now Puck was going to tell me how to feel, too?

I didn't need this shit from him and I didn't care if he was right—it wasn't his decision to make.

"It's time to end this. I've watched that bitch jerk you around for five years and I'm sick of it. No more. I'll get you set up at the hotel and then go straighten her ass out. We'll leave for Idaho in the morning."

The swirl of confused feelings in my head came together, turning into anger. I couldn't turn it loose on Mom because she'd run off, but Puck? He'd just painted a big ass target on his forehead and I didn't give a shit if attacking him was fair or not. I was an adult and I'd make my own damned choices.

"Who the fuck are you to tell me what to do?"

The muscle in his jaw flexed as Puck turned the key, the big truck roaring to life. "I'm your old man and it's my job to protect you. I'm serious about this, Becs. We're leaving tomorrow and you are never going to communicate with that bitch again."

Oh no. No way. He did not get talk to me like that.

"Fuck you," I growled. "You have no goddamn right to tell me what I can and can't do. You don't own me and you don't get to control me."

He turned to look at me, and the raw anger on his face stunned me. Holy shit. A small part of me wanted to cower back, to beg him not to hurt me. *No.* I wasn't that little girl anymore and Puck Redhouse didn't get to push me around.

"You'll do what I say, Becca. She lied to you. Put you through hell. What kind of psycho bitch tells her kid that she's dead just to make quick buck? If you still want anything to do with her, you're fucked in the head. We'll leave first thing in the morning."

Red rage filled my vision, no joke. As in, my vision literally turned red. That's how angry I was. I wanted to kill him, destroy him. Here he was, I realized. Here was the biker asshole coming out, the one I'd known was in there all along.

"This is why I'll never be your old lady," I hissed. "In the end, you're all the same."

The words fell between us with a thud.

"I'm too pissed to have this conversation with you right now," he said, slamming the truck into gear. He pulled out into traffic with a squeal of tires, just like my mom had. Crushing pain hit again, and I felt my anger deflate. Why would she do that? How could she do it? What the hell had I done to deserve that woman for my mother?

Fuck her.

And fuck Puck, too. Fuck him for being right about her, and for saying all the things I didn't want to think about out loud.

Fuck all of them.

I started to cry.

SIXTEEN

PUCK

My fingers itched to kill Becca's mom—her and her piece of shit husband. They'd been alive too long, polluting and destroying everything they touched. Fucking disease on the earth, both of them.

And now Becca was crying. Like I was the bad guy here?

Fuck. I knew I was being an asshole. Had known it the instant the words left my mouth. Not that what I'd said was wrong—this was absolutely the end for that bitch and her husband. I'd kill them both if they ever tried to contact her again.

Might still kill Teeny anyway.

But tearing into her like that? That'd been a tactical error, not to mention a dick move. Becca needed compassion and kindness and the right words. I'd never known how to do any of that shit.

Darcy.

I'd call Darcy and she'd tell me what to do. Relief hit as we pulled into yet another shitty little parking lot, attached to another shitty motel. Diesel was already here, waiting on the tiny scrap of grass clearly designated for smokers.

Cigarettes.

Fuck, I wanted one. I could taste it already. If I had a smoke, I'd be able to deal with Becca. That'd do it. Parking the truck, I glanced at her and winced. She was still crying. She wouldn't look at me, either. Nope, she just stared out of the passenger-side window, sniffling because her mother had ripped out her heart and then I'd acted like it was all her fault. Christ. Fucking day from hell. I needed to say something, even I was smart enough to know that. Too bad I had no idea what to say.

"I'll be right back," I told her, opening my door. Ten minutes later I came back with two keys to a room down at the end of the building. Becca wiped her eyes as I grabbed our shit, but she followed me toward the room. Then she caught sight of Diesel, pausing.

"That biker's watching us," she whispered.

"Yeah, I know," I replied, my voice tight. *Get her ass into the hotel, then you can have a smoke.* "I asked him to meet us here."

"Why?"

"For backup," I said. "I don't like heading into shit without someone behind me. He's an ally—that's all you need to know."

Balancing the bags in one hand, I opened the hotel room door and stepped inside. Looked just like every other crappy room in existence. Battered polyester bedspread, TV so old it probably had vacuum tubes.

"We need to talk," Becca quietly, shutting the door. I glanced over to find her staring at me, eyes like open wounds. Wow, this day was just getting better and better.

"What?"

"Will you answer a question for me?"

"Sure."

"Were you ever planning to let me kill Teeny?"

I studied her, realizing it was a trap. Even worse, it was a trap I'd set for myself. "Why do you ask that?"

"You wouldn't make a plan with me," she said slowly. "And now I find out you arranged for another guy to come. He wouldn't want some woman he's never met as a witness. Why were you playing me? I'm not a child, Puck."

"I'm not playing you and I sure as fuck don't think you're a child," I told her, running a hand through my hair. Christ I wanted a smoke. "But you're right—I wasn't planning to let you kill anyone. You've got enough bullshit and darkness in your life already, Becs. Trust me, you take a man's life, you're stuck carrying him forever. I understand why you wanted Teeny dead but no fucking way I'd lay that on you. I care about you too much."

"You seem to think I'm some sort of glass figurine. I'm not going to break, Puck. I'm an adult who's been through shit. I survived and now I'm moving forward. You should've trusted me."

"But it's my job to protect you," I said, wondering how the hell I could make all this go away.

"You can't protect me," Becca whispered. "Life doesn't work that way. Look, I'm sorry I lost it with you. I'm not stupid—I know Mom screwed me over and I know I need to cut her off. But that was something I had to figure out for myself. When you give me orders it pisses me off and then I stop listening."

I sighed. "Yeah, I get it. I'm sorry I was a dick, too. Look, I need to go out to talk to Diesel. Might hit a bar or something. Won't be more than an hour or two, that sound good? I think a little space might be good for both of us right now."

She nodded, looking away. "Yeah, space is good."

Her quick agreement didn't make me happy—shouldn't it bother her that I wanted out? Fuck, what did I want?

A smoke. Yeah. Smoke first. Calm down a little . . . then we could talk, figure everything out. Damn, but relationships were complicated. No wonder Painter couldn't keep his together.

BECCA

Puck had never taken me seriously.

No matter how I looked at it, I shouldn't have been so surprised. That's just how things were in the MC world. An old lady isn't supposed to ask questions. She certainly doesn't stick her nose in club business, not even when it's not club business at all.

Puck himself had told me the Silver Bastards were different from the Longnecks, but they weren't that different. Now what? We needed to find a compromise or this whole thing was dead in the water. That terrified me, because despite our fight I couldn't handle the thought of losing him on top of everything else.

I dropped back on the motel room bed, wondering what the hell was wrong with me. There had to be something, right? Puck treated me like a child and my mom treated me like I wasn't even a real person. Did it really matter that Puck hadn't planned to let me kill Teeny? That was a side issue. Ultimately, this was about my mom screwing me. Again.

She might as well be dead to me.

Rolling off the bed, I walked into the bathroom, washing my face with cool water. That felt better . . . When Puck got back, we'd have a real talk. He needed to know I wasn't going to be an old lady like he thought. I wanted to be with him, no question. But I'd never be happy as one of those puppets who nodded and smiled whenever her man said to.

My stomach growled and I bit back a smile. So what if my world had crashed down around my ears—apparently I still had to eat. I walked over to the window and looked out to see a Denny's on the far side of the parking lost. Maybe I'd treat myself, see how much fourteen bucks could buy at a place like that. Grabbing my burner, I dialed Puck's number.

"Hey," he said, answering on the first ring.

"Hey," I said back, feeling awkward. "Um, I'm sorry to bug you, but I'm kind of hungry. You mind if I walk over to Denny's? It's just across the way."

"Yeah, I can see it," he answered. "Okay. Go grab something and then head right back. Call and let me know when you're back in the room. I might be a while."

"Sure."

I grabbed my purse, checking to make sure the little gun Earl had given me was still inside. Not that I expected to need it, but after all that'd happened anything seemed possible.

As it turned out, fourteen dollars was enough to buy quite a bit at Denny's.

The food improved my mood. Enough that I was starting to feel some serious guilt about the way I'd taken my anger out on Puck. Not that I agreed with him on everything. I didn't. But it was time to face reality—I had an anger management problem and if I didn't figure out a better way to communicate with him, sooner or later it would drive us apart.

The waitress brought my bill and I counted out what I owed plus a thirty percent tip. That left me with exactly one dollar. I shook my head and dropped it on the table, because why the hell not? Then I hit the bathroom. Another woman walked in and took the stall next to me. I finished my business and set my purse on the counter to wash my hands. I'd just reached for a paper towel when I caught a glimpse of her stepping out of the stall.

It was my mother.

At the gas station I hadn't really looked at her. I'd been too startled. Now I took in every wrinkle around her eyes, the gray at her temples, the tremor in her hand . . . Mom still dressed like a biker babe, but she'd taken on that tough, dried-jerky look that comes from too much hard living.

"I'm sorry," she whispered, holding my gaze. The agony in her voice sounded so real I almost bought it. Then I remembered— Mom wasn't human. She didn't have real emotions, not like the rest of us. Nobody who felt real emotions would do what she'd done.

"I want to apologize," she said. "Please, baby. I fucked up. I see that now."

"Fuck off."

"I realized at the gas station—I haven't seen you in *five years*. You're different, baby. All grown up. I can't quite believe it, can't believe I almost threw you away again. Please let me talk to you."

"There's nothing you can say that I want to hear."

She frowned, reaching into her pocket. In that instant I knew something was terribly wrong and I reached for my purse right as she pulled out a gun.

"Drop it and step away from the counter," she said, her voice cold. I dropped it, staring her down.

"I wish he'd killed you," I whispered. She flinched, but her hand didn't falter.

"You're going to walk though the restaurant in front of me like everything is fine," she said told me. "We're going to leave through the door on the far side, away from the hotel. Once we're outside you'll get into the car and we'll leave."

I shook my head.

"Go ahead and shoot me. I'd rather die than get into a into a car with you."

"You're not the one who'll be dying. Teeny is outside, and he's got your boyfriend in his sights. If you don't do what I tell you, I'll call him and he'll take the shot. Start walking."

The backseat of the car was full of garbage and old fast food wrappers. I sat across from my mom, glaring at her as she held the gun on me with one hand. She held her phone against her ear with the other. She'd thrown my purse into the front seat.

"I've got her," she said.

Seconds later Teeny opened the driver's-side door and sat down. I screamed and lunged for my door, because I hadn't been joking when I said I'd rather die than go with them. Teeny slammed the car into gear, tearing out of the parking lot as Mom threw herself at me, smashing my head against the window. Someone had seen us. They had to have seen us. If I could just get out, they'd have to leave me behind.

"Calm the fuck down!" Teeny shouted over his shoulder. I took that as a sign that I should fight harder. Then he stomped on the brakes, sending me and Mom shooting forward into the front seats with a thud.

Teeny turned on me, raising his gun and pointing it at my head.

"I never liked you," he whispered. "Believe me—I want to pull this trigger."

"Don't be crazy," my mom begged. Was that a hint of real feeling in her eyes? "Becca, we don't want to hurt you. This will all work out just fine—you just need to do exactly what I tell you. First up, I'm going to tie your hands and feet with this duct tape. You gotta settle down, sweetie. Otherwise you'll hurt yourself."

I stared at the gun, mesmerized. This was really it—I had to make a choice because Teeny would do it. I saw it on his face.

Suddenly I wasn't so ready to die.

My stepfather glared at me, holding the gun as Mom fumbled with a roll of duct tape. I flexed my muscles, trying to buy a little extra wiggle room as she tied me up. Less than a minute later, she'd secured my hands, feet, and even put a strip of tape over my mouth.

Teeny grunted his approval and pulled back out into traffic.

"Don't worry, sweetheart," Mom said, wrapping an arm around my shoulders and pulling me close like I was a little girl . . . like she wasn't actively kidnapping me. "Mama's here. I'll take good care of you."

We drove for a good forty-five minutes out into the desert, past our old house and down along a dry riverbed. Finally Teeny stopped the car outside a motor home. One of those old ones, like the kind Walter White used to cook meth in *Breaking Bad*.

Knowing my mom, she'd seen the show and been inspired by it.

It'd obviously been parked there long term, and I wondered if the thing could still drive. Probably not. They pulled me out of the car and I hopped awkwardly inside, Mom on one side and Teeny on the other. Sure enough, the camper smelled like cat pee—they'd definitely been cooking in here. Great. Knowing my luck, the whole place would explode.

Mom helped lower me to a small couch on one side of the camper. I think I expected an interrogation, but instead she and Teeny grabbed seats at the little table across from me. Teeny tossed my purse down with a thunk, and then he had my wallet out.

"Nothing," Teeny said after a minute. "Where's your money?"

It took me a minute to realize he was talking to me. I shrugged, unable to answer. He growled and leaned forward, ripping the tape off my mouth. It took the top layer of my skin with it. God, that *hurt*.

"I've told you all along—I don't have any money. I'm a waitress and I'm going to school. I spent the last of what I had on breakfast."

"What about this boy of yours?" my mom asked, her voice almost playful. I decided she was trying to play "interested mom" to get information. I'd give her plenty.

"Do you remember that guy who took me to Idaho? The one who kicked your ass?" Teeny scowled and Mom had the grace to blush.

"That was such a confused time," she said quickly. "I think we all look back and wonder—"

"What about him?" Teeny demanded. Holy shit—he hadn't been holding a gun on Puck at all, I realized. There was no way Teeny would've forgotten his face.

"He's my old man now, and he brought some of his friends with him . . ." I said with a smirk. "They're probably on the way to find me already. You really sure you want to piss him off like this?"

They both stared at me blankly.

"Him?" Mom asked finally. "That same boy?"

"He's not a boy, and he's not going to be happy when he finds out what you did. Let me go now and I'll call him off. Otherwise you're fucked."

Teeny's mouth gaped and I laughed. I couldn't help myself. I could actually see the little ferret inside Teeny's head starting to run faster and faster on its wheel. He swallowed.

"We didn't mean any harm," he said quickly. "You know how impulsive I am. But I never mean anything by it."

"Eat shit, Teeny," I sneered. He bristled. Crap. *Don't piss off the asshole with the gun!*

"We have to kill her," Teeny announced. My heart froze and Mom looked between us, stunned.

"What do you mean?" she asked. "We can't kill her. She's my daughter."

"Like you care," he muttered. "I sold her ass to half the club, you never said a thing."

"She was a big girl—she could handle it," Mom hissed, narrowing her eyes at him. Any other time I might have found concern touching. Now? Now I mostly just didn't want to die. Looking around frantically, I tried to spot something I could use as a weapon. Anything. Unfortunately, the duct tape limited my options in a big way.

That's when Mom and Teeny started going at it. He shouted insults at her as she moved into a full-on hissy-fit, squawking and screeching My purse still sat on the table. The gun was zipped into a side pocket—so far as I could tell, Teeny hadn't noticed out yet. He'd been too focused on my wallet.

If I could get over to the gun, maybe I could . . . What? Grab it with my tied-up hands?

Fuck.

Suddenly Teeny's gun was in my face again. He stood over me, hands trembling, and I saw my death written in his eyes. This was happening. For real. They say your life flashes in front of you when you're about to die—that didn't happen to me. All I could think about was Puck and how much I loved him. Suddenly it was terrifyingly obvious that I'd been letting a good thing slip through my fingers. Why the fuck had I done that? I should've just enjoyed him.

"Teeny, you can't shoot her," my mom was saying, her voice growing hysterical. "That's my baby girl. I was okay with taking her money, but this is different. You don't get to kill her. I won't let you do it!"

"Shut the fuck up," Teeny growled at her. Then his attention focused back on me. "Stop looking at me. Close your eyes. Close them!"

I closed my eyes, mind racing. The gun clicked as he cocked the trigger.

Out of nowhere, I heard my mom howl with rage. Teeny shouted in surprise, then there was a cracking, squelching noise and believe me when I say those two sounds shouldn't go together.

Something hot and wet hit my face as a heavy weight crashed to the floor.

My eyes flew open to find my mom beating Teeny with a bat. A fucking aluminum bat. Holy crap. She smashed his head over and over again, blood spattering everywhere. Reality spun up again and I started to pick out her words.

"No! No! You don't get to hurt my baby, you cocksucking asshole!"

I scooted across the couch as far as I could, trying to avoid the spatters of blood and hair and gray chunks that I really, really didn't want touching me.

"Mom," I called, trying to keep my voice steady. She seemed oblivious. "Mom! You can stop, Mom. He's dead now."

She slowed, panting heavily. The bat dropped out of her hands and bounced against the faded linoleum.

"He's dead," Mom whispered. She looked like something out of a horror movie. Ragged, stringy hair hanging down in bloody chunks. Spatter all over her face and chest. Then she smiled at me, one of her front teeth rotten and gaping.

"I'm sorry about that," she said after a long pause, nodding toward Teeny. I swallowed, wondering what the hell I should say or do. I wasn't dead—that was a good thing. But despite the fact that she'd saved me, Mom was scary as fuck and obviously batshit crazy.

"I need to get going," she announced, and I couldn't tell if she was talking to me or herself. "Need to get out of here. Can't let them find me like this."

"Wait! You have to help me. Just help me get the tape off. You can just drop me in town. It'll all be over."

She glanced down at me, her face suspicious. Suspicious and almost feral . . . Like a cornered animal. I couldn't even tell if she recognized me.

Shit. Trapped in a motor home in the desert with a dead body and a crazy woman.

"Gotta go," she said again, grabbing my purse. She shoved my wallet back inside, then walked toward the back of the RV. I raised my hands and started tearing at the tape with my teeth. I needed to get myself free and get the hell out of here. I didn't think Mom would hurt me, but who knew? She'd obviously lost touch with reality.

I'd worked one strip of the tape loose when she came back carrying a bright red suitcase.

"Okay, then," she said, stepping over Teeny's body to give me a quick kiss on the cheek. "You just sit tight and I'll take care of everything. Don't worry, sweetheart."

She smiled at me, then turned and stepped out of the motor home. Seconds later I heard the sound of a car door closing before she drove off.

I looked down at Teeny's body and closed my eyes.

This really, really sucked.

SEVENTEEN

It took me about ten minutes to get my hands free. The feet were easy after that. Then I was up and moving toward the back of the RV. I don't know what I expected to find there—so long as it wasn't a bloody corpse, that would be an improvement.

Stepping into the tiny bathroom, I caught a look at myself in the mirror. There was blood on my face. Blood and . . . brains? Oh fuck. *Fuck*. Trying not to panic, I turned on the water and scrubbed myself frantically. After a couple minutes the sink wheezed and ran dry. I clutched the edges of the counter, trying to catch my breath.

At least my face was clean. Now what the hell should I do next? *You can do this.* My phone had been in the purse, along with my gun. Thank God for Puck and the fake ID he'd provided—if Mom ditched it somewhere, it wouldn't lead straight back to me.

Fuck, if only that was my biggest problem. That title went to the dead guy waiting for me outside the bathroom door. I didn't know where I was, didn't have a phone, and the only potential escape vehicle was a meth camper. Of course, odds were good the RV couldn't drive anyway, which made things even better, right?

I needed to look around, see what I could find to work with. Oh, and not lose my shit in the process.

Counting to ten, I opened the bathroom door and stepped back out into the hallway. There was a small bedroom to my right. I started searching it, which wasn't easy because Mom had obviously just ransacked the place. Lots of clothes everywhere. Couple bags of weed. I pulled open a drawer to find a purple dildo with dry, crusty stuff on it.

Ewwww . . .

I almost didn't open the second drawer, scared of what I'd find inside. *Get over it—you could die out here.* Sliding it open, I hit pay dirt in the form of a .38 semiautomatic smiling up at me. I grabbed the pistol and checked it for ammo. Fully loaded. Now *that* was a thing of beauty. Feeling better, I kept looking, hoping for a phone or some keys. Thirty minutes later and still no joy. Pisser. There was only one place left to look. The most obvious place, really.

I needed to search Teeny's body.

Biting my lip, I walked over and poked him with my foot cautiously. I knew he was dead, but somehow I kept expecting him to jump up and start yelling at me or something.

He didn't.

My stepdad seemed smaller now. He'd never been physically imposing—if I'd fought harder, could I have protected myself? I'd never really fought him that much, not after the first time. I'd been too afraid to try.

Now he just looked pathetic. Almost fake. When he'd raped me, he smelled like stale sweat and grain alcohol. Now he smelled like raw hamburger. It was so pathetically mundane—shouldn't a dead human smell like more than meat? If he'd managed to shoot me, I'd smell like that right now, too. Just another bag of burger.

Trying not to gag, I leaned forward and caught his hip, rolling the body to the side so I could reach his pockets. Inside I found a set of keys and a cell phone, my fingers leaving bloody streaks on the glass as I turned it on.

No service. Fuck.

Maybe the keys would work. I moved toward the front of the RV, wondering if I'd actually be able to drive the thing, assuming I could get it running.

Moot point—none of the keys even fit the ignition.

Now what?

I wasn't sure how long I'd been in the camper, but it felt like hours had passed. The sun was pounding down, superheating everything. A fly buzzed by, landing on Teeny's body. When I heard a motorcycle in the distance, my first reaction was a surge of excitement. *Puck is coming to save me!* Except Puck couldn't possibly be coming to save me, because his bike was still up in Idaho.

The roar of the bike's engine grew louder.

I ran over and locked the camper door, then darted into the tiny bedroom. Peering out from behind a faded curtain, I watched as a motorcycle pulled up next to the camper. A man wearing Longnecks colors swung off. He pulled his helmet free and I gasped.

It was Bax—Teeny's brother.

Crappity crap crap!

Frantically I grabbed the .38, sitting down with my back against the bedroom wall. What should I do? Hide? The whole vehicle shuddered as Bax pounded on the flimsy door. I heard him cussing at Teeny, then everything shook again as he took his shoulder to the door. Seconds later he stepped inside.

"Oh, Jesus," the man muttered, and I imagined the scene before him. His brother on the ground, chunks of brain and hair spattered around the room. The murder weapon still sitting right there, dripping with blood and slime. "Teeny, you little asshole."

More rocking as the big man shuffled around. A gasping,

wheezing noise. Was he crying? My tension grew as long seconds passed—would he search the bedroom? If he found me, I was fucked. I'd have to shoot him. Shoot to kill, preferably before he even realized I was here.

Looking down at the gun, I swallowed. Could I do this?

Another sound broke through my thoughts—a second vehicle was coming. I heard it turn toward the camper, growing louder as it pulled up. Bax must've heard it, too, because he scrambled to his feet, cocking his gun.

A door slammed. I clutched my own weapon, sliding toward the window to peek outside. Puck was just stepping out of his truck, semi-automatic pistol out and in front of him. His Reaper friend was climbing out the other side. I watched as they started around the camper in a wide circle, obviously scoping the place out.

No fucking way. How he'd found me I couldn't imagine, but one thing was certain—if I didn't so something, he'd walk right into an angry Longneck looking for revenge. A strange and terrible calm came over me and suddenly I understood why Puck had yelled at me earlier.

I had to protect him.

Nothing else mattered.

Pulling away from the window, I edged toward the door, easing it open in silence. Bax stood waiting, gun at his side. He stretched his neck and smiled. I focused on my target as reality narrowed down to just the two of us.

I'd seen that look on his face before. Smug. Sure of himself. Exactly the way he'd looked right before he raped me. Lifting my gun, I braced carefully as I took aim.

Then I pulled the trigger.

The gun bucked in my hands but I held it steady, watching as Bax jerked to the side and fell heavily to the floor. His weapon dropped and I stepped forward, ready to shoot again as the men outside started shouting.

Puck didn't sound like a very happy camper, I thought, wondering why that seemed so funny. It wasn't normal, wanting to laugh right after putting a bullet in a man . . . Maybe I'd finally lost it? Oh, well. As for Puck, I'd just have to worry about him later. Right now I needed to be sure Bax was down for real. Reaching his gun, I nudged it away with my foot, then stood over him, gun trained on his head.

"Puck, are you out there?" I shouted.

"Becs? Is that you?"

"Yeah," I yelled back. "I'm inside. There's two guys in here with me, but I think they're both dead. The door should be open, come inside."

I heard the door hinge squeak behind me, then the hiss of Puck's breath.

"Your girl doesn't fuck around," said the Reaper.

"Becs, drop your gun and step back," Puck told me. "I've got them covered, so get out of the line of fire."

Didn't have to ask me twice.

I moved back toward the bedroom, setting my gun carefully on the dirty countertop. Puck stepped into the camper, nudging the bodies with his foot. Neither moved. He gave me a quick glance, his eyes taking inventory of my body.

"I'm fine," I reassured him. "I mean, I think I just killed a guy, but aside from that it's all good."

Puck raised a brow.

"Sure you're all right?" he asked. I considered the question seriously—everything felt sort of detached. I could feel my heart pounding, but it didn't seem like a real part of me.

"I might be in shock," I admitted, swaying.

"Fuck," he muttered, ducking into the camper to catch me. I wrapped my arms around his neck, savoring the smell of his body. This was real—Puck was actually standing here, holding me. Everything would be all right.

"How did you find me?"

"Your mom called me from your cell," he murmured. "Gave me directions. She said you'd need my help cleaning up."

"She killed Teeny," I managed to say, my mind spinning. *And she called Puck to save me.* "He decided to shoot me after he learned you're my old man—figured you'd hunt him down if I told you what he'd done."

"So you were just going to disappear? He think I wasn't gonna notice?"

I gave a dark laugh. "Thinking's never really been his thing."

"Let's get her out of here," the big Reaper said. "You can talk shit through later. We'll have to torch the place—that should take care of any evidence leading in our direction."

"Won't someone see the fire?" I asked, frowning in confusion. He glanced at me and shrugged.

"Maybe," he admitted. "That's why we need to leave. With any luck, one more burned-out camper out here won't even hit the radar. Just another drug deal gone bad. We'll take care of it, then you two start driving for Idaho right away. I'll head another direction."

"Go get in the truck," Puck told me, and for once I decided following his orders wasn't such a bad idea. Apparently he had more experience with this kind of thing.

Two hours later we were heading north. The camper went up fast, then, as we drove away, it exploded. Guess that's what happens when you torch a meth lab.

Back in Santa Valeria, I'd stayed hidden in the back of the truck while Puck grabbed our shit out of the motel room. I had no idea whether anyone had seen my abduction outside the Denny's, and I didn't want to find out.

"So let's unravel this," Puck said once we'd made left the city limits. "How the hell did you end up in that camper?"

I looked down at my wrists, running a finger over the bruises forming from the tape. Mom had actually been fairly gentle, but I'd savaged myself trying to get free.

"Mom ambushed me at Denny's. Pulled a gun on me. I told her to fuck off, but she said Teeny was ready to shoot you if I didn't follow her orders. We walked out to the car and they kidnapped me, dragged me into the desert. They seemed to think I'd brought money to pay Teeny off."

Puck's jaw tightened, and he started to open his mouth.

"No," I told him, catching his arm. "I know you're pissed. I'm pissed too, but this time let's not take it out on each other. The situation sucked but at least we're both alive. That's more than Teeny can say. I just want to get the hell out of here and go home."

Puck frowned.

"You should at least thank me for saving your ass," he said finally, frustrated.

"Thank you for saving my ass," I said, feeling proud of the fact that we hadn't started fighting. "But I'd already saved myself, you know."

"Aside from being stranded in the desert with two bodies? Yeah, I guess you're right. You were practically home free by the time we got there."

"Bax's bike was there—I could've taken it."

"You know how to ride a bike?" he asked, obviously startled.

I rolled my eyes. "I grew up on a bike. Of course I know how to ride."

"Didn't realize that," he replied, glancing at me with new respect. "But what were you planning to do, ride into town covered in blood? And what about the forensic evidence? You can't just leave a trail of bodies behind you, Becs. Throw me a bone, here."

"Okay, you saved me," I admitted. "But I saved myself, too. And I saved you. Bax was ready for you—he would've shot you right through the door."

"That's probably true," Puck said. "Appreciate that, by the way."

We drove in silence for a few minutes.

"I can't believe she got me again," I finally said. "And just in case it isn't clear, I'm done with her. You were right all along. I should've stopped taking her calls a long time ago. They must've thought I was a complete idiot, falling for their bullshit over and over again."

To his credit, Puck didn't rub it in. He just reached over and caught my knee, giving it a squeeze.

"Were you surprised when she attacked Teeny?"

I shrugged, covering his hand with mine.

"I don't know what to think—I still don't know why she lied to me, or why she decided to stop him. I guess killing me crossed some sort of line in her head? I'll probably never know."

"Probably not," he agreed. I leaned over to turn on some music. Talking made me think too much.

"Becca, you should come to bed."

I stood next to the window, looking out across the darkened parking lot. If anything, the quality of our hotels had gone down a notch. Puck said the shittier the hotel, the less likely it was anyone would remember us. By that logic, we were now perfectly safe. I'd already seen two drug deals go down outside, and I'd be willing to bet that those two girls with lots of makeup and very high heels weren't just having a party in their room.

"I keep thinking about Teeny," I admitted. "Mom just kept hitting him, over and over. Blood sprayed everywhere. Like in a horror movie. Not only that, I killed a man today. It seems like I should feel something—guilt, or maybe excitement or triumph or something. I'm just tired, though."

"Come to bed," he repeated, pulling back the covers next to him. I walked over and climbed in, tucking myself into his side.

"Are you pissed at me?"

"For what?" he asked. "You're gonna have to narrow it down before I can answer that."

"For all of it. Answering her calls. Listening to Teeny . . . dragging us down here in the first place." Puck's fingers caught my hair, running through it lightly. Then he sighed.

"Maybe a little," he admitted. "But mostly I'm just happy you're alive. When your mom called, it's like everything around me just stopped. All I could think about was you lying dead somewhere out in the desert. It could've happened, too."

"I'm sorry that you had to go through that," I said. "But I can't seem to feel bad about Teeny or his brother. And I know this is fucked as hell, but I'm glad my mom saved me. Maybe in her own way she still loves me, even if she's a nut job. Probably sounds crazy to you, but that makes me feel a lot better. Not that I ever want to see or talk to her again—no worries there."

He kissed the top of my head, tucking me farther into his side.

"So what now?" I asked him.

"We should sleep," he declared. "If we get up early and keep driving then we'll hit Idaho tomorrow night."

"No, I mean what about us?"

"What about us?" he asked, his tone touched with humor. "I just drove across the country to commit murder for you. Earlier today I helped burn a couple bodies to cover your tracks. That implies a certain level of commitment on my part, don't you think?"

"Well, I guess when you put it that way . . ."

Puck kissed me. Hard. "Go to sleep. Long drive tomorrow."

I snuggled down, feeling myself start to relax. Then I remembered something important.

"Puck!" I said, pushing myself up. He lunged for his gun, ready for action. I froze.

"What is it?" he whispered urgently. "Did you hear something?"

I shook my head, staring at the weapon. "You think you could put that down?"

He nodded, then lowered it slowly.

"What is it?" he asked again. I laughed nervously, feeling stupid. "Um, well earlier today I thought I was going to die."

"Been trying not to think of that."

"So . . ." I said, then I shook my head. This wasn't the right time. "Let's just go back to sleep. We can talk tomorrow."

"Becs, whatever the fuck's got you worked up, spit it out."

"I love you. When Teeny was about to shoot me? It's all I could think about. I love you and I wish I'd spent less time fighting with you. We have a lot to work out between us and that kind of scares me, but whatever happens you should know how I feel. You don't have to say it back."

God, this was awkward. Puck turned and set down his gun. Then he reached out and caught the back of my neck, pulling me in to rest his forehead against mine.

"I love you too," he said. "Don't know when it happened, but somewhere along the line it did. They say love at first sight is bullshit, and they're probably right. But whatever I felt for you that first night? It turned into something real. I'm never letting you go."

"So what does that mean?" I asked. "I mean, I still feel the same way about controlling my own life."

Puck sighed, then gave a low chuckle.

"We'll have to figure it out later, because I'm really fuckin' tired," he admitted, falling back onto the bed. I snuggled into his side again, resting my hand on his chest as I closed my eyes.

EIGHTEEN

TWO MONTHS LATER
PUCK

I stepped out onto the roof, shutting my apartment window behind me. The air was chilly, and while it wasn't freezing just yet, I still smelled fall in the air. It'd be time to put the snow tires on the truck soon. I'd have to park my bike for the winter, too. I still had the snowmobile of course, and it was a hell of a lot of fun. Just not as good as riding my bike.

"Did you remember the bread?" Becca called through her own open window. I held the French loaf up for her and she smiled. Ouch. Like getting punched in the gut every time. If anything, the gut punches were getting worse. Crazy about that girl.

"Thanks," she said as I got close. I leaned over and kissed her, wondering whose bed we'd end up in tonight. I usually crashed at her place, but sometimes she liked to mix it up. She caught my hand as I stepped inside, tugging me toward the table.

"Come sit down," she said. "Have a drink."

"Wow, you went all out."

She had. The table was covered in a deep maroon cloth that I recognized—she'd hemmed it with the brand new Singer sewing machine Regina had delivered last week. It wasn't an antique, but it seemed to work all right. She'd bawled like a baby when she saw it.

That wasn't the only crying she'd done. Becs had been terrified her foster parents would never forgive her for what she'd done, avoiding Earl and his wife for two days after we got home. Finally I'd had enough, so I put her on my bike and drove out to their place without any warning. There'd been an awkward silence, followed by hugs and tears and more dessert than should be legal.

Danielle had been less forgiving—she'd yelled at Becca for close to an hour before she decided not to hold a grudge. Blake stood behind her, arms crossed as he glared at me the entire time. I think he was somehow convinced it was all my fault. Maybe he'd just wanted in on the action. Either way, I was just thankful I didn't have to fight him. Afterward, the girls erupted into tears and hugs, at which point Blake and I decided to join forces and get the hell out of there.

"So I've got your favorite beer here," Becca announced, opening the fridge. "And I made you a pie. The spaghetti will be ready in just a minute."

I took the beer and grabbed a chair, enjoying the sight of her cute little ass wiggling as she bustled around. Becca glanced at me, her face full of uncertainty. Then she blinked and I wondered if I'd imagined it.

"You have a good day at school?"

"Yes, it was fine," she replied. "Um, speaking of school . . . I may be changing up my schedule a little. I've decided I really can't wait four more months before graduation. They said I can start going full-time, accelerate things."

I frowned. "You're already crazy busy, between school and the Moose. How d'you figure you'll pull that off?"

Becca frowned at me, but before she could respond the timer went off.

"Pasta's ready."

Five minutes later she handed me a plate full enough to feed the whole damned club.

"That's a lot to eat," I said, glancing at her. Becca smiled uncertainly, setting down her own plate. I waited for her to say something but she didn't—just sipped her water, looking nervous. What the hell was going on here?

"You want a beer?"

Becca shook her head and sighed. "We should talk."

"Words every man wants to hear," I muttered. Leaning back in my chair, I crossed my arms over my chest, waiting. She twisted her fingers silently.

"Babe, you can just tell me," I finally said, feeling something dark unwind deep inside. Had her mom been in touch? I knew Becca had mixed feelings about that bitch, but I didn't. Sure, she'd stopped Teeny from killing Becca in the end. Of course, the only reason she'd needed to protect her was because she'd set her up in the first place.

I hoped she was dead. That'd be best for everyone.

"So, we've never really talked about the future," Becca said slowly. "Sometimes I wonder . . . Where do you see us going, Puck?"

I frowned at her.

"What do you mean?"

"Well, I mean do you see us together long term?"

"You're my old lady," I replied, taking a long pull of my beer. "What else is there?"

"We've got something good started here," she said, her words careful. "And you know I love you. But I don't want to trap you."

"Not trapped, Becca."

She stared at me, her gaze steady, hands folded on the table.

"I'm pregnant."

I blinked. "Excuse me?"

"I'm pregnant," she repeated and I realized her fingers were squeezing each other so tight they'd turned white. Fair enough. Something squeezed pretty damned tight in my chest, too.

"How did that happen?"

Becca stiffened.

"We forgot the condom a couple times, remember?" Her tone was hostile. Shit.

"So you're really pregnant?"

"Yeah, I'm pregnant," she replied, eyes narrowing. "If you're going to run, tell me now. I won't turn into my mom. I'm going to raise this kid right, and I won't be counting on some man to save our asses."

I frowned.

"I'm not some man, I'm the kid's father. And why the hell do you think I'd run off?"

"Because a family is a lot of work—it'll change everything."

The words hung heavy between us and suddenly I realized this was actually happening. *I was going to be a father!* A thousand thoughts exploded through my head, moving too fast for me to catch them all. We'd need a bigger place—not right away, but I wasn't going to raise a kid in an apartment overlooking Main Street. He might fall out the window.

Christ. Kids fell all the time. Ran off. Got kidnapped and murdered and . . . *Fuck.*

Better not be a girl. I couldn't handle a girl.

"That why you're finishing up school faster than you planned?" I asked Becca.

She nodded, biting her lip.

"I might not ever make it back if I don't finish now."

"Makes sense . . ." Shit. How could she work and finish school? That's when it hit me—a baby meant Becca would finally have to let me help her. 'Bout fuckin' time. I'd humored her on the whole *"I'm an independent woman who pays her own way"* thing so far, but no more. This were three of us now.

Three of us. Wow.

"Okay, so we need to pick an apartment," I told her, mind racing. "I don't care which one, but I don't see any reason to pay more than one rent bill. That'll save money, so you can quit at the Moose, finish up school . . ."

"Does that mean we're staying together?"

The words threw me off. I studied her face, full of nervous tension. Great. After all we'd been through, my girl still thought I'd dump her for getting pregnant.

"Jesus, Becca," I growled. "Who the fuck do you think I am?"

"I love you," she said, eyes welling with sudden tears. Shit. More crying . . . Holy fuck, maybe it was the pregnancy hormones. That explained a hell of a lot. Becca was like a faucet since we'd gotten back. "But I'm still getting to know you. We've never even talked about kids. Do you even like kids?"

"I'm your old man, Becs. That means we're in this together. And yeah, I like kids."

"We still can't even buy groceries together without fighting," she whispered. "I mean, I know we're getting better at it, but I'm only twenty-one years old, Puck. We've only been dating for two months. How the hell are we supposed to be parents together?"

I considered the question, then shook my head.

"We just do, babe."

"But—"

"No," I said, standing and pulling her away from the table. She came into my arms and I held her tight. Was her stomach bigger already? I reached down between us, cupping it. My kid was in there. I wondered what he looked like. Or was it a she?

Fuck. *You better be a boy, you little shit.*

"Becca, I promise . . ." I swallowed. "I promise I'll take care of you and the baby. We'll get through this."

"All right."

I put my face in her hair. Did she smell different? More . . . pregnant somehow? I couldn't decide.

"Puck?"

"Yeah, Becs?"

"I'm sorry. I guess I'm just a little scared. I love you."

I bit back a nervous laugh, because I was a little scared, too. Then I pictured a little baby wearing Becca's face, imagined her feeding it . . . My woman feeding my kid. Damn. How did that make me feel? Love seemed like such a pathetic word to describe something this intense.

"It's okay," I told her, hoping I was right. "I love you, too, Becs. And not just 'cause your tits are gonna get bigger . . . although I'm looking forward to that the most, I think."

"Fuck you," she said, slapping at my hand and laughing. I let her pull back just enough to think she might get away, then jerked her into my arms.

"Love you," I whispered again, kissing the top of her head. "Fuck, I can't believe you have a baby inside you."

"It's scary," she whispered. "Are we really going to do this?"

"Yeah. I think so."

"I don't want to fuck it up."

"Okay," I told her.

"Okay what?"

"We won't fuck it up. I promise."

"Are you sure?" she asked.

This time I couldn't bite back that nervous laugh, because I had no idea. I put my hand on her stomach again and shook my head.

Holy shit.

EPILOGUE

SIX YEARS LATER
BECCA

"You're definitely gonna fuck it up," I told Danielle, smirking at her. She sat at my kitchen table, clutching a cup of tea between fingers white from stress. "Everyone fucks it up. The good news is that kids are strong. They bounce. You'll be fine."

"But I want to be a perfect mom," she said, her voice strained. "I always thought I'd have my shit together first. I mean, things are good but we run a bar, for God's sake. How can I work at a bar and take care of a baby?"

"How could I finish school, start a relationship with Puck, and have a baby?" I asked, shrugging. "You just do it because you have to. I promise you—once that kid is born, you'll be way too busy and tired to worry about getting it right. If the kid is still alive at the end of the day, you win."

Danielle rolled her eyes and flipped me off. She thought I was playing around, trying to make her feel better. Hah . . . She'd learn.

"So, Regina wants to know what kind of cake to make for the baby shower."

"German chocolate," she answered, picking at a fingernail. "I still don't see why we can't invite the guys."

"Because Blake paid me fifty bucks to make sure he wasn't invited," I told her. Before she could reply, my boy, Gunnar, came tearing through the kitchen.

"Katy is trying to shoot me!" he screamed, his little three-year-old tongue twisting around the words. "She's going to kill me!"

I caught the boy and swung him up onto my hip.

"I'll be right back," I told Danielle. She nodded, scowling. Probably shouldn't have ratted out Blake.

Stepping through the door, I looked out across our small lawn toward my daughter. Our house wasn't much—just a little two-bedroom back in one of the canyons—but we were surrounded by woods and the kids loved running through the trees.

"Katy Redhouse!" I called. "Get over here!"

She came running, and I realized she'd been playing in the mud again. The kid was coated in it from the knees down. Covered her hands, too.

"Why are you trying to shoot your brother?" I asked. She grinned up at me, a large gap in the center of her smile.

"Because he pissed off the Silver Bastards," she said proudly. "We can't have that shit, you hear me?"

Oh, I heard all right. I heard her father's voice coming right out of her mouth.

"I'm pretty sure the Silver Bastards can take care of themselves," I replied, my tone dry. "Say you're sorry to your brother, and then you guys can play with the hose for a couple minutes. See how much of that mud you can get off without my help. Once you're totally clean, you can have a popsicle."

Katy and Gunnar looked at each other and started shrieking with excitement. Then they tore off around the house to find the hose.

Perfect.

Walking toward the garage, I heard the roar of a Harley engine coming to life—yet another of Puck's fixer-uppers. The first time he'd dragged one home, I'd thought he was crazy. Then he'd turned around and sold it for three thousand bucks profit. Suddenly he wasn't sounding so crazy after all.

I knocked on the door and pushed it open. Puck crouched next to the bike, poking at the engine until it died with a sputter.

"How's it going?"

"Good," he grunted. "Should be done with this in another week or so."

"Did you know your daughter is planning to shoot your son?"

Puck stopped and looked at me, raising a brow.

"No shit?"

"Yeah, apparently he pissed off the Silver Bastards, so she's gonna take him out."

Puck stood, brushing off his hands. Crap. Six years together and the asshole just got sexier. Seemed sort of unfair, given that I'd gone through two pregnancies.

Puck smirked and stalked toward me. "You're looking very sexy today, Mrs. Redhouse."

"That's *Ms.* Redhouse, and don't try to change the subject," I told him, biting back a smile. "You've got a lot to answer for. Your daughter seems to think she's a biker badass."

He caught me by the back of my neck, pulling me into his body the same way he had a thousand times over the years. Never failed to turn me on.

"Sounds like bad parenting to me," he muttered, kissing along my jawline. "Doesn't she know girls can't be in the club?"

"She doesn't seem to accept that logic," I told him. "Seriously—you shouldn't let the kids hear shit like that."

"This is who we are," he replied. I tried to argue, but he didn't give me the chance, taking my mouth in a kiss so heated I forgot to think. Then his hands cupped my ass, lifting me and carrying me over to his workbench.

"The kids are outside," I whispered. "They could walk in . . ."

"They're playing with the hose," he replied. "I can hear them around the house. We've got at least ten minutes."

I considered the situation. Danielle still waited at the table, but she was a big girl. And he was right about the kids.

"Okay," I whispered. Puck slid his fingers into my jeans, jerking them down around my knees. I balanced awkwardly, reaching down to take off a shoe. He caught me and spun me around, pushing me down across the bench as I started laughing.

"You should be taking this seriously, *Ms.* Redhouse." His fingers reached between my legs, smoothing up and down along my opening. Then he replaced them with his dick.

"Fuck . . ." I sighed as he pushed deep inside.

"That's the general idea. Christ, those Kegels should be mandatory for every woman on earth," he muttered. "Your cunt's tighter than it was before the kids, shit you not."

I squeezed down on him hard, because there's nothing like flattery to inspire a girl.

"Danielle's scared she'll ruin her baby's life."

Puck laughed. "You tell her that ship's already sailed?"

I opened my mouth to reply, but he thrust into me particularly hard and my brain stopped working. Oh *wow*. I heard the kids shouting outside. Was Katy trying to shoot her brother again? I decided I didn't care.

"You're so fucking hot," Puck whispered, fingers digging into my hips. He paused and I pushed back at him, not wanting him to stop. He reached around my body to find my clit.

"Oh crap!" I moaned, arching my back. "That's really good, babe."

Kissing the back of my neck, Puck started moving more quickly. Every stroke filled me and I wiggled, wanting more. I wasn't in the mood to play around or tease—I just wanted him to fuck me. Hard.

Not a problem.

Then again, it never was. Puck knew exactly what I liked, and all too soon he had me hovering at the edge.

"Say you want it."

"I want it."

"What?"

"Your cock."

"You got it, babe."

Letting himself go, Puck pounded deep inside as I whimpered, exploding around him. Seconds later he joined me, shuddering heavily. Finally he pulled free, and I managed to stand up unsteadily, legs like spaghetti. The fact that my jeans were still bunched around my thighs didn't help.

"You okay?"

"Great," I replied, tugging them upward. "You think you distracted me, but you didn't. We should talk about your daughter's love of violence."

"Mom!" Katy shouted. Scrambling to fasten my pants, I stumbled toward the door.

"Yeah?"

"Mail is here! Can I go check it?"

"Sure thing, baby."

Puck had just come up behind me—wrapping his arms around my waist—when Katy tore into the garage, waving a purple envelope.

"Look!" she said. "I bet it's a birthday party invitation."

Reaching out, I took the card and studied it. No return address, but it had a Chicago postmark. Frowning, I slipped a finger inside and tore it open.

It was a Mother's Day card, which seemed strange considering it was June already.

Dear Becca—I learned recently that you had another baby. Okay, so it's been three years, but I didn't know until now. I just want you to know that I'm happy for you and proud of all you've accomplished. I wish I could have been a better mother. Take care and kiss those little ones for me sometime. Love, Mom

Tucked into the card was a twenty-dollar bill.

"Damn," Puck said, reading over my shoulder.

"Damn," Katy echoed gravely. I folded the card closed and stuck it back in the envelope, along with the money. This marked the fourth time she'd written to me over the years, although it had been so long since the last message that I'd wondered if something had happened to her. Last time she'd sent a ten, along with a pressed daisy.

"Can I have a popsicle?" Gunnar asked, peeking his head through the door.

"Sure thing, kiddo," Puck said. He pulled away from me to walk over to an old fridge he'd put out here. I heard the freezer drawer slide open, and then he was handing treats out to both the kids. "You want one, Becs?"

Stuffing the envelope into my back pocket, I shook my head.

"No, I'm good," I told him. "I should go help Danielle."

He held my gaze for a second, then shrugged.

"Love you."

"Love you, too."

Leaving them, I headed back to the house, considering my mom's note. Six years, four cards . . . Maybe a total of a couple hundred words.

So much for that relationship.

When I'd first gotten pregnant with Katy, I'd spent months worrying about all the things I might do wrong. In the end, it turned out to be pretty simple—feed them, kiss their boo-boos. Make sure their clothes were clean, or at least cleanish.

Oh, and fucking stick around.

No matter what else happened, I had that part covered. Guess I wasn't my mother's daughter after all.

AUTHOR'S NOTE: This bonus scene takes place at the North-woods Academy the same night as the raid on the Vegas Belles Gentleman's Club in *Silver Bastard*.

BONUS EPILOGUE

SHANE

I floated on my back, staring up at the vaulted glass ceiling over the most beautiful pool house in the state of Idaho. Like the rest of my prison, it'd been built in the 1920s by my great-grandfather Keiran McDonogh—a monument to his wife. She'd never liked the place, or Keiran himself, for that matter. Just one of many McDonogh brides who loathed their husbands over the past hundred years, setting an example I supposed my own wife would follow one day.

Assuming I lived long enough to marry, that was.

Big assumption.

Hopefully after tonight my odds would be improving. My best friend and personal bodyguard, Rourke Malloy, was meeting with representatives from the Silver Bastard motorcycle club right now. With any luck, my stepfather—Jamie Callaghan—was dead already. I'd grown too cynical over the past four years to feel any real hope, but I guess this was the next best thing.

His death wouldn't solve all my problems, of course. My own mother had tried to poison me once this week already. The only thing saving my ass was the fact she couldn't risk actually killing me, which complicated the whole process. A permanent vegetative state would suit her purposes perfectly, though.

All because I'd been "lucky" enough to inherit the Laughing Tess silver mine. Now there was a fucking joke. Tess must be laughing at me specifically, because here I was, trapped in a luxurious prison just like my great-grandmother. Of course, she never had a court-ordered monitor strapped to her ankle. Lucky bitch.

Issues of personal dignity aside, that fucker chafed like hell.

The sound of a door slamming echoed through the vast chamber, and I righted myself. Roarke was back. He stood on the deck staring down at me and I could tell already that he didn't have good news.

Fuck.

I started swimming toward him, enjoying the stretch and pull of my muscles in the water. The pool was the only thing to like about this hellhole. If I somehow survived intact and took over the McDonogh Corporation in six months, the first thing I planned to do was evict the tenants and blow the place up.

Reaching the edge, I boosted myself up onto the deck. Water ran down my back as I walked over to Rourke, who handed me a towel. I wiped off my face, then looked at him.

"Jamie's not dead, is he?"

Rourke shrugged. "Not like we really expected it to work. According to Boonie, he's got some serious fucking leverage. If it's true."

I frowned.

"What kind of leverage?"

My best friend narrowed his eyes, studying me almost like he'd never seen me before. Then he shook his head.

"It's bad shit, Shane."

"Do we know what it is?"

"Yeah."

"And?"

"You aren't actually related to Seamus McDonogh. Callaghan did a DNA test on your mom—I got no idea whose kid she was, but she wasn't his. That gets out, you'll lose everything."

"Holy fucking shit," I whispered. Blood roared in my head, because this was something I'd not even started to imagine. "Grandma was fucking around on him?"

"Apparently," Rourke said. "The minute you kill Jamie, it'll blow sky high. He's only sitting on it because he's still hoping to use Christine to take over."

I looked away, trying to process what he'd just told me.

"Do we know he's telling the truth?"

"Only one way to find out," he replied. "You really wanna risk proving you aren't a real McDonogh? Hell, if I were you, I'd look into exhuming the whole damned family tree and cremating them."

Fuck. He was right. I had just opened my mouth to answer when a loud clopping sounded echoed through the entire chamber. Spinning around, I dropped into a defensive crouch. Next to me Rourke had done the same—it'd been a long time since we'd had to literally fight for our lives, but we kept our skills sharp.

I looked around, searching for whoever was in here. A spy? Jesus, this was the kind of secret men would kill to protect. Men like me.

"Come out," I said, keeping my tone conversational. Almost friendly. "We can talk about whatever you just heard, but we won't leave until we find you. Could be a long night, and the longer I wait the less patient I'll be feeling."

No response, but I thought I heard someone's breath catch. Good, they were smart enough to be afraid. I could use fear. Rourke and I shared a glance, communicating without words. He backed toward the door, blocking the entrance as I started circling around the pool. The sound had come from this side.

There was only one exit unless our spy was strong enough to shift the heavy sliding service bay doors on the far end. Unlikely, given the fact they weighed a couple hundred pounds each and had probably rusted shut by now.

I followed the line of bright blue and gold tiles circling the deck toward the bins of aquatic equipment—foam "weights" and other shit they used for the water aerobics classes. It was the most likely hiding space. I'd almost reached them when I heard the slam of the main door opening. I turned to see a girl walk in wearing a two-piece swimsuit that my grandma would've found too modest.

She stared at me, looking absolutely terrified.

I recognized her. Lola. Lola Sanders. She was one of the few students here without a court order, probably because her parents couldn't be bothered to do anything else with her.

Rourke slid into place behind her, closing the door with a loud click.

She gasped and spun around, all but shaking in terror. I'd never seen her any other way, actually. Lola was one of those ghostly girls who lived on the edges of our reality. She hid in her room, did all her classes online and I had no fucking idea how she managed to eat, because I never saw her in the dining room.

"Um, I'm just looking for Piper," she said. "She was in here a minute ago . . ."

A wave of savage satisfaction tore through me. Piper Givens I could control—she didn't have any money and I already had plenty of leverage on her. I'd avoided her until now, for any number of reasons. Not least of them was the fact that I spent far too much time imagining what she'd look like sucking my cock.

Unfortunately, that wouldn't exactly help my cause.

"Are you and Piper close?" Rourke asked, coming up behind her so quietly she jumped when he spoke. He pushed himself into her space, raising an arm to wrap it around her shoulders and neck. Almost like a hug, but this wasn't a hug.

If he pressed on her carotid artery she'd be unconscious in less than thirty seconds.

"We're friends," she replied, her eyes growing frantic. Rourke leaned in, whispering something in her ear. She gave a terrified squeak, then shook her head. He wrapped his other arm around her, spreading his hand over her bare stomach and pressing her back into his body.

He shot me a feral grin.

Guess my friend had found a new toy. Interesting, but maybe not so surprising. I'd never seen Lola in anything but shapeless sweats and giant T-shirts. For the first time I could actually see her figure—not bad. Not bad at all. Rourke enjoyed variety in his bed, something that wasn't easy to come by here at the academy.

Lola was in for a big surprise.

"Piper, you need to come out now," I called, my voice taunting. "I'd hate for anything unfortunate to happen to Lola. If you heard us talking, you'll know I'm not fucking around. It's not like you can get away, but you still have the chance to protect her. Otherwise I'll give her to Rourke."

My friend grinned, because we both knew I'd give her to him anyway.

I turned to watch as Piper rose slowly to her feet behind the exercise equipment. She wore a bright red bikini, and while it wasn't the most revealing I'd seen, it didn't do anything to hide her curves, either.

Fuck. I guess it was better than having one of the more connected students listening in, but she tempted me so much it was dangerous.

"Get out here."

She stepped around the bins, walking toward me slowly. She was one of the older students here—twenty, just like me—and I could see that she fully understood the implications of what she'd heard. Dread rolled off her, because she'd heard the stories about me and Rourke.

"I wasn't trying to spy on you," she whispered, coming to stand in front of me. It was the truth. That much was obvious. She wasn't a player, not like so many of the rest of us. "I'll never tell anyone, I promise. Just let me and Lola go. She wasn't even here."

I smiled at her, then glanced back at Rourke. He still held his prisoner, whispering quietly into her ear as his fingers smoothed across her stomach. I had no idea what he was saying, but Lola's eyes were wide and almost panicked.

Perfect.

Turning back to Piper, I shrugged. "I don't want to hurt you. You're not part of this and there's no reason you should have to suffer. At the same time, I can't just let you walk away . . ."

Behind me Lola gave a sudden, sharp scream and my friend laughed. Piper's gaze darted between us, and I sensed the exact instant she panicked. In total silence she started running for the door.

Rourke dropped Lola, beating Piper easily. I started toward them, refusing to move faster than a slow, stalking pace that would scare her even more. Maybe it sounds sadistic, but it really was for her own benefit. If I couldn't control Piper's mouth, I'd have to kill her.

That's when Lola startled the hell out of me—instead of crumbling into a ball of whimpering nothingness, she attacked Rourke. Not a flailing, pathetic little girl slap attack, either. She went straight for his balls and he might've been in trouble if his dad wasn't one of the most deadly contract killers in Callaghan history.

Rourke seemed utterly enchanted as he caught her by the foot, easily flipping her toward the floor. If she'd hit, it might've been fatal. Lucky girl, he'd decided to play with her instead. Seconds before she hit, he caught her head, cushioning it.

She'd still be bruised as fuck but no concussion.

Winking, Rourke turned to face Piper, who'd come to a full halt.

"Come back here," I told her, allowing a hint of impatience into my voice. "You can't get away from me. I'm still willing to talk to you, but you're running out of time."

"Go!" Lola hissed. Rourke clamped a hand over her mouth. She surprised me again, biting him. This time he laughed, the sound pure delight.

"Lola, you're making a big mistake," I said lightly. "If you play dead, he'll leave you alone."

"You're both fucking psychopaths!" Piper hissed, looking between us. I held her gaze for three long seconds. Then she bolted, and this time I couldn't resist. Piper was fast, but I was a foot taller and in far better shape. Still, she managed to stay ahead of me for close to a minute, tearing around the pool deck like a secretary running from her boss around a desk.

My dick was hard as a rock by now.

Rourke laughed the whole time, taunting me as Lola struggled in his arms. Then I caught Piper in the corner and she spun to face me, panting. A thin sheen of sweat covered her face, every breath she took bouncing her breasts.

Her waist was narrow and her hips were wide. Not fat, but perfectly designed to cradle a man.

Me.

"Give up," I whispered, holding her eyes. She shook her head. Time to end it.

In an instant I was on her, one hand covering her mouth as I wrestled her down to the deck. Even now, Piper fought hard, thrashing her body against mine until I thought I'd lose my mind.

Then I had her down on her belly, covering her with my hard cock buried in her ass with only the thin fabric of our suits to protect her. I kicked her legs apart on instinct, then pressed into her.

"You shouldn't have done that," I whispered in her ear, closing my eyes for a second as I fought for control. This had started out as a game, but here was the danger—I wanted Piper. I'd wanted her for a long time and now I had her. "I'm going to let your mouth go. If you scream, you'll pay."

I moved my hand.

"Please don't rape me," she whimpered. My ass flexed, the tip of my cock pressing right against her opening. Fuck.

Groaning, I pulled back.

In the distance I heard Lola squawk, but I couldn't be bothered to look at Rourke's new toy. Piper held my entire focus. I leaned down, my lips brushing against her ear as I spoke with calculated menace.

"If you were anyone else, I'd have to kill you for what you overheard tonight," I whispered. "But you're a lucky girl, because you don't have a stake in any of this. I'll give you one chance. One. You keep your mouth shut and you don't have to worry. But if I even imagine you talked, I won't just come after you. I'll come after Charlie, too. Do you understand."

She turned to stone.

"How do you know about Charlie?"

Triumph flashed through me—I had her.

"I know everything," I whispered. "I know about the trial. I know about the custody battle. I even know about what you were doing the night it happened. I don't want to hurt you, Piper. You're an innocent girl and you don't deserve any of this. Keep your fucking mouth shut and nobody ever has to know any of it."

"I will."

"I'm going to let you go now. You'll go back to your apartment and you'll never talk about this to anyone. Stay away from Lola and don't give anything away to your mom. You'll live happily ever after."

Piper nodded desperately. I inhaled, drinking in her scent, then forced myself to push away. She refused my offer of a hand up, edging away from me on her hands and knees. Then she was up and running.

Seconds later, Piper and Lola were gone.

I looked at Rourke and smirked.

"She's right," he said. "You really are a fucking psychopath."

"No, I'm not. If I was, I'd have killed her. That would be safest, and we both know it."

He laughed.

"That'd be a waste—I'll bet you never see her again. She'll be too scared to leave her room."

I shrugged.

"Better that than dead. I'll need you to take a message back to the MC. Just because we can't kill Jamie doesn't mean we shouldn't send him a message. In the long run, this may work to our benefit."

TURN THE PAGE FOR A
NEVER-BEFORE-PUBLISHED BONUS NOVELLA . . .

CHARMING BASTARD

AUTHOR'S NOTE: Darcy and Boonie are characters in their late thirties during the Reapers and Silver Valley novels. Their love story starts twenty years before the beginning of *Silver Bastard*.

CHAPTER ONE

CALLUP, IDAHO
TWENTY YEARS AGO

"There's no room for you in here!" Erin hissed, glaring up at me from a narrow hollow between two boulders. I clenched my fist, wishing I could punch her right in the face.

This was *my* spot—she only knew about it because I'd shown it to her. In the distance I could hear the boys shouting at each other, followed by a girl's shriek. We'd been playing a weird game of hide and seek on the way home from the bus stop all week, although it seemed a little unfair that the girls always had to hide. Unfortunately there were five guys and only four of us, so they called the shots.

"You suck," I told Erin, then started up the hill again. Bitch. See if I ever saved her ass in math again.

Pushing through the trees was hard work and after a couple minutes I was panting. Not only that, between the steep hillside

and the brush everywhere. I was making too much noise. Crap. I'd
bet Boonie five bucks that he wouldn't be able to catch me before
five p.m. I didn't actually have the money to pay up. It'd been stupid, but he'd been flipping me so much shit lately. For a couple
weeks, actually.

God only knew what he'd make me do if I couldn't pay up.
Knowing my luck he'd make me eat another damned worm.

I'd first met Riley Boone when I was four years old. We moved to
Callup, Idaho, after my dad blew out his back and had to go on
disability. Boonie's family lived next to ours. Every afternoon he'd
swagger off the school bus after kindergarten like a conquering
king. For the first week he ignored me, until I'd impressed him by
climbing nearly thirty feet up in the tree behind his trailer. They
had to call the fire department to get me down, but it'd been worth
it to see the respect in his five-year-old eyes.

He gave me a worm in honor of my accomplishment. I'd fallen
in love. The next day he made me eat the worm and our relationship has been complicated ever since.

Eight years later I was still getting myself in trouble trying to
impress him.

I was almost halfway to the ridge now, my backpack tugging me
downward as I climbed. I'd been up this high before—hell, I'd
explored most of the gulch over the years—but this was farther
than I'd usually go this late in the afternoon. It was a bit of a risk.
If I went too far I wouldn't make it home before it was time to fix
dinner for my dad.

Not a good scene.

On the other hand, Boonie probably wouldn't look for me up
here. He liked to think he was so sneaky and tough, but I was
pretty sneaky, too.

The distant shouting faded as I clambered higher. The hillside was really steep now. The soft trickle of a stream sang to me in the distance, the light hardly filtering through the thick evergreen branches overhead. Ferns and moss and pretty little flowers grew on everything.

Unfortunately, ferns and moss and flowers aren't big enough to hide behind.

Then I saw a fallen tree and smiled. The trunk itself wasn't that big, but it'd come down sideways, lodging against several other tree trunks to form a natural shelf on the slope.

It was perfect.

Climbing up and over it, I followed the length to where it'd crashed through a little thicket. If I crawled in there I'd be completely invisible. Seconds later I was flat on my stomach, peering down the hillside from my perch and feeling smug as hell. It was four thirty already. Another half hour and I'd be the winner. About time, too, because it seemed like Boonie was always ahead of me.

Not this time. Ha.

Something rattled on the slope below me and I froze, eyes darting. More rattling, and I saw some branches swaying about a hundred feet off to my right. Someone was down there, but if I stayed still they wouldn't be able to see me.

Don't move. Don't breathe. Don't let him win.

Then a boot landed on the middle of my back and I screamed.

"Hey, Darce," Boonie said. "Looks like I win again."

"Shit," I groaned, dropping my forehead into the pine needles. "How did you do that?"

"I've been right behind you the whole time," he said. "When will you learn? You can't beat me."

That wasn't worth an answer so I didn't bother giving one. Instead I pushed up with my hands, trying to get up but his booted foot held me down firmly.

"Jesus, Boonie. What's your problem?"

"Five bucks. Pay up."

I sighed, wondering why the hell I'd let him goad me into this. Time to 'fess up.

"I don't have the money," I admitted. Boonie didn't say anything at first, then he lifted his boot slowly, setting me free. Shit. Was he going to be a dick about this?

"Roll over," he said. I rolled over and looked up at him, wishing to hell I'd never opened my stupid mouth. Boonie wasn't a guy to mess with. He got in more trouble than any of the other freshmen. Even worse, he'd started running around with some of the older kids in the trailer park ever since he'd shot up last summer. Now he was six feet tall. It occurred to me that I didn't really know him that well anymore.

We were only six months apart in age, but I was just a lowly eighth grader.

Crap.

"Can I get up?"

"Do you have five bucks?"

"No," I admitted, feeling a little sick.

Boonie dropped to his knees next to me, a knowing smirk on his his face. "I knew you didn't when I made the bet."

"What do you mean?"

"You had to borrow a dollar from Erin to get a drink and there's no way you'd leave any cash at home. Your dad would take it."

Well. Looked like Boonie knew me a little too well.

I sat up and we faced each other, our faces a little closer than felt comfortable. A strange tension had come into the air. I'd known him most of my life, but these last few months he'd been more distant. Now I didn't know how to act around him or what to say.

Erin had a crush on him, said he was hot. Studying his face I could see it—he had strong features, and his short, dark hair was just shaggy enough that I wanted to touch it. Push it back, away from his face so I could see him better.

This was totally messed up—I shouldn't be thinking shit like this about Boonie. We'd always alternated between being friends and enemies.

This was different. Scary.

Boonie lifted a hand toward my hair and I flinched, feeling my cheeks heat.

"What do you want?" I whispered.

"What do you think?"

I licked my lips and his eyes followed the movement. My breath caught as he leaned forward just a little.

"You guys up there?" Erin called, her voice shrill. "Darcy! Where are you? Is Boonie with you?"

I eyed him warily. "Erin likes you."

He shrugged.

"So?"

"She's my friend."

"Come here."

"We should get going," I said, scooting back across the pine needles. My jeans caught on a branch, stopping me. Boonie leaned forward, crawling up and over my body. He wasn't touching me, but his knees straddled mine. Then his hands came down on either side of my head.

"Give me a kiss and we'll call it even."

I didn't know what to say. His eyes were dark, intense. I knew he'd kissed girls before, maybe even more than kissed. I'd even seen him coming out of Shanda Reed's trailer a few times. She was sixteen and everyone knew she slept around. Not that I judged her for it—she'd babysat me a couple of times when I was little and used to build tent forts for me. I liked her.

But I had a feeling she wasn't building forts with Boonie.

I licked my lips again, knowing I should kick him in the balls. Instead I watched as his head came closer. Then his lips brushed mine, ever so softly. Something strange and new started to uncurl deep inside. Something restless and needy. When his teeth nipped I opened my mouth with a soft sigh.

Then his tongue slipped inside.

Holy. Shit.

Erin said open-mouthed kissing was slutty. No wonder Shanda was slutty, because this was *amazing*. Boonie's body lowered over mine and I felt his weight press me back down into the pine needles.

The kiss was harder now, his tongue plunging deep into me and his fingers tangled into my hair. I couldn't think, couldn't breathe, couldn't do anything but feel as he thrust one of his strong thighs between my legs.

That's when I felt it.

Something hard, pushing against my stomach.

Was that . . . ?

Ohmygod!

"Darcy!" Erin yelled again. She was almost on top of us and we both froze. Boonie lifted his head, staring down at me in heated silence. Whole worlds burned in his eyes and I knew things would never be the same between us again. His hips shifted once, restlessly.

"Darcy, where the hell are you?" she shouted again. I opened my mouth to reply, but before any sound could come out Boonie put a finger across my lips.

"Stay quiet. She can't see us," he whispered. His pelvis pressed down into mine and suddenly I knew exactly where this was going. Boonie might only be six months older than me, but he was years ahead of me when it came to this kind of game.

I wasn't ready. Not at all.

"I'm coming, Erin!" I shouted abruptly. Boonie's eyes narrowed, but he pushed away, letting me sit up. Then he was pulling me to my feet. Watching him warily, I reached for my backpack and slung it over my shoulder.

"I'll be right down!" I yelled, backing away.

"Stop," Boonie said.

I shook my head.

"Your hair is full of pine needles," he added quietly. "Let me fix it. Otherwise you'll catch shit."

Crap. He caught my shoulders and turned me around, fingers combing through my hair. The touch sent shivers running down my spine. I wanted to lean back into him, to feel him wrap his arms around me.

Instead I waited for him to finish then started down the hill.

"Erin, I'm headed down," I called, glancing back at him. "Wait for me and I'll be right there."

Boonie watched as I left, making no move to follow. That was different, too. We'd fought with each other as much as we'd played through the years, but more often than not it'd been us against the world—I was used to having him at my back. That boy was gone now. He'd turned into someone else. Someone hard and fierce and maybe even a little scary.

I wanted him to kiss me again. Desperately.

Erin started babbling about the eighth-grade graduation dance when I reached her, oblivious to the world-shaking events that'd taken place farther up the slope. I followed her down the hill to the road and we started walking along the gravel toward the trailer park.

"Everyone else already went home," she declared. "It took me forever to find you. What were you doing?"

I shrugged. "I didn't have five bucks. I couldn't let Boonie find me."

"Whatever," she replied, and I wondered if she'd even been listening. Probably not. She never did. That usually pissed me off but today it was exactly what I needed.

It was just after five when we slid through the ancient wooden fence surrounding Six Mile Gulch trailer park, which was missing at least half its boards. My dad would be zoned out in front of the

TV with his beer and Mom was working swing shift at the grocery store. That gave me plenty of time to get dinner started on a normal night.

But as soon as we reached the central dirt driveway I realized this wasn't a normal night.

My steps faltered as I took in the clumps of anxious, upset adults. Some of them were crying. Children sat on steps, watching with wide eyes. Over at the Blackthorne place, Granny Aurora stood on the porch looking lost. I'd never seen her like that—usually she was the rock holding all of us together, always ready with a hot cookie and a cold glass of milk. My stomach sank. This was bad. Really bad. Fear and something worse hung in the air.

"What's going on?" Erin asked, her voice wavering. Shanda ran over to us, her face smeared with streaks of black mascara.

"Have you seen Boonie?" she asked breathlessly.

"He's probably right behind us," I told her, ignoring Erin's sharp look. "What happened?"

"There's a fire at the silver mine—it's bad. Real bad."

"That's impossible," I said, confused. "It's solid rock down there. What could be burning?"

"Nobody knows, but it's definitely on fire. Boonie's stepdad was underground today. So were Jim Heller, Pete Glisson, and Buck Blackthorne. We need to find Boonie and get him up there because his mom's lost her shit. Nobody knows if they got out or not."

Oh crap. Boonie's mom had gone downhill over the years. Not that his stepdad was that hot, but Candy Gilpin was a basket case on a good day. In a genuine crisis she'd be uncontrollable. Like, shooting at people uncontrollable.

"Fuck," I whispered, running across the dusty ground to my place. Tossing my backpack on the porch, I grabbed my bike and pedaled down the driveway and out onto the road. Boonie couldn't be that far behind, could he?

Two minutes later I saw him, looking more like a man than a

boy as he walked toward me. My bike skidded to a stop so hard I nearly crashed.

"What the fuck?"

"The mine," I gasped. "There's a fire at the Laughing Tess. Your stepdad's underground and your mom needs you."

Boonie's face paled and I started to climb off my bike, planning to give it to him. He was already off and running. That's when I happened to glance up at the sky and I saw it.

A pillar of thick, black, oily-looking smoke was rising slowly over the ridge.

Holy shit. What the hell had happened down there, half a mile underground in the darkness?

Funny how we turn disasters into dry, sterile numbers.

Three. That's how many days it took for the fire to burn out. Sixty-six. That's how many self-rescuing breathing devices failed because they hadn't been repaired or replaced on schedule. Eighty-nine men died, most within the first hour. Some were found sitting in front of open lunch boxes—that's how fast the smoke took them out.

And then there was the worst number of all. Two hundred four-teen. Two hundred and fourteen children lost their fathers that day. One of them wasn't born until months after the last funeral.

Seven days after the fire started, they pulled out two men alive. They'd sheltered under an air vent nearly a full mile below the surface, breathing shallowly and praying as tendrils of dark, poisonous smoke ebbed and flowed less than twenty feet away.

Boonie's stepdad was one of them.

The *New York Times* plastered a picture of the survivors as they stumbled out into the light for the first time. Afterward there were congressional hearings on mine safety, although according to the local union it didn't change anything. The Laughing Tess shut down for six months. Then she was up and running again, business as usual because the price of silver was up.

None of this mattered to Boonie and me. His stepdad announced on live TV that he'd never go underground again. Then he packed up the family and they left Callup for eastern Montana.

I didn't see Riley Boone again until my junior year of high school. By then I'd been dating Farell Evans for nearly eighteen months.

CHAPTER TWO

"Get your ass up here!" Erin yelled, laughing so hard I could hardly understand her words. She'd already scrambled to the top of the embankment ahead of me. My boyfriend, Farell, boosted me up behind her, and I didn't miss how his fingers slipped under my jean skirt to grope my ass. Someone was horny. He'd started drinking before the graduation ceremony, although I hadn't realized how much until we were driving up the gulch toward Six Mile Cemetery for the after party. He'd nearly gone off the road twice, scaring the hell out of me.

I hated it when he got like this.

Fortunately, we made it okay and I was definitely ready to party. There were only forty-two students in the class of 1992, so they were more than happy to have us juniors along for the ride. I'd probably be here even if my boyfriend wasn't a senior. Half the high school was.

I'll never forget the first time he'd asked me out—it was one of those Cinderella moments. He was tall and strong and smart. Not only that, he played quarterback on our football team. His family had lived in the valley for a hundred years and they owned the White Baker mine. Practically royalty by Silver Valley standards.

My mom already had my wedding dress picked out, although I had my doubts. Farell would be heading to the University of Idaho in the fall and I'd seen way too many couples break up when that happened.

Fortunately, I'd only have to get through another a year before joining him. My family was broke, but I'd always worked hard in school. I wanted to get a business degree. The school counselor told me that between my grades and our family income I'd have lots of scholarship opportunities.

I planned to make the most of them.

Popping up and over the top of the bank, I staggered to the side. Farell, Colby, and Bryce followed, then we all started across the darkened cemetery toward the party.

Six Mile had close to eight thousand graves, although you'd never guess it. Back during the gold rush, thousands of people flooded the valley. Callup might only have eight hundred residents now, but in those days we'd been the biggest city in north Idaho— home to a strange mix of miners, whores, gunfighters, and preachers. Even a bunch of nuns. You name it, they came here and when they died, they'd been buried on the steep hillside above Six Mile Creek. Now pine trees had taken over. From the road you couldn't even see the place.

I loved it here.

Peaceful graves stretched along the thickly forested hillside in every direction, covered in moss and brush. Stone markers, wooden crosses, statues, and crudely built crypts . . . thousands of memorials for people long forgotten.

At night it turned into something else entirely.

"This place is creepy as fuck," Erin whispered with thrilled glee. She clutched my arm as the boys whooped and wandered off. I couldn't argue with that. We stumbled along the slope toward the party, which was back behind the memorial for the men who died fighting the 1910 wildfires. A terrace overlooking the grounds had been built out of smooth river stones, and was lined with benches. A rough concrete bowl sat in the center. I think once upon a time it was supposed to be a pond or something. Tonight it would be our fire pit, with the terrace itself providing the perfect place to set out the kegs.

Yeah, I know. We were horrible kids.

We were also the third generation of Callup residents to party up here, so at least we came by it honestly. Everyone in town knew where the graduation party would be, of course. Same place it'd been for the last twenty years—traditionally the cops gave a free pass on graduation night.

I stumbled on a tree root and tripped, falling into a headstone. Farell came out of nowhere to scoop me up, throwing me over his shoulder and running up the slope like I was a football. I screamed and slapped at his back.

"You're gonna kill me!" I shouted. Farell laughed and his buddies cheered us on. Then Bryce caught Erin and it turned into a race. We reached the memorial at the same time to the sound of hooting and clapping. Farell lowered me to the ground and pulled me in for a kiss, tongue shoving deep into my mouth. He tasted like beer and the taquitos we'd eaten at his house during the reception.

I liked kissing Farell. Hell, I liked more than kissing him—we'd been sleeping together since I was sixteen and he was usually in tune with my needs. He pulled away and looked down at me, grinning like an idiot.

"Fuckin' love you, Darce."

Then he let me go and swaggered off, sharing high fives with the other football players before heading over to the keg. My eyes followed him, feeling that strange sense of loneliness that always came when he turned away. Farell was a bright, shining spotlight. When he focused on me it was like staring into the sun. When he left I found myself blinking, blinded and startled by the sudden loss of warmth.

I looked away, searching for Erin. Instead I saw Riley Boone watching me with those cold black eyes of his.

He leaned back against a tree just outside the circle of firelight. People swirled all around but Boonie stood apart, studying me with an intensity that scared me. Like always, the sight of him reminded me of that kiss we'd shared so many years ago. We'd hardly been more than kids, but they say you never forget your first.

Gave me chills every time I thought about it.

Boonie lifted his chin in silent greeting and I nodded in return. Then someone stumbled into me, breaking the spell. Good thing, too.

Riley Boone was nothing but trouble.

I'd hardly recognized him when he returned to Callup. I guess his stepdad ran off with a younger woman last summer, so his mom came running home to lick her wounds. Took her less than two weeks to hook up with one of the Silver Bastards, a member of the motorcycle club here in town. Boonie's dad had been one, too, although he'd died when Boonie was just a baby.

I'd heard he was back, of course. Callup was the kind of place where everyone was up in each other's business. Still, that didn't prepare me to see him again in person.

He'd pulled up to the high school on a midnight blue Harley Davidson, looking like the hero in a movie. You know, one of those teenage tragedies where the naive and foolish heroine falls in love with the gangster? Then she has to watch him get gunned down in the end, leaving her alone and pregnant because things can never work out with guys like that.

I hadn't recognized him at first. I mean, Boonie had been cute as hell when he'd left, but for all his height, he'd still been a boy. Now he was all man. Six foot three, with a bulky, muscular body and dark hair. His eyes held secrets and he still walked like a conqueror, only now he was the kind of conqueror who'd cut off your head for crossing him. Farell and his friends learned that fast, too.

Until Boonie came home, Farell had been the king of the school. Now Boonie was, even if he wasn't interested in taking on the role.

Farell hated him for that.

That was reason enough for me to avoid Boonie—Farell had an ugly temper. While I didn't think it was reasonable for him to say I couldn't talk to my old friend, I didn't want to lose him, either. I compromised by staying friendly but distant. It'd been a tense year, made more tense by the fact that no matter where I went, Boonie's eyes followed me.

I didn't know for sure, but I think he and Farell even fought a couple of times—either that or Farell was running into an awful lot of doors. I couldn't think of anyone else brave enough to take him on.

When they'd finally graduated I think half the town sighed in relief.

Now the party swirled around me in a blur of red Solo cups and cheap beer, punctuated by the occasional kiss or swat on the ass from my boyfriend. By two in the morning, I had a good buzz going. I also needed to pee. I hadn't seen Farell for a while, but that didn't mean much. I figured he was off smoking pot, which he seemed to think I didn't know about. Not that I cared—compared to the Oxycontin my dad popped like candy, pot was nothing. That's when I saw my old neighbor Shanda Reed.

"When did you get here!" I shouted, running over to her. "I didn't see you at graduation."

"I couldn't make it in time," she said, laughing and pulling me into a hug. "Had a work thing."

Her words broke through the haze and I felt awkward. Shanda's "job" wasn't what I'd want, although she drove a shiny new cherry red Mustang these days.

Not my place to judge how she earned her money.

Shaking my dark thoughts off, I looked her over. "I really like your hair like that. The blonde is perfect on you."

"Thanks," she said. I wondered if she was here for Boonie, not that it was any of my business. "Damn, I need to pee. Wanna go with?"

As soon as she said it I remembered my bladder was about ready to explode. "Yeah."

"Great. You can tell me all the gossip."

I followed her back into the trees, stumbling over roots as the firelight and music faded. The night air was warm without being hot, and the sound of crickets surrounded us.

"Here, this spot looks good," she said, pointing to a clump of bushes. It was completely shielded from the party. Five minutes later we'd finished our business and headed back down the hill. About halfway back I heard a girl laughing, along with the rhythmic grunting that could only mean one thing. I bit back my own giggle, shooting a glance at Shanda. She smirked, catching my arm.

"Hold on," she whispered. "I want to see who it is."

"What?" I asked, scandalized. "No. No, we can't!"

Her wicked grin flashed. "Sure we can. They're in the open—fair game."

I shook my head, but I followed her as she crept through the darkness. Then I stepped on a branch, making a loud snapping noise. The laughter stopped.

"What was that?" a girl asked. I recognized the voice—Allie Stockwell. Well, wasn't that nice . . . Allie made a huge production last year about wearing her purity ring, announcing she would never sleep with a boy before she was married. Not only that, she'd done it while staring me down in the locker room pointedly. I hated the bitch.

"It's fine, baby," her partner said, the words heavily slurred.

I froze.

"Farell?" I asked, my voice unsteady. No. I'd heard wrong. Farell would never cheat on me—Farell *loved* me. I heard Allie gasp as I swayed, dizzy. This wasn't real. *It couldn't be real.*

"Who the fuck is in there?" Shanda demanded, her voice ringing out in accusation. She started forward, pushing through the weeds and I followed, praying I'd been wrong. We'd find Colby back there with Allie, or some other guy. Obviously I hadn't heard right. Too much booze.

I stepped into a clearing to find them, half naked in the moonlight. My drunken boyfriend had rolled to his back, dick flopping as he tried to pull up his pants. Allie gaped at us like a fucking goldfish.

"Farell . . ." I whispered, my world shattering around me. "Oh, shit. Why? Why did you do this?"

He tried to say something, then Shanda had my arm and was dragging me away.

This was what it felt like to be punched in the gut.

I literally lost my breath. I couldn't take in air, couldn't focus, couldn't do anything but try not to fall on my face as Shanda hauled me away from my future ex-boyfriend.

"Fuck off, asshole!" she shouted over her shoulder. "You eat shit and die."

Finally my head stopped spinning and I realized I was crying. Sobbing. We were nearly back to the party and I dug in my heels, pulling back against Shanda's grip.

"I can't go back there," I hissed. "I can't let them see me like this. Oh my God, how did this happen? Why would he do this?"

Shanda caught my shoulders, giving me a shake.

"I've got no idea why the hell he'd cheat on you," she said. "I don't care why, either. Here's what I do know—if he's been fucking her, then all of his friends know about it and so do all of hers. That means everyone at the party but you and your best girls are in on this bullshit. You've got two choices here. You can run off and hide like you've done something wrong, or you can walk back down there, grab a drink, and then wait for him. When he comes back, you'll throw that drink in his face and dump his pathetic ass. Then we're going to dance and have fun and maybe get you laid by a real man, because he does *not* get to win."

I stared at her, blinking.

"I don't think I can do that," I whispered. Shanda's eyes narrowed.

"Listen to me—the world's tough for girls like us, Darce. Girls from the trailer park. They think that because we're poor, we're trash, and that's how they treat us. But we're not trash. I don't care how much money Farell has. He's the trashy one here, not you. Sometimes you just gotta cowgirl up."

She was right. I hadn't done anything wrong, so why the hell should I run away? Lifting the edge of my halter top, I wiped off my face, trying not to sniffle.

"How do I look?"

"You'll do in the dark," she said, winking at me. "Hold your head high and remember, I've got your back. Six Mile trailer park forever, baby."

Boonie was the first person I saw back at the party.

He leaned against a pickup truck full of massive speakers the senior boys had hooked to car batteries. Something had gone wrong with the system early on, and they'd stopped working. Still, the truck's own stereo wasn't too bad when they cranked it all the way.

Now the fire burned high and girls were dancing all around it.

I saw Erin wander up to Boonie and lean into him. He gave her a hug then pushed her away firmly when her hands started to wander.

Shanda marched us straight over to them.

"What happened to you?" Erin asked, so drunk I could hardly understand her words.

"I caught Farell fucking Allie Stockwell," I said bitterly, wishing I could kill the hateful bitch. "Now I'm going to dump his ass."

"Holy shit."

Boonie didn't say anything, but his eyes flared with sudden intensity. Shanda looked between us, a strange smile playing at her lips. I think she was about to say something.

Then Farell stumbled out of the dark and back into the party.

"Darcy!" he shouted, lurching toward us. People turned to stare. "Darcy! Darcy, it was a mistake. Let me explain."

"Showtime," Shanda said, pushing me forward. I felt an almost palpable wave of excitement from the crowd. Great. Nothing like a little drama to make a party memorable.

"We're done, Farell," I announced before I lost my nerve. I was supposed to love him . . . but he was supposed to love *me*, too. Asshole. "Go back to Allie."

He swayed, confused shock all over his face.

"But Darcy . . . I didn't mean it."

"You heard her," Boonie said, stepping forward. Erin straightened and lurched into Shanda, clearly trying to show her support no matter how drunk she was. "You're done. Go away."

"Shut up, you fucking loser," Farell said, swaying. "She's my girl. You want her but you can't have her."

"No, I *used* to be your girl," I said, the words cutting through me like knives. In the firelight he looked almost homeless, his clothes covered in dirt and pine needles. "It's over. You made your choice."

Farell looked confused, eyes blinking. Slowly he started to sneer.

"I see how it is," he said. "You're fucking him, aren't you? I guess trash calls to trash."

Boonie growled and stepped forward, reaching for him. Farell took a drunken swing and then they were all over each other. Shanda pulled me and Erin back as the students started shouting and screaming, "Fight! Fight! Fight!"

Farell was drunk off his ass, which should've made him an easy target. And he was—for every hit he landed, Boonie got him twice. The alcohol seemed to be dulling his senses, though. I wasn't sure he even felt the pain.

He couldn't possibly last long.

Not only that, Boonie was fast and more savage than I'd ever seen him. He threw a sudden flurry of punches, his face cold with fury. Then Farell went down hard and it was over. A hush fell over the crowd as Boonie swirled around and stalked over to me, chest still heaving. I'd never seen his eyes so wild.

"C'mon," he said. I looked around, wondering what to do. He didn't wait for me to answer, catching my hand and all but dragging me down the hillside. That's when I heard Farell shouting after us.

"Fuck you, whore! Go fuck your trashy boyfriend. He's *nothing,* just like you're nothing!"

Boonie stopped short, every muscle in his body rigid. Then he turned slowly to face Farell one last time.

"If you ever talk to her like that again, I'll kill you."

Nobody there could doubt him—Boonie meant every word. My former boyfriend blinked, and I saw raw terror. Then Boonie pulled on my hand again and we were off.

I stumbled along in shock for a while, finally realizing I had no idea where we were going, or even why I was with him, but I did know this—something monumental had just happened.

"Why did you fight with Farell?" I asked. Boonie turned on me, backing me into a small crypt surrounded by brush. The plaster-covered bricks hit my butt and I stared up at him, wide-eyed.

"Because he's an asshole," Boonie said. "Why the fuck did you let him stick his dick in you, Darcy?"

I gasped, shaking my head.

"I can't talk to you about this."

Boonie pushed forward into my space, reaching down to catch my waist as he lifted me to sit on the monument. Then he was standing between my bare legs, staring down into my face. A muscle in his jaw flexed. I felt one of his hands reach down and around my waist, spreading across the flat of my back.

His other hand rose to cup the back of my head, fingers burrowing into my hair.

"Been thinkin' about this all year," he whispered. "I come home and my fuckin' girl is with the biggest prick in the valley. Took you too long to figure it out, babe. Such a goddamn waste."

His fuckin' girl?

I hardly had time to process his words before he jerked me into his body, wrenching my head back for his kiss. I gasped and he took the opportunity to shove his tongue into my mouth.

I thought I'd been kissed before.

I was wrong. This was nothing like what I'd experienced with Farell—nothing like the first kiss Boonie had given me, either. This was a man's kiss, his mouth taking everything from me without mercy. I felt his cock hard between my legs and God help me, but I wanted him. Then his hips started moving in a slow, steady swivel that pressed my clit right into my pelvic bone. Lightning sheets of need shot down the length of my spine.

Boonie tore his mouth away suddenly, resting his forehead against mine. His body shuddered and mine answered like we'd been made for each other.

I'd never wanted Farell like this.

Not even close.

"Tell me no right now," he said, the words a low growl. "Otherwise we're doing this."

Reaching down, I slipped my hands under his shirt on either side of his body, sliding them along the sculpted curves of his muscles.

"I want this, too."

That was enough. Groaning, Boonie caught my mouth again, even as he shoved up my skirt. I spread for him and his fingers traced the lines of my opening through the silky fabric of my panties. Then he found my clit, creating waves of sensation and need as my body recognized his.

He teased me like that for an eternity. Boonie still hadn't touched my skin directly but I felt the pressure building. Finally he pushed the thin fabric of my thong aside and slid one strong, roughened finger into me.

Holy. Hell. I squeezed around him, unable to control myself. He ripped his mouth free to look at me. His eyes were wild and his breath came in deep, shuddering gasps.

"That's the hottest fucking pussy I've ever felt," he said, and while the words might not've been romantic, they were about the sexiest thing I'd ever heard.

"It'll feel better around your cock," I whispered, feeling a thrill of feminine power.

Boonie closed his eyes at my word, those little muscles in his jaw flexing over and over. He seemed to be fighting some sort of battle with himself. I took the opportunity to push up his shirt.

Then I leaned forward and very deliberately licked his nipple.

He exploded into action, ripping his finger out of me. He took a step back and I felt suddenly cold and alone. For an instant, I thought he was leaving me.

That devastated me.

He was mine. *We belonged together.*

Then Boonie's hands found his pants, jerking his fly open, and I realized he wasn't going anywhere. He'd gone commando, and my mouth fell open as his stiffened cock burst free. It was big and hard and all too ready to fill me.

I couldn't take my eyes off it.

The sound of a condom package opening reached my ears, and then Boonie caught his dick in his hand, pumping it twice before smoothing the rubber down its length.

I shifted, meaning to slip off my thong. He didn't give me the chance, catching my hips and jerking them just off the edge of the tomb. I fell back on my hands. His fingers shoved the narrow strip of fabric to the side, then I felt the head of his cock pressing into my opening.

"So fuckin' good," he groaned, sliding into me with an endless stroke that stretched me to the limits of my capacity. Reality narrowed, every part of me utterly focused on the feel of him deep inside. I closed my eyes and let my head fall back.

Strong hands caught my hips, sliding me closer to him.

His hips started moving faster, but it wasn't quite enough. I needed more. Reaching down between us, I found my clit and started rubbing it in time with his strokes.

His cock swelled and he moaned.

"Keep doing that," he gasped. "Hottest fuckin' thing I've ever seen."

Didn't have to ask me twice. I rubbed harder, feeling the pulsing waves of pleasure just out of my reach. Boonie's hands slid down around my ass, grabbing my cheeks and squeezing them roughly. That changed his angle. Suddenly his cock was slamming into some spot deep inside me that I'd never felt before.

"Oh, shit . . ." I whimpered, fingers flying aganst my clit. So close. *So. Fucking. Clo*—the orgasm slammed through me, my back arching as I clamped down around him. Hard.

Boonie's cock thickened and pulsed as he came, grinding his hips against mine.

I opened my eyes slowly, looking overhead to see a thousand stars floating overhead. Reality filtered in. In the distance I heard faint music and shouting.

Boonie leaned down, kissing me soft and slow.

"Fuck, I can't believe this is happening now," he whispered. "You should've dumped his ass earlier, before I signed papers."

Stretching like a cat, I savored the ache between my legs. Who knew sex could be that good? And to think, I'd thought sleeping with Farell was nice . . . he had nothing on Boonie.

"Signed papers for what?" I whispered, wondering how long it would take him to recover. I definitely wanted to do this again. Soon.

"The Marines. I leave for San Diego the day after tomorrow. Basic training."

My breath caught.

"Why?" I asked, wondering how the thought could hurt so much. We weren't dating. I had no hold on him—hell, up until an hour ago I'd been with someone else. Someone I was supposed to love. But how could you love one guy and then sleep with another?

Boonie gave a harsh laugh.

"Because there's nothing for me in Callup," he replied, his tone bitter. "You've made that pretty fuckin' clear this year, Darce. I finally got the message. My dad was a jarhead, figured if it was good enough for him, it'll be good enough for me."

I had no idea what to say. More shouting cut the air, louder this time, and the music stopped. Shit, that was Farell. I recognized his angry, drunken ranting. A truck door slammed, and I heard the sound of wheels spinning out on gravel and the roar of an engine.

Boonie leaned his forehead against mine.

"I want you in my bed," he said. "I want—"

A sudden, horrific crashing noise filled the air, all shrieking metal and shattering glass. Boonie pulled away and I sat up, adrenaline surging.

"What was that?"

"Car accident," he muttered, zipping up his pants. I heard screams in the distance. "Stay here."

Boonie took off down the hillside toward the road. I followed him, lurching through gravestones in the darkness, hoping I didn't fall and break my neck.

When I reached the embankment overlooking the road, I nearly fainted.

The pickup truck from the party—the one holding the big speakers and that they'd used to haul the kegs—had rolled sideways down the bank from the cemetery driveway, crashing across the road below to land in the creek.

"Dear God . . ."

Someone was screaming in the wreckage, and I heard shouting all around. Boonie was already climbing down to the shattered vehicle.

More boys followed him, falling over their own feet as they ran.

I slid down the bank on my butt, to find Boonie on his knees, peering inside the cab of the upside down truck. High-pitched, horrific cries came from inside.

"Jesus Christ," Boonie shouted, looking up to find me. "Stay back, Darce. You shouldn't see this."

"Who is it?" I asked, my throat tight. He shook his head, refusing the answer. The screams turned to a high-pitched, pain-filled keening.

"Who is it?!" I shrieked. "Tell me!"

"We need an ambulance," he yelled back. "The trailer park's less than a mile away. Someone needs to get down there, make the call."

"Answer my fucking question—who is it?"

"It's Farell," he said, unreadable emotions flashing across his face. "He was driving. Allie's in there, too. It's bad, Darcy. Real bad."

I wasn't sure if I should go to the hospital—what do you do when the guy you just broke up with gets in an accident? Even though Farell and I weren't together any more, when Boonie asked me to come home with him I said no. My head was too confused, a mass of emotion, guilt, and raw terror that Farell would die.

I hadn't been driving the truck, but I knew my boyfriend. Knew how he was when he got drunk. I'd humiliated him publicly and then left the party with his biggest rival—I should've seen this coming. Stopped it somehow.

Instead I'd been busy fucking Riley Boone on a grave. Jesus. What the hell was wrong with me?

Shanda offered me a ride, which I took over Boonie's protests. I couldn't look at him right now. Not that he'd done anything wrong—I just felt so guilty. What kind of girl sleeps with another guy right after breaking up with the boy she loved?

We planned to go back to the trailer park but found ourselves driving around aimlessly instead, neither of us sure what to say. Eventually I couldn't stand it anymore—I had to know if he was all right—so we drove to the hospital in Kellogg. Even so, when we pulled up to the emergency room I wasn't sure it was the right move.

"Should I go inside?" I asked Shanda, feeling sick to my stomach. "What if he's dead?"

The thought was almost unbearable. Yes, I'd broken up with Farell—after dating him for *eighteen months*. He was my first and I'd thought he'd be my last. *Oh, God . . .*

"I'm here with you," Shanda said, reaching over to catch my hand. "We'll just check and see how they're doing."

I nodded, unfastening my seat belt. The sliding ER doors gaped obscenely as we walked in together, holding hands.

Half the high school waited in the lobby.

I saw Bryce and Erin huddled together along the wall. Both were crying. Clumps of young people I'd grown up with surrounded them, wiping their eyes.

"Bitch," someone hissed as I walked past. Shanda spun around, glaring, but everyone looked away.

"Jesus Christ, shut the fuck up," Colby said, striding toward me. *Wow*. Hadn't seen that coming. He caught me up in a tight hug, and I felt myself start to tremble. Finally I pulled free, and swallowed.

I had to know.

"Tell me," I said. "Are they . . . ?"

Colby swallowed, his eyes red and puffy.

"Allie is gone."

The words cut through me. *No*. It couldn't be true.

"But she was screaming," I said, shaking my head. "She was awake. We all heard her. How can she be . . . dead?"

My throat choked as I whispered the word. This was too awful, too real. How had a stupid party turned into Allie dying? Suddenly I didn't care that I'd hated her, or that she'd slept with my boyfriend—we'd known each other since kindergarten, and now I'd never see her again. Not even a bitch like Allie deserved that.

And if *she* was dead, what about *him*?

"She lost consciousness in the ambulance," Colby continued. "She was bleeding inside her head. They did emergency surgery but her heart stopped on the table. They couldn't save her."

"Oh my God," I whispered. More guilt slammed through me— I'd wished her dead and now she was. I felt like I was going to throw up. Swallowing, I forced myself to ask the hardest question of all. "What about Farell?"

"He's in surgery right now," Colby said. "Nobody knows what's going on. His parents are waiting in the chapel."

He nodded toward a small door against the far wall.

"His mom's been asking for you," he added, his voice cracking.

Now I *really* needed to throw up. Renee Evans had been so incredibly good to me. When I'd first met her I expected her to hate me—after all, her golden boy had dragged home a girl from the trailer park. By valley standards I wasn't even close to good enough for him. But Renee never cared about any of that. She'd welcomed me with open arms, and eventually I spent more time at their house than my own. I hadn't let myself think about that until now—breaking up with Farell meant giving her up, too.

Pulling away from Colby, I walked over to the bathroom as fast I could without drawing even more attention. Thankfully it was clearly labeled and easy to find, because I barely made it inside before I started puking.

Everything tasted like beer and bile and betrayal.

"Darcy, is that you?" a familiar voice asked outside the stall. I stilled, clutching the toilet for support. Renee.

"I'm in here," I managed to say.

"Thank God," she replied. "Are you all right?"

Better than Allie, I thought, feeling a touch hysterical.

"I don't think any of us are all right."

"Come out," Renee replied softly. "I need to see you, sweetheart."

She didn't know, I realized. She still thought me and Farell were together, that I had a right to be here. What would she say when she found out? I flushed the toilet and stood, bracing myself. Then I stepped out of the stall.

Renee looked like hell.

Her hair hadn't been combed and her clothes didn't match. Way out of character, but I guess when your son's been in an accident you don't take the time to coordinate your outfit. Her eyes were red and puffy, but she gave me a small, brave smile as she held out her arms.

I couldn't do it.

"Renee, I need to tell you something."

"I already know—or at least I know enough," she said softly. "Bryce told me about your fight. Farell had another girl with him. But I know you care about him and right now I could really use your support."

Falling into her arms, I hugged her tight and sobbed. Everything was still awful and I was confused and scared, but just being close to her I felt better than I had all night.

"How is he?" I finally managed to ask.

"He's in surgery right now," she said, rubbing my back. "They told me his spine was crushed. We're not sure exactly what that will mean in the long run, but it can't be good. I don't know what's going to happen next, Darcy. I just don't know. I'd like you to come wait with us, though. I think Farell would want that."

I shook my head—she was wrong. Farell wouldn't want that at all.

"You know, Marcus and I have been married for twenty years now," she said softly. "That's a long time—you learn after a while that you can't judge a relationship by any one thing. People make mistakes. You have to look at all of it when you judge a man. Please come with me, Darcy. Maybe you don't want to do it for Farell right now, so do it for me. You've been like my own daughter this past year. Help me get through this. Please."

I nodded slowly, because what else could I do? Taking a minute to wash my face, I followed her back to the chapel.

He didn't get out of surgery until nine the next morning. It was a success, in that he was still alive. We wouldn't know about brain damage until he woke up.

If he woke up.

I stayed at the hospital with Renee and her husband, Marcus, until late afternoon. That's when Shanda came looking for me.

"Let me take you home," she said. "You need a shower and some rest."

"Will you be all right?" I asked Renee. She nodded, her eyes heavy.

"Get some sleep," she replied softly. "I'll call you if anything changes."

Thankfully, Shanda seemed to understand that I needed quiet so she didn't pester me with questions as we drove. We pulled into the trailer park around six p.m., and I saw a motorcycle in front of my house.

Boonie.

He was waiting on the porch, his face shadowed. I got out of the car and walked over to him.

"Hey," I said.

"Hey."

We studied each other, and for once I didn't feel any kind of attraction. I didn't feel anything at all—I was hollow. Used up.

Exhausted.

"I heard about Allie," he said quietly. "Bad shit."

"Yeah," I said, my voice catching. "Farell's in bad shape, too. They don't know when he'll wake up, or whether he'll ever walk again. I guess it's pretty unlikely. It was a bad accident."

"So you were with his family . . . What does that mean?"

I shrugged, wishing I had an answer.

"I have no idea," I replied softly. "I don't know what to think about any of it. I'm just so tired . . ."

"And us?"

His eyes bore through me, black as coals. I studied him, remembering how he'd felt deep inside me. It'd been good. The best I'd ever had, that was for sure. But what did having sex together really mean? He'd slept with half the senior girls this past year.

"So you're leaving tomorrow?" I asked after a long pause. He nodded.

"Yeah, I have to be at the Spokane airport by five in the morning."

"Wow."

"You need to sleep," he said finally. I blinked. He was right—I did.

"You want to come inside?" I asked. "My dad's home, but he won't care."

He probably wouldn't notice. Between the beer and the painkillers, he'd turned into a permanent lump in front of the TV. Boonie nodded, standing and reaching out his hand. I took it, then led him to my bedroom, where we collapsed together on my twin-sized bed. I'd love to say we made sweet love all night, or that we talked and it was beautiful and special.

The truth is that I passed out in his arms and didn't wake up for fourteen hours.

He left a note, said he'd write to me.

I took a shower and went back to the hospital.

FOUR DAYS LATER

"He wants to talk to you privately," Marcus told me, his eyes weary. Farell had been in a medically induced coma since the accident to let his brain heal. They'd woken him that morning, but I'd had to work and couldn't be there. I'd come over right after finishing my shift, still wearing my uniform.

Glancing toward the ICU door, I swallowed. I felt like a giant phony, waiting at the hospital like I had a right to be here. Renee seemed to appreciate it so much, though, and even Marcus looked happy to see me.

I couldn't understand it at first. Then Shanda pointed out that I was more than someone to sit with in the waiting room. I was a living, breathing tie to their son.

It was a lot of pressure.

Now I found myself walking into Farell's room, wondering why the hell I was putting myself through this. He lay on the bed, hardly looking like himself. Between the bruises, the tubes, and the casts, he could've been an extra on a hospital drama.

His eyes opened as I sat beside him carefully.

"Darcy?" he asked in a rough, painful whisper. "Are you really here? I've been having dreams . . ."

"It's me," I said, blinking back tears. Fuck. I stilled cared about him—I'd come to that unwelcome realization after the second day of sitting in the hospital. Guess that's one of life's little jokes.

Feelings don't just turn off.

"I talked to Bryce earlier," he said. "I don't remember graduation at all, or the accident. Dad told me Allie Stockwell is dead"—his voice broke—"and that I was driving the car. I killed her, Darcy. I was drunk."

I cleared my throat, blinking rapidly.

"Yeah, that's what happened."

"He also told me we broke up right before it happened. I don't remember any of it."

I reached for a tissue, wiping at my eyes.

"Let's not talk about that right now."

"No," he said, and while his voice was weak, his gaze on my face was strong. "Tell me. I need to know what happened. Nobody will tell me anything. They're all trying to protect me, but I really need to know what I did."

I sighed, then nodded my head.

"We were at the party, you know that much," I started. "You'd had a lot to drink. Everyone was just hanging out and after a while I lost track of you. Finally I went into the trees with Shanda to pee. On the way back we found you and Allie having sex."

Saying the words hurt.

"When you came back, I broke up with you and left the party.

Colby said you kept drinking more, then you and Allie left in Greg Krafft's truck and crashed it. Greg said he tried to stop you but you wouldn't listen."

Farell's eyes blinked rapidly, turning red.

"I'm so sorry," he whispered. "I don't know what happened, Darcy. They say I probably won't ever remember that night. I never meant to hurt Allie—I didn't even know her that well. And I can't think of any reason that I'd want to cheat on you. I love you."

The words hung heavy between us—what was he expecting from me?

"I slept with Riley Boone," I blurted out suddenly, feeling my stomach clench. "After you and I fought, we went off and had sex."

Farell's eyes widened, and I saw a flash of hurt.

"I guess I don't get to complain about that," he whispered. "Does . . . does this mean it's done between us?"

I felt a bittersweet pang. I'd loved him, or I thought I had.

But I couldn't stop thinking about Boonie, either.

"I don't know," I said finally. "Boonie left for basic training. He says he wants to stay in touch."

Farell grimaced. "Where does that leave us?"

"I don't know," I whispered. "I guess we just take things one day at a time."

"I love you, Darcy. However this works out, I want you to know that wasn't a lie. I fucked up, and I have no idea why I did it. I'll never forgive myself for what I did to Allie."

"Were you sleeping with her all along?" I asked. Farell met my gaze head on, his face anguished. The silence hung between us, punctuated only by the hum of the machines surrounding him.

"No," he said finally. "It's always been you, Darcy. You're the one I love. But right now I'm really fucking scared."

He tried to shift his arm to take my hand, a tear running down his face. Leaning over, I wrapped my fingers around his.

"They're taking good care of you," I whispered.

"It doesn't matter," he replied, his voice breaking. "The doctor said I'll probably never walk again. It's over, Darce. All of it. My whole life is over. I don't even have you anymore—I've lost everything."

His expression was so sad, so desperate. I couldn't leave him like this—so what if we weren't together anymore. I could be his friend, right? Taking a deep breath, I smiled at him.

"It's not over, Farell—I still care about you. So things have changed and that's hard, but you can't give up, okay? It's not time to give up."

He squeezed my hand.

"You promise?"

"Yeah, I promise."

July 20

Dear Boonie,

I'm glad to hear training is going well. Things are weird here in Callup. Everyone looks at me and whispers . . . I'd forgotten how they used to do that, before Farell and I started dating. Now they don't know what to make of the situation. Everything went crazy that night and it's still not right. Maybe it never will be.

As for me, I think about our time together a lot. I'm sort of embarrassed to write about it, but I hope you know what I mean when I say I wish you were here.

One thing I need to tell you—Renee Evans asked me to come by sometimes and help out once Farell comes home. It looks like he'll be on house arrest or probation for a long time (they're still talking to the prosecutors) but the judge is a family friend, so he's probably not looking at jail time. I think they figure he already paid for what he did, since he's paralyzed (and you know how this stuff goes in the valley anyway). I heard they gave Allie's family a lot of money but nobody knows for sure.

I hope you are okay.

Take care,
Darcy

———

October 1

Dear Boonie,

I hope you're feeling better now. Sucks that you got sick, but at least you still managed to graduate training. I was so disappointed you couldn't make it up to Callup on leave, tho. So far senior year isn't bad. Renee hired me to come after school and help take care of Farell, officially. Now that school started I couldn't help and still work, so this was a good solution for everyone. We got official word—he's not looking at jail time. Lots of probation, community service, all that. He's doing better now, too. Up and moving around in the wheelchair. They've been renovating the house to make everything work.

I still think about you a lot, and I'm sorry that when you tried to call the phone didn't work. We lost it after Dad ran up the bill. Mom and Dad had a huge fight over it. I guess I'm out of luck, unless you want to call me at Farell's house. That might be kind of weird because I told him about us.

Have you found out yet whether you'll have leave at Christmas? I know you aren't real close with your mom, but I'd really like to see you.

Hang in there,
Darcy

January 15

Dear Boonie,

I hope your holiday was good. I feel sort of stupid saying this, but are you getting my letters? Did I do something to make you mad? Maybe I was reading too much into that night together . . . I really thought you'd stay in touch.

Now I feel stupid for even writing this. Obviously you're choosing not to reply and I know you must have had some kind of leave by now. I heard your mom's back in Montana, so maybe you went there?

I hope your Christmas was good. Mom and Dad gave me a gift card to buy some clothes, although I've got no idea where the money came from. Things are still tight here since Mom's hours were cut. I'm chipping in to help out now—it takes most of what I earn.

Unless I hear from you again, I'm going to stop writing. It's been nearly three months without a letter. I still have some dignity left.

Your friend (or at least I thought was),
Darcy

November 10

Dear Boonie,

I really debated about writing this, but I wanted to let you know I'm getting married. You'll probably think I'm crazy. Here's the thing—Farell has changed a lot this past year and a half. He's quieter now, and he doesn't take life for granted the same way.

Back in high school I loved him, but then he cheated on me and . . . well, you know. We both learned a lot since then, and like Renee says, you can't judge a man on just one action. Anyway, I know he'll never cheat on me again—at least, he can't cheat on me like he did with Allie. I probably shouldn't go into details, you don't want to hear them and it's embarrassing.

I guess what I'm trying to say is that what we have is different than I expected from my life, but it's good. I'm happy. I hope you can be happy for me.

And yes, I know you probably won't even read this. That's okay, because I'm not writing it for you, really. I just need to put this part of my life behind me.

Wherever you are, I hope you're happy,
Darcy

CHAPTER THREE

COEUR D'ALENE, IDAHO
ELEVEN YEARS AGO
DARCY

"You up for a walk-in?" Kelly asked, popping her head into the break room. I glanced up from my cup of noodles, hoping I didn't have one hanging off my chin. "He's hot as hell. Lori's got an opening but he asked for you by name. Said he got a referral. Wants an eighty-minute massage."

I ran the math mentally—a longer session would throw my schedule off, because theoretically it would take up two full slots . . . but that was only if I had two clients to fill them. Right now I didn't.

"Sure, I can take him," I said, wiping off my face and studying my soup mournfully. I hadn't had time to eat much, but it's not like ramen technically qualified as food anyway. "He look like a big tipper?"

She shrugged.

"He looks like a sex god and you get to touch him all over. Who cares how he tips?"

I sighed. Kelly and I might be the same age, but I felt like I was decades older than her sometimes. Of course, she still lived in her mom's basement and went dancing every weekend. She was fond of pointing out that a pretty girl doesn't need money to party—that's what men are for. Buying drinks. Well, buying drinks and occasionally killing spiders.

These days I preferred paying my own way, thank you very much. (I could kill my own spiders, too.)

"Give me five and I'll come get him," I said. "Let me check the room first."

"Sounds good," she said with a wink. "That'll be enough time to get his number out of him. Maybe he's free to come out tonight with us? You're meeting me at ten down at the Ironhorse. No excuses this time."

It took everything I had not to roll my eyes. Five minutes later I'd checked my room, straightened the sheets on the massage table, and turned on the built-in warmer. A small fountain bubbled happily on my supply cabinet and a candle flickered on a shelf in the corner.

Ready.

I walked down the hall to the reception area, pasted on a professional smile, and stopped dead in my tracks. Riley Boone sat on a chair in the waiting room, one muscular leg propped up casually across his knee and a smug grin on his big stupid sexy face.

Absolutely no fucking way.

"Long time, no see," he drawled. "How's it goin', Darce? I hear you have good hands. Nice and strong, never too tired to finish . . ."

"Uh uh," I said firmly, shaking my head. "Kelly, he's all yours. I don't need this shit today."

"Oh, I think you do," he said, his eyes hard. He stood up slowly and walked toward me, dominating the room. "We got unfinished business."

I swallowed, eyes darting toward the leather vest he wore. Boonie had joined the Silver Bastards motorcycle club right after he got out of the Marines. He'd never been an easygoing guy, but his time in the service made him tougher. Meaner. Mix that with his club affiliation and suddenly you had some real potential for ugliness . . .

Did Farell owe the MC money? Probably.

Shit.

"Okay, let's go," I said, my voice shaking. Once upon a time he hadn't scared me. Times change. "C'mon through. Room three."

Kelly cleared her throat nervously.

"I'll be out here. Just let me know if you need anything, Darcy. Sign says we reserve the right to refuse customers." She glared at Boonie, reminding me why I loved her so much. Was Boonie hot? Absolutely. But Kelly would always put a friend ahead of a pretty face. Not that he was pretty, exactly . . . he was a little too rugged for that. Even more rugged since he'd broken his nose.

Don't pay attention to what he looks like! Been there, done that. It didn't end well, remember?

"It's all good," I told her, although I wasn't exactly confident. "He'll behave, won't you Boonie?"

He gave me a chin lift and I knew he had no intentions of behaving. I had a pretty good idea why he was waiting for me today. It had nothing to do with therapeutic massage. Shit. How long would Farell's baggage weigh me down?

"Come on back," I told him. "Third room on the left."

Holding the waiting room door open, I gestured for him to walk through. I hadn't seen him for three months at least. We'd run into each other occasionally in Callup, but I'd been avoiding town since I left Farell.

My new life was here in Coeur d'Alene and I liked it that way.

Boonie stepped through the door and started down the hall. I didn't deliberately look at his ass, I swear. But as he strolled past me I couldn't help myself. His jeans hugged his heavy thighs, cradling a world class butt I'd never gotten to fully explore. Tight and muscular, not big but not flat, either. Throw in the broad shoulders and aura of control, and there wasn't a woman on earth who wouldn't spontaneously ovulate when she saw him.

Unfortunately, covering that strong, broad back of his was a leather vest with a miner's skull and the words "Silver Bastards MC," branding him as someone I should avoid at all costs.

Everyone knew the Silver Bastards were into some shady shit— I'd learned growing up that when they came to the trailer park for a "talk" with someone, it was best to go inside and pretend you hadn't seen anything. If you left them alone, they wouldn't bother you. If Boonie said we had unfinished business, that could only mean one thing.

My soon-to-be ex-husband must owe them a lot more than I realized.

I shouldn't be surprised. He spent most of his days gambling, and not even Renee could keep making excuses after they repossessed the car. He'd been lying to them as much as he lied to me. When his folks finally cut him off—*after* I left, for the record—he'd panicked.

For the first time in his life, Farell Evans was having to take full responsibility for himself and he didn't like it one bit.

Not that I cared. I was over his shit. Now I just needed to convince the club that I had nothing to offer them. Boonie had been a friend, once upon a time. Maybe I could convince him to show me mercy?

He stepped into my tiny massage room and I followed, closing the door silently behind us. His oversized presence filled the entire space. Seeing him here was unnatural and out of place. Boonie belonged in the wild, or at the very least in the kind of place that could erupt into a bar fight at any time. Not in a small, dim room with a massage table and aromatherapy candles.

Best to face him straight up.

"How much does he owe you?" I asked, crossing my arms. He cocked his head, studying me. Silence filled the air and I swallowed. "Whatever he owes you, it's his problem. I moved out three months ago. We may not be divorced yet, but it's definitely over and I have nothing to do with his finances. We never even had a joint checking account and my name's not on anything."

"What makes you think I'm here to collect money?"

I snorted. "Right, you're here for a massage? Come off it, Boonie. If the club wants money from Farell, great. Go talk to him about it. I've got nothing—I didn't even take my engagement ring when I left. He's probably pawned it by now."

Boonie shook his head, all leashed tension and predatory menace.

"I'm not here to talk to you about money. But you bring up a good point."

"What's that?" I asked. The room really felt too small. I was used to my clients lying down on the table—I liked it that way. I was in control, powerful. Boonie was way too tall, and he was definitely using up more than his fair share of the oxygen in here.

"I'd already heard you left him."

"Right . . ." I replied, confused.

"Why?"

"Because he's an asshole and I couldn't take it anymore."

"What happened to taking care of him?" he asked, mocking me. "I thought it was your *job*?"

Shit. He wasn't playing fair.

"I was just a kid," I said. "I thought he needed me, that he loved me. Maybe he did, in his own way, but that was a long time ago. Now all he does is drink and gamble. At this rate he'll be dead in a few years anyway, because he ignores his doctors. I guess I woke up one morning and realized I'd married my dad. Sooner or later we all have to grow up."

He studied me, those dark eyes of his impossible to read as ever.

"I had to hear about it in a bar," he said finally, his voice tight.

"What?"

"I learned you left your *husband*"—he said, spitting the word out—"in a bar. Jake Preston and Chad Gunn were talking about how much they wanted to tap your ass now that it was on the market again."

I swallowed, feeling a little sick to my stomach. Callup never changed, apparently. Good thing I lived in Coeur d'Alene.

"That's . . . flattering," I managed to say. "But I'm not quite sure what that has to do with you being here."

Boonie gave me a tight smile that never quite reached his eyes.

"Now you're just being difficult," he said, his voice low and rough. A spark of tension raced down my spine, settling low between my legs. Thank God my arms were crossed, because I was pretty sure my nipples had gotten hard. So what if I wanted Boonie? That wasn't a big deal—so did every other woman who met him.

"I have no idea what you're talking about."

No, but you've got a fantasy, my traitorous brain whispered. Right, because *that* had turned out so well last time.

"So that's really how you're gonna play it? Fine. Tell me about the massage," he said abruptly. I blinked, caught off guard.

"Well, treatment depends on what kind of issues you're having. We can do everything from deep tissue to simple relaxation." I swallowed, frowning. "Boonie, I don't think this is a good idea. If Farell doesn't owe you money then I don't think you should be in here."

"Why not?" he taunted. "Do you have a problem touching me? If that's the case, lay it out for me. How is rubbing your hands all over my body a problem for you? 'Cause it sure as fuck isn't one for me."

Hearing those words should really piss me off, because this wasn't some cheap massage parlor where they hand out happy endings. Unfortunately, hearing him talk like that was a turn on, which seemed deeply unfair.

He was the last man I should be attracted to.

I'd just gotten *out* of one shitty relationship, and while I might not see Boonie very often, I knew far too much about him. He was Callup born and bred, and we kept track of our own whether they liked it or not. He'd given the ladies down at the Breakfast Table more than his fair share of good gossip since he'd come home last year.

According to them, the man was hornier than an alley cat.

Shit. I couldn't think about that right now.

"I'm a professional, Boonie," I told him firmly. "I'll step outside and let you get ready. Undress to your comfort level and lie face down under the sheet. I'll be back in just a couple of minutes."

I stepped out of the room and shut the door, leaning back against it. Could I do this? I wasn't sure. If I'd had any idea he'd actually expected me to *touch* him I wouldn't have let him back into the room at all.

Liar.

Why hadn't he gotten fat? Or started losing his hair? Granted, twenty-three was young to start balding but that hadn't prevented it from happening to Farell.

God, I wished I could go back in time. Maybe if I'd walked out of the hospital without talking to Renee that night, things would be different right now.

Except they wouldn't. Even if I'd been free, Boonie hadn't been. And now the Bastards held him tighter than any woman ever could.

"You okay?" Kelly asked, peering through the small pass-through window between the rooms and the reception area.

Say you can't do it. Just tell her you're not feeling good, you're going to throw up, anything to get out of walking back into that room.

But I'd only been working here for six months. For three of those, Farell had been leaving nasty phone messages and while Gloria had been patient, did I really want to risk causing trouble? Because getting rid of Boonie would be trouble, no question. He wouldn't just get up and walk away without a fight.

Boonie never, ever backed away from a fight.

I knocked on the door, then stepped inside. The man who'd beat up my boyfriend before fucking me on a stranger's grave lay on his stomach, watching me speculatively as I came toward him. Everything about the situation was completely appropriate on the surface—the sheet covered him to the middle of his back, just like it was supposed to. He should have been just another massage client, one of hundreds I'd seen since graduation.

He wasn't, though. Not even a little bit.

I swallowed, then came to stand next to him. "Everything comfortable?"

"Yeah."

"All right. Just go ahead and relax. Let me know if the pressure's all right or if there's anywhere I should concentrate on."

Once again, the words were the same I'd used a thousand times, but somehow they seemed different today. Dirty.

Thankfully I could ease into this. Pumping my hand full of lotion, I reached down and touched his back for the first time. Oh crap . . . All these years I'd told myself I'd imagined how good his body felt. That I'd been drunk, that whatever Boonie and I had between us had been a figment of the booze and the fire and all the adrenaline that followed.

I was wrong.

His skin felt smooth and hot against my fingers, silky soft over a layer of hard muscles. My heart skipped a beat and I stilled.

"You okay?" he asked, his voice low. I swallowed.

"Fine. How's the pressure?"

The words hung between us and I bit back a giggle. What was wrong with me?

"Give me everything," he finally said. It took everything I had to force my hands to keep moving. I warmed up his back with slow, steady strokes, studying his Marine Corps tattoos. Every touch reminded me of that brief, incredible moment when he'd pulled me out of the party and taken me in the darkness. I still had dreams about it. I wondered if that night even stuck out in his memory. He'd fallen out of touch so fast—it'd obviously meant a lot more to me than it had to him.

Not a huge surprise, I guess. We'd never even had a date. Just a fast, hard fuck. One of many in his life.

"So you're living in Coeur d'Alene now?" he asked as I started working his shoulder.

"Uh-huh," I answered, falling into the rhythm of my strokes. "I moved out three months ago. They tell me the divorce should be easy—I don't want anything from him."

The words came out sharper than I planned, and I felt his body tense.

"Did he hurt you?"

Fuck, how to answer that one? I considered my response carefully and I smoothed down the length of his arm.

"Not physically," I finally said. "But that night changed him . . ."

Boonie snorted, muscles growing tighter.

"According to your letters that was a good thing."

"You read them?"

"Yeah, I fuckin' read them."

Then why didn't you answer?

I didn't ask, moving down to his lower body instead. Reaching for the sheet, I folded it back to tuck behind his leg, fingers brushing the back of his right glute in the process. The technique called for me to fold it across, revealing the sides as I tucked it down between his legs. His muscles flexed, and he took in a harsh breath.

Oh, wow. My nipples were hard as rocks and need twisted me up into a tight knot. That strange, intense chemistry between us sure as fuck hadn't faded.

I started massaging his feet, giving myself permission to enjoy the interplay of muscle and skin as I worked him over. By the time I reached his upper thigh, we were both breathing hard. I felt a bead of sweat on my forehead, and reached up to brush it off with the back of my hand.

Despite the tension hanging in the air—or perhaps because of it?—Boonie stayed perfectly still. I was starting to actually believe this wasn't about the money Farell owed.

"Why are you really here, Boonie?" I asked him softly as I adjusted the drape, moving to the other side. He shifted, hips pressing down into the table. Without thinking, I smoothed my hand down his back. A light sheen of sweat covered it.

"Are you too warm?" I asked, moving back into professional mode. "I can turn down the heat on the table."

"That won't help," he gritted out. Okay. I dropped my hands back down, fingers trailing over his ass as I tucked the sheet between his legs. I pushed it down a little too far and brushed what could only be his erection.

We both froze, me in utter shock and horror. Men got them of course. It was a basic biological function, and I was a professional providing a therapeutic service. Like a nurse, I knew better than to take it personally.

But this was very, very personal.

Boonie pushed to his elbows, turning back to look at me.

"Either grab it right or move your fuckin' hand," he growled. "Because I'm about five seconds away from bending you over this table."

I jerked away, stepping back from the table. We stared at each other, history hanging heavy.

"I think you should go," I managed to whisper. "There won't be a charge. Just leave, Boonie. I can't do this."

He gave me a slow, predatory smile. Like a shark.

"Farell owes the club twenty-five thousand. But that's nothing. He owes the Reapers, too. He spends it faster than the Evans family can bail him out. It's not gonna end well. So far I've kept them off you, babe. Let's hope it stays that way."

I swallowed at his veiled threat.

"That's unfortunate," I replied after a long pause. "But I don't see what it has to do with me. Renee gave me an allowance—it's the only cash I ever had. I have two thousand dollars saved up and that took me three years. That's all I can give you. It doesn't matter what you threaten. I can't give you money that doesn't exist."

"I don't want your money," he said, eyes burning. We stared at each other, a whole world of unspoken words between us.

"Why did you stop writing to me?" I asked him suddenly. I'd spent years wondering . . . Now I had nothing to lose by asking.

"Every letter you sent was full of *him*," Boonie replied, almost snarling. "You never said a goddamned thing about us. Then I realized there wasn't an us, at least not to you. I'm not a fuckin' masochist, Darce. You think I didn't see what was happening?"

"I felt guilty," I whispered. "You don't understand—you weren't here. Everywhere I went, people looked at me. They talked about me, called me a slut. Said it was my fault, because of our fight. Someone at that party saw us together, did you know that? I never found out who, but the whole school knew about it. You beat him up and then we fucked on a grave while Allie died. You think it was easy, walking into that school every day?"

Once the words started flowing, I found I couldn't stop them. It felt good to let it all out. The only person I'd ever talked to about it before was Shanda.

She knew exactly what it felt like to be judged.

"So long as Renee stood up for me, I could handle it," I continued, my voice rising. "And I *liked* helping her. She was good to me, Boonie. She always had been. Treated me like a family member, and it felt good. Their house was clean, their food was good, and they listened to nice music and actually talked to each other in the evenings. You were *gone*, Boonie. You have no fucking idea what I was up against. And you know what? I liked helping Farell, too. It felt good to be needed because nobody else gave a shit about me. You didn't even fucking write back!"

I practically shouted the last sentence, and my body trembled. Someone knocked at the door.

"You all right in there, Darcy?" Kelly asked, her voice hard. I held Boonie's eyes.

"Yeah," I replied. "Everything's just peachy keen in here."

"Okay, but I'm right here," she said, sounding skeptical. "Gloria has no problem with us asking a customer to leave if they aren't appropriate. You might want to remind Mr. Boone of that."

Boonie stared me down.

"I don't have a problem right now," he said slowly. "But if you don't finish, I will."

Asshole.

"I can do my job."

He nodded, lowering back down to the table. I pumped more lotion and started in on his thigh. This time my hands were rougher, harder. He'd said he could take whatever I gave out? Well, he was about to learn I wasn't the same weak little girl he'd known in Callup.

My hands were strong now, just like the rest of me.

Boonie grunted as my fingers dug in, finding each muscle and working it until I knew he'd be sore the next day.

"Is that too much?" I asked ten minutes later. He gave a low laugh.

"I'll take everything you have and more, Darce. You should know that by now."

After that it was a contest of wills. No matter how hard I worked him, he refused to complain.

"I'm ready for you to roll over," I said finally, feeling frustrated. "I'll hold the sheet for you."

"You don't want me on my back right now," he said, pushing his hips lewdly into the table. I watched the flex of his butt and thigh, his meaning all too clear.

Goddammit.

"Um, I can just do a relaxing massage on your back for the rest of the time, I guess."

"Darcy?"

"Yes?"

"I think it's time for this to end," he told me, his voice strained.

"Sounds great," I said quickly, not even pausing to gloat. "I'll step out so you can get dressed. We didn't go the full time, so I'll tell Kelly that—"

"Sit down."

It wasn't a request. *Fuck.* I reached for my small rolling stool and sat down. Boonie pushed to his elbows, putting us face to face. For the first time his face softened.

"Renee Evans came to my graduation from basic training," he said slowly. "Did you know that?"

His words stunned me.

"What?"

"She came to my graduation," he said again slowly. "Afterward she talked to me. She said that you were doing well, but that life had gotten hard for you. She told me how people were, and she told me how big a help you were to their family. Then she told me that if I cared about you at all, I'd let you go."

I swayed on the stool, trying to process what he was saying.

"Why?" I asked. "Why would she do that?"

"I think she believed it," he replied slowly. "She said she'd protect you, but only if I stopped writing. Otherwise you'd be on your own, at the mercy of that whole damned town. So I stopped writing. I couldn't be here for you and you weren't even a legal adult yet . . . She said your life would be a living hell. I knew she was right."

Every word was like a knife cutting me.

"Is that why you never came back to Callup?"

"I did come back," he replied. "The summer you finished high school. I saw you with Farell at the park. He was in his chair and you were racing each other. You were both laughing and you looked so happy together, Darcy. I had nothing to give you and he had everything. Not even I'm that big of an asshole."

I swallowed, studying his face. He was telling the truth, absolutely no question. I couldn't believe Renee had done it. Even now she was like a mother to me. Why?

To protect Farell, of course.

She'd been his mother first.

"That fucking sucks," I whispered.

"Were you happy with him?"

I sighed, wishing I'd never gotten out of bed that morning. It was too much. All of it.

"At first, maybe. He didn't get bad until after we'd been married for close to a year. He's got a lot of pain—the nerve damage makes it almost constant. He was drinking more and more, and he burned through pain pills like you wouldn't believe. Then he started gambling and things got ugly. His parents spent more than six hundred thousand bucks bailing him out that I know of. Like I said, they've finally cut him off."

"You never answered my question—did he hurt you?"

"He never hit me. My lawyer tells me he was verbally abusive, whatever that means. All I know is that I was dying inside. I'm not ready to be dead."

We stared at each other, then he reached out to wipe something off my cheek. A tear. I hadn't even realized I was crying.

"I want you, Darce," he said, his words more intense than anything I'd ever heard in my life. "I never stopped wanting you. Not for one day. You've been in my blood since we were kids."

Swallowing, I closed my eyes, desperate to carve out enough space to think. This was huge, all of it. Him still wanting me, learning that Renee had set me up.

That hurt. I'd trusted her.

I guess there wasn't much I wouldn't put past the Evans family. There was a reason I hadn't asked for anything in the divorce— their money didn't just come with strings.

It came with chains.

"I'm not ready for a relationship yet," I said, looking at him again. "For the first time in my life, I'm free. I'm not sure I can give that up again."

Boonie's eyes darkened.

"Give me a chance," he said softly. "That's all I'm asking."

"I'll think about it."

I spent the rest of the day obsessing about our talk. Part of me wanted to call Farell's mom and confront her—she'd been my ally, my savior, even my friend for so long now.

I couldn't believe she'd done this to me.

Of course, she probably thought she'd been doing me a favor. In her mind, I was a poor girl who'd done well for herself, marrying into one of the most prominent families in the valley. I knew better than that now.

You can't buy happiness.

By that evening I was tired of thinking, so a night partying with

Kelly and her friends sounded perfect. I didn't know the girls that well, but we'd gone out a few times and they were all fun and nice. Not only that, there was a huge car show going on downtown. Thousands of people were flooding the streets to see the hot rods parading, which meant lots of good music, cheap booze, and dancing in my future. So what if Boonie confused me? That didn't mean I shouldn't go out and have fun.

Tomorrow was soon enough to figure him out.

Popping a beer, I pulled on a short skirt and a sexy thong/bra combo I'd bought for myself to celebrate the divorce. I finished it off with a low-cut top that showed off my shoulders, and cute sandals. My hair was long and free, my makeup was just this side of slutty, and I was ready for action.

Unfortunately, it was still two hours before I was supposed to meet my friends. I decided to go down early, finding a spot on Sherman Avenue to sit on the curb and watch the cars drive by. All around me little children jumped and squealed, their parents drinking beer and arguing about whether Ford or Chevy should rule the world.

Time passed as the kids disappeared and younger people started filling the bars. It felt good to be out. Farell didn't like being around people after his accident, so it seemed like we always ended up staying home.

The Ironhorse had a live band for the night, and they'd opened up their big sliding glass doors onto the street, creating a beer garden outside. Kelly was already there when I came in, along with her friend Cherise. I knew there were more girls on the way, but they weren't going to join us until later. We did a round of shots before hitting the dance floor, and by midnight I couldn't remember why the hell I'd ever considered staying home.

"I need water!" I yelled in Kelly's ear, lurching toward the bar. We had a table staked out in the back corner, but flagging down a waitress was next to impossible.

"Grab a pitcher for the table!" she replied, turning back to the dance floor. I wound my way through the crowds of people, trying not to fall on my face. I'd lost track of how many shots we'd done. More than a lot, but not *too* many. Yet. I giggled at the thought— when was the last time I went out and just let myself go?

The bar was slammed, of course. Not exactly a huge surprise, but I didn't mind waiting my turn. I could use the break. Even though I was in good shape, all that dancing left me out of breath and covered in sweat. I probably looked like hell, but that didn't matter—I wasn't here to find a man.

Fuck romance. Being single kicked ass.

I should tell that to Boonie, I decided. He might be hot and have a nice dick, but I wasn't going to let any man tie me down. *Ha!*

"Can I buy you a drink?" asked a guy next to me, and I turned to look at him. He was cute—probably around my age or a little older, with a shock of dark black hair and green eyes. He was all frat boy, coated in a thick layer of Abercrombie and Fitch. Kelly would be all over him.

I opened my mouth to tell him I was married, then snapped it shut again *because I wasn't married anymore!*

Holy *crap*, that was awesome. Suddenly I grinned at him like an idiot, leaning toward him to say, "No, but thanks for asking."

I turned away to find the bartender smirking at our little exchange, and shrugged my shoulders in a "whatcha gonna do?" kind of move.

"Can I get a pitcher of water?"

"And a round of kamikazes," a deep voice said behind me. I froze as big arms reached down to grasp the bar on either side of me.

Boonie?

I could see his reflection in the mirror behind the bartender. He stepped closer, crowding and covering me with his powerful body. Then he leaned down, smoothing aside my hair to speak directly in my ear.

"That guy sitting next to you looks like he wants to eat you," he said. "You give him anything that should be mine?"

I stiffened, refusing to reply as the bartender set a tray of shots in front of us. Then I reached into a pocket to pay for them, because like I said—I buy my own drinks.

Boonie wrapped an arm around my waist, trapping my hand as he handed the bartender a wad of bills.

"I ordered the fuckin' shots," he rumbled in my ear. "What's got your panties in a knot?"

I smelled alcohol on his breath and I wondered who he'd been drinking with. Was it a woman? I turned in his arms to frown at him.

"I've decided to stay single for the rest of my life," I announced grandly. "I don't care how good you are at sex—I'm not interested."

Boonie gave a shit-eating grin as he tipped the bartender.

"So you think I'm good at sex?"

"Don't be a dumbass," I said, rolling my eyes. Uh oh. That made me dizzy. I caught his arm and steadied myself, wondering what I'd been planning to say.

"Where's your table?" he asked. I glared at him.

"It's full," I declared. "We don't have room for you."

"You can sit on my lap."

He wasn't kidding about sitting on his lap. Kelly and the others squealed with excitement when they saw the tray of kamikazes, and they squealed harder when five big men wearing Silver Bastard and Reapers MC colors came to join us.

"You know," Kelly slurred, leaning toward Boonie. "I didn't like you very much this afternoon—even wished I hadn't told you where to find us. I'm really glad I did."

I turned on her.

"You told him?" I demanded. "I thought you were on my team!"

"I'm sorry! It was before you took him back with you—remember I said I was trying for his phone number? And he bought us shots. He's a good guy."

I frowned, not liking how he'd pumped my friend for information. In all fairness, though, she'd probably been the one doing the pumping.

Pumping. Ha. A fit of giggles overtook me as I reached for another tiny glass.

"What's so funny?" Boonie asked, his lips tracing the edges of my ear. It distracted me long enough for him to take away my drink and set it out of reach, which was really unfair. Then his hand started running up and down my thigh under the table and I forgot all about the booze.

"Kelly pumped you," I said, giggling again.

He gave a low laugh. "Darce, you're hot as hell but I got no fuckin' idea what you're talking about."

I let my head flop back on his shoulder, smiling at him. God, he was beautiful. Kelly squawked as one of the bikers caught her hand, dragging her off toward the dance floor.

"You want to dance?" Boonie asked. I nodded, grinning at him. "I take it that means you're over your snit?"

I frowned. "What snit?"

"At the bar. You looked pissed to see me. I wondered what'd been going through that brain of yours."

I frowned, trying to remember. Oh, yeah. I wasn't married anymore. That was pretty fabulous.

"I like being single," I informed him. "I like how nobody tells me what to do. If you tell me what to do, that'll piss me off."

He laughed, then leaned close.

"Babe, I'm not Farell."

I shifted in his lap, feeling the bulge of his cock flex under my ass. A wave of heated need ran through me, and my drunken mouth spoke before giving my brain a chance to weigh in.

"The last time I had any real penis/vagina action was with you in that cemetery," I said, trying to focus on his face. Unfortunately things had started to spin, making it damned. Ha. *Hard.* I liked hard things. "Farell couldn't get it up after the accident. We still fooled around and he got me off, but even that hasn't happened for at least a year."

"Jesus Christ," he groaned, turning me toward him. One hand caught my hair, and then he was kissing me hard, tongue diving deep into my mouth. His dick turned rock solid under my ass and I wiggled happily because everything was tingly between my legs— *woohoo!*

Things got real fuzzy after that.

I know we danced for a long time. We also made out a bunch, which was perfectly fine because after every kiss I reminded him that I absolutely, positively wasn't interested in a relationship.

Boonie just nodded and smiled—then he'd kiss me again.

The only part that wasn't so great were the other bikers. Now that I knew how much money Farell owed, I was a little scared they might ask me about it. Fortunately, they were too busy trying to convince Kelly and the others to come back to their clubhouse and party to pay attention to me.

By last call, I was exhausted, starving, and horny as hell.

That's when Kelly stood and informed us we needed a "potty break." We all trouped to the bathroom in a giggly, wobbling clump, taking turns using the disgusting little stall as Kelly called for a vote.

"So what's next, girls? We going to that party or doing our own thing?"

I frowned into the mirror, then made fish lips at myself. *Glub. Glub.* Funny . . . Sudden, loud shouting broke through my alcoholic fog and I blinked. This wasn't happy, "We're at the bar!" shouting. These were definitely "Holy shit, something's really wrong!" noises.

"What the fuck?" Kelly asked as we looked at each other with wide eyes. Creeping to the door, I opened it a smidge. People were rushing through the hall toward the emergency exit. Not good.

"We gotta get out of here," I told her. Someone pushed against the door and I stepped back as Boonie opened it, his face dead serious.

"C'mon, all of you," he said, grabbing my wrist to pull me out into the hall. The rest of the girls followed and then his friends were with us as we joined the tide of people. I still had no idea what the hell was going on. After a few long, confusing minutes the flow of bodies burst out into the alley and I saw flashing lights everywhere.

"Fuck," Boonie said, jerking me closer. Good thing, too, because people were lurching and falling all around us. I heard someone shouting over a loudspeaker, but I couldn't tell what they were saying.

We started following the back of the building, trying to get away from the crowd. In the distance I heard the roar of more shouting and screams. I couldn't see Kelly anymore. I couldn't really see anything—just random people rushing in all directions, their faces panicked.

After an eternity of waiting, we reached the end of the alley and ran into the street. That's when I saw the line of cops wearing riot gear and carrying plastic shields. They were shouting something . . . "Get back!"

"Oh, fuck," Boonie said, looking around. Suddenly a rock flew over our heads. It hit one of the cops. Then a glass beer bottle shattered against a shield. The police line faltered, and one of them stepped out of line, lifting his baton to hit a man who'd been standing too close. Suddenly the others started hitting people, too, and the crowd panicked. Everyone surged back but there was nowhere to run—the wall of people behind us just kept pressing forward. I felt Boonie's grip on me slip.

"Boonie!" a man shouted. I looked over to see one of his biker friends waving at us. He plowed into the crowd, cutting a line toward us. Boonie caught me up, throwing me over his shoulder as he moved toward his friend. People were throwing more rocks now as the police kept fighting them.

What the hell? *Things like this don't happen in Coeur d'Alene!*

The crowd ebbed and surged around us as Boonie fought free, then we were running across Lakeside Avenue into the neighborhood just north of downtown. We weren't the only ones fleeing— all around people ran up the street, shouting and crying. I'd never seen anything like it.

"You okay?" Boonie asked, setting me back down. I nodded.

"The others already left," his friend replied.

"Thanks, brother," Boonie said. I looked at him, noticing the Silver Bastard patches he wore. This man had thrown himself into a rioting crowd to guide us to safety, I realized. No wonder Boonie considered him a brother. I think that's the first time I realized the club might be more than a criminal gang . . .

"Thank you," I told him, and the man gave me a toothy smile. That's when I saw a trail of blood trickling down his forehead.

"Are you hurt?"

"No worries," he said, wiping at it. "One of 'em got me, but I got him back."

The sudden, bright light of a spotlight filled my eyes.

"Stay where you are," a voice said over a loudspeaker.

"Let's go!" Boonie's friend shouted, then we were running again as the sound of the rioting crowd grew louder behind us.

Ten minutes later, Boonie and I had slowed to a walk as we moved up Fifth Street. I had no idea where his friend had gone, or where Kelly was.

"Would your friends have taken the girls with them?" I asked

Boonie as we stopped to lean against a wooden privacy fence. My breath came hard and my side hurt from running. At least I wasn't feeling drunk anymore. Way too much adrenaline . . .

"Yeah, they should be fine," he said, rubbing the back of his neck. "We planned it out when we came looking for you. Fuck. Don't take this the wrong way, but every time I kiss you something blows up. I'm startin' to think we're cursed."

I looked at him, and realized he was right. First the mine, then Farell's crash . . . now whatever the ever-loving fuck this had been.

"Damn. What do you think would happen if we actually made it to a second date?"

He stared at me, then his face cracked and he started laughing. I caught his mood, and then we were both laughing so hard tears ran down my face

"Fuck if I know," he said admitted finally. "Apocalypse or some shit?"

I sobered, frowning at him. He was joking, of course, but he raised a point. Bad things really did seem to happen every time we got together.

"Maybe for the good of humanity we should call it quits?"

"No way," he said, pulling me into his body for a hard kiss. My insides heated and I guess I wasn't totally sober after all, because I felt absolutely no inhibitions.

A car sped by and someone shouted, "Cops are coming!"

Boonie dropped me abruptly. Down the street I saw the flash of blue lights.

"Are you kiddin' me?" he asked, glancing around. "Over here."

I followed him into the alley behind the fence. It had a gate, but it was locked. Not a problem for Boonie—he caught the edge of the fence and jumped, boosting himself up and over. Seconds later it opened from the inside. I ran through right before the squad car turned down the alley. Boonie slammed it shut behind me, and we both leaned back against it, panting.

"Are they looking for us?" I asked, confused.

"Doubt it," he replied. "I mean, they always target the club, but I'm thinkin' they just want to clear out downtown."

"What the hell happened? Did you see anything?"

"Yeah," he said. "There was a biker outside the bar. The cops were givin' him shit, and then some guys in the crowd started arguing with them. By the time I realized what was happening, the biker was already gone. Still not quite sure how it turned into a riot."

I glanced at him sharply. "Was he one of your friends?"

"Nope. Never saw him before and he wasn't wearing club colors. All happened pretty damned fast. I think the cops panicked."

Beyond the fence more lights flashed. We heard the police car pull into the alley, then it stopped and the lights went dark. I heard the crackle of the cop's radio—he'd parked there. Crap.

"So now what?" I whispered. "I think we're stuck here."

Boonie shook his head, lifting a finger to his lips but it was too late.

"You hear something?" a voice asked. Suddenly a flashlight hit the other side of the fence, narrow strips of light shining through the cracks in the boards. I gasped. In an instant, Boonie caught my head, covering my mouth with his hand.

"Boost me up," said another man. "I'll look over the top, maybe I'll see something."

Boonie let my mouth go, holding my gaze intently. As the cops shifted just inches from us, he jerked his chin behind me. I glanced around to see an overgrown lilac shrub—it was more than big enough to hide us . . . assuming we could reach it.

Fortunately we'd been in this situation before.

Not with the cops, of course. But when we'd been kids we'd had a far more terrifying nemesis.

Granny Blackthorne.

Twice a week she baked bread for her family, which she'd set out to on her back porch. She also put out cookies, cupcakes, and even the occasional pie.

Looking back, it's obvious that she was leaving the food for the kids in the trailer park. Most of us had enough to eat—at least during the school year, when we could get free lunches at school—but a lot of it was cheap, prepackaged shit. Not long after the worm incident, Boonie had judged me worthy to join his raiding party. Because I'd been a cute little girl, they'd used me as bait. I'd pick a handful of wildflowers, then go knock at Granny's door. After a few minutes—her hearing wasn't so good—she'd answer and I'd hold them out, offering my best gap-toothed smile and lisping about how much I liked her roses.

It was my job to keep her talking as long as possible, while Boonie and the boys went raiding. I'd wait for the signal and then run off to share get my share of the booty.

She never caught on to us—or so we assumed—but no matter how much we stole, she put out more. Along the way, we'd developed a whole secret language of elaborate hand gestures, winks, et cetera, because you never knew what might happen during a highly dangerous food raid.

Now Boonie blinked at me twice in the old pattern.

Back up.

The cops were talking again, then I heard a flashlight hitting the boards. I nodded understanding, taking two steps backward as Boonie guided me. He caught my hands and lowered me to the ground. Seconds later I'd scooted silently into the safety of the shrub. Boonie followed, crawling over my body just in time.

Behind him—through the leaves—I saw the cop peering over the fence, shining his light into the back yard. Boonie looked down on me, his body heavy as we lay perfectly still.

"You see anything?" the cop asked his partner.

"Nope, looks clear."

The man grunted as he dropped back down, his radio crackling again. I became more aware of Boonie's weight pinning me in the darkness. His legs tangled with mine, reminding me of that afternoon in the woods above the trailer park.

He'd been heavy on me then, too. Now his hips pressed down and his mouth dropped over mine.

I wanted to protest—the cops were less than five feet away—but he didn't give me a chance. He nipped at my lip, then shoved his tongue deep inside as I gasped. My head started to spin as he kissed me, taking advantage of the fact that I couldn't risk making a sound.

When his hand trailed down my side, sliding between us to catch my thigh, I started getting nervous. When he pushed my leg out to grind his pelvis into me I felt something like panic, knowing there wasn't much Boonie wouldn't dare.

How far would he take this?

Farther than was comfortable. His cock pushed into the softness between my legs and like always, the chemistry between us was instant and powerful. He shifted, his hard cock rubbing against my clit. For long minutes he swiveled his hips slowly, pressing me back into the dirt silently as fire raced up my spine.

I wanted to strain against him but I couldn't—he was already being so reckless, so crazy. No matter what I did, I'd risk making noise. Not that they had any reason to arrest us.

Not any legitimate reason.

But not half an hour ago I'd watched the police start beating people with clubs, people just like me—and that was in front of *witnesses*. What would they do here in the dark, where nobody could see them?

Boonie pushed up on one arm, still holding my lips captive as he reached down to catch my shirt. Then his fingers caught my left nipple, pinching it lightly and tugging as his hips kept their steady rhythm.

We heard thudding footsteps as a group of people ran by, the police parked beyond the fence racing to meet them. Someone screamed. I couldn't move, couldn't think, couldn't do anything. Boonie wasn't so inhibited.

Taking advantage of the distraction, he lifted his hips and reached down to unzip his pants. Then he pulled up my skirt and I felt my ass hit the bare dirt.

I really needed to stop wearing skirts. Seconds later his fingers slid inside me and I'm embarrassed to admit how wet I was already. Okay, make that stop wearing skirts and invest in some serious granny panties, because these thongs weren't providing any protection at all.

His thumb found my clit as his fingers hit my g-spot. I arched my back, and I would've cried out if he hadn't caught my mouth with his again, swallowing the sound.

Overhead lights flashed and outside the fence people shouted. I hardly even noticed, because Boonie pulled out and grabbed his cock, lining it up with my entrance.

Then he pushed inside.

Looking back, it's hard to keep all of it straight. I know the chaos around seemed to be moving away, but I could still hear the police radio on the other side of the fence. Boonie's strokes were steady and smooth, not to mention so achingly slow that they were torture. I pushed my hands down into his jeans and cupped his ass, urging him to go faster. He ignored me, maintaining his pace as more people ran by. The chemistry between us had always been insane, but this time it was explosive and by the time I came, he had to cover my mouth with his hand to keep me silent. At the last minute he pulled out, blowing his wad on my stomach as the fireworks were still exploding in my head.

Then he shifted, rolling us to our sides and then pulling me onto his body, rubbing one hand through my hair as the noises around us faded. It was just me and him, joined in our own private world.

You'd think the adrenaline would've kept me up all night, but apparently it wasn't enough to overpower the sex and the booze. At some point I drifted off, despite the lights and the noise.

Boonie woke me with a kiss, raising one knee up between my legs as I squirmed against him restlessly.

Then a branch poked my ass and I remembered where we were.

"What the hell was that all about?" I asked, my voice a soft whisper.

"I think it was a riot. Although I still can't quite figure out how it started. Never heard of one around here before."

I shivered, and he tightened his arms around me, rubbing up and down my back.

"That's pretty fucked up."

"No shit," he said, then distracted me with another kiss. I pushed back against his leg, realizing my skirt was still up around my waist.

Slutty, much?

"Um . . . I'm not sure—" I started to say, but he cut me off.

"Don't think about it too much. Not gonna end well for either of us. Just consider this—every time we've gotten together, some big disaster hits. This time it missed us. Maybe that means we're home free."

I frowned at him, flinching as pain shot through my skull.

"Hangover?" he asked. I nodded. "You need some coffee and some food."

"And a shower."

"Great," he said. "We've got all of that at my friend's place. It's not far—will take us about ten minutes to walk there."

There are walks of shame, and Walks of Shame. I think when you come dragging in after a riot, covered in dirt, leaves, and dried come, you qualify for capital letters by default. We saw a few police cars along the way, but things seemed to be settled. Early light traced the sky. If I hadn't known better, I'd never have guessed there'd been people fighting in the streets just hours before.

His friend's place was just an apartment over a garage. When we walked in, the first thing I saw was Kelly asleep on the couch. Well, she was on top of a man on the couch—the same man who'd helped rescue us from the crowd.

He opened his eyes briefly, then closed them again. More people slept in the bedroom, but at least the bathroom was empty. I followed Boonie through the wooden door, then frowned when he reached for his leather cut.

"Maybe we should shower separately?"

He shook his head.

"No way. Took me long enough to pin you down. I let you out of my sight you might go marry someone else."

I think he meant it as a joke, but I frowned.

"Boonie, I was serious when I said I wasn't ready for a relationship. The divorce isn't even final yet—I can't handle anything new."

He pulled off his leather, hanging it carefully on a hook. Then he reached for the edges of his shirt.

"I get that," he said, tugging it over his head. The sight of his bare chest caught me. Damn, this man was beautiful . . . "But what we have between us isn't new, Darce. It's always been here. I had to walk away twice. I won't do it again."

He was right, I realized. There really had always been something between us. And not just when it came to sex. As children he'd always protected me . . . well, protected me from everyone but himself. He'd fought Farell for me, and even when he'd stopped returning my letters, he'd thought he was doing it for my benefit.

This wasn't new at all.

"I'm not willing to give up what I have," I insisted, refusing to roll over. I'd had my fill of *that* with Farell. "My whole life I've had to live for other people. This is my time. I'm not willing to let that go, not even for you."

"Does having 'your time' involve you fucking guys who aren't me?"

I rubbed my stomach, a thrill running through me at the memory of him, deep inside. Could I imagine doing that with someone else?

Not really.

"No, but it doesn't involve me moving back to Callup and giving up my career, either. I want to own my own spa some day—one of those places where people come to, get their hair done, and manicures and massages and all that."

"Sounds great, so long as I don't have to get my nails done," he said, shrugging. "But I definitely want more of those massages. Wouldn't mind a happy ending, either."

"Not funny," I snapped. "I'm a therapist, Boonie. I help people who are in pain. You should respect that."

The smiled dropped from his face and he caught my hands, pulling me close.

"It was just a joke, Darce," he said. "I don't need you giving up on your dreams. Hell, I've got my own life. The last thing I want is you all whiny and dependent. My mom was like that. Sucked. I just want to know that at the end of the day you'll be in my bed."

I leaned into him, laying my head on his chest.

"I could probably make that work. But no more riots, okay? My ass is covered in scratches. Let's keep it boring from now on."

"Boring. I can work with that."

A sudden knocking pounded the door.

"Boonie, get out here!" his friend shouted. "You won't believe what just happened."

Boonie pulled away, running a hand through his hair in frustration.

"I think we're going to have to be bored later," he muttered. I sighed, realizing I should probably get used to it.

"We really are cursed."

Boonie shook his head, then gave my nose a quick kiss.

"We're just normality-challenged. It'll be okay."

Wrapping my arms around him, I gave a squeeze then let him go. Might as well get used to it—boring was probably overrated anyway, right?

HISTORICAL NOTE

The events in this story are based loosely on real events that took place at different times in the Silver Valley and Coeur d'Alene, Idaho.

The "riot" in downtown Coeur d'Alene took place in June 1999, during the annual Car d'Alene classic car show. It began outside the Iron Horse Saloon when police stopped a biker and were booed by the crowd. Things grew out of control when more officers arrived in riot gear. While the exact timeline of events is controversial, many witnesses (including my own friends who were present) stated that the police attacked them violently. Fourteen people were arrested and it led to a challenge in the Idaho State Supreme Court over whether police officers are immune from prosecution.

The Sunshine Mine Fire is one of the darkest chapters in Silver Valley history. On May 9, 1972, the second deadliest hard-rock mining disaster in U.S. history killed ninety-one men deep underground, many of whom were overcome so quickly they were found still sitting in front of their open lunch boxes. Escape efforts were hampered by out-of-date rescue equipment and leadership issues. Eight days later, two survivors were found 4,800 feet under the surface. No other men would come out alive. The oldest victim was sixty-one years old and the youngest was nineteen. They left behind seventy-seven widows and more than two hundred children, three of whom were still unborn. If you're interested in learning more, I highly recommend *The Deep Dark* by Gregg Olsen.